THE NAMELESS HEIR

This is a work of fiction. Names, characters, places, and incidents either are the product of the author's imagination or are used fictitiously. Any resemblance to actual persons, living or dead, events, or locations is entirely coincidental.

Copywrite © 2024 Emma Arch

All rights reserved. No part of this book may be reproduced or used in any matter without written permission of the copywrite owner except for the use of quotations in a book review.

First edition 2024

*For the nameless, the misfits, and the broken,
I claim you.*

PART ONE
Barwyn's Bastard

ONE

Fallon Solveij always believed her name would be remembered for generations. Legends would be made. Tapestries of her great conquests would hang in every grand hall, her grandchildren and their great grandchildren would be regaled with the tales of her reign.

Alas, the strings of fate are not ours to puppeteer.

Had it not been for the voice in Fallon's head rousing her from the grave, she would still be lying face-down in the snow. Doomed for death. *Get up, Fallon. Get to the river*, it said again and again.

Even when she rolled over and fought her way to her knees, the voice never stopped. One sentence, one plea, one goal: get to the river.

That was three days ago, and Fallon was still running. The frozen woods were a white haze around her as Fallon stumbled through them. Every breath felt as if she was inhaling hot nails as she gulped down bile and blood.

He tried to *kill* her.

She always assumed it would come one day, but not now. Not before she had even seen the age of twenty. Fallon let the anger fester inside of her until she could no longer see straight. She kept feeding the hot coals of rage until it was the only thing keeping her warm anymore.

Dying was not her fear, it was not even her biggest concern at the moment. Dying like *this* though—weaponless, banished, broken, her title ripped from her … That was unacceptable. Fallon Solveij was born to be on a throne, and let the gods hear her when she swore she would sit upon one again. No matter what it took.

Cupping her hands over her mouth, she used her breath to melt away the frostbite creeping up her fingers. Fallon had been raised in the ice lands of Barwyn, so she'd once considered the cold an old friend. Now, surely to die from it, she felt nothing but the burning rage within.

The river. She had to reach the Calder River. Even if it meant crawling on her hands and knees to get there. Every time her skin touched the snow, ice cold memories melted onto her. She felt sticky and adulterated. Fallon needed *out* of Barwyn before she lost her mind.

But never once had she gone out into the barren woods without a proper cloak or furs. The simple drape of fabric she wore over her shoulders had no hood, and she knew that was no coincidence. Her rust-colored hair did her no justice in the snow. They wanted predators to find her. Wanted her to resemble the spilled blood she would soon be.

Fallon wanted to just let go, to let her body sink into the earth where she would finally remain untouched and unburdened. But death had abandoned her in her time of need. She was certain he had found her there in the snow. But instead of taking her into his arms, he simply laid a kiss upon her brow and walked away.

Fallon got the message: live to fight another day. She had blood to draw, and a birthright to reclaim.

The journey across the country of Valdimir was not an easy one. Luckily, they had thrown her in the very direction she needed to go. She was only another two nights away from the Calder River. Even if she made it there, that was just the beginning.

Stories said three ancient brothers were the first to arrive on this land. They named the country after their family name, Valdimir. Some would say they fought so much, the earth split under the weight of their hatred. Others—like Fallon's mother—believed the brothers freed nature spirits from the caves of a waterfall. In return, the spirits created the Calder River to divide the land into three parts, giving one to each brother. The three promptly named the individual territories after themselves: Barwyn, Halvar, and Audhild.

That same waterfall would be Fallon's salvation. Its waters fed the fifteen-meter-wide river that ran through the country. There was no simple way to cross, boats and men alike would capsize in seconds at the hands of current. No, her goal was to best the waterfall itself. If she could climb it, she could escape into the southern territory of Halvar.

Her long, shivering nights were filled with planning. Fallon never really slept, she just had episodes of fading in and out of reality. Maybe this was what people called madness. Sometimes, she would open her eyes to find she was on the ground, having passed out for who knows how long. Fallon knew she had truly gone mad, though, because she became optimistic. Within her hunger, ire, and misery, she found drive. Fallon would survive because everyone else in this world wanted her dead.

When she reached Halvar, Fallon would seek asylum with the Haedilla Clan. They would recognize her as a Blodvinger, and if they knew who she was, they would kill her on sight. Fallon had to offer them something. Something good enough to slacken the bows of an entire clan.

Blodvinger. The taste of her old clan's name was foul on her tongue. She spat it out on the snow and hugged her body closer for warmth. Morality was not high in Fallon's nature, but loyalty was. If she was going to do this, she would have to get used to the idea of betrayal. Luckily the Blodvingers, the Royal House, and the chief were pretty damn easy to hate right now.

Fortunately, most of her trek was downhill. Thrown from the icy mountains of Amory Village, she knew each aching step got her closer to warmer weather. It seemed like it was taking forever, though, because every few minutes Fallon had to lean against a naked tree to catch her breath.

After she found somewhere to safely heal and recover, Fallon would return as a relentless storm. The calamity she would unleash upon these lands will be like none other. Fallon could not risk making a fire right now, so she burned from within. Molding a plan in a forge of flaming vengeance and spite.

The Haedilla would accept her plea, because she had something they could not refuse: information. The clans were at peace for now, but the mountains rumbled underfoot. It only took one rock to start an avalanche, and Fallon came bearing boulders. She knew the ins and outs of the Blodvinger Clan, and the Haedilla Chief would have no better choice than to listen. Even if it meant Fallon would be branded as a traitor and never return home.

You have no home anymore, she reminded herself. *They made sure of that when they threw you off a cliff.*

Fallon shook out the negative thoughts, the movement causing her chest to scream. Her eyes burned from searching the snow for any sign of an animal. She would settle for a squirrel or even a plump bird at this point. Fallon doubted she would even have the patience to cook it—she was ready to sink her teeth into its warm, still-pulsing neck.

All those years of ruthless training, and here she was. Dawdling around like a novice. What was the point of muscles if she had no energy to use them? What was the use of bones if they were all broken? Her rigorous daily routines had been pointless, a mere task to keep her busy and out of her father's way. Every time she thought she had done it all, he simply came up with a new challenge.

A new punishment for the daughter he couldn't get rid of.

Feeling her energy steadily deplete, Fallon allowed herself a few moments of rest. If she completely exhausted herself, there was a fair chance she would not wake back up. So, she had to ride a steady line and listen to her body, even if that meant moving at a glacial pace. She tried to always keep her fingers moving so they would not stiffen up and fall off. Sitting with her back against a tree, she braided a few small strands of her hair. An awful habit of hers.

She had not gotten her looks from her father, thank the gods. He was a big, brown-haired brute. Fallon had waves of red hair and freckles that she inherited from her mother. A woman who Fallon barely remembered.

A small crunch of snow from behind made her blood run still. Her hand went instinctively to her side to reach for a weapon, but found nothing to grasp but empty air. Cursing, she quickly picked up a nearby rock and peeked around the tree trunk.

Please be food, she prayed. A herd of elk, maybe. Or bison. Fallon would gut a rabbit then wear its fur.

Her eyes focused on something about ten feet away. A bright orange blob stuck out wildly in the monochromatic landscape. Confused and intrigued, Fallon carefully walked clockwise, keeping behind the trees. Once she was close enough, she was able to make out each little ...

Berry.

Cloudberries, if she wasn't mistaken. They only grew in certain parts of Halvar, and they were expensive to buy. Fallon had always gotten some at trade posts. How did a perfect pile of them magically appear ten feet away from her?

A biting wind pushed through her hair. A voice, that same vaguely familiar voice from three nights ago susurrated within it: *you remember the stories.*

With a large sigh, she plopped back down against the tree, cradling her ribs with her arms. She'd tried her best to ignore those memories, to think of other explanations.

The first sign was a flower at her feet when she'd first woken up from the fall. Then, she found a small doll made of sticks and twigs. This morning, she found a ring woven from grass on her middle finger—which she was in fact still wearing, for it gave her hope. Reminding her that there existed a place beyond the snow, beyond Barwyn and the Blodvingers.

She told herself it was all because she was nearing the Calder. Water Catchers might have dropped things off their wagons as they rode to and from the river with their large basins of water. Either way, she was not going to eat the berries. She had come too far to be poisoned by a pile of brightly colored bush fruit.

She leaned her head back against the tree and closed her eyes. The stories. Yes, Fallon remembered them. Her mind started to wander, and she once again found herself in that place between sleep and awake.

In a blink, she was four years old again, sitting in her room by the fire. It was snowing violently outside; it had been the worst winter Barwyn had seen in centuries. Her mother placed a heavy blanket around her shoulders and started to brush her hair, just as she always did during a storm.

"Tell me about the forest creatures again, mother," Fallon said, "about the little ones."

Her mother's laugh was so gentle and warm, Fallon swore it could melt the ice coating her window. "You mean the Little Folk? Yes, my light, the Little Folk live in the woods beyond the villages of men. Little tricksters they are. They see and hear everything we don't. Some think they even see things that haven't happened yet." Her mother spoke as if she had known them personally.

Fallon turned to face her. "What do they look like?"

She turned Fallon back around and attempted to braid her endless rush of hair. "No one knows for certain, as they have mastered the art of living unseen. All we know, all they have allowed us to see, are their little hands. They have long, white fingers. Perfect for weaving their way through worlds."

Fallon held up her own pudgy, pale hands. "Like mine?"

"Aye," her mother laughed. "Like yours. The younger Little Folk love the human villages. Sometimes, they even leave small gifts. Though only the best of children who tidy their rooms get gifts."

Mother tied off her braid and gave a sigh of contempt. Fallon turned to peer up into the woman's eyes. An ever-changing field of green and gold that mirrored Fallon's own.

Asta Solveij could stop battles with one beautiful smile, but Fallon recognized the look her mother was giving her then. A look she knew all too well. She locked her arms around Asta's small waist. "You're leaving again, aren't you?"

Her mother's breath caught, but she tried a sad smile anyway. "Yes, my light, I am afraid so."

Asta had secrets. Fallon knew that. It seemed as if she only got to see her mother three times a month. This time, Fallon asked her not to leave. It didn't matter because she still did. It didn't matter because that was the last day Fallon ever saw her mother.

Her eyes fluttered open, but her vision was still black. She stood as fast as her aching body would allow and whipped her head around. The berries were gone, and so was the sun. She'd fallen asleep in the open again. Her heartbeat was a drum in her ears, filling her with the adrenaline to run.

Keeping her damaged arm tight at her side, Fallon moved as quickly as she could through the trees. Luckily, her dark Blodvinger clothes hid her well within the night's darkness. The only source of light was the dim beam of the moon and the wink of the stars.

The voice, the stories, the berries ... the ghost of her past was chasing her. Maybe death had changed his mind and sent hounds of dread after her. Panic set in, sending her into an aimless flee. She was no more than a wounded elk running from the wolf: no thoughts, no pain. Just survival. She didn't even realize how long she'd been running until the taste of blood flooded her mouth and she stumbled to a halt.

She felt a kick to her in the ribs with every beat of her heart. Fallon tried to control her breathing, but she coughed her throat raw. After spitting a mouthful of blood onto the ground, she collapsed onto her knees.

It took a lot of hacking and retching for her to realize her mistake. From the distance, she heard wet panting and footsteps drawing near. Following the trail of fresh blood she has been leaving for miles.

Fallon wasn't ready to run, not even close. She had no time to register where she was or if she was even going the right way. Blood spurted from between her teeth as she seethed with frustration. Fallon scanned her surroundings desperately as the scent of fur and rancid breath filled her nose.

She had nothing but the stars as her witness. All she could do was back up against a tree and wait for them to find her. Nowhere to run, nowhere to hide.

Six glowing eyes broke through the shadows before her. As the cold snow soaked through her trousers, Fallon realized she was finally, truly defeated. After all she had been through.

No. This time, her own voice echoed through her head—*I am Fallon Solveij.*

Sure, she had been banished by her people and disowned by her family, but she was still able to stand. Even if it was all she had left. She wiped the crusted blood from around her mouth, "I am Fallon Solveij," she repeated aloud. "And I do not kneel to Death."

As the silhouette of the wolves' bodies became clear, she pushed herself onto one foot, then the other. Knees wobbling, she took a step forward. Valhalla would never accept her with no weapon, this was not a warrior's death, but she planned to make sure her battle cry rang through whatever afterlife consumed her.

The first wolf, fur of gleaming silver, wasted no time. As soon as it was close enough that Fallon could see the moon's reflection in its golden eyes, it angled its powerful body and lunged. Instinctively, she crossed her arms in front of her face to brace for the pain.

The world slowed down.

Pain.

She almost laughed. If Fallon knew anything in this life, it would be pain. Physical and emotional, spiritual, and mental. Every fiber of her being had been pushed to its limits. Yet she was still standing.

Fallon shoved every horrible memory, every regret, nightmare, and loss deep into her chest until the pressure was too much to bear. She didn't feel the cold anymore; she didn't even feel afraid. Peeking through her fingers, she saw the beautiful wolf's jaw a foot from her face. For a fraction of a second, their eyes met.

You want my pain? She closed her eyes for the last time. *You can have it.*

With a sky-rattling scream, Fallon released it all. She slammed back against the tree as night turned into day. A bright flash blinded her through her eyelids, heat rushing through her bones in a warmth she had never felt before.

It seeped into every crease of her skin. Fallon felt weightless. She felt akin to gods.

When the light faded, she felt frozen in place. It was still nighttime, but the air buzzed around her with energy. She felt it pop and sizzle against her skin, doing dances across her arms and through her hair. Raising her eyes, she saw the bodies of three wolves ten yards away from her. Unmoving.

Before she could process what just happened, a chorus of howls broke through the air. The rest of the pack was coming, and she had just made a royal announcement of her location.

Around her feet was a perfect circle of melted snow, revealing a patch of bright green grass she never knew laid underneath. Outlining that circle were ten beautiful white flowers.

Fallon knelt, slowly reaching out to graze its teardrop-shaped petal with her finger, just to see if it was real. The energy in the air simmered down, and the entire forest turned quiet once again. Fallon remembered these … peace lilies. Her mother used to paint them.

Somehow, all her energy returned. Fallon moved her broken arm to test its mobility, and sure enough—no pain. Not in her ribs, her head, her knees, nothing. Fallon was ready to run. Frankly, she felt as if she could go for miles. She just did not know where to go.

She stood again, taking in the scene before her. This was too much. The light, the flowers, the wolves … it was all too strange for her mind to wrap around. Then, a small series of taps stopped her from spiraling. Her head whipped in the direction of the noise where a single cloudberry lay in the snow. Fallon ran towards it, finding a trail of bright orange berries making a path through the trees.

Well, she'd seen what happened the last time she ignored them. So, Fallon Solveij ran strong, and very much alive, through the trees and toward the Calder River.

TWO

Fallon ran through the night as a storm given flesh; relentless, determined, and hungry for carnage.

Her sudden rush of energy lasted long enough for her to regain her bearings. According to the setting moon and the position of the stars, she was still headed in the right direction towards Halvar. And, judging by the thinning of the snow, Fallon was nearing the Calder already. Days passed by quickly when you were already half-dead.

Her lust to get out of Barwyn, find the Haedilla chief, and spill all her secrets was insatiable. She needed it just as much as she needed air. Though now, there was one secret she would keep to herself. Perhaps all the way to the grave. How a girl made of pain exploded into a ball of light, leaving nothing but a ring of flowers in a frozen wasteland.

Sneaking around here was no game, so Fallon kept her distance from the river. The Haedilla were advanced archers, and they were known for poisoning their arrows. Fallon came to the horrifying realization that she knew so little about her enemy. She hardly ever left her home village, let alone Barwyn. All she knew of the land beyond Amory Village was from war maps she studied in secret. Fallon could still see the oil from her lantern dripping onto the aged parchment as she memorized everything she could while her father slept.

Fallon soon found herself back to normal and struggling to catch her breath. Or at least she thought she was herself again. Her definition of normal had changed drastically within the last two hours. Had that explosion come from her? No. That was impossible. Heimdal, the ever-vigilant guardian of Asgard, must have seen her from his post at the Bifrost and killed the wolves. He was said to see everything in all the nine realms, but why save one girl? *Why me?*

She kept walking at a steady pace until she could hear the loud rush of the river's current. That beautiful sound … it made her dry lips crack in a smile. Alas, her thirst would have to wait until she reached the waterfall.

Perhaps Heimdal knew exactly what he was doing, because her timing was perfect. As the moon set, the night patrol would be switching out with the morning patrol. Leaving time for one sneaking bastard to slip through.

She stopped for a moment to listen to her surroundings. The ache of her ribs was growing into a throb, and a hot line of pain ran from her shoulder down to her wrist. Her pain coming back with the rising sun.

This close to the border, the snow did not stick to the bare trees, but the night's chill still made her fingers feel heavy. Fallon could not wait for the warmth she knew came with day in Halvar.

Fallon kept walking upstream before her thoughts caught up with her. Slowing down meant thinking. Fallon has been focused on surviving and finding shelter if only to avoid processing what happened nearly four days ago. But none of it mattered now. Because the gods had kept her alive twice now. It has to be for a reason. Fallon needed to complete one last task in this life: to take down the Blodvinger Royal House and watch her old clan burn. Then she could die.

Being who she was, Fallon always had easy access to all Blodvinger war plans and procedures. She knew there were currently fifty-four groups of guards positioned all along the river, each two miles apart. Judging by the fact that there was not currently a spear through her chest, Fallon guessed the trail of berries had led her to a safe distance between patrols.

She knew the layout of the Royal House brick by brick. She knew all the entrances, escape tunnels, what guards liked to sleep on shift, where their treasury was. She knew everything down to what side of the bed the Blodvinger Chief slept on. Fallon would find the Haedilla Chief, and together they would conquer these lands.

Gazing up into the cloudy sky, she took a deep breath in and out. Every time she closed her eyes, she saw those elegant, white peace lilies. Memories of the storybooks her mother used to read flashed through Fallon's mind. Ones that spoke of Faerie Circles terrifyingly similar to the one she just saw. Fallon had always held onto those stories; her mother's soft-spoken voice filled her dreams at night. Stories of Faeries that lived underwater, or wild beasts that were half horse and half man.

The thoughts she tried to keep at bay were breaking through her mental dam. They trickled in, one by one, each more troublesome than the last. Her injuries were coming back, meaning at one point they had healed. She had to see it as the gods pushing her towards her destiny. Towards her birthright.

Fallon had known her life was going to change the moment she woke up four nights earlier. It wasn't noise that had jostled her from her sleep that morning, but the absolute silence. No wind, no shouts, no clanging of metal from the blacksmiths next door. Even the air had tasted stale and dry. It felt as if the whole world was holding its breath. She'd sat in bed for a whole minute, listening. Then, the Vali burst into her chambers, shattering the silence.

The Vali were the Royal House guard, sworn to personally protect the chieftain and his family. When the strongest of them all had approached her with chains in his hands, Fallon knew the day she'd expected for months had finally come.

"On behalf of the Chief—" he started to say, but Fallon had simply raised her hand for silence.

"I know why you're here. Don't torture me with the formalities, Hagen."

Hagen was a dark and muscular nightmare that death himself cowered before. Some think the chief summoned him from Helheim to do his bidding, a descendant of

Surtr himself. But to Fallon, he was just Hagen. Her mentor, her friend.

The leader of the Vali took another step forward, his chainmail armor reflecting the sun into her eyes. "Please, Fallon. Let this go easy and maybe you will be given a fair fate." He hadn't even tried to sound convincing. They both knew what was to come.

Hagen had known Fallon all her life. The wolf of the House, he called her. Because while her father chained her outside with the dogs, Hagen saw potential. A beast worth training. Now, nineteen years later, he was to carry her to her death.

Fallon slowly reached for the blade under her pillow. "I thought you knew me better than that. You'll have to drag my breathless body to that pyre."

Never in her life had she seen the leader of the Vali hesitate. But for a count of three, he stared at her with pleading eyes. The chief chose Hagen specifically for this task, they both knew it. He wanted the *one* person Fallon trusted to be the one to walk her to her end. To put down the animal he raised.

Hagen rolled his shoulders back, remembering his position and his oath to the chieftain. He owed Fallon nothing.

"So be it."

And it was. Fallon had been impressed with herself; she'd lasted almost two minutes against three of the best trained warriors in Barwyn. Blow after blow, tossed to the ground, her hair ripped from her scalp, Fallon fought on relentlessly. This was her last chance to die a warrior's death, she needed them to kill her. She *wanted* them to kill her.

Desperate to lose, Fallon fought dirty. She sliced their faces and kicked them where she knew it would hurt. "Come on! Bloody cowards!" she shouted, letting them hit her again and again. She never dodged a single blow, practically running into their fists. She bit and screamed as if she were a rabid animal.

Blood gushed from her nose, and she felt a crack as one spear whacked against the backs of her knees. Fallon hit the ground and wheezed out more insults, staring at the ceiling in an unfocused daze. "Is that all you can do?"

Unfortunately, Hagen caught on. He walked over and placed a massive boot on her gut, stepping down hard. "Enough of your childishness. We were ordered to bring you alive."

Fallon smiled, blood filling the spaces in between her teeth. "I have been wrongly accused. I demand a trial."

He loomed over her, blocking the sunlight like a lunar eclipse. "It has already been decided," he said. His eyes were so dark you could not see his pupils. His shaved head showed ink buried deep across his skull and onto his jaw. If she were to search for mercy, she would find none with him.

She blinked the water from her swollen eyes. "Pyre or gallows?" she gasped as Hagen ripped the blade from her hand. Two others flipped her over and not-so-gently tied her hands together with ice-cold chains.

His silence awoke a fear in her she thought had died long ago. "*Pyre or gallows?*" she demanded again.

He still did not answer as they lifted her, dragging her by the chain out of the door and into the freezing winds.

"Blood eagle?" she whispered, more to herself than to the others. It was a form of torture the Blodvingers was known for; grotesque and graphic enough to make the blood drain from her face.

Her crimes did not warrant that execution. Surely, she would be burned or hanged. But Hagen just peered over his shoulder and shook his head slightly. Why was he not answering her? It was bad enough they had the entire trial without her.

So, Fallon was carried to her execution by someone she trusted. Someone she had been naive enough to look up to. Even though she was innocent, he still sided with the chief. It was at that moment, as her bare knees painted the icy earth red, Fallon understood what true power was. Because after every beating and broken bone, Hagen had been the one she ran to. Despite all the time she and Hagen had spent together, all it took was one sentence, one order from the *chief*, and it was as if it never happened.

Never again would Fallon let herself trust someone like that. *Never* again.

Now, the sky was already starting to lighten. Fallon knew she was approaching the waterfall as the sound of water grew from a rush to a roar. That also meant she was getting closer to the guards on both sides of the river.

For a while now, Fallon had the feeling she was being followed, but by beings too small to be men. She didn't know whether to take it as a comfort or as a warning that they were still with her, but tiny eyes watched her every footstep. Had they been there that day, too? Did they see what her people did to her?

As she climbed over the peak of a small hill, the waterfall finally came into view. If she weren't in immediate danger, Fallon might have stopped to admire the beauty of the scene before her for hours. Seventy-foot falls crashed down into a crystal-clear plunge pool. The sky's reflection danced in the crystalline water, causing her dry tongue to stick to the roof of her mouth in desperation. If she was to be killed within the next hour, Fallon was thankful she got to see this.

Shaking herself from her trance, she moved slowly through the trees. Fallon might have been spared from death, but her life had never been short of misfortune. Across the rushing river, Fallon could see green. *Green* grass. Only a blanket of frost covered the earth under her now. Fallon tilted her head back, smiling up at a partly cloudy sky. No gray storms. Just … blue.

As usual, joy was quickly snatched from her grasp. A sneeze, a human sneeze, echoed in the distance. Fallon quickly hid with her back against a tree, gulping down her waves of fear. Blodvinger border patrol. His footsteps grew closer, and soon Fallon could hear the scraping of his metal armor. She needed a plan—now.

THREE

Finding a dead guard would set off the Blodvingers. They would know Fallon was still alive and had made it this far. Or worse, they could blame the Haedilla and start a war too soon. She had to handle this correctly, which meant ignoring the lust for blood roaring in her ears.

She had to make a move before her injuries got any worse, otherwise she would not be able to fight at all. After this she would have a weapon, a proper cloak, and a small bit of satisfaction to hold her over until she came back for the rest of them.

Fallon simply walked out from the trees. One guard, moderately armed, took a moment to see her approaching. "Oi! Stop right there!" the man shouted, hoisting his spear.

He stared at her in confusion. She was not sure if it was the pure shock of seeing a Blodvinger woman this close to the river, or because Fallon resembled a walking corpse.

"Would you mind pointing me in the direction of Halvar? I think I'm lost," she said snidely.

Clad in Blodvinger silver, black, and red, he stopped a few feet away from her. The bearded man assessed her clothes, her figure, and then finally his eyes registered on her waves of rustic hair.

"You," was all he said, his whole body visibly tensing.

Fallon kept walking closer. "Surprised to see me?" Grabbing the end of his spear to yank him closer, she turned her hips to kick the guard straight in the chest with her good ankle. The movement made her body scream in protest, but she didn't listen. Unfortunately, the guard was almost twice her size and in full armor, so Fallon's blow only stunned him for a moment. She used it to twist and pull the metal spear from his hands.

He smiled down at her through his thick beard. "You're a long way from home, lass." He pivoted and thrust his elbow into Fallon's jaw, causing her to fall to one knee. She was weak and slow, but she still held the weapon.

Ignoring the heat building on the left side of her face, Fallon swung the metal spear at the guard's knees. The weight of his armor did him no good as he fell down beside her. Fallon quickly twirled around, pressing one knee right into his sternum. She pressed the tip of the spear down on his neck, but then she made a big mistake.

Her eyes trailed down to the patch sewn onto his cloak: a decapitated raven with three spears sticking out of its neck.

The sigil of the Blodvinger Royal House.

The three spears represented the three honored traits of the Blodvinger Clan: loyalty, discipline, and brutality. By killing this guard, she would become not only an outcast, but an enemy of her clan. Fallon would never bleed Blodvinger red again.

The guard took advantage of her emotions. Pushing the butt of the spear into her chin, he sent her toppling backwards. Warm, thick blood collected in her mouth. Fallon spat to the side, the splatter of bright blood staining the snow, and along with it lay one of her teeth.

"Too weak to fight, too big of a coward to kill," the guard mocked. Fallon recognized him now: Gormun. She had spent enough time with all the warriors here to know them by name, but they only knew hers for a completely different reason.

She tried to stand, but she had crashed right onto her already broken ribs. Even with adrenaline, she was starting to get dizzy with pain. Gormun was taunting her. He didn't want to just slit her throat. He put the spear point under her chin and lifted her face to meet his round and ugly one. Her eyes drifted back to the sigil over his breast. Gormun caught her gaze and laughed humorlessly.

"What's wrong, traitor? Don't fancy this symbol? I wear it with pride. It is an honor to protect the Royal House." He knelt and pushed the spear harder against her jugular, smiling to reveal a collection of yellowed teeth. "Do you know which House I serve, bastard?"

The emptiness inside her was quickly refilled with fresh, ravenous hatred. The air around them popped and sizzled. "Say it."

Gormun's breath smelt of rancid meat. "I serve Chief Beowulf, of House Solveij."

Something inside her snapped at the sound of his name. The familiar warmth of energy rushed through her body, but this time she didn't close her eyes. The tip of the spear against her neck tingled for a moment, then Gormun yelped and dropped it as if it burned his skin.

He looked at her with eyes full of anger and confusion. Fallon took that moment to grab the sides of his head with her hands, releasing the anger and resentment she had for that damn name; her father's name. The same man who ordered her execution. Her vision went white, and Gormun screamed in agony. Fallon had never heard screams like that before. Through the white haze, she could see him clawing at his face and neck. She didn't take her eyes off him until he stopped moving.

Blinking away the spots that danced in her vision, she no longer felt the pain of her injuries. But when her eyes focused on the dead Vali before her, she fell to her knees.

Charred blood streaked down Gormun's face, dripping from now hollow sockets. His lips were black and cracked. The smell of burnt flesh was enough to make her gag as she watched a pinkish liquid trickle from his ears. Fallon has witnessed plenty of men be burned alive ... but never from the inside out.

The sky was lightening quickly. Morning patrol would be here any moment and she still needed to get to the other side of the river. She quickly recovered, as she had no choice. Her brain was in paralyzed shock and jittering in panic at the same time. She ripped the thick cloak off the corpse and swung it around herself.

Brutality.

Fallon grabbed the spear off the ground and attached his dagger to the belt around her waist with fumbling fingers.

Discipline.

Leaving the body here was sloppy, but no one could trace this back to her. In fact, she didn't know what people would think when they saw what had happened to him. Quickly, she used the dagger to cut the patch from the cloak and bury it in the snow.

Loyalty.

She ran, aware she might fall into complete shock at any moment. Dawn was breaking the sky, filling it with beautiful colors that helped to cleanse her eyes of what she had done. Her mouth stopped bleeding, but the dull ache was already returning.

Fallon didn't even notice the tears streaming down her face until she had to stop to catch her breath. Half gagging and half sobbing, her whole body shook and heaved but her stomach had nothing to offer. Her hands trembled violently as she grabbed onto a tree to steady herself. Fallon pressed her brow against the rough bark and took a long breath.

Then, the sun touched her skin.

As the sun finally rose over the land, its beams reached out and grabbed her in a comforting embrace. She leaned into it, trying to let the light touch as much of her as possible. It had been so long.

Her mother used to tell her that long ago, the Sun fell in love with the Earth. But they could never be together, or the Earth would burn. So, the Sun made a promise to forever provide Earth's children with light and warmth, and Earth promised to never leave. If the Earth ever left the Sun, or if the Sun stopped providing light, all life in Barwyn would perish.

She could almost hear her mother's voice now. *You see now, my light? Love is one of the most powerful forces in our lives. No matter where you go, no matter who you choose to become, promise me you will remember that.*

I promise, Fallon had said then.

"Please, forgive me," she whispered now.

The air was so much warmer already. It was strange not having the cold nipping at her lungs. Looking up at the immense beauty of the water before her, she did not see an easy way across.

The waterfall was tall and steep, as if it had just dropped from the sky. There were plenty of ledges and niches within the gray stone, but everything was wet. But if she could keep the pouring water close to her right, it might provide cover.

Fallon saw no other option but to start climbing. Swimming through the large plunge pool was against Valdimir law. Even though she hated everyone in this country, Fallon did not wish her current filth to be drunk by anyone. Plus, she did not believe guards would mistake her for a fish. If she was seen, there would be nowhere to go.

The volume of the waterfall was deafening up close. Fallon could not escape getting sprayed and soaked by the water as she climbed straight up the cliff side, but at least she was getting clean. She made the mistake of looking down and seeing nothing but the fifteen-foot fall onto the jagged rocks below.

Her vision went blurry as the familiar sensation of falling tugged at her gut, causing her entire body to go numb. Fallon did not remember how long it took to hit the ground after they threw her off the cliff, but she remembered being weightless. Nothing to grab onto, nothing to fight. Her body was out of her control.

Don't look down. She would never look down ever again.

Her fingertips were bleeding as her arms trembled with the strain of hauling her bodyweight. Blood, moss, and water mixed to make every handhold a slippery mess, but she kept going. *Keep your eyes up, and you won't die.*

Planting her feet and finding a strong grip with her good arm, Fallon reached out to grab a handful of water. The strength of the falls almost ripped her arm out of its socket. But when she put the cold liquid to her lips, everything seemed worth it. Smiling with euphoria, she drank handful after handful. Fallon Solveij was drinking sun-kissed water halfway up a cliff. Despite everything they tried to do to stop her.

They had tossed her down, and here she was climbing back up. Fallon Solveij *survived*. Her father would live to regret not slitting her throat himself. He should have watched her burn. He should have watched the light leave her eyes as she swung by her neck like a pendulum. Because now, Fallon will return. And she will not make the same mistake Beowulf Solveij did.

Hand over hand, she kept climbing until she could no longer feel her arms. Still refusing to drop her gaze. *I'm not high up*, she kept telling herself, *I'm right by the ground.* She was completely soaked and shivering, but the sun was a gentle hand on her back, pushing her forward encouragingly.

Fallon scouted the rocks for another handhold, but to her right she saw a winding ledge that led to an indentation in the cliff—going right *behind* the waterfall. On that path no wider than her foot, lay a single orange cloudberry.

Seeing no other way to advance upwards, Fallon sighed and prayed to the gods, "Please don't let them be trying to kill me."

She shuffled across the ledge with her chest to the rocks, begging her feet to not slip. *Don't. Look. Down.*

It was a slow, nerve-racking process. She needed to move faster, but her knees were shaking dangerously. The rough cliff wall shredded her cheeks until finally the crashing water was to her back. Everything was even wetter, louder, and slipperier than before. Splendid.

Maybe she spoke too soon about being a survivor. Because just after Fallon had developed a rhythm, her right foot fell from under her.

Screaming in panic, she clawed at the gray stone for a saving grasp. Her nails ripped up from their beds as they dug into the rock. She cursed and cursed, squeezing her eyes shut. If she fell, she did not want to watch this time.

Miraculously, she managed to regain her balance. She squatted with one foot on the ledge and one in the air like a confused bug. Looking around, she saw the problem: the path ended abruptly, with nowhere to go but a stomach-twisting drop.

Oh, gods above …

The sound of the water was drowned out by her pounding heartbeat. Was she hyperventilating, or not breathing at all? Her leg wobbled under her weight, the tendons in her knee slowly tearing like dry twine. Fallon had only seconds before she lost balance and went toppling backwards into a fall she could not walk away from twice.

Her eyes shot around frantically, seeing her only option. About five feet to the right was another ledge. This one was larger, and she could see daylight shining through an opening in the rocks behind it.

With no time to be afraid, Fallon jumped with everything she had left.

As her fingers closed on the ledge, her body slammed into the rock wall. Pain flashed through her ribs and nose so intense she almost blacked out. Using the last of her strength, she kicked her legs and pulled herself up.

Fallon plopped flat on her back. She pressed her palms onto the rock beneath her to ground herself, savoring every moment until her stomach settled. She tilted her head back and caught a glimpse of the sun leaking through the rocks.

The hair on the back of her neck tingled as she felt multiple eyes on her. "Whoever you are," she croaked, "or whatever you are, if I see another bloody berry, I am going to step on it. Then I am going to find you, and step on you."

Fallon let them watch her struggle to her feet. "I hope you enjoyed the show," she added bitterly. Wrapping an arm around her throbbing chest, she turned to leave this gods-forsaken waterfall. She found a narrow break in the rocks that was barely wide enough for her to shimmy through.

Fallon had to shield the sun from her eyes as she beheld a scene straight out of her mother's storybooks. A thin layer of frost coated the open fields as a shimmering blanket. Trees with *leaves* covered the rolling hills before her. Fallon saw so much green, red, blue, and orange.

Transfixed by its allure, Fallon took her first step into Halvar territory.

There was an unpleasant *squish* under her boot. Her eyes slowly trailed down to see a pile of brightly colored berries at her feet.

Pain wreaked havoc on her body, but still Fallon smiled and shook her head. "I think we might just get along after all," she said to herself.

Fallon reached down and popped a few in her mouth. The bittersweet taste awoke her senses and, admittedly, lifted her spirits. Fallon made her way down the hill. Ready for whatever Halvar had to offer.

As she trotted down the steep decline, her mind kept going back to the bright light that had saved her life twice now. She's heard of heroes and warriors blessed with temporary strength or wisdom, but not the power of the sun. Fallon was no hero, and her actions were anything but heroic.

The sound of the waterfall became a distant rumble as she walked along the base of the Calder. Fallon stopped behind a large pile of boulders to wring out her cloak. It was made for a grown man, so she cut off some extra length to use as bandages for her shredded hands.

Fallon was so thankful she could not see her own reflection. The left side of her jaw was swollen and no doubt purple. In addition to the new wounds across her cheeks courtesy of a rock wall, her mound of filthy hair stuck up at odd angles like a matted cat. Her tongue ran over the empty socket in her mouth where her left canine had once resided.

She had a foul scent on her, and if Halvar used hounds as hunters as the Blodvingers did, she was finished. Shaking her head, she threw back on her cloak and peered around the boulder. No one was there, but it would be safe to assume there were many archers in the trees that littered the land. There was so much color over here, she had to strain her eyes to focus on any one thing.

Her ear twitched. Fallon turned her head to see a wagon rolling up to the river from the grasslands beyond the hills. It was a simple wooden wagon, pulled by two beautiful white steeds. The man driving wore Haedilla colors—greens, browns, and blues, but no armor. Two women sat in the back with many large water jugs.

Water catchers. Perfect. If she could just find a way to get on that water wagon, they would lead her back to the village where she could demand to see the chief. Or she could distract them long enough to steal the wagon, and hope the horses knew their way home.

Then, from across the way she heard the familiar sound of men shouting at each other. Fallon moved to peer over the other side of the rock, where five Blodvinger Vali on horseback stood at the far brink of the river.

From the trees, five equally terrifying men came running to the Halvar side of the river, all armed with full quivers and swords. Gods ... Fallon had not even seen them.

They met at the Calder, having to shout through cornucopia-shaped horns in order to hear one another. This had to be about the guard Fallon killed. She could hear some words, but not enough to understand. The water catchers approached the scene, and the man and two women all got out to get a better look. Seeing an opportunity, Fallon ran for it.

She would have to thank the Vali sometime for providing the perfect distraction for her. The three water catchers had their backs to the wagon, noses deep in the

Vali's conversation. She ran in a wide arc, jumping behind boulders or crouching in the grass to remain unseen.

Coming from the back of the wagon, she gently spoke to the horses, careful not to spook them. She grabbed the stolen dagger from her belt and began to cut the reins. She needed to make it look like the horse had chewed its way through the rope. It took time—time she did not have.

As the rope finally gave, Fallon peered over her shoulder to see the two clans still bickering. She untangled the horse and used the wagon wheel to help her climb on. As she turned her gentle steed to run south towards Halvar, she glanced back one last time to make sure she was not seen.

Straight across the river from her, Fallon locked eyes with Hagen. The leader of the Vali; the man who tossed her off a cliff.

Her breath died in her throat as the world around her wilted away. Hagen rode a massive steed as large and dark as he was. A storm cloud coming to rain on all her triumphs.

Everything was over. Every breath she has taken since the cliff was just borrowed time. Fallon was paralyzed in her defeat. She was ready for the worst, but her old mentor had a gleam of pride in his eyes as he soundlessly turned and continued toward his men.

The gentle, familiar voice in her head spoke to her once again: *Go now, Fallon!*

Remembering how to breathe, Fallon used her heel to kick her horse into a run. She rode a winding path through the trees, avoiding main roads where more guards were surely posted. With her eyes set straight for the heart of Halvar, Fallon leaned back and laughed for the first time in weeks.

FOUR

Ronen was powerful. He could feel it thrumming through his veins with every heartbeat. Every blade of grass, waterdrop, and speck of pollen let out a whisper of existence, and his pointed ears could hear it. Finally, this is what it was like to be one of the most ethereal beings in all the realms—this is what it was to be Fae.

The world buzzed around him in a golden haze as he walked through the forests of Elphyne, playing their games and running amongst them freely. His tongue ran across his long canines, causing him to break into a smile. He was *finally* one of them.

Still laughing, Ronen ran faster than any animal through the trees and over the hills. Elphyne was his; he finally felt at home here. Twenty-one years he has been waiting for this. Ronen approached the Golden Castle, knowing this time they would not turn him away.

But before he could get there, his world faltered as the smell of old earth filled his nostrils and dribbled into his mouth.

Spitting and cursing, Ronen awoke to the sound of that old man yelling, "Get up you worthless *orlendr*!" directly into his ear.

Wiping the mud out of his eyes, Ronen sat up from his rickety wooden cot, back into the cold grasp of reality. "Really, Urg? Just yelling would have sufficed," he hissed.

Looking down, he saw he was unfortunately still Ronen Nøkken. Still in dirty clothes, with greasy hair and filth-covered skin. No gleam of immortality, no fangs, just calluses and bruises. And body odor.

"Come on, you know I can't wash this out!" Ronen grumbled as he walked out of the small storage closet that also doubled as his bedroom.

Urg huffed. "Go stand by the forge to burn that smell off if you're going to cry about it."

Urg was not his actual name; that was just what Ronen called him, since it was the noise he made all the time. Urg repaid him by calling him things along the lines of *worthless orlendr*—outsider.

Ronen had to constantly remind himself to be thankful though, as Urg was the only Fae in Elphyne that would give him work and a place to sleep. The elderly Fae was the best blacksmith Elphyne had ever seen, but he was getting old, even by Fae standards. Ronen called himself Urg's apprentice. Urg called him a useful headache.

Urg shoved a roll of parchment into his arms. "Today's order," he said. "It's a big one. So get to work!" The Fae's frail white hair showed his age. He was pushing three hundred—a respectable Fae elder.

Unrolling the paper, Ronen read its contents and got angrier with every word. "Are they serious? Two hundred orichalcum knives? The Valdyr blow through weapons faster than we can make them."

Whipping back around, Urg made a noise worthy of his name. "It is a great honor to produce weapons for our warriors, and you would be wise to remember it," he sneered. "I did not take a chance on you so you could go around disrespecting the castle guard!"

Ronen rolled his eyes. "I meant no disrespect. I was only suggesting that if they effectively used the weapons instead of breaking them, they might not need so many replacements," he said casually.

Eyes burning, Urg stepped closer to him. "Do you know what would happen if anyone but me heard you say that, boy?"

"They would break their weapons upon my head?"

"Exactly. Now, get to work! Try to keep up."

Ronen sat down at his small workstation as the other smiths started to arrive. They sat far away from him, pretending he was not there. Ronen didn't mind; at least he did not have to share any of his tools.

The shop was a moderately-sized, rectangular room lit only by forge fire and whatever light came down through the chimney. Yes, weapons hung everywhere and the walls were covered in soot, but it was home.

Ronen began his flow of melt, shape, hammer, and repeat. The others were faster, but sloppy. He had once tried to offer advice and almost got killed for it. Ronen wanted to pay attention to the blades, make sure the curves were even and check the balance. When he had extra time, he even carved small intricate details within the metal. Not that anyone would notice or care as they used it to gut someone.

Because of what he was, Ronen was not allowed to bathe or be around water in general. His kind had been exiled from this realm eons ago. Somewhere out there, Ronen's mother died giving birth to him. Seeing nothing but a helpless newborn, the Little Folk of the forest had brought him to Elphyne. But after determining his bloodline, he was shunned. Growing up, it was just him and his family of Little Folk.

Working in the smith's shop made Ronen strong, but still, he was barely comparable to a Fae child. Their kind were born with enhanced strength and senses, while he was born with a curse. Every time he saw those pointed ears and elegant faces, a wave of hot envy washed over him.

Hours passed until it was midday. Urg kicked everyone out for lunch as usual. "No crumbs on my worktables!"

Ronen walked outside, using the back door instead of the front. The weather was nice, as it always was in Lysserah. This side of Elphyne was a land of perfection and beauty, and the temperature was no exception. Ronen, on the other hand, belonged on the other side of Elphyne—Ondorr. The dark, monster-filled hills of nightmares. Ronen had only heard stories about the things that lurked within those woods. It was a place absent of sunlight, which was a Faerie deathtrap. All Faerie Folk alike needed sunlight constantly to survive.

The smith's shop was on the outskirts of Athol Village, so Ronen did not see many people besides those he worked with. Rather, he had come to know them by the backs of their heads, since that's all they ever showed him.

It did not matter to him, though. He enjoyed having the back of the shop to himself. He sat on the creaky wooden steps and gazed into the endless green woods before him. If he turned around, he would see the busy stone roads filled with people rushing in and out of their wooden homes. He chose to look at the trees.

He heard a faint *tap tap, scratch,* and Ronen turned to see a wrapped loaf of bread behind him.

"Thanks, guys. I was starting to think you'd forgotten about me. I would have gone to get myself some lunch this time, really. It's just ..." He gestured to his filthy state. He did not need to give the villagers another reason to hate him. Being the only Nøkken in Elphyne was bad enough.

To anyone walking by, Ronen would probably seem mad for talking to someone that was not there. Or at least, someone they could not see. The Little Folk have provided for him his whole life. He has somewhat learned to interpret their strange language of small sounds, or sometimes they left him letters in a peculiar alphabet they taught him as a child.

"Extra big order today. What's happening up in the castle?" he asked.

Tap, tap, tap, tap, snap, snap, scratch.

"Yeah, yeah, I know. Confidential court business. That's what you always say."

Snap, snap, tap, tap, tap, pop.

"Well, maybe I'd stop asking if you actually told me what's going on!"

Ronen chose the wrong moment to raise his voice. Walking around the corner, Munjor laughed mockingly.

Munjor was one of the Fae Ronen hated most. Which said a lot because he hated all of them. He was huge, loud, and horribly narcissistic. Which was strange, because all Fae were inherently beautiful; one would think appearance would mean nothing to them. Munjor was living evidence such a thing was false. And nothing made him feel better about himself than ruining Ronen's life.

Wearing fabrics far too nice to be in a workshop, Munjor was followed by his two best friends. Ronen did not know their names because he did not care.

"Talking to yourself again, Gronen?" Munjor asked. "Or is that pebble your friend now?"

Taking a bite of his bread, Ronen stood and silently shooed away the Little Folk. They'd fought his battles when he was a child, but now they knew to leave him be.

"It's Ronen, actually, and I was talking to *that* pebble." He pointed appropriately. "So if you don't mind, I'd like to get back to our discussion on landscape."

He turned and walked away, the bread in his mouth nothing but a dry, tasteless lump. Just one day. Ronen wanted just *one* day free of torment.

He was almost in the clear until a familiar pebble struck him in the back of the head with enough force to knock some dried mud from his hair. Ronen cursed and spun around, the motion causing the pain to rush in between his eyes. "Really?"

Munjor laughed while he pulled back his dirty blond hair, exposing his pointed ears. In Elphyne, only the warriors grew their hair out. The fact that Munjor had enough to pin up meant he was ready to leave on this year's recruit camp.

"I heard you and that old radish talking about the Valdyr. I think you'll find we know damn well how to use our weapons. You need to watch your mouth, *Nøkken*," he said scornfully.

Ronen's body twitched upon hearing that word. Still, he kept his composure. "What are you going to do? Beat me up?" He would rather be beaten senseless than be called by his species again. Munjor was not actually a Valdyr, not yet at least. But everyone knew his father was high up in the castle guard. It was impossible *not* to know, as he told everyone at least twice a day.

Munjor only smiled, exposing his long canines. The wave of envy that followed made Ronen's skin feel hot. "I can do worse." Reaching behind him, Munjor grabbed the flask of liquid about his friend's waist. Both of his companions looked at him as if he'd gone mad when he threw it at Ronen's feet.

"The Nøkken has water!" he shouted with fake panic.

The two other Fae turned and fled with genuine fear in their eyes. The windows of the surrounding houses filled with panicked faces staring at him.

Laughing hysterically, Munjor followed them, but not before giving Ronen a very impolite gesture Urg would have thrown a fit about. Shouts grew louder as panic spread, but Ronen stayed still, staring at the flask of water in the grass.

Without hesitation, Ronen kicked the flask with all his strength, hoping it would fly far, far away from him to where it belonged.

Instead, it was snatched from the air by a hand so fast, his brain struggled to register it. Ronen's eyes focused on a large figure a few yards in front of him that had appeared out of thin air.

The bread dropped from Ronen's hand.

Bhaltair Herleif stormed towards him with murder in his eyes. Never before had Ronen felt the urge to bow before a Fae. He had heard stories of Bhaltair, but they did not do him justice. His presence broke through the air like an oncoming storm—mighty, ruthless, and inescapable.

He was so muscular it was surprising the spear he held didn't snap in his hand. Not to mention, just like all of them, Bhaltair was aggravatingly attractive.

Remembering how to speak, Ronen's voice came out a few octaves higher than he wanted. "They sent the General of the Valdyr to deal with a little misunderstanding? Are you guys understaffed up there?" *Why would you say that?* Ronen scolded himself.

Munjor must have known the Valdyr were in the area. He wanted Ronen to get in trouble. Why couldn't everyone just leave him alone?

Bhaltair examined the water flask within his hand. "Misunderstanding? No, I understand just fine what you are." His face contorted into one of beautiful anger as he threw the flask over his shoulder. His golden eyes, a rare gift for a Fae, bore into Ronen's soul.

"No, you have it all wrong. It was—"

"Enough!" he snapped, pointing his spear at Ronen, "Apprehend him. We are to return to the castle." The towering palace of pure gold was home to only the royal family. Though it seemed Ronen would be getting a personal tour. Bhaltair turned, his long black hair pulled back in many braids and twists. Two more Valdyr dressed in their green and gold uniforms approached him.

Ronen was filled with blinding rage as their massive hands clamped around his arms. He hated them. He hated *all* of them. Every last soul in this worthless realm. How could they be so smart, yet so stupid?

Ronen fought as hard as he could, he spit at them and called them foul names. He hoped his stench would make their noses bleed. He knew he was only drawing more attention to himself, but what was the point anymore? A crowd had already gathered to watch the big bad Nøkken of Athol Village be taken away.

Then an old, cranky voice made them all halt. "Wait! What do you think you are doing?" Urg came stumbling from the shop, already wheezing. Even though the two guards held each of Ronen's arms in a bone-cracking grip, Urg still felt as though he had a say in the matter. "Let him go! He has work to do!"

Ronen guessed the general had never been shouted at by an old Fae before, because Bhaltair blinked twice before responding. "This boy is accused of treason and will speak before the King's Court." *Boy*. Not male. Not even man.

Urg examined Ronen, a definite glimmer of sadness welling up in the old Fae's eyes. "No, no. He works here, he stays here, he—"

The general raised his hand for silence, and Urg could do nothing but swallow in fear and obey.

Urg shook his head, "What did you do, boy?" he whispered sadly. The guards holding Ronen started to walk, dragging his seemingly weightless body with them.

"Urg!" Ronen tried to say goodbye, to say thank you, but the general flashed him a look poisonous enough to kill.

Mothers clutched their children close, and families watched from the windows as they made their way down the stone road. Why was this happening? He had done nothing wrong, nothing but be born. Ronen was officially done with Elphyne, and it appeared it was finally done with him.

Ronen whipped his head over his shoulder, shouting, "Urg, it was Munjor! I-I didn't ... I would never—"

Crack. One blow over his temple and Ronen went limp. The last thing he heard was people clapping.

The taste of blood was strong enough to stir him from unconsciousness. It dribbled from his nose and into his mouth until he gagged and sat up. His head was foggy and throbbing, but at least from what he could tell he was alone.

Things started to come back slowly; Munjor's stupid face, Urg yelling, people cheering, and two golden eyes coming towards him. He tried to look around the dark room. *Where am I?*

Judging by the thick, murky air and darkness, Ronen realized he was not in the Golden Castle. He was under it. The room was pitch black and smelt awful. If they were going to kill him, he hoped he would get to bathe first so he would not go smelling up the afterlife. Then they would hate him there, too.

Ronen felt absolutely no attraction to water, no desire to control it. Just the lust for taking a nice bath. His only Nøkken feature was his blue left eye, in contrast to his brown right eye. A sign of his half heritage.

Nøkken were known as seductive water creatures. Appearing mostly Fae, they played their beautiful music, luring people into the water where they drowned them slowly. Some stories said that Nøkken ate his victims, others said he added to his collection of children's skulls. All stories had the same moral: don't go near them. So, that's how he was treated his whole life. Even to this day, he sat in a dungeon without a cellmate. Or perhaps there was one somewhere, but it was too dark to see. The thought made him scoot his back closer to the wall.

Ronen always thought it was hypocritical of the Fae to treat him this way. He showed no sign of water manipulation, but they did. It was rare for a Fae to have elemental powers, but it happened. Ronen knew the current leader of Elphyne, Fritjof Aodh, was a Fire Fae.

After the queen died, there were no more royals, so the position of power went to that psychotic military general. Fire Fae were the rarest and most powerful. Water, Air, and Earth Fae tended to be more peaceful.

They could be trusted to control water because *they* were beautiful pure beings. Nøkken could not be trusted because they were regarded as monsters. Even though no one here had ever even seen one until baby Ronen arrived with nothing but a note from the Little Folk and a loaded nappy.

His eyes slowly adjusted to the intense darkness around him. The unnerving silence made his pulse sound loud in his ears. He could hear every breath and every blink of his eyes. Panic. Yes, Ronen was going to panic.

He could not see, but he could hear and smell. The walls felt lumpy, like compact dirt. He stood and walked the perimeter of the room, waiting to feel metal bars. He had encircled the medium-sized square room almost three times before he came to the horrifying conclusion:

No door.

He must have made a mistake. He got back down on his knees and felt around the floor, but nothing. If he got in here, there had to be a way out. The only option left was the ceiling. Ronen tried looking up but saw nothing but the looming abyss above. He was certain there was some kind of hatch or door he could not see. A cell would have been bad enough, but a *pit*? This was just offensive.

Ronen was of average height, but even when he jumped with all his might his fingers never touched the ceiling. He was completely trapped in a dirt pit underground. Or as some called it: a grave.

Underground ... Ronen knew people underground. He ran over to the dirt wall and did his best attempt at tapping *help* in Little Spoke, the smallest bit of hope building in his chest. He was not positive he was doing it right, but he kept trying until his knuckles started to swell and bruise. If there was anyone who could break him out of here, it was them. They were also the only ones who would want to.

A thought cold as ice struck him then, and his hand fell to his side. *What if they don't try to find me?* Only Urg even knew his real name. Ronen would die here, a worthless half-blood with no family. Just like everyone said he would. It was all because of Munjor and his little games. If Ronen ever got out of here, he swore he would make Munjor pay. As would anyone else who got in his way.

Ronen wished he was as evil as everyone thought he was. He wished he could control water. Because if everyone was going to hate him for something, it might as well be true. But deep inside, Ronen knew he could never become the monster they painted him to be.

Metallic creaking came from above, and Ronen let himself get excited only to be disappointed by two golden eyes glaring down on him. "You're awake," Bhaltair called down a good ten feet, his face illuminated by torchlight.

Ronen tilted his head back and tried his best for a smile, shoving aside his thoughts. A skill he has unfortunately mastered.

"You're taller than I remember," he called up. An annoyed grunt was the general's only response as one end of a thick rope dropped at his feet. Ronen took the rope in one hand. He was so desperate to get out of this dark place before shade-poisoning set in, he started to ascend despite his better judgment.

"You should be nicer to me you know," he said, climbing up the rope with ease. "I could drown you with your own snot and tears."

Ronen knew he was joking, but Bhaltair did not. The general gave him a wary expression as he locked chains around Ronen's wrists and ankles. The torch Bhaltair held was the only source of light, so it appeared as if the room stretched on for miles. Nothing but hundreds of square hatches littered the floor as they slowly walked away from his pit, the sounds of screaming and banging growing louder as they passed each one.

"So, where are we going?" Ronen asked, needing to distract himself.

"Silence."

"Never been there before."

A backhand to the nose shut Ronen's mouth promptly.

He followed—or was dragged, more like—behind the moody general. Bhaltair was alone; maybe they were starting to realize what little threat Ronen actually posed. He had never been taught to fight. Growing up fatherless, Ronen imagined there were many things he'd never been taught. One of which was when to stop talking. But at least he knew how to hold a sword. He made so many of them, sometimes he would sneak out to the woods and practice against the trees. Only to be laughed at by Anthousai, the tiny flower Faeries that lived for gossip.

They finally reached a wall and started to head up a stone spiral staircase. Ronen noticed Bhaltair trying to cover his nose, wincing occasionally. He smelt bad to himself, so he couldn't even imagine how he smelt to someone with an enhanced sense of smell.

"What are you smiling about?" Bhaltair snapped, offended that Ronen was not cowering in fear.

"Oh, I'm just excited to finally see the castle—"

Another blow to the nose sent him toppling down a step. It was obvious Bhaltair was pulling his punches, but it still made his head spin. This time, blood dripped onto Ronen's lips, washing away any trace of a smile that had been there before.

They finally breached the surface to a slightly less terrifying corridor. Caged doors lined both sides of the hall, and Ronen had to avert his eyes from what he saw inside them. A thought clicked through his head, escaping through his mouth before he could catch it. "There *are* cells. What made me qualify for an empty pit?"

Bhaltair just ignored him, leading him up another set of stairs at the end of the chamber of despair.

No punch to the face. At least he was making progress.

Or maybe the general didn't know the answer. The only time Bhaltair seemed wary of Ronen was when he fake-boasted about his abilities. Maybe he didn't think Ronen deserved this kind of treatment, either.

This is the General of the Valdyr who has knocked you in the face three times just within the morning, he is not your friend, Ronen reminded himself.

He had only seen the Golden Castle from a distance, and even then, he had to admit it was incredible. It was the jewel of Lysserah, built into the side of a mountain where waterfalls cascaded through and around its great towers and arches. Every inch was pure gold or shining ivory. The most talented Earth Fae kept incredible gardens surrounded by fountains and statues made in the gods' likeness.

Perhaps the most impressive features were the Valdyr and their Barguest companions. Barguests were a species of massive, protective, loyal canines. Standing almost as tall as their warrior owners, they were bred and trained within the castle. Each bonded for life with a Valdyr.

Together, Fae and beast stood watch on the crooks of the mountainside, atop towers and bridges, and posted around the surrounding villages. Both clad in golden armor.

He would die before he ever let Bhaltair know, but Ronen had been obsessed with the war dogs when he was a boy. He dreamed of having one of his own. If only he had understood the consequences of hope back then, it would have saved him years of heartache.

Now inside the castle himself, Ronen could confirm it was just as entrancing up close. Ignoring where he had just come from, the Golden Castle was the most beautiful place Ronen had ever seen. He and his captor came out of a large set of wooden double doors onto an open-air bridge leading into the main palace. From hundreds of feet up, Ronen could see the entire valley.

The sun kissed his skin once again, and the shadows that lingered on him melted away. Bhaltair had his back turned to him, but Ronen could still see all the pale scars that covered the general's tanned olive skin.

Bhaltair tugged on his chains as Ronen drifted towards the railing. "Don't get any ideas."

He was touched that the general was concerned about his mental health, but suicide by bridge was not on Ronen's to-do list. He had to kill Munjor first, which meant surviving the next three hours.

Ronen shrugged him off. "Wouldn't matter if I jumped. Nøkken can fly," he snorted. He was not sure if Bhaltair believed him, but he did hold a tighter grip on Ronen's chains.

The wind was strong this high up, causing the general's long, raven-black braids to fly majestically around his face. All whilst Ronen stood filthy, his horrid stench whisked away by the wind and probably gagging some poor Fae three miles downwind.

Bhaltair kept walking at a brisk pace. "Nøkken cannot fly."

"How would you know? Have you ever asked one?"

The general went quiet for a few moments. Ronen thought the conversation was over, but he spoke again without turning around as if he felt more comfortable talking to the air. "What are you, really?"

"I'm Ronen."

"I didn't ask *who* you were."

"Is it not the same thing?"

More silence. This time it lasted until they reached the end of the bridge. Ronen could not help but wonder if this was going to be his last time outside. Would they lock him up forever, or just kill him? He couldn't decide which was worse.

Ronen had only a small second to glance once more at the valley below before the general yanked him through the doors. The moment he stepped inside, it was like he entered a new world: the air was perfumed with the scent of freshly bloomed flowers and vanilla. Ronen thought the gold walls would be distractingly tacky, but they were like waterfalls of pure light. Soft, beautiful music played in the distance creating an ethereal ambiance.

"Woah," was all he managed to say. Bhaltair smirked proudly and pulled him down the hall. Ronen's filthy boots walked along a fine red rug, leaving a trail of mud in their wake. Good.

Two Valdyr in their gold and green uniform walked towards them, their waist-length hair swaying back and forth in unison. The general nodded to his men, who bowed in respect and kept going, holding their noses as they passed him. Ronen lifted his chained hands to wave, but Bhaltair pulled on them hard enough to pop his shoulders out of their sockets.

"What are they doing?" Ronen asked.

The general bit the inside of his cheek in annoyance. "Patrol."

"Where are their Barguests?"

"They do not come inside the castle."

"Well, you let me in here, so you obviously don't have high standards—"

Bhaltair growled. Animalistically *growled* at him. "They have their own kennels within the gardens. They hate it inside," he said angrily.

This was the most Bhaltair has spoken, so Ronen didn't push his luck with another question. His nose could not take another Fae backhand.

They walked through hall after hall, each more extravagant than the last. Stained glass windows depicted stories he did not know, vines of flowers grew and hung from wherever they pleased, and enchanting female servants rushed around carrying wine or fine silks. Each of them turned their noses up at Ronen as if he were a flayed rodent. Between the blood dripping down his chin and his stench, he probably came off as a madman. Little did they know, the true madman was at the other end of the chains.

As they turned the corner, Ronen knew they had reached their destination. The set of doors at the end of the long hall before them appeared different than the others. They were massive, made from polished ivory with gold and silver detail. The worst part of it all was the line of Valdyr on either side of the wide hallway, each with a silver claymore in their hands. Each staring right at him.

A room this guarded and grand could only be one thing. His fears were confirmed when Bhaltair turned to face him, face set in ice-cold stone.

"You are about to enter the throne room. You will not speak unless asked, you will not move unless told, and if you show any sign of disrespect, you will be killed without hesitation," he explained.

Ronen could feel the heat of Bhaltair's breath on his face, the power of a true general's tone almost knocking him over. It was clear he was used to giving orders, and used to being obeyed.

Ronen raised his hand in question, waiting for permission to speak. He swore steam came out of the Fae's pointed ears as he let out a low growl. "What?" he snapped.

Ronen wiped some of the blood off his mouth. "Who exactly am I talking to? Or, I suppose, *not* talking to?"

A sinister grin crossed Bhaltair's face, and his golden eyes lit up with malice. "Fritjof Aodh."

That was enough to shut Ronen up. Possibly for the rest of his life. One of the last living Fire Fae, who was also the leader of Elphyne, was running Ronen's trial.

He had heard terrible stories of Fritjof. Some were merely rumors—a store owner once told him Fritjof had a hunger for stillborns and menstrual blood. Other stories of the red-eyed monster were more plausible, which made them the most horrifying. Some say he killed the last queen for power.

Now, Ronen had to stand before him. Bhaltair chuckled humorlessly, drinking up the fear all over his face. This was it. Ronen was going to be burned alive.

Something in his gut twisted so hard he thought he might be sick as they made their way down the hall. Bhaltair ordered the Valdyr to open the doors. It took four of them to do so, moving synchronously. A gust of air smacked him in the face, blowing his hair back.

The Ash Throne. It was real.

There was really a *tree* in the middle of the castle. Unlike any other, the trunk of the towering ash tree before him curved and bent to form a perfect seat. Its vibrantly green leaves were so glossy they reflected the sunlight coming from the open-dome ceiling above. The round room consisted of stained-glass walls telling the story of creation, then leading to the royal family tree.

The Ash Throne sat atop a golden staircase, with a green rug leading down to the doorway where Ronen stood shaking in his boots.

This was one of two powerful trees in Elphyne. Its sister was the Entrance Tree, another towering ash that was the only portal in or out of this realm: precisely where Ronen wished he was right now.

He could not explain it, but the Throne Tree was pulsing with power. He felt every wave of it pass through his body as Bhaltair shoved him forward. Ronen had never really been around true magic; save for the few Fae he had met with elemental powers (that they used against him). But it was as if the tree had a soul of its own. It was the heart of Elphyne, pumping power into the land with every regal heartbeat.

Encircling the room and passing under the Ash Throne was an empty brook where water would usually flow. Lotus flowers and lily pads lay dying on the dry ground. Obviously, they had gone to extreme measures in preparation for this trial ... Ronen could almost blush.

Bhaltair kept pushing him forward until they stood before the stairs leading up the throne, where nobody sat. Ronen was pushed onto his knees as they waited in ear-shattering silence.

Ronen looked around awkwardly. "Does he know we—"

"SILENCE!" a booming voice rang.

Suddenly, all the moisture was sucked out of the air, and a wave of hatred filled the room. Fritjof Aodh was like no other Fae. Others seemed to add on to the beauty in nature; he burned the life out of it. Even the water in Ronen's blood squirmed as his pores were swept dry.

Draped in only shades of red, and hair so blonde it was barely visible, the High Lord certainly dressed for the occasion.

"Ronen Nøkken." Ronen's adopted last name. "You stand here accused of going against your agreements and using impure powers of water with the intent to harm."

He paused as if waiting for Ronen to plead for his life. For once, Ronen took the general's advice on keeping his mouth shut. If only because Fritjof was even more intimidating than Bhaltair, something Ronen had thought was impossible.

He heard the large doors close behind him, and Fritjof took his place standing in front of the throne he did not have the blood to sit upon. If he tried, if *anyone* without royal blood tried, they would die a slow and painful death. Maybe that is how they would execute him.

More figures walked forward, and Ronen's eyes adjusted on three Buguls. Despite their gnome-like stature, bulbous noses, and protruding eyes, Buguls were highly intelligent. They served as representatives of all small nature folk and handled most legal business. Although in this particular moment, Ronen didn't feel all that represented.

The tallest of the three spoke in a voice so high it was hard to tell if they were male for female. "Does the accused have anyone willing to speak on his behalf?" They spoke to Bhaltair rather than Ronen.

The general shook his head. "He has no one."

No one.

The last pillar holding Ronen together crumbled. He no longer felt the pulse of the Ash Throne's ancient power, he no longer heard the people talking around him, he no longer felt anything at all. Even his anger abandoned him, leaving Ronen with the empty abyss in his chest. He had no one. Even those he thought he could trust were absent in his time of need.

Ronen was ready to erupt, not caring about this stupid court or trial. Forget punishment. Forget Elphyne and every last Fae within it. Ronen was going to die today, but he refused to admit guilt.

He opened his mouth, ready to give the High Lord the cussing of a lifetime, but was interrupted.

The large doors were loudly shoved open, and two Valdyr ran forward. Fritjof whipped back his long cape and walked down the stairs, passing Ronen without even acknowledging him. A surge of heat hit Ronen so hard, the blood on his face crusted and fell to the floor.

The Valdyr stopped before him and got down on their knees, one holding up something in his hand. "My apologies for interrupting, my lord, but this could not wait. This came through the Entrance Tree only hours ago."

Fritjof picked a small scroll out of the guard's palm and unrolled it. His red eyes scanned the parchment, top lip arched in a permanent look of disgust. Slimy. Heinous. Ugly. Fritjof was the first *ugly* Fae Ronen had ever seen.

After a moment, he turned back towards the Buguls. "I do not recognize this language. Translate this for me."

The three small creatures rushed forward but stepped back in defeat. "This tongue is beyond us, my lord." They bowed. "We can offer nothing."

As Fritjof turned back, Ronen caught a glimpse of the letter. Before he could think, he blurted out, "I can read it!"

All eyes turned to him. Fritjof's eyes blazed as he demanded an explanation. Seeing no way out now,

Ronen went with it. "That language, I know it. I can read it to you."

For five seconds, everyone stood motionless. Bhaltair raised his brows with genuine surprise, like he could not believe someone so dumb could exist.

Fritjof pointed at his guards, then at him. In an instant, Ronen had seven Valdyr surrounding him. The High Lord approached him, absolute revulsion in his expression. His eyebrows were even lighter than his hair, almost disappearing on his fair skin. Pale eyelashes surrounded his red eyes that bore into Ronen's soul.

He took a long breath. "Any games or lies, and—"

"I get it," Ronen snapped.

A wave of heat slapped him in the face, but he ignored it, not giving Fritjof the satisfaction of seeing him cower. Slowly, Fritjof held out the paper for him to read. Only one sentence was written in the small letters of Little Spoke. It consisted of only straight lines: crossed or dashed across a longer line that connected them all. Ronen squinted, only speaking when he was sure he had translated it correctly:

"We found her."

These words meant nothing to Ronen. He started to worry he read it wrong. But when he looked back up, Ronen almost leaped out of his skin. Two red eyes full of fury stared right back at him. Everyone went even stiller than before.

Fritjof held the letter in his palm, and Ronen watched as it burst into flames and melted into ashes. Perhaps no one else noticed, but Ronen saw the way Fritjof studied that paper: worry. Those three words had shaken the High Lord.

Ronen must have been right, because Fritjof turned his fiery gaze to Bhaltair and calmly said, "Everyone in this room dies. Come to my chambers afterward. We have an issue to address."

FIVE

It turned out Fallon made a rather good Haedilla. No one stopped her as she pushed her steed to its limits though the trees. She knew there had to be a few hidden warriors watching her, but she supposed the Haedilla did not have the same "kill on sight" law that the Blodvingers did.

After a short ride, Fallon stumbled upon a small village. She immediately disposed of her dark cloak and stole a new one, desperate to cover her hair and face. Fallon knew the Royal House would not be in this small, plain village so close to the Calder. She just hoped it was not a four-day walk as her own home village, Amory, had been.

Her teeth grit together. *Amory is not your homeland.* Fallon had to remember that. As far as she was concerned, her homeland was her mother's womb that she had clawed her way out of, bloody and screaming.

Fallon pulled her steed by the reins as she walked through the dirt roads. She knew no words in any language to describe how amazing the warm sun felt against her deprived skin. The Barwyn sky she'd become accustomed to was full of thick gray clouds, even in the summers.

Her new cloak was so thin compared to those in Barwyn made to keep off the snow. Audhild, the third territory, must make them specifically for each land. The Avvore Clan produced the fine fabrics for all Valdimir—just like the Blodvingers made weapons, and the Haedilla grew food. Trade was what kept them from war, but Fallon believed soon even that would not be enough to soothe men's lust for blood.

Though the people could not be more different, Fallon found similarities between this village and the small Barwyn towns she had visited. Same wooden longhouses and huts, same blacksmiths and meat houses—architecturally they were almost identical. But their shops strung bows instead of whacking red-hot axes. Their bakeries sold cakes instead of ale, and beyond the fences of the village Fallon could see farms growing crops she didn't even recognize. No brothels were in sight, and no fights took up the streets.

Fallon did not let the scenery fool her, the Haedilla were no pansies. There was a reason even Beowulf Solveij failed to claim these lands.

Maybe it was the anonymity she now had, maybe it was the smell of rosemary in the air, but Fallon felt more comfortable here than in Amory. How had her life been so miserable for so long, she felt safer with her enemies? The people who were supposed to be her family were her biggest threat.

For a while she made her way through the streets, keeping close to the shadows. People kept on turning back to her with grimacing faces, no doubt because of her smell and horrid appearance. Fallon needed to find a bathhouse, but if they were the same as in Barwyn, they'd be public ones. There would be no worse way to announce her illegal presence than to undress in front of the enemy and have a nice soak. So, she turned into the trees east of the village, hoping to find a spring or stream.

There were hundreds of flowers littering the ground, and the trees were bursting with leaves. Fallon had never seen so many colors in her life. Why did she never come here when the royal families met to discuss trade? Her father always left her behind. As the sound of the busy village died off in the distance, Fallon realized why.

This place reminded her of her mother.

Yes, Asta would have loved it here. Where the fields matched her eyes, and the sky mirrored her spirit. Her mother had been the world Fallon never saw. All she had to do was carry out this last task and die a glorious death. Then the pain could finally end, and she and Asta would be reunited. Hopefully in a place much like this one.

Her ear twitched towards the sound of trickling water, and Fallon's heart rushed with excitement. She quickened her pace, dragging her horse along towards the sound. Soon enough, there it was. A bit underwhelming, yes; it was only a small creek as wide as her body, but it was enough.

Fallon tied off her horse, encouraging it to drink. Then she walked a few paces downstream and peered down at her broken reflection.

She knelt and shoved off her hood, breathing in the crisp afternoon air. Alas, Fallon did not get to so much as touch the water, because staring back up at her were two more pairs of eyes that were not hers.

She saw them on either side of her own reflection—in the trees above her, bows drawn tight. Her whole body buzzed with anxiety as she calmly walked back to her horse. They might not know she saw them; she might be able to make it back to the village and lose them in the crowd if she just acted calm.

"Stop right there, and raise your hands," a male voice said.

Fallon quickly scanned the ground, but still saw no one. Luckily, she had slipped her dagger up her sleeve the moment she saw them. She did as she was told, using the cloak to obscure her misshapen forearm.

Finally, she heard them. Two faint *thuds* as they jumped down from the trees onto the soft earth. They were graceful and swift, as all Haedilla were trained to be.

She turned to face them. Two men: one short and stout, the other tall and youthful. The older one, balding on the top, approached Fallon slowly. Both of their bows were knocked with wicked-looking arrows.

"Jaeger, send falcon to those water catchers. I believe we found their missing steed," he said in a gruff voice.

But the younger one, Jaeger, did not take his eyes off Fallon. He scanned her once over with enough intensity to make Fallon start to sweat. "I think we found more than a lost steed," he said, cocking his head to the side. An innocent gesture that made Fallon want to roundhouse kick him in the face.

She saw it in his eyes that he knew. Not everything, but he knew Fallon did not belong here. If only she had gotten a change of clothes while she was in the town and fixed her broken face …

Well, too late now. Fallon flicked her wrist, summoning the blade in hand and gave the horse's rear a quick swipe. It let out a cry, rearing up on its hind legs before coming down into a full charge towards the men.

Fallon took off in the opposite direction. The men shouted at one another, compelled on who to chase down first. She headed for a dense grove of trees to lose them in, but she was in their territory. Thus, it took only a minute of running aimlessly for Jaeger to catch up to her. Fallon never even heard him coming.

He was soundless, winding through the trees as if he were a phantom in the wind. He was in front of her in seconds, bow drawn and ready. She came to a stumbling halt, her eyes barely had time to focus on the tip of the arrow before it was flying towards her.

A stinging pain shot through her right ear and echoed in her skull. Suddenly she was pinned to the tree behind her, like a painting nailed to a wall.

By the time she had her wits about her, Jaeger already had another arrow knocked. He watched her carefully with those striking hazel eyes. His head and gaze seemed to move separately, like a bird of prey.

"Stop, that was a warning shot. I will not miss next time," he said, and Fallon believed him.

"Are you part of the royal guard?" she asked. She needed someone to take her to the chief. Jaeger and his fat friend wore uniforms—simple, but official. Dark green tunics lined in gold tucked into brown trousers. The Halvar Royal House crest was patched onto their breast: a golden crown around the trunk of a leafless tree. No cloaks, No capes, just a quiver full of arrows.

He let out a small laugh. "You need to learn to roll your *R*s less, northerner," he said, adjusting his grip on his aspen bow. "Even if you blend in, your mouth is stained by the Blodvingers."

Fallon hissed through her teeth. "I am no more a Blodvinger than you are. You have the horse, now just let me go," she said, as more of a warning than a request. She could hear the second man's footsteps approaching behind her.

Jaeger shook his head, dark brown curls bouncing from in front of his eyes. "You have no rights to be on this land," he said slowly. Little did he know, Fallon didn't really have the right to be on *any* land.

The second man was a wheezing mess as he reached them. Jaeger rolled his eyes. "Norman, grab her weapon," he instructed.

"I beg your pardon? Who is shadowing who here?" Norman asked in annoyance. Clearly, they were working on their own issues. "I already had to chase down a bloody horse, you take it!"

While they were distracted, Fallon bit her lip, counted to three, and jerked her head to the side. She felt the lobe of her ear split as she yanked herself free. Pulling the arrow from the bark, she stepped back and held out her dagger in one hand and the arrow tip in the other.

Already captured, she had one option left. It was a risky, foolish move. One laced with cowardice, but Fallon was desperate.

"I demand *grio*," she announced in a panic.

They both stared at her with shocked expressions. Jaeger's eyes were on her bleeding ear, and Norman just cursed aloud multiple times.

Fallon slowly lowered her weapons, and she let out an internal sigh of relief as the men did the same. In the old age, *grio* was a truce between traveler and leader. Fallon now had temporary protection while she was brought before the chief to speak. Only after she voiced her part could they decide to kill her.

It was a coward's move, but Fallon was outmatched and completely out of her element. She had been a fool to think she could somehow find the Royal House alone and unseen. A cocky fool.

"Who are you to invoke such a thing?" Norman asked, sneering at her. "Why should we even honor it?"

Fallon was at least three inches taller than him, but he had about fifty pounds on her. He had a pig's nose and bull's breath. She could probably take him, but Jaeger was a far more formidable challenge.

"I already told you. I am no Blodvinger. I am seeking asylum within Halvar, in exchange for information the chief wants," she explained.

They both tensed. "How would a northern girl know what Chief Sigurd wants?" Jaeger asked, scanning her again with those multicolored eyes. His gaze shifted impossibly fast. Watching her breathe and speak all while counting every freckle on her face.

Sigurd. Chief Sigurd of House Osmund. Fallon had not been able to remember the names until just now. "I suppose you'll just have to trust me, and abide by tradition," she said.

She recalled her father speaking of their chieftain, calling him weak and a coward because he wanted no place in war. Her father tried to make an alliance with him once; together they would take Audhild and split the territory and spoil fifty-fifty. But Chief Sigurd was no fool. Beowulf Solveij never went by his word and never left any survivors. Fallon was walking proof of that.

Sigurd Osmund had his young, beautiful wife and seven children. The eldest son was the perfect heir waiting for Sigurd to die or retire. If only everything had been that simple at House Solveij.

Neither of them appeared enthusiastic about her proposal. They glanced at each other, having a silent conversation before slowly nodding. Norman spat on the grass, shaking his small head. "Twenty years in the Keepers and never once has anyone called for *grio*, not once," he grumbled, turning to Jaeger. "I will call for some Reapers to come down and escort her to Reinhart," he said.

But Jaeger shook his head vehemently. "We must be the ones to take her. She has *grio* with us, not them. Reinhart is only a two-day journey by horse, we can make it."

Fallon turned to him in surprise. She did not know what a Reaper was, but they sounded far more equipped to handle her than these two did.

"Now is not the time to be showin' off to the chief, lad," Norman warned. But Jaeger's face was set in stone. He was almost handsome, with a square jaw and a nose that had obviously been broken before. He could not have been older than twenty-five, with bronze skin that glowed like burnt caramel in the sunlight.

Seeing there was no point in arguing, Norman let out a sigh through his nose. "Fine. But the girl will be restrained and without a horse," he added, a greasy smile on his face.

Jaeger opened his mouth, but Fallon butted in. She did not need him arguing and ruining this perfect opportunity for her. "Very well," she said.

Norman, appearing just into his forties, let out a dramatic groan and took a seat at the trunk of a nearby tree. "You fetch the horses then, lad, I have done enough wrangling for today."

This was not the *grio* Fallon had imagined.

There was a rope tied loosely around her neck, the other end tied to Jaeger's horse who stalked a yard behind her. Another rope bound her wrists together, leading up to Norman's brilliant white steed in front of her. If she acted outside of *grio*, they could simply run in opposite directions and decapitate her. Or drag her in the mud until she decides to behave. Norman kept the pace; the ropes had been his idea in the first place. Saying it was, "better to be safe than sorry" with women such as Fallon.

She did not mind the walk at first. She got to take in the beautiful landscape before her. She moved through the lush, rolling green hills with occasional groves of trees. They even passed a flower meadow a mile back, and Fallon had to resist the urge to run to it. But as the hours passed, each hill became an obstacle. She swore each one was taller than the last. Death had turned a blind eye to her for now, but sleep whispered beautiful things in her ear as she fought to keep her eyes open.

Fallon demanded one leg in front of the other, and she kept doing so as two hours turned into five. With Fallon on foot, it would take closer to three or four days to reach the Royal House. But Fallon did not complain. She did not ask for water or a break for one single reason:

Fallon was tied with ropes, not chains.

Three days in the Royal House dungeons had her licking the sweating stone walls for water. Three days had felt like a lifetime chained up outside with the frozen metal ripping the skin from her bones. But *this* ... being warm under a blue sky with the end in sight, she could bear this for however long it took. She did not feel guilty for taking in breath after breath, as there was no one to tell her she was a waste of air. It was the freest Fallon had felt in a terribly long time.

Even though the path they were on was invisible to Fallon, she knew it was the right way. There was a small, barely noticeable tugging feeling within her that only got stronger the farther they went. As if someone had tied a piece of string around her sternum and was pulling her forward. Fallon knew Reinhart was where she was meant to go.

The Norns had unraveled a ball of golden thread to lead her to her destiny, and Fallon planned to follow it until her legs gave out. And if they did, she would crawl to it. Fallon would cut off her legs to get rid of the dead weight so she could drag herself to it. Because her fate was the only thing she had left. Fate, and a bottomless well of anger was all that kept her together these last few days. It was probably the only thing that kept her going long before her banishment.

Jaeger was always closer to her, so the rope around her neck never actually choked her. At one point he even sped up so they were side by side, trying for conversation.

"Who is your chief, if not Chieftain Beowulf?" he asked.

"I do not belong to a clan," she simply stated, trying to not scowl at his name.

He snorted. "Everyone in Valdimir belongs to a clan," he said. And for the most part, he was right.

When she said nothing, he continued anyway. "So, you are a nomad? That explains ..." he eyed her up and down. "... A lot."

Fallon turned to hide her red cheeks. A small part of her was embarrassed that he thought she presented herself this way all the time: matted hair clumped with dirt, filthy clothes, covered with wounds old and new. So she changed the subject as she trudged through the knee-high grass.

"You don't speak a peasant's tongue. Did you grow up in Reinhart?" she asked. If he did, she might be able to get details about what to expect when she arrived.

He shook his head, brown curls swaying across his brow. "Not exactly."

She looked up at him for the first time. He held the reins with his left hand, his right tapping on his thigh. Did she make him nervous? He sure did not seem eager to share any information, but Fallon could respect that. Because neither was she.

Up ahead, behind the next tree line, Fallon saw the smoke from a chimney blowing into the wind. *Another village already?* In Barwyn, the lands were so unforgiving that there were few places where it was even possible to build a village. Amory was the largest, as the royal village usually was. But every lord of every village still answered to the Royal House; to Chieftain Beowulf. And one day, they will answer to Chieftess Fallon.

She smiled at the thought. That smile vanished as a familiar, warm voice spoke up once again from behind her.

"How long has it been since you've eaten?" Jaeger asked, probably having seen her drool over the smell of meat that was pouring over the hills.

She shrugged. "A day, maybe two." She lied. Fallon did not need, nor want his pity. His hazel eyes already watched her with enough emotion to make her vomit.

Jaeger called ahead, "Norman! Let us stop in Elinbar. We should pack a bag for the next two days, as well as for the journey home."

The grumpy man looked over his shoulder with a sneer. "Very well. I will get rations. You watch the banshee. Consider this part of your training, lad. The Keepers rarely have hostages, but as you can see there are always exceptions."

Fallon spit in the direction of his horse. Curse them. One day soon she would be leading them in her ranks. She would make sure Norman was in the back, without a horse and wrists bound.

Norman glared at her scornfully. Rather than a verbal punishment, he kicked his horse hard in the sides. Before she could shout the most vulgar insult she could muster, Fallon was yanked from her feet. Her face smacked the earth as she was dragged through the dirt by her wrists. If Jaeger had not been so close to her, she might have lost her head.

Jaeger was quick to whip his own horse into a run. He shouted at Norman to stop, but the old man was laughing heartily as they rode through the trees. Fallon shouted curses as dirt was shoved down her shirt and up her nose. Her face was bombarded by rocks and tree roots until common sense kicked in. Fallon flipped onto her back, only to face the horrifying sight of horse hooves stomping an inch from her face.

After what felt like a century of screaming and watching the world fly by in a blurry haze, Norman cut the rope attached to his horse. Fallon came to a tumbling halt, stopping only an inch from a cobblestone road that would have ripped her to shreds.

Her head was spinning as Fallon laid still for a moment, trying to ease the storm of anger within her. A familiar warmth was building in her chest: a warning of what was to come if she did not calm down. They reached the village, and Fallon had already made a spectacle out of herself. She did not need anyone to see her explode into a ball of light like a comet falling from the sky, nothing but destruction in her wake.

Not yet at least.

Jaeger jumped down from his horse and reached for her. Fallon quickly shoved him off, hitting his arm with enough force to make her hand sting. "Get off me! I'm fine," she shouted, the air pressure rose until her ears hurt, she hoped he did not notice.

She grabbed her cloak and tried to rub the dirt and blood from her face. Jaeger knelt next to her, hazel eyes full of concern. Fallon wanted to punch him in the face.

"Don't be foolish, you might infect your …" he blinked at her. "Your ear?"

Fallon instantly reached up. Sure enough, the slice through her ear had mended. Nothing but crusted blood and dirt. She touched the side of her face that had been the size of her fist hours ago, but the skin was smooth. In Barwyn, her wounds came back with time. But ever since entering Halvar, she has stayed healed.

Fallon shook her head, "You missed. It was just a nick."

The boy stared at her for a long while. His hawk's gaze engulfed her soul. Fallon turned, biting the inside of her lip and gritting her teeth through the pain that only fueled the wildfire spreading through her veins.

"What is your name?" he asked at last.

She needed to calm down. For no reason other than that, she answered him. "Rhodeia," she lied, her throat as dry as straw.

He nodded. "Well, Rhodeia, it seems as though we will be spending some time together since you pissed off my mentor and everyone else wants to kill you." He raised a disciplinary brow at her as if she were supposed to feel guilty about the fact. She did not, as this was a fairly average day for Fallon.

She shrugged. "What is his deal, anyways?" she asked. The village consisted of no more than ten buildings, with a single longhouse and well in the center. Fallon and Jaeger—along with the horse—stayed in the trees off the cobble roads, if only to hide the terrible sight that was Fallon's face.

Jaeger took a seat on the soft grass, pulling his quiver over his shoulder and tending to the feathers of his arrows.

"Do not let Norman trouble you. Two decades in the Keepers can turn men more sour than month old milk," he joked.

Fallon studied him for a few moments. She slowly sat down, refusing to let the pain of doing so show on her face.

She licked her cracked lips. "These Keepers and Reapers you speak of, what does it mean?" she asked.

"Reapers are our ground warriors. They do all the raiding, combat, and get all the glory. Keepers stay within the trees, mostly along the border. We are archers. The eye in the sky that sees and knows all," he explained, waving his hands dramatically.

Fallon nodded. It was an interesting tactic, having a legion of foot warriors along with a second, hidden army. If even half of them could shoot as good as Jaeger ... Fallon could post them at the many cliffs surrounding Amory to shoot down anyone who tried to escape.

"Why did you choose to be a Keeper?" she asked.

Jaeger quickly went back to fiddling with his arrows. "I am not a fighter. So much so that Norman was the only one I could find who agreed to allow me to shadow him," he admitted.

Fallon nodded. "I had a mentor too, once," she said dryly. He must have seen the coldness in her face because he did not pry.

The lush grass around them brought out the green in his eyes. Though she knew the next moment they would be blue again, or gray, as they changed with the surrounding light. They sat in almost-comfortable silence, watching the trees lean in the wind.

Alas, as she quickly found with Jaeger, the silence never lasted long. He threw his quiver back over his shoulder and turned toward the sun that was slowly descending over the western hills.

"As only an apprentice, I had no hopes of being assigned to watch the border. It is a great honor to protect our side of the Calder. Keepers who prove themselves worthy enough to be permanently stationed there get the title of Muninn Spirit," he said.

This was the first thing about Halvar that made perfect sense to Fallon. Muninn and Huginn were Odin's pet ravens; the three were rarely depicted apart. The ravens' mission each morning was to circumnavigate the world, acting as his eyes and ears as they accumulate a wealth of information and relay it back to Odin. They were what made him so wise.

Jaeger went on with a sigh. "So, I was disappointed to find Norman had volunteered us to post around *Penswallow*," he snorted. "Possibly the most boring and least eventful village in Halvar. At first, I thought it was because Norman did not trust me, but after the first week I figured out he just preferred not to work. I often found him dozing off in his perch, the flask he swore was filled with water always bone dry." He shook his head, eyes still on the setting sun.

Fallon was not sure what she was supposed to say. This was the first real conversation she'd had in days, and she was finding it difficult to pay attention let alone care about this archer's life story. Exhaustion was tugging at her eyelids, the soft earth around her growing more comfortable by the second.

"That was until early this morning." He went on. "When I saw a girl in dark clothing racing through the trees like her life depended on it. I tried to signal Norman, but he was either asleep or ignoring me, because nothing *ever* happens in Penswallow."

Fallon stared at him. At his long chin, perfectly straight teeth, and naively kind eyes. "Then you should have just left me alone."

He gave her a slight smile, thin lips barely curling at the edges. "I almost did. But I watched you steal that cloak. I saw the bruises on your face and the way you hid within the crowd. You know I could not just let that go. I went back to get Norman, but I kept stepping on …" He trailed off and shook his head, eyebrows scrunched in deep thought.

Fallon leaned forward, glazing at the bottom of Jaeger's boots. Hidden within the groves, within the mud and grass, were many bright orange seeds.

"Cloudberries?"

Jaeger watched her carefully as he slowly nodded. "Yes, cloudberries. By the time I woke up Norman and returned, I lost you. I used the squashed berries to retrace my steps, and eventually there were fresh ones headed towards the west creek. So, I trusted the path they left me."

A sickening, dropping sensation made Fallon blanch as she repeated, "*They?*"

Before Jaeger could answer, the sound of horse hooves approaching made them both jump to their feet. Norman, in all his tubby glory, came to a halt before them. He jumped down without a word, untied some bags from the saddle, tossed one to each of them, then walked deeper into the trees. The bags under his eyes were heavier than the one Fallon held in her arms. For the first time, she saw a dark, haunted guise in the man's brown eyes.

Jaeger gave her an apologetic smile. "He gets this way when the sun goes down. Best not to talk to him until after he drinks himself to sleep," he said. He pulled a loaf of crusty bread out of his bag and began to chew loudly.

Fallon, still in shock, could barely get out the words, "Wasn't planning on it," she assured him before she collapsed back down. Had Jaeger grown up with the same stories she had? Ones of Little Folk and nymphs and Faeries?

She scarfed down everything in her bag while Jaeger made a small fire. A bread loaf, three apples, some hard cheese, dried meat, and a canteen of water were all gone in minutes. She hardly noticed him staring at her until she had to come up for air.

He blinked, the fire lighting up his face in an eerie glow. "How long has it been since you've eaten, really?" he asked.

Why did the Little Folk help you, too? She wanted to ask in return. Instead, she folded up her cloak into a pillow and laid down. With a full stomach and the warm fire against her skin, Fallon let sleep consume her. But not before she quietly mumbled to the man she could feel staring at her.

"Five days."

SIX

As Fritjof Aodh made his dramatic exit out of the throne room, Ronen Nøkken internalized that he was going to die.

He thought about his eight years at the shop. The sweltering nights in the storage closet that he had come to love. Occasionally, when the nymphs came out and danced to summon the rain, Urg gave them the day off. He always said it was because of the leaky roof—he did not want to risk putting out the forge and ruining their work. The truth, however, was that Urg made everyone leave so Ronen could go stand on the back porch. He took his shirt off and let the rain wash over him, ravishing every second.

That was the memory he wanted in his head as he lived out his final moments. So when Bhaltair closed the massive doors and turned to them all, Ronen was able to stay calm. He let the memory of the water pouring down over his face take over his mind. Not the fact that he was alone, not that nobody would remember him. Just the calm that came with the rain.

Because now, his lifelong torment was over. Ronen did not listen as Bhaltair spoke to the three Buguls, did not watch as they and two guards vanished somewhere in the back of the room. Ronen was too busy staring out of the stained-glass window, memorizing the way sunlight felt on his face.

The late Queen of Elphyne had been added to the royal family tree where she would remain eternally. She was young when she died, leaving behind no heirs. She wore a billowing dress of white, hands clasped gently together. The way the sun was coming in, it made her green eyes glow gold as they stared at him.

The hair on Ronen's arms stood as they held eye-contact. Perhaps it was the mastery of the artwork, but the gaze felt so *real,* like she truly was staring right back at him. It made him feel less alone. At least one person would know what happened to him here today.

Two black boots stepped in his line of vision. Ronen raised his head from where he still knelt on the floor. Bhaltair loomed down at him, completely expressionless as usual. Ronen turned back to the window and muttered his last words.

"Don't mark my grave."

Bhaltair unsheathed his sword. The pummel was curved, with a golden set of wings and a diamond in the center. It appeared to outdate Ronen's smith shop, possibly even outdating Urg. Swords such as that usually had a name, passed down generation to generation. Generals thousands of years before Bhaltair probably used that sword to execute other innocent Faeries. Ronen could practically see the blood dripping from it.

"Why?" the general asked. But Ronen did not answer. He let Bhaltair put the pieces together; that Ronen had been desecrated and segregated his entire life. If he was truly going to die, he wanted to finally rest in *peace*, six feet under, where no one could bother him ever again.

Bhaltair raised the blood-soaked blade, and Ronen swallowed down the ball in his throat. He kept staring at the queen's eyes, so intensely that red and purple circles took over his vision. His heart was racing as thick, heavy fear consumed his system.

Ronen flinched embarrassingly hard as Bhaltair's blade came down right in between his wrists. There was a horrible screeching as metal cut metal, and Ronen's chains fell to the floor.

He blinked. Or maybe he yelped. Honestly, Ronen almost threw up as Bhaltair pulled him to his feet and got uncomfortably close to his face.

"Are you going to stay quiet and act dead, or do I need to knock you unconscious?" he hissed.

Ronen's brain hurt. His eyes burned. He looked around, down, up, everywhere but the Fae warrior before him. He even turned to the queen trapped in glass for help, but she had nothing to offer. *Why am I not dead?*

Bhaltair shook his head. "Forget it. Your mortal brain is failing you," he grumbled.

Before Ronen's mortal brain could even form a sentence, Bhaltair loaded his fist back and Ronen finally fell into the darkness he had been waiting for.

Death, as it seemed, smelled of body odor and dirt.

As Ronen slowly opened his eyes, he was lying on his back in complete darkness. He did not feel dead, but he felt sore. A pounding pain above his eyebrow alerted him to his still-beating heart. His own breath was the only sound in the empty room.

The room that he knew was square. He knew if he crawled, he would find nothing but compacted dirt walls. Ronen knew climbing, screaming, or fighting was pointless. Because he was back in his underground pit, buried alive.

He was surprised, and a little afraid, of how disappointed he was. Ronen sat up and touched his brow, wincing at the large lump that was there. What happened?

The throne room. There was never a verdict on his trial—if that even counted as a trial. Ronen shook his head, wiping his hands down his face. Three words. The three simple words on that letter had been more important than Ronen. He was so dismissible, so useless, they forgot to kill him.

He sat there for a long while taking that in. It could have been minutes or hours. Long enough that the sudden sound of the hatch above him creaking open was enough to make him leap out of his skin.

Then he nearly soiled himself as a large, cloaked figure jumped down, soundlessly landing a mere foot in front of him. Ronen's useless mortal eyes strained to see in the dark. The open hatch let in just enough light from above that he could make out the figure's silhouette. He could do nothing but watch in horror as they reached into their cloak.

But rather than the glint of metal coming out, an eerie green glow lit up the brooding face of Bhaltair Herleif. The last person Ronen expected to ever see again.

An endless stream of questions rushed through his head, but the first one to make it out of his mouth was, "are those mushrooms?"

He pointed to the large jar in the general's hand that was the source of the ghostly green glow. Bhaltair gave Ronen a strange look, glancing back and forth between him and the jar. "Yes, foxfire. They grow almost everywhere, but with the sun always in the sky, few people know about their bioluminescence."

Ronen was speechless. What business did the General of the Valdyr have knowing such botanical wonders? "Were they all out of torches?" Ronen joked, trying to calm his nerves.

Bhaltair's eyes shifted up towards the hatch, then pushed Ronen closer toward the wall. "No torches. No flames," he said quietly.

The seriousness in his voice made Ronen shiver. No flames—no Fritjof.

The green light made Bhaltair's golden eyes glow yellow. He scanned Ronen over carefully before speaking. "Hold out your arm," he instructed.

"Why am I not dead?" Ronen finally got the courage to ask.

The general snarled. "Do you want to be? Hold out your arm," he said again, and Ronen had the feeling this would be the last time he asked nicely.

So he complied. Taking a step back, Ronen held out his grime-covered skin. He had no idea what to expect. He watched as Bhaltair used his free hand to grab something tucked into his belt. Ronen heard the familiar sound of a popping cork, then the cool sensation of water rushing down his skin.

A shiver ran up and down Ronen's spine, his entire scalp tingled as he shook off his soaked arm, cursing in surprise. He was not sure what shocked him more—the fact that Bhaltair Herleif had just poured a jug of salty water on him, or that the general seemed hesitant about it.

Those feline eyes watched Ronen carefully for a few seconds before nodding, his lips pressing into a straight line. "I apologize, but I had to be sure," he said.

Ronen rolled his eyes. Bhaltair balked at his disrespect, but Ronen already had a death sentence. What did he have to lose?

"There, you see? The Nøkken monster can't hurt anybody," he mocked. He thought this would be over, but so long as he was alive people would never trust him. All they saw in Ronen was his blue left eye.

The general stared at him as if debating what to say. He stood straight, his presence radiating power even through his obscuring cloak. It was more than the primal power all Fae carried. Bhaltair's deep set eyes, strong jaw, and permanent scowl demanded submission.

"There are much worse things from Ondorr than Nøkken," he said quietly.

"Sentinels?" Ronen whispered. "You think I'm a *Sentinel*?" The shadow-men were Elphyne's biggest threat. They were born in the darkness of Ondorr; soldiers of the sunless woods. Every so often, a group of them would cross into Lysserah. The main purpose of the Valdyr was to kill them, round them back into their side of Elphyne, or die trying. Ronen had been accused of many things, but this insult rammed deep into his soul.

"Not a Sentinel." Bhaltair shook his head, lost in thought.

Ronen racked his memory, trying to remember everything he had ever heard about Ondorr. During the day, he could often hear his coworkers murmuring about such things. Sentinels were no secret, they encountered them firsthand during the Elphynian War over a thousand years ago. It was a panacea mission to push the shadow of Ondorr back. Many, many died fighting wave after wave of monsters.

Blights were dark clouds with wings, they stole your senses one by one until you were too helpless to run. A Fodden was a personification of decay. A creature assembled from bones and carcasses. They all had no soul, felt no pain, and understood nothing but sickness and death. The perfect, disposable soldiers.

Elphyne only won that war because some Valdyr accidentally discovered Ondorr's weakness. Seawater, it seemed, mixed with their inky-like forms and absorbed them into nothingness. Any creature from Ondorr who encountered it hissed and melted like a slug stuck in salt. Because the seawater surrounding this land is sacred. It is *made* of souls. That is why tears are salty, too. When we cry, it is just our soul bleeding.

A slug in salt. That is exactly what Bhaltair had been waiting to see when he poured that seawater on his arm. Ronen did not resemble a Sentinel—thank the gods—but there was a creature far more primordial than shadow soldiers who could resemble *him*.

A creature Ronen had not heard of since he was a young boy. Oftentimes he would sneak out of the orphanage and run to different houses to peek through all the windows. He wanted to know what families were like, what they did and how they spoke to one another. Even no older than seven, Ronen knew the way the orphanage matrons spoke to him was wrong. He just wished that little boy understood that it was not his fault the Little folk chose to leave him there.

Sitting under open windows or crouched on porches, Ronen listened to their bedtime stories. He heard them laugh and could smell their dinners. But when the children went to sleep, he also heard the parents speak in hushed tones.

He remembered the one-bedroom, spruce wood house on the corner of the street. It was the middle of the night, but the sun still shined just as bright, so it was hard to hide. He ducked under the windowsill filled with chrysanthemums and listened to the story that kept him up all night for weeks. About an ancient threat to Elphyne long thought extinct, but many believed one remained. One that survived the huntings during the war because it was stronger than its brethren—smarter.

Ronen felt the blood drain from his face. His body felt ice cold as he prepared to say the word. He only mustered a whisper. "The last Shapeshifter?"

The glow of the foxfire mushrooms seemed to dim in response. Bhaltair nodded grimly. "What would be a better cover for a Shapeshifter, than a foul Nøkken orphan?" he said. Not cruelly, but honestly.

It hurt, but Ronen understood. "Someone not allowed near the water that could kill it. Someone people turned away from, with no family to account for." He nodded. "You were smart to think as much. I'm sorry to disappoint you, but I really am just a foul Nøkken orphan who *really* needs a toilet," he admitted.

Bhaltair started to pace the room, stalking back and forth like the predator he was. "It *is* disappointing. Over a decade as general, and I have made no progress tracking her down." He gritted his teeth.

"Her?" Ronen asked. "You think the Shapeshifter is female?" Could a Shapeshifter even have a true gender?

Bhaltair suddenly stopped walking. He looked up at the hatch and his face fell, surely hearing something Ronen's mortal ears could not. "I have reasons to believe what I do. Whatever you think you know about Ondorr and Shapeshifters, boy, I promise it is only a quarter of the truth."

Given how little Ronen knew, the general was probably right. Someone told him Shapeshifters were blood-drinkers, that's how they changed forms. The more blood they had, the more powerful they became. But they could only mimic appearance, not powers or knowledge.

A rope dropped down from the hatch. Bhaltair grabbed hold. "Stay here and ... Listen," was all he said before he climbed the rope, not bothering to use his legs. A second later, Ronen heard the hatch close and lock above him.

"Yeah, I'll stay here!" Ronen shouted up pointlessly, throwing his arms up. "Like I have another choice!"

SEVEN

Fallon swore her legs were made of lead as they trudged over hill, after hill, after hill. She *should* feel great after being fed and well rested. The only rope on her was one that bound her wrists, and she even got to bathe at an abandoned bathhouse Jaeger found.

But Jaeger was the source of her uneasiness.

Early this morning, when her eyes barely started to flutter, she heard the men talking. They needed to find Fallon new clothes and a way to get rid of her smell. Jaeger suggested Norman go back into the village to find clothes while he sought out a small pond, but Norman was not having it. He was audibly annoyed as he shouted, "Are there any more errands, Lord Osmund, that I can do for you?" he asked sardonically.

Fallon's eyes had shot open. Jaeger did not protest the name, he just chuckled and told the old man off. *Lord Osmund.*

The name had been haunting her ever since they left three hours ago. Fallon thought it over while munching on breakfast. She thought about it while bathing, while lacing up the new brown vest over her green undershirt. Jaeger Osmund, of House Osmund. No wonder he wore boots so much finer than Norman's and how he knew the way to Reinhart by memory.

But now, with the lord following on horseback behind her, Fallon could not make sense of it. She worked on braiding her tangled hair to the side while she was deep in thought. Sigurd Osmund's eldest son was only a year or two older than Hakon, Fallon's half-brother and false heir to the Blodvinger throne. That could make him no older than fifteen. Yet here Jaeger was, well into his twenties.

As far as she remembered, the Osmund family were all of fair hair and blue eyes. Jaeger held neither. Perhaps Norman had only been joking when he called him a lord. Or, just maybe, Jaeger had been born into the same unfortunate fate as Fallon.

She did not want to let herself believe it. She did not want to have that hope ... The dream that someone might understand her pain. Even *if* Jaeger was Sigurd Osmund's bastard son, he was alive. He was still living in Halvar. The man even worked for the bloody Royal House.

She shook her head in disbelief. Mercy. Compassion. Opportunity. These were actions not given to Fallon. No, Fallon was thrown off a cliff for being a bastard. Her father had claimed she was abusing privileges by living in the Royal House and wrongly acclaiming herself heir.

In her defense, she was not even a bastard until her father remarried. Her mother's very existence faded from the people's memory, leaving Fallon as the only proof of their marriage. As years passed, assumptions were born about Fallon's real mother being only a harlot passing through due to her wild red hair and green eyes. All respect for her had been lost by the time she had her first bleed. She was just a rat living in the walls after that.

No, Jaeger understood nothing of her pain. He never had to fight other children for meals. He was never forced to kill the horse he loved. Fallon did. So if this was all a set up, and he was taking her back to his father as an offering, she would kill him. Fallon would hold a knife to his neck until they agreed to her terms. As of right now, they were each other's hostages.

"Rhodeia?"

She nearly forgot her own fake name. She responded a few seconds late. "What?"

Jaeger sped up to trot next to her. "How are you feeling?"

She could not bring herself to look at him. She did not know how she felt. She was so mad that she was calm, her anger was a flame that snuffed itself out. That ball of energy in her chest pounded against her ribs like a caged animal, a constant reminder of what lingered inside of her. Unable to see straight, she said the first thing that came to her mind. "Warm."

He chuckled nervously. "I suppose to a northern wolf, that is a rare feeling."

She nodded. "In Barwyn, children train for the cold. They are given frostbite on purpose to condition the skin. Babies breathe frozen air until it's all they know." she explained.

Jaeger released the reins, holding his hands up in surrender. "I'm not saying I have seen worse. I'm just trying to understand. Sometimes in the spring, it rains so hard for so long I worry the sky will never clear again," he said quietly. When Fallon said nothing, he probed, "What *is* the worst weather you have ever seen?"

Fallon finally met his eyes. It was the genuine curiosity and naive innocence that lured Fallon into answering. The warmth in her slowly died out, replaced by the stone-cold memories that sent frost crawling over her skin.

"How old were you when Audhild invaded both our lands ten years ago?" she asked.

"I was fifteen," he said solemnly. He jutted his chin forward, gesturing to Norman who trotted ahead, ignoring them as usual. "Just keep your voice down."

That war had been devastating to them both. It was not born of violence, or greed or lust, but revenge. A different kind of fury that brought out the monster in men. Norman was old enough to have fought in it. Perhaps that was the source of the blackness behind his eyes.

Audhild was a labyrinth of dense trees, the Crosby Royal House tucked away under the lush canopy. One day, a fire of unknown origins began to rage. It spread, village after village left in embers. House Osmund and House Solveij sent no aid. They sat back, ready to watch a clan collapse.

Somewhere under the ashes, a young woman with a baby half out of her womb lay scorched. The wife of Chief

Destin, in the middle of delivering their fifth child, was in no condition to flee the flames. No one ever found that house, the woman, or the baby.

Chief Destin was beside himself with grief and rage. He sent army after army into Halvar and Barwyn, their only order: *make them pay.*

Fallon set her gaze forward, letting the memories play in the back of her mind. "I was eight when the fires started, and nine when the legions came marching," she explained. "It was not the war-horn that raised people from their slumber that night, but a different kind of alarm. A warning far worse than any battle ever waged. I was trying to fall asleep when the guards sounded the squall-horn," she explained.

Jaeger blinked. "A squall?"

She nodded. "A type of storm made by gods, to kill gods. It only comes around once or twice a century, but the winds from that fire blew north. Winds full of lost souls and last breaths. Imagine the biggest, darkest, angriest cloud you have ever seen. Except it was not high in the sky, but rolling on the ground. If you saw it, you would think the days of Ragnarok had come," she said.

"You really saw it?" he breathed. His eyes were wide, like a child listening to a bedtime story.

She chucked humorlessly. "All of Amory was consumed by the storm. The Avvore legions marching towards us never stood a chance, their frozen corpses still stand as statues in the fields. Buildings in Barwyn have protocols for such storms. Metal or wooden barricades are made to block every door and window. Anything to keep the cold out. The Royal House itself is built into the hollow of a mountain, the curvature keeps the worst of the winds away." She explained.

In Jaeger's silence, she went on. "Five minutes. After the squall-horn sounds, the doors to the Royal House grand hall open for five minutes. If you can make it before they lock everything down, you will be safe through the storm. People kill to get through those doors," she said quietly.

For once, Jaeger avoided her gaze. He stared straight ahead, hazel eyes transfixed on Norman's back. "Is it fair to assume you were not one of the lucky ones?" he asked.

"They closed the doors right in my face," she lied.

He did not need to know that she had been safe in her rooms, sitting by the warm fire. That her father's wife had barged in, holding baby Hakon in her arms. Once the grand hall was full, people would fill the halls, the kitchens, even the servant's chambers. Anywhere they could fit. Her stepmother had gotten overwhelmed, demanding her own room. So she grabbed Fallon by the hair and tossed her out of the window.

Fallon did not even get out a scream before the latch on the window was locked and a metal plate slid into place. She was still in her nightgown, not even wearing shoes as she ran through the chaos.

"How did you survive?" Jaeger asked gently.

Fallon wished he knew. She wished he could see the snow that had been on her hair and eyelashes. She wished that he could see the nine-year-old girl pushing her way through the frozen sea of screaming bodies, and the sound of that god-awful horn.

A soul. That storm had a soul. A wave of darkness made of nothing but wind and ice. Yes, the cold was intolerable, but the wind was fatal. With it came tiny shards of ice that ripped your flesh off in one gust. It tore down houses and devastated entire continents, leaving nothing but carnage and five feet of snow in its wake. It was moving impossibly fast, headed straight for the Royal House.

How had she survived?

A little girl with red hair and bleeding feet stood on a hilltop, staring into the eyes of calamity. A gale of icy wind hit her so hard it ripped the freckles from her cheeks, but she did not falter. The cloud with demon eyes seemed to stare back at her. They stood, storm against storm.

Then, the clouds broke. Beams of white light clawed their way through the haze. It started to slow down—as if the storm was dazed. It gave her just enough time to get to the stables.

Most horses ran upon sensing the storm, but some were trapped inside. Fallon locked the sliding door behind her, using all her tiny body to push bale after bale of hay in front of the doors. Finally, she hopped one of the pens and laid under a pregnant mare.

The horse's body heat was the only thing that kept her alive. It took two days for the storm to pass and another two before anyone found her. The sound of the wind breaking through the wood …

Fallon cleared her throat. "I managed."

In one motion smoother than running honey, Jaeger dismounted his horse and began walking next to her. Fallon had to look up and over his slim shoulder to see his face. "And your parents?" he asked carefully.

"Dead," she said, perhaps too fast. Too fast to not be suspicious. She quickly went on, stringing together whatever scraps of truth she could. "My mother died when I was around four. And my father …" She licked her lips. "He is gone too."

The late afternoon sun gleamed against his skin. She could only describe it as the color of hardened tree sap. He smiled, ruggedly square jaw now shadowed with stubble. "If you and I have nothing else in common, Rhodeia, at least we can both sympathize over that," he said.

"You lost your parents?" she asked, trying to soften her voice.

"My mother disappeared fifteen years ago, when I was ten. Father said she had somewhere to visit, but she never returned." He shook his head. "In terms of my father, he is still breathing, but he is dead in my mind," he said.

Fallon dropped her head, pretending to be interested by the grass at her feet. "I can sympathize with having a poor relationship with your father," she admitted.

He nudged her shoulder with his own. "Oh, don't be mistaken my lady. We had a wonderful relationship! Especially after my mother left, he was always there for me. He tried to ease the pain by telling me the same stories she had." He smiled sadly.

Once again, her hopes of someone possibly understanding her were kicked out from under her feet. Now, more annoyed than optimistic, she had to know the full truth.

She stopped walking and turned to face him "Jaeger, is your father—"

She was interrupted by the cries of Norman's horse. The white steed reared up on its hind legs, obviously offended at whatever was before them. Norman, however, said nothing as he soothed the horse.

"Norman! What—" But Jaeger stopped talking as he peered around his friend. Fallon moved to see for herself, but Jaeger swiftly put himself in front of her. "Stay still," he whispered.

Not feeling much of a need to listen, Fallon stepped out anyways. Four men—four *large* men—prowled towards them. They wore similar uniforms as her two companions, but they were wrapped head to toe in leather armor. They all had full quivers on their backs and strange staffs Fallon did not recognize. They were shorter than a spear, with nothing but a lead ball on the end. Swung with enough force, that could cause some serious damage.

"Reapers?" Fallon whispered.

Jaeger gave her a barely perceptible nod as she watched them approach.

She let out a low whistle. "Now these are the men I'm used to."

The man who Fallon decided was the leader, based on his position and gait, was first to speak. He was an older man, handsome face worn and torn. He had the classic Halvarian fair hair and blue eyes.

"Keepers!" he shouted in greeting. "What are you doing this far from the border? Surely two trees somewhere are really missing all the dead weight," he barked. He had an awful, snickering laugh that made Fallon physically blanch.

Her movement caught everyone's attention. "And with a prize!" he added.

Jaeger put on an impressively convincing smile. "We are simply escorting Lady Rhodeia back to her village. An errand I'm sure the guards of the hills have no time for." He bowed his head in obedience, but his tone and smirk implied challenge.

"What village?" another guard asked. His hair was so black, it gleamed almost blue in the light.

Norman, who had been uncharacteristically quiet, finally cleared his throat. "Falmoore. So we best be gettin, we wish to return before nightfall," he said, mustache bristling. They were both covering for her. They were lying to their own people's faces. *Why?*

The four Reapers still shifted around uneasily. They gripped those skull-bashing spears tightly in their hands. The blond man sized Fallon up, "What were you doing so far from your village, las?" he asked.

Fallon took Jaeger's advice from the previous day, holding down her *R*s and trying to mimic the lilt to Jaeger's voice. "Hunting rabbits. My father sells their furs," she lied. Halvar sold the furs to Audhild, who sewed them into boots and cloaks to sell to Barwyn. Fallon bought them herself at trade posts.

This answer, however, did not seem to satisfy the men. They looked at each other, having wordless conversation. But they all shrugged and seemed to continue on their way, tossing out a few more insults towards the Keepers.

Fallon leaned closer to Jaeger, trying to obscure her bound hands. As the group stalked past them, the blond man stopped next to Fallon. She kept her face neutral, resisting the urge to bite him as he reached for her. He grabbed a braided lock of her red hair, twirling the silver bead between his fingers. "What a unique color," he said quietly, his hot breath rolling across her face.

"Thank you," Fallon made herself say. She could feel Jaeger's back muscles tense. They did not relax until both parties began walking their separate ways. No one spoke a word.

Not until Norman turned around, face squashed and purple. "Do you understand—" he began his lecture, but Fallon did not want to hear it.

"You lied for me," she interrupted. "Why?"

After a few deep breaths, Norman finally relaxed his shoulders. "The rules of *grio*. We must protect you," he huffed.

"You have to protect me from your own people?"

Jaeger's head stayed low as he spoke. "The Reapers are much less ... Accommodating than Norman and I.

They would take their time getting you to Reinhart," he warned. "Your best chance is with us."

She thought for a few moments. This cordiality did not exist in Amory. The royal guard, the Vali, fought valiantly and together. This division within Halvar's own ranks was a weakness. One Fallon could abuse one day, once she became chieftess.

Jaeger mounted his horse, then held an arm out to Fallon. She stared at his empty palm. "What?"

"You have been walking for days. Take a break," he urged, reaching for her again.

She searched his eyes for any sign of ill intent. They were green today, green and full of warmth. Fallon reminded herself that they were not enemies, not where clans were concerned. Fallon had meant what she said: she was no more a Blodvinger than them.

She took his hand. It was difficult with her wrists still tied together, but they got her on and adjusted.

Norman gave them a disapproving glance. But Jaeger just smiled. "Do you want to get to Falmoore by nightfall or not?"

The old man grunted, reaching down to pull a flask from his belt. Fallon had seen this many times before: men returning from war desperate to numb the pain. To block out the nightmares. Jaeger said the old man needed to drink to fall asleep, but Fallon imagined his demons followed him well into the day. War was a sickness. And who it did not claim, it lived and festered within.

From here, she could use her restrained hands to reach over Jaeger's head and choke him out. Then, she could take the horse and ride into Reinhart herself. But not right now. Her eyelids weighed down as if they were made of lead. Fallon really did need to rest for a moment. She closed her eyes, pressed her forehead against Jaeger's back, and let the sun pour down on her.

Her dreams were bright, vivid, and strange. For a while all she saw was a blinding light. She saw faces she could not place and heard voices she did not know. Then, everything came to a standing halt.

Before her, standing in stunning regality, was a massive tree.

Its trunk was wider than Fallon was tall. Its branches loomed over her, covered with bright green leaves. It was beautiful. It called to her the way birds chase north: soundlessly, deeply, and naturally.

Every bone in her body settled into a safe, content joy as she reached out to touch the brown bark. Fallon felt like she was seeing an old friend, but the memory was just out of reach. This tree, this feeling, she had felt it once before.

A sudden flash of light made Fallon shield her eyes. As her eyes focused through the haze, she took a step back in horror.

The tree was up in flames.

The heat quickly doubled in intensity as each leaf crumpled to ashes. Fallon tried to run, but she was paralyzed. It had no voice, it had no face, but the tree was calling out in pain. Fallon felt its despair in the depths of her own soul, as real and as painful as the flames around her. They curled as hissed around the trunk, and Fallon felt her own skin scream in pain as if they were one. They both screamed in terror until—

Fallon's eyes opened.

She hissed as she jerked her hands back from where it had been on the ground, inches away from a billowing campfire.

Hands that were still tied together. Fallon quickly assessed her surroundings. The sun had long set. In fact, it was almost rising again. The only sound was the crackling fire and Norman's snoring. The man was pressed up against another tree, head limp on his shoulder with a steady stream of drool pouring out.

She fell asleep. On the back of a horse. She did not even wake when they made camp. Her cheeks flushed with embarrassment as she thought about her head comfortably pressed against Jaeger's back for hours.

Jaeger. Where was he? Fallon saw Norman's horse tied nearby, but no sign of the other Keeper. Perhaps he went to find food in that village, Falmoore.

If that were true, then Fallon could get more rest before he returned. She looked down at her hand, the skin of her knuckles was pink and shiny from the mild burns. Memories of the crying tree were still clear in her mind. Fallon never remembered her dreams. It was all so vivid, it hardly felt like a dream at all.

But as she lay her head back down, a lead ball formed in her gut. Something was not letting her eyes close ... something triggered her internal guard. Trusting her instincts, Fallon sat up and swept the area one more time.

The trees felt wrong. Something about the way their shadows moved was wrong.

There. A glint of metal, reflecting the fire's light. Fallon was instantly on her feet. "Norman—"

But she was too late. A massive hand from behind clamped over her mouth and nose, "Quiet, las." That familiar, hot breath licked over her ear. "You're our prize now."

Fallon bit down, the sensation of her teeth sinking through flesh making her gag. The man cursed, lifting his grip just enough for Fallon to maneuver out of his grasp. Her hands were still bound and worthless, so she kicked her leg and landed somewhere that truly hurt.

His scream was obscured by the barking laugh of the raven-haired man, who had a sword to Norman's neck. "Aye, Darby, she's a Blodvinger alright," he snorted.

The blond man called Darby rose from his knees, glaring hatefully at Fallon. "I expected more from Beowulf's own daughter." He tried to grin through the pain.

Fallon's stomach dropped into her boots. She immediately turned to Norman, ready to explain herself, but thankfully the old drunk was still snoring soundly.

The men laughed. Darby clutched his manhood in one hand and in the other held his bone-cracking weapon. She needed to get her hands on something sharp. Or heavy. Or both.

"I cannot imagine the prize Beowulf has in line for your return." He grinned, displaying teeth almost as yellow as his hair.

At that, Fallon could not help but laugh. Then it turned into a cackle. The more she thought about it, the funnier it became. Eventually she was on her knees, clutching her sides as she laughed so hard her eyes watered. They watched her, confusion and anger contorting their faces.

Darby pounded the butt of his weapon on the ground. "Is something funny?"

Fallon wiped her eyes with her sleeve, still unable to stop the giggles falling from her mouth as she spoke. "You think my father *wants* me back?" she snorted. "He is the reason I'm here. He wanted me dead—tried to kill me himself. If you take me back, he would kill us all just for wasting his time."

"The burden of a bastard child. I would try to erase you from existence too," the raven-haired man sneered.

She slowly got to her feet and faced them both. "How did you know?" she asked. A mere distraction to give her time to formulate a plan.

"Your border patrol warned us of a red-haired vigilante that escaped into Halvar's territory. A few days prior, we had heard about the execution of Beowulf's red-haired bastard. It was not hard to put two and two together," he explained. "Alas, if Beowulf will not pay us for you, Chief Sigurd will. You are still breaking clan law by trespassing." He shrugged.

That was punishable by death. They all knew it. So, Fallon rolled her shoulders and cracked her neck. "Well, one chief already tried to kill me. Why do you think yours will be any more successful?" she cooed.

"We will do it ourselves, then," the raven-haired man growled. He took two steps towards her, but Fallon was ready. She kicked one of the scorching logs of the fire straight into the man's face.

As the man screamed in pain, Fallon ducked just in time to save her head from Darby's fatal swing. The weapon was heavy, so the momentum carried his body into a full rotation. His back exposed, Fallon kicked him in the liver.

She felt a crunch under her foot, and Darby gasped as he collapsed in on himself. Fallon had never hit someone that hard before … she should not be able to.

From there it turned into a dance. He swung, she dodged. He nicked her shoulder with a dagger, sliced her forearm and cheek, but Fallon hardly felt it. She smiled with joy; she ravished in every drop of blood falling from her. *This* is what she understood: strain, exhaustion, anger, and pain. This is what Fallon was good at. This man merely exploited malice, Fallon was its master.

The man whose face was now burned swung wide with his sword, just as Fallon anticipated. She leaned back, seeing her own smiling reflection in the blade as it passed over her face.

Interested in her new strength, she went for a headbutt while he crouched at her level. There was a *crack* before he went stiff and fell inches from the fire. Fallon had to blink a few times but felt nothing.

She picked up his sword with her tied hands and turned back around, Darby was breathing hard through his teeth. "You little bitch. Where did you learn to fight?"

She did not have time to cut her hands free before he swung again. This time Fallon jumped *over* his strike, tucking her knees into her chest. She twisted her hips to kick him in the jaw. His head turned farther than it was meant to, and he too dropped motionless to the earthen floor.

"I wasn't given a choice," she panted.

Finally, Norman awoke. He slurped up his drool and looked around in shock. Seeing nothing but two unconscious men and Fallon standing over them.

He sloppily got to his feet, unsheathing his own sword and pointing it at her. "What have you done?" he demanded.

She rolled her eyes. "Only save your life."

He spun in a full circle. "Where is Jaeger?" he asked.

Fallon felt bile rise to her throat. Jaeger was still not back. She stared at the two men on the ground. Where were the other two that approached them that afternoon?

Fallon held her hands out. "Cut me loose, quickly!"

Norman scoffed and pulled back. "Absolutely not."

But she reached out, grabbing his sword by the blade. She felt the edges sink into her palm and fingers. "I need my hands free or that boy is going to die!" She shouted. "He doesn't fight, and you couldn't take on a flight of stairs let alone two Reapers."

He stared at her. That sad, hollow look in his eyes was enough to tell her what he wanted to say. *Not him, too.*

Fallon used the blade to slice the ropes at her wrists, and Norman did not stop her. She poked around the fallen Reaper, taking a set one one-sided axes from his belt. Fingers fumbling, she untied Norman's horse and jumped on.

"Where did he go?" she asked, rolling out her sore wrists.

Norman pointed east. "Through there, towards Falmoore," he said. As Fallon whipped her horse into a sprint, she watched the old man sit back down against the tree and pull out his flask.

Fallon was protecting her bounty. Protecting her *grio,* that was all. Just as Norman said—they had to protect each other. Nothing more.

Shouts up ahead made her pull the reins. If she spooked them, they might just kill him right away. Demanding her feet to be quiet, she dismounted and walked on in a low crouch.

She saw their silhouettes. Jaeger's bow was lying a few feet away from him, his horse lying motionless on the ground. They had taken out his *horse* to stop him … Fallon bared her teeth, her face getting hot.

They had Jaeger cornered, one man's blade pressing against his jugular. The other was stalking back and forth. He had not been in the group from earlier, Fallon would have remembered a man such as him. He was the biggest out of the four—a mountain of a man with a bald head and tangled beard. Fallon could hear his footsteps from here.

Their body language indicated they were waiting. This was an obvious trap made for Fallon, with Jaeger as the bait. But the first rule of hunting was to make sure your snare was big enough for your prey. These men had no idea a wolf was about to step in their little rabbit trap.

Odin favored the bold and brave. Fallon could use another blessing, so she stepped out from behind the trees, axes at the ready. Everyone's head turned at once.

"Let him go," she ordered.

Jaeger's eyes widened. "Rhodeia, no! You must run!"

The bald man laughed. "Finally. Come, Barwyn's bastard, let us get a look at you," he said, voice as rough as stone on stone.

Jaeger's lips pressed together when he heard her title. Well, now he knows. At least now it will be easier to convince him to run.

"Let him go, and I'll go with you," she lied. Once they let go of him, he could run and she could bury her axe in their chest.

Both Reapers laughed once again. "I think the girl is confused, Goron."

Goron, the man with biceps as big as Fallon's head, nodded. "The bounty is not for your *safe return* to Barwyn, las, it's for your head." He grinned, missing half his teeth.

She refused to face Jaeger. She did not want to see the hurt of betrayal that was surely in his eyes. "You knew I would get past the other two and come," she said. He had wanted her to kill them so he would only have to split the reward two ways.

Goron nodded, peering down at her with black eyes. *Betrayal.* It had once been a disgusting, foreign concept to her. Now it was her truth. Her entire reason for breathing was to betray the ones she once called her people. Fallon was no better than the men before her, she was no better than anyone. Barwyn's Bastard.

Her emotions once again caused her to pause, and Goron took full advantage. He lunged at her. Fallon barely had time to parlay his strike before he slammed her into the ground. The wind left her lungs, only to be replaced by a growing heat as the words echoed in her head; Barwyn's Bastard.

Oh no.

She rolled, avoiding a swift beheading as Goron's blade sunk into the earth. She got onto her knees and sliced the back of his knee, but he barely flinched before turning to land a punch to her nose. She gasped, eyes swelling with tears as she scooted on her rear to get some distance between them.

Jaeger kept yelling at her to run. But Fallon could barely fight right now. Her limbs zapped and tingled uncontrollably, and the pressure building in her chest was unbearable. This was different than the time with the wolves ... this was *more*. More power. More destruction. She had to stay focused.

Her nose already stopped bleeding. Fallon's teeth were chattering as Goron grabbed her by the hair and tossed her aside like dirty rag, sending her crashing into Jaeger. They came to a tumbling stop as both Reapers pointed blades at them.

Fallon landed on her stomach. She pressed her brow into the earth, pounding her fists on the ground. *Calm down. You need to calm down.*

Her step-mother had grabbed her hair like that. Her father had dragged her by her braids and tossed her into the dog kennels. Dragged. Restrained. Forced. Fallon felt wildfire raging in her lungs.

"Rhodeia?" Jaeger's soft voice spoke. He reached out and placed a tan hand on her arm. He winced but did not let go. "You're burning up."

His small gesture made the swelling pressure inside of her slow down. She was breathing raggedly as her eyes wandered between them all. She felt the sweat drip down the side of her face.

"You need to close your eyes," she rasped, sitting up. The ball inside her was unraveling, she was losing whatever grip she had on this power.

"What?"

The Reapers advanced, ready to end this.

"You know who I am. I lied—our *grio* is broken. You can turn your back on me now. You can hate me for the rest of your life, but for the love of Odin close your eyes and run!" she instructed. Her vision was going white around the edges.

The boy turned pale but nodded his head. As the Reapers raised their swords, he slowly crept backwards on all fours.

Another one. Another good, fair person Fallon failed to keep in her life. Something dark and unlovable had taken root within her soul. No matter where she went, no matter what name she used, no one wanted her. *Barwyn's Bastard.*

Fallon shifted all her focus to her hand. One inch at a time, she raised it until she saw the men's smiling faces through her fingers. Maybe, just maybe she could control this.

When she could hold her breath no longer, she let go. Then Fallon blew up.

EIGHT

When she was little, Fallon's mother always called her *my light*.

If she ever asked why, mother would tell her the same thing: that Fallon was her north star, the eternal light that always led her home. And that someday, Fallon would find her own north star. A love so bright, so true and pure, all the other stars felt dull in comparison.

Today, however, Fallon did not feel like her mother's little star.

No, she was a flaming comet ripping its way through the fabric of the sky. Beams of light arched and swirled in and out of her skin. They were as radiant as solar flares, but felt like barbed wire being threaded through her flesh. Fallon could do nothing but writhe on the ground in agony.

Everyone watched her in shock and horror. The men were flung back initially, but quickly recovered. Fallon screamed again and again; her bones were burning rods trapped inside of her. From what she could see through the golden haze, the others were unharmed. The power was not attacking them. No, it was attacking *her*. Fallon was trapped.

Her muscles all flexed at once, incapacitating her. She was put back together just as quickly as she was pulled apart. She tried to scream it away, Fallon fought and fought but the light was relentless.

Goron's skin turned red as he got closer, his clothes beginning to smoke.

Fallon was still convulsing in agony as he approached. She turned on her side into a fetal position, covering her ears with her palms. The air pressure tripled, pushing her eardrums to the breaking point. Release. She wanted release, she wanted this to all go away.

Time passed in lapses. One blink, Goron was gone. Two blinks, he had a sword above her head. But then, his body went rigid. When Fallon blinked again, he was on the ground next to her with an arrow through his head.

In one ear, out the other. Only one person could make that shot.

Fallon let out another cry—out of misery, out of hope, and out of *pain*. There was so much pain. She felt it from the roots of her teeth to the creases in her palms.

"Rhodeia!" A voice called through the light. It took so much effort just to turn her head. The heat distorted his features, but she recognized Jaeger instantly.

He kept saying her fake name. She gave him a fake name. Why did she feel so guilty about it? She swallowed, taking three deep breaths.

"Fallon!" she said as loud as she could. The name her mother gave her was Fallon.

Jaeger gave her a nod of encouragement. "Alright, Fallon, you need to calm down," he said. He was on all fours, slowly inching closer to her as the light swirled around them in a glittering tempest.

He came back. He had every right to hate her at this moment, but he was helping her. Fallon locked her gaze on him, letting those hazel eyes be a steady rock in the raging storm she was in.

Jaeger smiled, sweat pouring down his face. "Good! Just like that," he said, coming a bit closer. "Look around you, you're safe. Everything is fine."

The men were dead. Jaeger was here. Fallon still had a chance.

Slowly, the pressure lifted from her ears. She was able to pick up her head, then her arms. Breath after breath, Fallon watched as the golden rays sizzled and settled back into her pale skin.

Spots danced in her vision as Fallon fought to stay conscious. She felt as though every drop of blood had been drained from her body. It confirmed her fears that without a shadow of a doubt—this power came from within her. Not a god.

Jaeger was right next to her. "You're okay," he kept repeating, placing a hand on her clenched fist.

Soon, she felt normal again. As if every molecule in her body had not been charged with the power of ten suns only seconds ago. Both of them were drenched in sweat but did not speak. Fallon had trained hard for years, but she had never felt her muscles be this sore before.

But the *silence*. The pure, still silence was as refreshing as a crisp mountain stream. No more roaring of power or screaming.

Jaeger moved slowly, trying to help her up. "We need to go. We are still too close to Falmoore, someone might have seen," he warned.

The sun was a single golden line above the horizon as Jaeger helped her to her feet. His nose and cheeks were an angry red, as were his bare hands. She had heard of this before. On the rare days the sun broke through the Barwyn clouds and reflected off the snow, people came back with these burns. Sunburns.

She let him assist her through the trees and back to Norman's horse, who was hiding behind some bushes.

"Stay here," he instructed. "I will be right back."

Fallon leaned against the saddle, holding on tightly as her knees wobbled under her. She shivered, remembering the sensation of the light traveling *inside of* her. Through her veins and up her bones.

She sniffed the air, the tinge of smoke coating her nostrils. Jaeger came bouncing through the trees. "You set a fire?" she asked.

He nodded, "Now the villagers have a cause for the light. An unattended bonfire, with two drunken Reapers who were playing with a bow," he said.

She looked at him in disbelief. "Why?" she asked quietly. A million questions wrapped into one simple word.

He examined her face closely. Fallon was too weak to stop him as he pushed aside her hair, tucking it behind her ear. Then he ran his finger along the bridge of her nose, sending a chill up her scalp.

"You were really raised in Barwyn?" he asked sternly.

She nodded.

Jaeger gave her a sad smile. "How did you survive so far away from home?" he asked, more to himself.

Before she could ask more, the sound of heavy breathing and footsteps interrupted them. They both turned, to see their inebriated knight in shining armor approach. Norman was sweating just as much as them as he took in the scene before him.

"I-I saw the, the light," he stammered.

"Norman, we need to go," Jaeger said. It took an embarrassing amount of effort, but they got Fallon onto the saddle. Jaeger hopped on behind her, reaching around her to grab the reins. She would have protested, but she genuinely questioned her ability to keep herself upright.

"We will meet you at the lake southeast of here. Rent a horse from the Falmoore stables," Jaeger instructed before whipping the steed into a run.

They rode for a while in silence as the morning finally came, lighting up the sky in blues and purples. The constant jostling made Fallon's aching head howl in pain, but she was able to rest her eyes for a while and let her body remember how to function.

Norman never asked any questions. Fallon appreciated he was that kind of man, but Fallon was not that kind of woman. As they finally slowed their horses to a trot, Fallon nudged Jaeger's side with her elbow.

"Is your name really Jaeger Osmund?" she finally asked.

She felt him stiffen behind her. "Yes, but it is not what you think. My father is Gus Osmund, elder brother to Sigurd Osmund. The chief is my uncle," he explained.

She loosened the breath she did not realize she was holding. He hadn't lied to her after all.

"If he is older, why is he not chief?" she asked. She had heard of siblings—even cousins—battling for the throne, but there had not been a conclave in centuries.

He hesitated. "My father stepped down. The people shamed and hated him for his beliefs and ideas. The tension between the clans was high when my grandfather retired, the people needed a warrior—a beast. And that was my crazy uncle Sigurd. He called for a conclave, and my father knew he could never win. So he gave the throne to his brother. Since then, my father has just been a lord of a village far west from here," he said.

They rode in silence for many minutes while Fallon processed his words. The rightful chief gave up his throne. *Gave it up*, while Fallon was here fighting tooth and nail to get to hers. It was unfathomable.

"What did he believe in so strongly that he gave up the throne for it?" she asked. Fallon could not think of something she would not do to get her birthright back.

He chuckled. "That question has a long answer."

They peaked over a hill. Fallon let loose a breath as she took in the view before her; a massive, glimmering lake.

The sunlight danced on its perfect blue surface. It looked as if someone had cut out a piece of the sky and laid it on the grass as a heavenly blanket. Pale sand, rocky shores, and people surrounded the lake.

Jaeger noticed her eyeing them. "It's alright, this is a peaceful area. Most call this Mimir's Lake," he explained as they trotted to an unoccupied area tucked within a tall cluster of gray boulders.

"Mimir." She repeated, "Like Mimir's Well, where Odin traded his eye for wisdom?"

He nodded. "Yes, the waters that could answer any question if you drank them. It is said Odin poured three drops of Mimir's water into this lake. People come here to pray, practice divination, and sometimes to just get some peace and quiet," he explained. "And we could use all three."

Fallon felt Jaeger's warm body leave from behind her as he jumped down and tied off the horse. After helping Fallon get down and sit comfortably against some rocks, he rummaged through his saddlebags and pulled out a few apples and full skins of water.

"I did manage to get to Falmoore before those barbarians cornered me," he said, tossing Fallon a beautifully full bag of food.

They ate in silence. Though Fallon could feel his questions lingering in the air. He looked at her less, spoke less, and for the first time seemed uncomfortable around her.

Fallon could bear the awkwardness no longer. "There is no point in us pretending you did not see what you did, so we might as well address it," she said at last. Tossing her apple core towards the horse who happily obliged.

Jaeger picked at the calluses on his hands instead. He sat straight across from her, barely an arm's length away. He peered out onto the water's surface, confliction clear on his face.

"When your mother was alive, did she ever read you Faerietales?" he asked after a few minutes.

"Yes," she said softly. "Most of my memories are of her reading to me. I always remembered them, because I felt like as long as those stories were alive, so was she," she said. Fallon never admitted that to herself, let alone aloud.

"My grandfather—the old chief—*lived* by those stories. He told all his sons and daughters about the Fae. About dancing nymphs and the ancient Little Folk. About the flowers that turned into Faeries and beautiful women with a cow's tail," he smiled, locking eyes with her. "He talked about them so much, because he had met them before."

Fallon blinked. "Met … Faeries?" Maybe Jaeger was still in shock.

He rolled his eyes. "You do not have to believe me, but yes. For a long time, the Fae realm and this one shared a bond. There was a portal hidden within Halvar. For hundreds of years, it was the Halvar Royal House's duty to protect that portal and protect those who came through," he said.

He spoke with all the confidence in the world. Fallon scanned his eyes but found no humor. He was being serious. "Alright, then where does this Fae realm lie within Yggdrasil?" she challenged. Their world was only one of nine on the World Tree. Other realms were said to be home to frost giants, dwarves, and dark elves. Yet none of them spoke of Fae.

He scooted closer to her, their knees touching. He used his hands and slow words, as if explaining something to a child. "Imagine Yggdrasil as a house, rather than a tree. In the house are nine rooms: the nine realms. And some of those rooms are connected. Like a bedroom with an antechamber."

Fallon raised a brow. "So, this Fae realm is an extension of Midgard? Through a portal?" she asked.

He nodded excitedly. "All on the same branch of Yggdrasil."

"Right." Fallon nodded, pressing her lips together. "Did your grandfather tell you that?"

He shook his head. "He died when I was only three, so my father carried on the tradition. He told everyone, as was his duty, and they made a mockery of him. Deemed him unfit to rule, just because he wanted to protect those who needed protecting. My family was the last who believed in the stories, and now that even my father and I don't speak, I think the Fae don't trust us anymore. I never saw any sign of them since my mother disappeared. Not until …" He trailed off after seeing the unimpressed look on Fallon's face.

A cloud passed overhead, casting a shadow over his already tanned skin. He pointed at the lake beside them, his tone stern and a bit fed up. "You believe a god poured three drops of magical water into this lake, but not in Faeries? You are a fool to think there are only nine realms. And an even bigger fool if you think it took you putting on that show for me to know that *you* are from there."

Fallon was stunned at his words. For a few seconds they just stared at each other, as still as the wise lake.

"Your ear healed too fast." Jaeger went on. "You walked for *days* without rest. Flowers bloom around you when you sleep. And when you're angry, the air around you creates a moving mirage like it does above a fire. Shall I go on?" he asked.

"No."

Fallon did not want this. She did not want her fears confirmed. Yet here she was, sitting by a lake blessed with wisdom, getting answers to the questions she never wanted to ask.

She felt pathetic at how timid and shaky her voice was as she spoke, "I didn't believe—I didn't *want* to believe. Because all throughout my mother's stories I've never heard of this power. Not in this world, or the next," she said quietly.

Fallon still can't say the power was *hers*. That would mean taking claim to it. How could she? It terrified her— it nearly killed her.

As always, Jaeger seemed to sense her emotions. The warmth in his eyes came back, and he placed a hand on her knee. "If I am to be honest, neither have I. But we can go on that journey together if you'd like," he smiled.

Fallon shook her head. "I-I don't know if I'm ready for that yet. I have things I need to do first, there are debts that need to be paid," she insisted.

Fallon needed to fulfill her purpose by siding with Halvar and killing Beowulf. If she survived that, then she would come back here. She and Jaeger could find the source of her power, and maybe even find out what happened to their mothers fifteen years ago.

But the first thing on Fallon's mind was getting her throne back. She knew Jaeger understood that because pure disappointment and pain washed down the man's face.

"Then in the meantime, can I at least offer some advice? As someone who doesn't want to see you fall down the wrong path?" He tilted his head to the side playfully, giving her a slight smile.

Fallon snorted. "Oh, this will be good."

Jaeger leaned forward, grabbing her face between his hands. "Everything about your old life is gone, so take this as a chance to *start over*, not go back to the same patterns. My advice, Fallon: find something that sets your soul on fire and follow it. Live by it. Protect it. So when the entire world is crashing down on you, you have a reason to stand back up. Otherwise, you will just crumble into bitterness. Hate. Never. Wins." His eyes were hypnotizing. Fallon wanted to fall into his words, she wanted to savor them and let them seep into her soul. But she was just so utterly broken, it all fell right through the cracks. She felt nothing.

"I'm afraid I'm not that good of a person," she whispered.

"No," Jaeger said, leaning back in defeat. "You are afraid of choosing to be, when all you know is the feeling of an empty heart."

Whatever he thought he knew about her, he was wrong. Just because they spent some time together did not make them friends. Fallon had a purpose. Her fate was her purpose. One day soon, when Fallon sat on the Blodvinger throne, he would see. They all would.

"Well, then, I will take your advice. Beowulf needs to be stopped," she said. Even though saying it made her feel even more empty. Nothing ignited inside of her. *Find something that sets your soul on fire.*

Jaeger had nothing else to say to her. They sat and finished their scraps of food until Norman came trotting over the hill. Fallon was surprised he came at all; the man did not seem to be motivated by much. But when he had come running after Jaeger, and the relief on his face when he saw the man was alright, it was clear the warrior still lived within him. Even if it was deep, deep down.

"Well, we are all out of coin, so we better get movin' if we're going to reach Reinhart by tonight," he said. "I'm going to pour my own wisdom water into this lake, then we're leaving," he aanounced.

"Charming." Fallon grimaced, getting a chuckle from Jaeger.

The birds started to chirp, and a strong breeze swept through the valley. She smelt pollen, leather, and freshly churned dirt on it.

"What do you believe in so strongly that you gave up being a lord?" she asked at last, if only to distract herself.

"That love is love, and that it is no one's to change, control, or question," he stated simply, his eyes twinkling behind those curls.

She nodded. "Did you have an arranged marriage?" The idea was common. It was a barbaric business deal, bringing together two lords thus doubling their production.

Jaeger chuckled nervously. "My father tried and tried again, but he could not find someone to match my … taste."

Fallon smiled at the playfulness in his eyes as he waited for her to pick up the pieces. "Your father did not let you become lord, because you would not take a wife."

Jaeger nodded, watching her reaction carefully. Fallon did not particularly care. She had walked past enough opium-scented brothels to know it was not foreign in Barwyn for a man to take another man to bed. Fallon never put too much thought into it herself, no man *or* woman would be caught dead with Barwyn's Bastard.

"He gave me a deal," he continued, "saying I could do whatever I wanted if I just married a woman, gave her children, and acted *appropriately* on the surface." He scoffed.

Fallon struggled with what to say, not knowing if it was even her place to say anything at all. "That does not sound ... horrible," she tried.

"Why should I change myself to meet someone else's comfort level?"

"Don't," Fallon smiled. "Don't you ever yield. Not for them."

He gave her a smile just as wicked as hers, she felt his unapologetic, fearless spirit dance with her own. For the first time, Fallon saw a warrior who did not kill. He fought a silent, ruthless battle unknown and unseen by most. She saw it in his eyes—that fire he spoke of that burned within. He found it.

"If you don't, then others will be given the courage to follow. That is how revolutions are started. It is truly your father's loss. They would be blessed to have you as lord," she said, and she meant it. "What is the name of the village, anyways? So I can pay your father a special visit when I take over." She gave him a playful wink.

"Cordelia, named after my mother. It is not far from the southwest Calder, where Halvar meets Audhild." He poked her right above her sternum. "Get that heart in the right place, and you will make a brilliant chieftess, Fallon Solveij." He smiled.

"No." She shook her head. "Not Solveij."

Jaeger shrugged, sticking out his hand. "Well, then, it is an honor to officially make your acquaintance, Fallon Not-Solveij."

She clasped his hand. "And you, Jaeger ..."

"Hulderson."

"Jaeger Hulderson." She gave his hand a strong shake.

Norman came back around and they all got on their horses, Fallon sitting behind Jaeger. As they headed out on their last stretch to Reinhart, to the next phase in Fallon's plan, she turned back to Mimir's Lake.

If not Solveij, then who?

Fallon. She would face these next few days as Fallon, as her mother's daughter. Yet as the lake turned into nothing more than a silver dot in the distance, Fallon could not stop herself from asking:

Who am I?

If there was an answer, she was too far away to hear it.

NINE

In Elphyne, the only way to tell apart night and day was the presence of the moon.

The sun held a permanent position in the middle of the sky, giving life to those below. Every twelve hours, however, another astral body joined it. The moon made a twelve-hour journey across the sky passing right under the eternal star. For one minute, at exactly midnight, the two touched edges. Everyone grew up calling this Dag and Dagmar's kiss. Their two gods in their heavenly forms, coming together every night for eternity.

All Faeries needed the sun—more so than food and water. Without it they become ill, a sickness known as shade-poisoning. The first sign was a devastating loss of energy, then nausea, then headaches and violent chills.

That was how Ronen knew, despite all he had been told, that Nøkken originally *were* from Lysserah. Because on his second day in that pit, he could hardly lift his head.

Every corner of his dirt cage was full of vomit. He was drenched in sweat even though he had not moved for the better part of the day. He laid there, chills rattling his bones, finally understanding the purpose of these lower-level dungeons.

Ronen did not get the luxury of a cell, because the cells were for people who had a chance.

That long hallway full of cells on either side, that was where he should have been. That was for petty crimes and detentions, a little scare to get people on the right track. There had been a barred window in every cell because they needed to stay alive.

But below that, was *this* chasm of torment. They buried them, blocking out every molecule of light, and let them die. He went over the memory of his short time above his pit again and again in his head. The hatches were of novice make, the dug-out pits were not reinforced, even the stone stairs leading down here from lockup seemed rushed. All of this had to be new. And Ronen was willing to bet he knew exactly when this addition was built.

Fritjof Aodh. He thought of this. There was just no way the royal family would approve. Shade-poisoning was a slow and miserable way to die. So, hopefully soon, Ronen would just seize and go into a coma he would never awake from.

Every so often, Ronen's death was interrupted. Someone would open his hatch and he would be blinded by a torchlight. It never lasted long, just enough time to confirm he was still indeed breathing. If he was right and they checked on him twice a day, it was on the morning of the third day when he heard it.

Ronen was lying flat on his back, as usual. It seemed to be the only way to stop his head from spinning. The guards had just checked on him, the slam of the hatch closing echoed painfully in his skull.

"Still alive," he groaned into the void.

Ronen had decided to live out of spite, for as long as he could manage. His mortal blood was the only reason his body was coping. The mortal blood that had come from his mother. Ronen wondered if she had brown hair, too. If he had inherited his cleft chin from her or his father. What if she hummed when she was bored, just like him? Did she write with her left or right hand? Was her last breath whispering his name?

Ronen was terribly afraid he was days away from getting those answers. Would his parents be on the other side, waiting for him? Maybe they forgot about him, or turned away from the bitter soul he has become. How would Ronen face them like this? How could he even begin to explain how he ended up here? *It wasn't my fault,* he wanted to cry. *They never gave me a chance.*

The pounding in his head never ceased. He reached up and pressed his palms against his eyes, but minutes passed without relent. It did not even sound like a drum anymore ... just *bang, bang, scree, bang bang scree.* Over and over. Seeming to only grow louder.

Ronen's eyes shot wide open.

Tap, tap, scratch.

His name. That was his name in Little Spoke.

How did he not recognize it sooner? With all the strength left in him, Ronen sat up. After dry heaving nothing but bitter bile for a few seconds, he scooted on his rear to the closest wall. *Bang, bang, scree.* It was an aggressive version of his name, the equivalent of someone calling out to him.

He pounded his fist against the dirt wall twice, then racked his nails down it. *I'm here.* He wanted to scream it until his throat bled, but he knew he could not waste the energy. *I'm here! I'm alive!*

The sudden urge to live gave him enough strength to keep pounding the wall. If the Little Folk did not find him, he would die here. Ronen was only twenty-one. He wanted his own house, he wanted to see the rest of Elphyne and find love, gods—Ronen had not even made a *friend* in a decade. He would not face his parents as a loser. As a dirty, worthless *orlendr*.

So he punched the wall until he felt blood pouring down his fingers.

He punched until he felt his knuckles splinter.

He punched until he fell.

And when he did, he started kicking. For a moment, he convinced himself it had all been in his head. An illusion created by his own misplaced hope. His legs dropped uselessly to the ground as the emptiness of the room swallowed him whole.

The darkness seemed to seep into his skin, moving like ice through his veins as he lay motionless on the floor. His throat burned as he fought back his sobs, but it was pointless. Ronen let himself cry.

Dying felt like turning to stone. He was calcifying in his own misery. He thought about the painting in the throne room; the queen trapped in the glass. He could still see her red hair and kind smile. The sunlight ... Ronen still remembered the way the sunlight glowed in her eyes. It was real. Warmth was real, the smell of soot and metal were real. He kept those memories close as the tears poured down his cheeks, squeezing his eyes together in fear at what could be waiting for him in the afterlife.

But it never came.

Instead, a small warmth spread across his open palm. Ronen opened his eyes, taking a few labored breaths. Turning his head to the side, he almost yelped in surprise. Something was *glowing*. A soft, green light lit up his hand. It was not bright, but Ronen still had to squint.

He slowly sat up, twirling the small mushroom in his hand. He looked up to see yet another before him. It lit up a small hole in the wall, right where Ronen had been punching.

"Foxfire," he whispered, his voice swimming through the silent eeriness of the room.

He clamored forward. The hole was barely big enough for his shoulders to fit through, but he could squeeze. Ronen stuck his head in and saw the hole continued into a tunnel, a foxfire mushroom every few feet to light the way.

They came for him. Just as they had come for him when he was nothing more than a wailing baby on the side of a river. His heart pounded with emotion, his eyes already full of fresh tears. Ronen turned it into determination. He lasted this long, he could make it out of here.

Each of his limbs weighed a hundred pounds as he dragged himself through. Ronen coughed up dirt and scraped his stomach raw, but eventually he got into a rhythm. He took a hard left, then a right, followed by another two lefts.

Ronen was *so* tired. Sleep called to him, but he had to keep going. Eventually the tunnel got so steep, he could use his knees to awkwardly waddle upwards to give his arms a break. The green glow of the foxfire got farther and farther apart until he could see nothing but darkness up ahead.

What Ronen *thought* was darkness, though, turned out to be yet another solid wall of dirt. He ran smack into it. He rubbed his throbbing nose, cursing.

Well, the tunnel ended. Ronen flipped on his back and looked up, but it was still dark. No, this could not be right. It had to lead somewhere.

Suddenly his world shook, and Ronen nearly soiled himself as thuds and stomps came from above. Footsteps—heavy footsteps. He was right under the surface, he made it. But, where?

Ronen reached up, almost crying with glee as he finally touched something that wasn't dirt. He used both hands and pushed as hard as he could, hearing the beautiful sound of wood splintering until a final *snap* as it gave out.

Light.

Light poured down on him, so unbelievably bright he had to shield his eyes. He was still half-buried as he sat and let the sunlight burn away the fog in his head. It melted the frost off his bones and every breath came easier.

As his eyes finally focused, though, he saw no blue sky above him. A second later he started to gag on the scent of fur, drool, and feces.

Pulling himself up, he took in his surroundings and the reality of the situation sank in. Ronen's stomach dropped: the kennels. He was in the Barguest Kennels.

Thank the gods they were currently unoccupied. Otherwise, Ronen surely would have been eaten alive by now. The guard dogs were raised here—bred and raised to hunt, kill, and readily die protecting their Valdyr partners.

It could be described as a luxury horse stable. The set up was the same, but each stall was twice the size of the storage closet Ronen lived in. He walked over to the cotton-stuffed bed, his boots crunching the hay-covered floor. He had never actually seen a Barguest up close, so seeing the scale of everything in the kennel was slightly unsettling. There was a barrel of water in the corner and an even bigger crate of half-eaten vegetables and meat chunks. In the other corner ... Well, Ronen found the source of the unpleasant smell.

He looked down to see a paw print embedded in the hay. It was larger than his boot, with claws as long as his finger.

Yes, Ronen needed to get out of here.

Nothing but a simple gate held these beasts in their assigned kennel. Ronen hopped over it and headed down the single hall, careful to listen for anyone that might be around the corner.

He slid open the barn door and peered outside. Bhaltair had said the kennels were in the gardens, so at least he was not inside the castle anymore. Sure enough, nothing but blooming bushes, full garden beds, and tree groves surrounded him.

Ronen spotted someone kneeling next to a rosebush. Everywhere the man touched, another blossom opened. An Earth Fae, employed by the castle judging by his fine brown robes laced with golden detail. He paid no attention to Ronen as he slipped out and ran for the cover of trees.

He ran until he felt his lungs falling apart. Ronen did not know this area. He had never even left Athol Village. Anywhere near Castletowne was too crowded for Ronen—too many people to stare and point at him.

The moon was already on the other side of the sun. If the Barguests were out of their kennels, that meant they were out on guard with their Valdyr. Hopefully his stench would keep them away. If Ronen had a Barguest's sense of smell, he would probably run in the *opposite* direction.

He had to stop to gather his thoughts, kneeling inside the hollow of a tree and catching his breath. He opened and closed his fingers nervously, flinching in pain. He raised his hands to his face—

Oh no. His hands.

Blackened, bruised, and bleeding. Not a single knuckle had escaped his psychotic break against that dirt wall. His nails were so full of dirt they ripped up from their beds, yet they still managed to leave deep cuts in his palms.

He made sure as much of him was in the sun as possible and rested his head back against the tree. Staring at the sun for as long as his eyes could bear.

The people of Elphyne believed the sun and moon were the final forms of Dag and Dagmar Alfrothul, the very first male and female Fae. They were born from the two Sister Trees—Dagmar was first, coming from the Throne Tree. She spent twelve hours alone, until Dag emerged from the Entrance Tree and found her. Together they created all life on Elphyne.

So, Ronen asked not to be alone. He asked if he did fall asleep, that they would allow him to wake back up. He was glad he did, because only seconds after he closed his eyes did the darkness take over again.

It was not until Ronen was having a wonderful dream about a Hulder girl that he opened his eyes again. He felt something small hit him in the face. Multiple times, with growing intensity.

Ronen's eyes fluttered open just in time to watch a red dot fly into his forehead. He flinched as it struck, bouncing right off and rolling on the grass: a Chillberry.

He yawned and looked around, absolutely horrified at what he saw.

Ronen was covered in Faeries. All over his arms, his outstretched legs, shoulders, even on the top of his head lie sleeping Anthousai. The tiny Flower Faeries snores sounded like wind chimes as Ronen abruptly interrupted their slumber.

"Get off!" he shouted, flailing his every limb and swatting the glowing Faeries away. Stupid, loud-mouthed gnats. Each Anthousai gave off her own faint glow, always matching the flower petals she wore as clothes. Some had butterfly wings, some had dragonfly wings, but *all* of them were gossiping little pests.

They screamed and giggled, flying away in a rainbow haze. Ronen rubbed the sleep from his eyes just to be hit in the nose with yet another Chillberry.

He looked in the direction it had come and saw a pile of the purple-red fruit laying in the grass. "I'm up, I'm up." He yawned.

Ronen took a long breath, thankful for how easy it came. He did not know how long he was asleep, but the worst of his shade-poisoning seemed to be gone. That was the one mercy the illness showed: it was easily cured with sun exposure.

Ronen leaned over and took a handful of the berries. They got their name from the cold, minty feeling they left in your mouth. After he devoured the whole pile, Ronen got to his feet. "Thank you, guys," he said quietly. "You didn't have to get me out, but you did. Thank you."

Of course, there was no response. The only sign that the Little Folk were truly there was a single Chillberry rolling onto his boot. His eyes followed a trail of red dots leading through the trees.

He stretched his arms out and nodded. "Alright, let's go home."

※

When the Valdyr took Ronen from his shop, he was knocked unconscious for the majority of the trip. Now walking it on his own, he realized just how far it was.

Using the back trails the Little Folk led him on, it took Ronen nearly four days to make it back to Athol. His hometown was just a single stone street, lined with businesses and houses of the people who worked there. It was known to be the street that a Nøkken lived on, so people only lived here as a last resort. It was full of males and females like Urg—elderly, retired workers who could not afford anything nicer.

The smith's shop was at the end of the street, its backdoor facing the woods behind. Over the tree line was a mountain range no one really ventured to, as it was known to be occupied by Centaurs. The ancient, primal predators were mostly peaceful to Fae, but they were vehemently territorial. People knew the risks of venturing to the Longback Knolls.

Which is why Ronen was sweating the whole time he was even within sight of the knolls. The Little Folk's trail ended, knowing Ronen could get home from here. He often ran to these woods to escape ridicule or to get out some anger by practicing his swordplay on a tree.

The wooden backdoor of the shop finally came into view, and Ronen let out a sigh of relief. He realized he did not even know what day it was. By the lack of smoke pouring out of the chimneys, Ronen guessed it was a weekend as the shop was closed. Tomorrow, though, he could not wait to see the look on Munjor's face when he saw he was still alive.

Ronen walked up the creaky steps and easily picked the lock as he had done a hundred times before. The familiar scent of metal fumes and smoke coated the inside of his nose. It was dark, save for the glowing embers of the forge and the sunlight coming down from the chimney. Multiple workstations lined the square room, including Ronen's own forge and anvil which seemed to be untouched.

He heard a small scuffle and turned to see Urg emerge from his own room holding a lantern—wearing nothing but a stained white nightgown.

"By Dag." Ronen shielded his eyes. "That is not the warm welcome I wanted."

But Urg said nothing. He just stood, staring at Ronen. The old Fae took in Ronen's tattered clothes, his bloodied hands, and the dirt that covered his face. It was devastatingly clear Urg had expected to never see him again.

"*Orlendr*?" he whispered after a few moments. His wispy white hair was pressed down on one side, markings of a good sleep Ronen had interrupted.

"Yeah, old man, it's me. If you didn't already rent out my room to another orphan, could I have my job back?" he asked with a smile.

The shop was so warm. Ronen could hear his spring-ridden cot calling to him. He planned to sleep for at least three days, then work until he passed out for another four.

But Urg's thin lips pressed into a line. He did not even appear happy to see him. Ronen could feel his heart start to pound in his chest.

"I will go outside and wash up, I promise." He chuckled nervously. But the look in Urg's eyes made his palms sweat.

When the old Fae *still* said nothing, all the blood drained from his head. "No." Ronen shook his head, "No, Urg … you can't do this to me. Not now," he whispered, his voice wobbling.

Urg turned away, timidly cleaning some tools on the table next to him with a dirty rag. "They will come for you. And this will be the first place they check," he said in a distressed tone. "It is a miracle they are not here already."

Indeed, Ronen knew they could not be far behind. He assumed he was only a day or two ahead of them unless the Little Folk were keeping them off his trail.

Ronen covered his face with his hands, unable to comprehend what was truly happening. The thick, smoke-tinged air that had once smelt of home now suffocated him. This was supposed to be the end. Ronen thought if he just made it home, his trials would be over. All hope started to melt away like the skin was peeling from his bones. Leaving him naked and vulnerable. One by one, the pieces that held him together began to fall.

"I-I will hide," he stammered. "I will work nights. they won't hurt you or anyone else I promise, just *please—*"

"Boy," Urg interrupted, slamming down the bridle in his hands. "That is no life, that is a prolonged death sentence. You won't be able to hide forever. Not from them ... not here."

"Then where do you suggest I go?" Ronen shouted. He was so confounded, he was laughing as tears started to stream down his face. "Should I run to Merrow Cove? Maybe the Merfolk will be more accepting of me. Or-or maybe the Orculli giants will put me in a cage as a spectacle to laugh at," he shouted, throwing up his hands.

No. He refused to believe Urg would turn him away. The Fae had raised him. He taught him to work hard and respect others, and given Ronen whatever means of a home he could.

Ronen grabbed the old man's shoulders with shaking hands, turning him to look Ronen in the eyes: *Please, please don't give up on me.*

Urg's blue eyes were dewy, but stern. Rooted. He had already made up his mind about this. "I did what the Little Folk asked me to. You are a grown man now, it is time you go out on your own," he said, gently pushing away Ronen's hands.

There was a painful, buzzing silence that filled the room. "I was nothing more than a favor to you?" he asked in a broken whisper. It was true then ... Ronen had truly been the burden he felt like all these years. Urg never came searching for him. He did not speak at Ronen's trail, because he thought he finally got rid of him.

The same Fae who had taught Ronen how to read and write reached for him now, but Ronen pulled back. "Boy," Urg tried, but Ronen had heard enough.

"Is this what you have been waiting for?" Ronen took a few steps back. "To push the baby bird with broken wings out of its nest? Because you *knew* from the moment it was born it was destined to die at the hands of the wind anyways?" he shouted. The walls were closing in on him. All sense of home and familiarity vanished. He had to get out of here.

As the foundation of Ronen's life fell away, he stormed over to his old room. He practically knocked the door down and began shoving whatever pathetic possessions he had into a bag. A lie. A dream. Ronen had been a fool to think he could change people's minds. He hated them all. And most of all, he hated himself. He hated his blue eye and the power he did not even possess.

"I'm leaving Elphyne," he announced, slinging his satchel over his head and shoulder. Urg was right, he would never have a normal life here. Not anymore.

Urg rushed for him. "The Entrance Tree—the guards—"

"I will figure it out," Ronen spat, opening the door. "And congratulations on your good graces with the gods. I'm sure your years of charity work will earn you a good afterlife in Dag's waters," he hissed, the words leaving his mouth as a striking snake.

He saw the impact they had on Urg—the pain of an old, broken heart. *Good*. Ronen did not even know where his own heart was anymore. He could not find it among all the wreckage inside of him.

He slammed the door behind him, blocking out whatever last words Urg had to say.

The Entrance Tree was south of here. He had only ever seen it on maps, but he could get there. This realm was not a home to him or his kind, it never has been. So why did the Little Folk bring him here? As some kind of cruel experiment? Well Ronen was done playing the game. He did not know what realm his parents were from, but he was determined to find it. He would never stop searching for acceptance, even if it meant walking to the ends of every realm to do so.

What was the next realm? Did they already have a bias on Nøkken? Where would he go there, and who would he be?

It did not matter. Because right now, Ronen was *nothing*. Fresh tears soaked his cheeks as he walked, knee-deep in the broken pieces of the life he once had. Of the person he used to be. He ran his fingers through them, trying to find anything salvageable to put himself back together.

A black, empty void. That is all he felt, all he saw, and all he dreamed of the days and nights traveling to another doomed life.

TEN

Bhaltair Herleif sat at the head of a long table, staring at the man he hated the most. Fritjof Aodh stood adjacent to him, handing over a glass of freshly poured wine.

"My most trusted friend," he spoke, slurring his words as they slipped off his inebriated tongue. "Everything's coming together. Isn't it?"

He sauntered his way over to the opposite end of the table, where an armchair of velvet and gold awaited him. An armchair that could have paid for a month's worth of food for the castle servants, or ten shields for their guards. Unfortunately, the High Lord put the comfort of his ass before his own people.

Bhaltair set down his crystal goblet, licking his fangs. "As I assured you it would, my lord."

Fritjof went on, his words as uselessly theatrical as his blood-colored dress robes. Bhaltair focused on keeping an eye on the rest of the King's Court around him. Just as he had focused on keeping an entire kingdom running for the past fifteen years, all while playing his role as the High Lord's obedient general.

Keeping Elphyne from falling into chaos from behind the curtain was not an easy task. Luckily, Bhaltair was not alone. His captain, Enok, and two other court members were on his side. It was an insult to merely call Enok his second in command—he was also his lifelong friend.

"General Herleif?"

He snapped back into attention. Fritjof stared expectantly at him with crimson eyes, waiting for an answer. Luckily, Bhaltair knew the one thing the tyrant loved to hear. "Yes, my Lord," he answered.

Nodding in satisfaction, Fritjof continued his lecture.

Bhaltair checked everyone's plates, making sure no one had touched their food or drinks. Only the High Lord ate within the dining hall; the rest of them were to watch. Seven males and two females occupied the table: a few lords, a lady, the best farmer in the kingdom, himself, and Fritjof. The tenth spot at their table remained empty, as it had been for the past forty-so years. A king. Elphyne needed a king.

The room had a massive fireplace, three chandeliers, and yet Bhaltair felt none of the Golden Castle's once mighty regality. He had not felt the heartbeat of the Throne Tree or its sister, the Entrance Tree, in a very long time. Not since the day Fritjof took power.

Fritjof's years as General of the Valdyr were long over. He did not deserve to grow his hair as they did, no more than he deserved to sit upon the Ash Throne. His brows, hair, and eyelashes were just as fair as his porcelain skin, making him appear more animalistic than Fae. Every year that passed, less and less of the General

Aodh Bhaltair once knew remained. Worthy or not; he was one of the last remaining Fire Fae. It did not take much for him to take control of a room.

The candles in the grand glass chandeliers above them flickered with warning, and all eyes turned back to the Lord of Fire himself.

He stood tall and loomed over the table. His sunken, sickly face twisted in a sour scowl. For a moment, Bhaltair feared he heard about the Nøkken in the pits. Even though Bhaltair did not believe the boy was guilty of anything other than being obscenely irritating, he could not set him free without being certain. If it were up to him, he would have left Ronen in there a little longer to build some character. But the Little Folk pestered him endlessly to release him.

The Shapeshifter was not in the castle, but it did not give Bhaltair any peace of mind. He was back to square one on his search. Luckily, Fritjof was none the wiser to what was happening within the castle. As usual.

"Elphyne has needed a change for some time now. We have come to a lull since the king died, and to be frank, since long before that. Do you not remember, my brothers and sisters, when Fae were treated as the god's children? We ruled this realm with power and glory. Then, the Elphynian War happened, and suddenly the Fae were not on top anymore. We got afraid, hiding amongst the lower, mutated peoples such as the Anso and Orculli. Well, I say it's time to stop being afraid. I say, it is high time for the Fae to stand back up," he shouted, making his way around the table. Some people clapped, some nodded in agreement, but others stayed quiet.

Bhaltair did not understand why the High Lord selected these people to join the King's Court. The title was a joke within itself—they had no king, and this was no court. What did Fritjof plan for these lords and farmers to do? He spoke of war, yet Bhaltair was the only warrior in the room.

He went on. "Something happened recently that reminded me—inspired me, if you will—that it is my duty as your High Lord to lead this realm back to its former glory. Thus, on the first day of the coming month, there will be a meeting in which all of you will be attending. Clearly, all matter will be extremely confidential. I want every soldier here." He pressed his index finger into the table. "In the castle. No one comes in, no one comes out. Understood?"

"Yes, my lord," they all chanted. All but Bhaltair. He was focused on keeping his heart rate in check so no one could hear it pumping rage through his system.

Because a retired King's Court member had sent Bhaltair seven letters in seven days, and he did not think it was a coincidence. Bhaltair had not even had the time to read them yet. He had been too busy hunting down Shapeshifters and babysitting Nøkken. As soon as he was relieved for the day, he was going to tear open those envelopes the Little Folk delivered to his nightstand.

Ever since the queen died, the court had been in shambles, with only Bhaltair left to pick up the slack. Most of the court was loyal to Fritjof, they had to be. The

Lord of Fire could burn their entire village or farm in a single day. Even with half an army on his side, Bhaltair was powerless to stop him. For now.

He hoped the letters would have some sort of answer for Fritjof's strange request. This felt like more than his usual antics. Bhaltair has not seen Fritjof make such a laid-out plan since his days as general. Something did not feel right. Nothing felt right since Bhaltair caught glimpse of that tiny scroll from the Little Folk that Fritjof burned to ashes.

We found her.

And if it is who Bhaltair suspected it was, he was about to have a problem bigger than any Shapeshifter, Fire Fae, or King's Court meeting. If this is who he thought it was, the tables were about to turn.

ELEVEN

"But what does it *feel* like?" Jaeger asked yet again. Not seeming to see nor care about the annoyance written all over Fallon's face.

He bombarded her with questions the entire ride to Reinhart. Fallon knew he had good intentions and was only trying to solve the mystery of her life and power, but it was starting to get tiresome. Not to mention, her rear was sore from riding for so long, and the blazing sun was making her sweat. Fallon was not used to sweating, and she immediately decided she hated it.

She grit her teeth, trying to form an answer to his question. "Have you ever run your cold hands under hot water?" she asked. "Imagine that deep, strange tingling, but all over your body," she explained slowly.

Jaeger nodded. Surely another stupid question was forming in his head, so Fallon interrupted it with her own. "Tell me more about House Osmund."

"Has anyone ever told you you're a bit paranoid?" he asked, poking her in the side.

She sneered. "Has anyone ever told you not to poke a bear?"

"But what if the bear scrunches its nose every time it's mad?" He laughed. "It is awfully cute."

Fallon was going to rip her hair out. She groaned and ran her hands down her face in defeat, causing Jaeger to laugh triumphantly.

"There are no Keepers in Reinhart, only Reapers. The Royal House is on the top of a hill, surrounded by a large moat. A single, heavily guarded bridge is the only way across," he explained.

Fallon mapped out everything in her head as he spoke, exactly how she was trained. Fallon believed that bridge was the only way *in*, but there had to be a secret escape system to get the royal family out. If something went wrong, she needed to find that secret passage.

"How do the guard's rotations work?" she asked.

"Why does it matter?" he asked suspiciously, "I thought you wanted to only speak to the chief, make your deal, and live to wage war another day?"

"That is exactly my plan. But plans go wrong, Jaeger. The chief could reject my *grio* and send me to the gallows with one wave of the hand," she said.

She felt him tense up behind her. "You seem to be confident he won't," he said wearily.

Fallon shrugged. "I wouldn't. Not with the information I have. If he really wants to take Barwyn one day, he will need me," she explained.

"You believe he wants to take Barwyn?"

"I believe men will always choose selfishness."

They rode for a while in silence after that.

After a few breaks to eat and relieve themselves, Fallon, Jaeger, and Norman arrived. If the Solveij Royal House was a stone fortress, House Osmund was a towering ivory castle. Fallon had to crank her head back to see the top of it, where green flags bearing the royal sigil flew.

Reinhart. Fallon made it.

The city itself consisted of streets full of oak houses. Their red-brown clay roofs, smooth stone roads, and fountains screamed wealth. This was nothing like Amory. Fallon's confidence started to deflate in her chest—the chief might not want Barwyn after all. They did not need it.

They boarded their horses and walked through what Jaeger called a business street. A wisp of a glorious smell passed under her nose, and Fallon followed it like a bloodhound. She peeked through the open window, taking in all the cakes and pastries of her wildest dreams.

Norman had to remind her they were out of money and on a mission. Fallon growled at him, letting him know she would sell him out for one cream puff.

The massive crowds made it easy to hide, but they occasionally had to shield their faces from Reapers on patrol. Men with the sunken eyes of a beaten soul kept walking past them. Their faces were covered in thick, black smears, their clothing torn and filthy. When another group of them walked by, Fallon walked closer to Jaeger. "Where are they coming from?" she asked quietly.

"The mines," he answered. "The lands of Halvar are rich with natural resources if you can get to them. Collectors, as they call them, get paid even better than Reapers and Keepers combined. But it is brutal, brutal work. Few can handle it."

In Barwyn, there was no such thing. You were either a warrior or a victim. You could be a shop owner or a seamstress or even a lord, but at the end of the day the warriors took what they wanted. That had once been Fallon's dream. To be so strong, respected, and worthy, that no one would ever try to take anything from her ever again. But being here, being with Jaeger, seeing this city ...

"Fallon?" Jaeger nudged her shoulder. He turned down a small alley, stopping behind some crates.

Norman stayed behind, keeping watch at the front of the alley while Jaeger held out something to her. A piece of rope.

Fallon rolled her eyes, "Really?"

"We have *grio*, but they must see submission. Any wrong move can get us all killed. That is assuming Chief Sigurd will even accept our *grio*," he said. He was worried, Fallon could see it dancing in the blue of his eyes, but his hands were steady as he bound hers together.

She snorted. "This is *not* how you tied me up last time," she noted, gesturing to the shabby knot.

He watched her carefully. "Plans can go wrong."

If it came down to it, he wanted her to escape. Fallon decided that if she did need to run, she was dragging the brave young lord and the fat man with her. Even if she had to haul their three bodies across that moat herself. She owed them a life debt.

Norman smiled at her and nodded, his mustache twitching to the side. Fallon reached out and tapped his wrist with her tied fingers. "You can go now if you choose. The last step is over that bridge, we can take it from here."

"Las," he shook his head, chuckling. "Before you could tie your own boots, I led legions. Believe it or not, my house was just down this road." He smiled, eyes twinkling with memory.

"*Was* down the road? With a general's pay, you could afford something much nicer," Fallon noted.

That twinkle quickly faded. "All of my pension goes to the widows of my men. I don't need it or deserve it." He swallowed. "I couldn't save their husbands, but I can save their children from being hungry."

Fallon turned to Jaeger in surprise, but he kept his eyes on the ground. The demons Norman ran from, the ones he kept at bay with alcohol and bitterness, they were the shadows of his friends. And here Fallon was, bringing on another worthless war.

"Maybe a new chief, with new ideas, is exactly what this country needs." Norman jerked his chin to the side, urging her forward. "Now hurry up. I will walk your sorry arses to the gate, but they will only let two through," he said, turning on his heel and quickly waddling up the road.

A new, strange pain spread in her gut. She wanted to call Norman back, shake his shoulders, and beg him not to have any faith in her. *Don't hope,* she had to warn him. *Hope hurts.* Norman wanted her to stop a war, and Jaeger wanted to use her to find his mother. And Fallon was going to disappoint them both.

Fallon felt a boulder resting on her shoulders as they walked up the street. On their left was a large archway, guarded by four grubby Reapers. They locked their sights on Fallon almost instantly, inching for their weapons.

Norman rested his thumbs in his belt, nodding at the men. "G'evening, lads. Permission to cross?" he asked.

"Denied," one simply said, not even looking at Norman.

He scoffed. While the two men went back and forth, Fallon scanned the bridge and surrounding towers. Two stone pillars erected on either side of the archway, big enough for at least one man to fit in. She felt the hairs on the back of her neck rise.

Fallon knew the feeling of an arrow pointed at her head all too well.

The ivory castle was square in shape, four walls connected by four even larger towers. Along the top of the wall, cannons and catapults were pointed directly at them. Fallon watched as a man slowly walked behind one.

"Jaeger," she said quietly. "Now would be a good time to let them know about our *grio*."

There was barely a sliver of sun left peaking over the horizon. It was enough to shoot a reflective beam—

probably from a mirror—from the top of the castle down to the stone towers adjacent to her. A signal.

She felt an invisible shove from behind, and the voice that had never led her astray shouted: *Move!*

Fallon kicked Norman forward and slammed her body into Jaeger. All she heard was the zip of the wind before a piercing pain ripped through her shoulder.

She bit down so hard her jaw quivered, eating in the pain until she could stand straight again. Making sure she could still wiggle her fingers, she gawked at the arrow skewering her left shoulder. Tracing the trajectory, it came from the left tower.

Fallon glared up at the archer hiding within the stones. "Really?"

Jaeger reacted quickly. He stepped in front of Fallon, arms up in surrender. "Enough!" he shouted. "She is with us, protected under the old ways of *grio*."

The Reapers, who all held their weapons in hand, looked at each other carefully. Fallon stepped out from behind Jaeger, swallowing down the pulsing pain. "I have information for Chief Sigurd, for which I seek safe asylum in exchange."

She took small, quick breaths. Swallowing down each wave of pain as it came. *Don't blow up. Don't blow up.*

Norman was a huffing and puffing mess. He straightened out his collar. "It appears the rules have already been broken." he grumbled, putting up his pudgy fists.

"They did not know." Fallon said. She needed to get into that castle, even if it meant shoving her pride deep,

deep down. "Lucky for me, there was not a Keeper in that tower. Any decent shot and I would have been dead." She flashed them all a cheeky grin.

Jaeger let out a gleeful chuckle as all the Reaper's faces twisted in anger. Three more men were running down the bridge towards them, all clad in dark green uniforms.

One man with a beard as long as Fallon's hair grunted for attention. "We will take the girl up. *Only* the girl."

"No," Jaeger said without missing a beat. "Her *grio* is with us. We must escort her for protection."

The man scanned Jaeger up and down. "It's been a long time, young lord. Your father would be proud to see you standing this close to a woman," he said, laughter erupting from the other guards. Fallon even heard snorts coming from the top of the two stone towers. Blood roared in her ears, but as always, Jaeger did not falter. He did not yield.

"We all want to make our fathers proud. Your son told me so last night." He winked. "Tell him I'll be back around next spring."

Fallon had to bite down her laughter as the man's face turned green, then purple. He slammed his staff on the ground twice. "*Only* the girl!" he growled again.

Two men approached her. One snapped off the tip of the arrow in her shoulder while the other ripped it out the rest. Fallon's vision went blurry for a few moments, but she let only a gasp of pain escape her mouth. She would not scream for them. She hoped they did not note how little blood trickled from her already healing wound.

As they each took one of her arms in a bone-cracking grip, Fallon turned to her companions.

No, friends. She could call them friends.

Norman had his arms crossed, giving her a nod of approval. Jaeger, however, locked eyes with her. The hues of the dying sky around them danced in his irises, damp with emotion. Fallon got the message written all over his face: *Whatever you do, don't blow up.*

She could do that. Fallon could do this. She made it this far after all.

Before she could think of anything to say to them, the Reapers dragged her over the bridge. The thuds of their footsteps pounded to the drum of her beating heart. It worked.

The iron gate was lifted for them, and she was met by even more guards, swords, and catapults. She counted the steps they took, assigning them to the turns they made. The inside was nice—dark, polished wood walls and green rugs lining the halls. It sure beat the bland gray stone of the Solveij House.

It was after the third flight of stairs that Fallon knew something was wrong. The chief and his family had thrones at the head of the Grand Hall, but no Grand Hall was this far underground.

"Where are we going?" she demanded, her heart racing. Her shoulder stopped bleeding, and the pain stopped minutes ago. She knew the injury should be far worse, so she kept her left arm tense.

Their only answer was a smug grunt. Fallon knew she had made a grave mistake when they turned the next corner and were met with nothing but a solid stone door.

Her knees turned to liquid as she stared at it. The memory surfaced before she could stop it, encompassing her mind until she was surrounded by those four stone walls again.

"You know the rules," Beowulf's voice echoed through the empty room. "You cannot leave until you stop flinching like a coward."

He threw another knife that hit the wall inches from Fallon's head. The sound of metal scraping the stone made her teeth ache.

She stood, blindfolded, trying to stop her hands from shaking in anger and fear. The area around her feet was littered with various blades, but Beowulf was the real weapon. He could paralyze her, spill her guts on the floor, and rip out her heart. All without laying a hand on her.

Fallon knew the blindfold was just to invoke more fear. The dungeons had no light, anyways. She heard her father draw another dagger, and Fallon braced for it. She knew it would not hit her. If Beowulf wanted to draw blood—he would. He had before. But this was just another one of his "lessons".

She knew it was coming, but Fallon was only ten. Time after time, she flinched at the sound of metal sparking against the wall.

He sighed disappointedly. "Failure. As always." He picked up the only axe in the pile of old, rusted weapons next to him. "If you are going to act like prey, then I will treat you as such. Rabbits flee at the sight of wolves, so go ahead and leave," he said. She was blindfolded, but she could still see the smile on his face.

Fallon had known it was a trap. He never let her go. Fallon had spent more time in this dungeon than her own room, so she knew she could make it to the door and up the stairs while blind. She wondered what part of her Beowulf would go for. The smart thing would be to slice the backs of her ankles, but he might send the blade straight into her thigh just for the glee of it.

Fallon balled her frozen hands into fists and turned on her heel to run. Even before it hit her, she knew she was not quick enough. She never was.

A hot line of pain rushed across her face as the axe ripped its way across the bridge of her nose. She stumbled back, yelping in pain as she used the blindfold to press against her gushing face. The tan fabric turned bright red in seconds.

For a moment she thought her whole nose was gone, but it was just a deep laceration. He could have killed her—she wished he had just killed her.

He stalked past her as she choked down her sobs. Beowulf tsked in disapproval. "A Blodvinger does not bleed. He only draws blood," he growled. He wore that bear skin on his back, as always. So when he walked up the stairs and disappeared into the shadows, he looked like the monster he was.

Fallon was left alone to bleed out on the stone floor. She had waited five minutes before running to find Hagen …

"*Move!*" a harsh, male voice shouted.

Fallon was shoved forward, stirring her from her nightmares. But that scar was still on her face. She had to see that thick line across the bridge of her nose every time she glanced in the mirror. A constant reminder of how slow, useless, and weak she was. Just as Beowulf had wanted.

Her legs were not working, and her mind was absent enough she did not remember passing through the stone doorway or being led down this hall. Before she knew it, the two men tossed her into a cell and the bars were closed in front of her face.

"No!" Fallon shouted, shaking the iron bars as if he had a chance against them. "Wait! I am to see the chief!"

The blond man with a scar down his eyebrow dropped a key into his breast pocket. "You didn't say when. Could be tomorrow, could be in sixty years." He laughed. "Either way, you're a trespasser."

No. No, no! Panic surged through her system. *Don't blow up, don't blow up*. But she could feel her fingers and toes start to tingle. Not wanting a repeat of last time, Fallon tried to scream it out. Cursing the two men laughing at her as they walked down the torch-lit hall and shut the door behind them.

She had to get out. Fallon turned to gather her surroundings: her cell was small, maybe a five by seven-foot square. The only thing in here beside her was some molding hay on the ground and a bucket in the corner.

Fallon counted seven cells on either side of the hall, all of them empty except the one adjacent to hers. There was a small form huddled in the corner, almost completely obscured by a curtain of snow-white hair. That old woman must have been here for a long, long time. The thought of being here until she was that old and frail made her nauseous. Fallon had been locked away for far too long already. She crouched, hugging her knees and trying to calm her racing heart. Failure, misfortune … why did this cloud of defeat follow her every move—

"Hello?"

Fallon jumped, falling to her side in surprise. She did not think the old woman was breathing, let alone could speak. Fallon gathered her composure and turned to the bars that separated their cells.

But as the woman tucked her hair behind her tall ears, Fallon gasped. Her face was not ancient and wrinkled, but stunningly, *absurdly* beautiful, and full of youth.

Fallon was too shocked to speak. But the girl reached through the bars, holding out her tan hand as if Fallon was a warm fire. "You feel like the sun." She smiled softly.

"S-sorry?" Fallon stammered.

The girl scooted closer to the bars. All she wore was a simple green dress that was dirty and torn. Her eyes were the palest shade of green, like a drop of morning dew resting on a leaf. As enchanting as she was, exhaustion covered her angelic face.

Fallon scooted out of reach, resting her back against the far wall. She stared the girl down, who was staring right back at her. "How long have you been here?" Fallon asked.

She scrunched her brows. "Three days, I think." Then she cocked her head to the side playfully, a wave of white hair cascading down her slim shoulder. "You look like a marigold flower."

"Thank you?" Fallon almost smiled. As far as being red-haired went, that was probably the kindest comment she had ever received about it. Even if it was strange.

The girl slouched against the bars as if she could hardly hold herself up. Fallon could not make sense of what she was seeing. Something about the girl seemed drained, like an under-watered flower. That stark white hair—so long and yet still shining with health. And those tall, almost droopy ears …

"What is your name?" Fallon asked, officially intrigued.

"Elowen, Elowen Middlemist. What's yours?"

"Fallon. Just Fallon."

The girl spoke with a strange accent. Fallon could understand her clearly, but her words seemed to flow differently. It was like Elowen spoke in poetry. Her lips were full and beautiful, but pale. Her face was perfectly heart-shaped, but a darkness was spreading under her eyes.

"What happened to you?" Elowen asked, eyes trailing to the blood stain on her shoulder.

"My plan went wrong," Fallon said quietly.

The girl swiveled her head around the hall. "Do you have a flower on you?" she asked, as if it were a normal question.

Fallon snorted. "No." But she could tell Elowen was not joking.

She thought Jaeger was strange, but this girl was the most peculiar person Fallon had ever met. Yet no alarms in Fallon's head went off. She sensed no threat. On the contrary, her instincts were telling her to *trust* her.

That was, until she stood up.

Elowen used the bars to pull herself up, the action taking obvious effort. "I will find something," she said to herself. "Something green."

Her dirty green dress went to her ankles, and her ivory hair fell to her hips. Fallon could not help but stare as she paced around her cell on her bare feet. At first, Fallon thought it was just a strange belt. But when the girl turned around, Fallon's jaw hit the stone floor.

Impossible.

Fallon blinked. She rubbed her eyes and tried to make sense of it, but it was clear as day. A tail—the girl had gods-damned a tail. A *cow's* tail. Just like the stories.

Fallon's mind flashed with storybooks full of beautiful women with cow tails dancing and singing, always close to the tree they were connected to. She saw one oil painting in particular; it had been one of her mother's favorites.

It was in an old fable about a huntsman who fell madly in love with a woman whose beauty was out of this world, but he did not respect nature. One day, he carelessly dumped a bucket of rotten ale outside. It soaked into the earth, poisoning the roots of a nearby tree. The next morning, he found his love lying dead in the grass. Overcome with grief and guilt, he swore to never treat the earth unfairly again, having seen the effect of his actions.

The last page was a picture of the woman he killed. She had a lavender dress as simple and elegant as the one on Elowen's shoulders. Her brown hair was unbound, and she wore no shoes or stockings. Most importantly, a cow's tail swung at her side.

The woman died because she and that tree were connected as one. The title of her story was written in gold at the top of the page: *The Huntsman and the* …

"Hulder." Fallon breathed. "You—you're a Hulder."

Elowen turned around with a bright smile. "Yes! I have not seen anyone else in a very long time. When did they open the tree?" she asked, still on the hunt for a single flower in their underground prison.

Fallon's mouth opened and closed but no words came out. It was real. There was a *real* Hulder sitting in front of her, straight out of her mother's stories. That meant Jaeger had been right all along. Gods, she had been so rude to him. Just because she did not want to accept it.

She stubbornly shook her head. *So what?* So what if Faeries were real? This did not affect her life. This changed nothing. Because Fallon was still trapped in the dungeon of the Osmund Royal House with no visible way out. She still had to convince the chief to march on

Barwyn so Fallon could get the revenge she deserved. Faeries or not, Fallon was going to be chieftess.

Elowen pressed her face in the space between the bars. "Are you alright?" she asked gently. "You seem cold."

But Fallon said nothing. An awful pain was consuming her heart. She told herself long ago she was over her mother's death. But seeing Elowen and thinking of these stories again, it felt like a part of her mother was back. Pulled right from the grave.

Asta had spoken of Faeries as if she knew them personally. Now, Fallon understood she did. In this world, Elowen was a swan among geese. Too beautiful, too pure, too *good* for this realm. And that was exactly how Asta Solveij had been.

Fallon met Elowen at the bars and brought her face close. The girl raised her hand to Fallon's face and, just as Jaeger had done, ran her finger down the bridge of Fallon's nose, pausing over her scar.

"How strange," she said softly.

"You asked me if the tree was open, do you mean a portal?" Fallon dared to ask. Elowen's slim, pointy nose was an inch from her own.

"Yes. Can you open it? Can you get us back home?"

Fallon gripped the cold bars so hard she thought they would snap. The malice of this world had tainted her mother. Fallon was too young and selfish to understand it then, but she understood it now. If Fallon was able to save this Faerie from Asta's same fate, maybe her mother would forgive her for all she had done and all she planned to do. If she did this, maybe Fallon could even try to forgive herself one day.

So, she nodded her head. "Where, exactly, is home?"

"Elphyne, of course. The realm of the Fae."

TWELVE

The days passed slowly, and the nights lasted centuries in those cells. Fallon and Elowen were tired and hungry, with the Hulder falling more ill with each passing hour. They filled their time by sitting back-to-back against the metal bars, talking and asking questions.

Fallon only planned to share her name, but before she knew it, she was telling the tragic tale of a bastard girl and her journey to the southern lands. The girl who miraculously survived a death sentence, scaled a waterfall, befriended the enemy, and killed her way through Halvar. Only to be a failure in the end. She left out the details about her powers, but she told her about Jaeger and Norman. Their names made her throat burn.

Elowen returned the favor by telling her the equally melodramatic story of how she ended up here. Faeries used to be free to go back and forth between the two realms. Until one day when she was eight, the portal she called the Entrance Tree did not open back up. Trapped and alone, she feared for the well-being of her tree back in

Elphyne. Their spirits were one in the same; whatever happened to one, the other felt it.

She was captured a few days ago. "I saw the lights and the music," she said dreamily after finishing up yet another episode of shaking and vomiting. "I thought maybe this time would be different. That they would be nicer to me. I just wanted to dance, I wanted to sing and make friends," she said. Her voice cracked at the word *friends*.

People must have been afraid of her, maybe even appalled by the sight of her hair and tail. She said a group of men dragged her here, and Fallon could only hope her strangeness was enough to keep the men out of her cell.

The Hulder was pressed up against the bars separating their cells, as usual. Elowen was always adamant that as much of her body touched Fallon's as possible. She said it made her feel better, so Fallon allowed it.

Elowen's tail kept twitching while she slept—the sight making Fallon feel queasy. There was a slit in the back of her dress, allowing the tan appendage to move freely. There was even a small tuft of fur at the end, as white and shining as the hair on her head. It was so strange; Fallon could not help but stare. She was still adjusting to the idea of Faeries being real, despite all the stories Elowen told her about who and what lived in Elphyne. To think there was really an entire realm full of people like her …

Which meant a realm without people like Fallon.

Without dungeons and chiefs and lost birthrights. If she were any more of a coward, she might consider going to Elphyne herself. But Fallon did not run from a fight, especially when there was so much at stake.

She did not know how long her thoughts kept her up that night, but by the time Elowen started stirring Fallon already had another storm of questions lined up.

"Is it true Huldra can make people ill?" she asked.

Elowen rubbed her reddening eyes. "Yes, but if you learn to control it then you don't hurt anybody."

Fallon arched a brow. "There are some who can't control it?"

She shrugged. "Watch." And proceeded to sneeze into her hands.

A second later, Fallon's nose started to tingle. Surely enough, she sneezed twice into her elbow.

Elowen laughed. A light, bubbly giggle that made this prison feel a little less dark. "See. And if I just had something green, even just a single flower, I could help heal you," she said sadly.

"You can heal people as well?" Fallon whispered, wiping the snot from her nose.

"In a way, yes. But the healing doesn't come from me. It is more of an … exchange. Life demands life. That is the way of nature."

Fallon nodded. She understood that better than anyone. Beowulf had taken everything from Fallon, so she was going to return the favor tenfold. Life demands life—blood must have blood.

"So." Elowen crossed her legs and smiled at Fallon. "When are we leaving?"

"As soon as I talk with the chief. I will make a deal with him, one of the conditions being your release," she said. Elowen was clearly ill, she needed to find help soon.

The Hulder seemed to wilt to the side, surveying Fallon with wide eyes. "You're not coming with me?" her rosebud lips folded into a pout.

For a count of three, Fallon Solveij hesitated. She heard a small, barely audible whisper: *Go*.

She stared at Elowen, trying to find the words to explain her gratitude. Because for the first time in her life, Fallon was not alone in a dungeon cell. Simply having *someone* there with her had kept Fallon from falling into a pit of memory and despair she doubted she would ever come back from.

But before she could say a word, before she could explain why she could not go, the door at the end of the hall creaked open. They whipped their heads around to see two men stalking towards them, both wearing metal armor. All the Reapers she had seen thus far wore reinforced leather armor. These must be royal guards, then. Which meant Fallon's plan might have worked after all.

Which meant that she would not in fact go with Elowen. Even though her fate was leading her elsewhere, Fallon was happy she got to meet the Hulder. Hearing all of her stories had felt like speaking with her mother again.

The guards stopped in front of her cell. Out of the corner of her eyes, she saw Elowen scoot into the wall and lie very still. As Fallon stood, one man tossed a pile of fabric through the bars.

"Change."

She picked up a too-large blouse and pair of tan trousers. At first, she was confused. The fabric was a disgusting, dark yellow. In Valdimir, colors mattered just as much as names. They showed allegiance and piety. This was not southern greens and browns, northern black and reds, or western purples and silver. This was nothing.

Seeing no other choice, Fallon turned to the side as she changed. Leaving on the wrap of fabric around her breasts and her undergarments. Fallon did not care that the men were watching her; she was only happy they stayed quiet. She knew she was not impressive. Life in Barwyn had left her skin pale and barely nourished. And not to mention, two weeks on the run left her muscles the only thing pulling skin from bone.

There was also a thick, brown belt that she tied around her waist in an attempt to make the clothes fit. Once she finished tying back on her boots, Fallon gave Elowen a sidelong glance: *I'll be back. I promise.*

"Give me your wrists," the man ordered. He was as average as they came; big, gruff, long beard and even longer hair. The only thing that made him special were his hands. As Fallon stuck out her arms to allow him to handcuff her, she stared at his ink-covered fingers. Words in the old language were tattooed into his skin, fingertip to wrist. Fallon stopped studying the Runes long ago, it was not a warrior's job to partake in divination.

He opened the door and grabbed Fallon by the chains, pulling her forward.

"It's about time." She rolled her neck and stretched her legs, trying to shake the exhaustion out of her system. But Fallon had not eaten in days, so a task as simple as changing her clothes left her out of breath and woozy.

The men sneered at her in disgust. "You should be honored that the chief made time for you at all. You are not worth a single breath, bastard."

Fallon lurched forward, grabbing him by the collar. "Call me a bastard one more time and I will skin those Runes from your hands and wear them as gloves," she hissed.

Just as she hoped, he pushed her back into the bars of Elowen's cell and gave her a good smack across the face. The sound of the impact was loud enough to obscure Fallon tossing the key she had snagged from his breast pocket into Elowen's cell. The faint clank of metal hitting the stone floor was nothing more than an echo as the men growled and grabbed her by the neck.

Fallon knew there was a chance she would not make it to sunset. This meeting would end or restart her life, but that did not change her promise to Elowen. If Fallon did not come back, the Hulder would have her own way out now.

She knew Elowen saw and understood, because Elowen started singing softly as the guards dragged her down the hall. The light, gentle sound sent a wave of relaxation through Fallon's body, easing her mind enough to keep her power under control. A small, parting gift from Elowen. From a warm body in a cold dungeon who saved her from being alone.

They climbed the stairs and started to follow the same path she had entered from. For a moment she thought she was simply being thrown out, but then they turned down a hall she had yet to see. The ceiling got taller, the wooden floors turned into mosaic tiles, and more guards in metal breastplates stamped with the Royal House sigil walked past them.

Fallon practiced what she wanted to say in her head, but it was hard to concentrate when she was being vigorously manhandled.

"Where are we going?" she demanded.

"To the Great Hall," the man answered. "Where you will keep your barking mouth shut. You will kneel before Chief Sigurd," he said.

She balked at the thought. If someone had spoken to her that way a month ago, Fallon would have spilled his throat on the floor. But now, Fallon had no pride to protect. No honor to uphold. So she kept her mouth shut and let them drag her so she could save her energy.

Servants in simple, beige clothing rushed past them in fear. Her apprehension grew with every clamoring step they took. Every waking moment since she chose to get up from that cliff had led up to his. Every detour, every failure, every breath had gotten her here. To fulfill her destiny. She had to keep reminding herself that Beowulf failed, too. And he was about to be so, so sorry for it.

At last, two massive mahogany doors came into view. They were slightly ajar, and through them she could see a man on a wooden throne. Nothing but quiet whispers met her ears as they approached. But when she stepped through the threshold, a silence as still as death overtook the room.

The Grand Hall did not impress her. They were all the same to an extent: tall ceilings spiderwebbed with wood beams. Always ten or so long tables on either side of a long rug that led straight up the stairs to the podium.

What Fallon was *not* expecting, however, was every single seat on those long tables to be full.

This was a bigger crowd than the one at her execution. Her heart pounded so violently in her chest, she feared the men gripping her arms could feel it through her clothes. They kept walking, the clank of her chains the only sound as she was shoved to her knees before the small set of stairs.

She inclined her head slightly, meeting the cold gaze of Sigurd Osmund.

He was not a large man, not in the way Beowulf was. Chief Osmund was of normal build, above average height, and reasonably handsome. His blue eyes pierced her to the ground as he did not bother to stand upon her entrance. None of them had.

This room felt wrong … something was not right. It felt like she interrupted a funeral service.

There was a slightly smaller throne to his right, and one even smaller to his left—both empty. Not even his wife or heir was interested in this meeting.

After a few moments of paralyzing silence, he rested his hands on the arms of his birchwood throne and spoke. "What is the name of the first person to call upon *grio* in the last hundred years?" he asked, sounding rather bored as he picked at the cuffs of his dark gold robes.

A test. He knew exactly who she was. Fallon glanced over to the man holding her chains with his Rune covered hands, making sure this counted as permission to speak. He gave her a curt nod, and Fallon turned back to the southern chief.

She rolled her shoulders back, trying to stand as tall as she could while still on her knees. She banished all exhaustion and weakness from her voice, speaking directly from her chest. "I am Fallon, with no forebears to name. I come not as a plague from the north, but a cure. Barwyn has weaknesses, this I know for certain. But if you ever dream of finding them, you will need my help. All I ask in return for my information are three conditions," she finished, letting the chief take the next move.

He rubbed his stubbled chin, grinning slyly. "Let us hear it, then." The crowd murmured behind her. She felt their breaths move around her, grazing and licking her skin. The air was laced with anticipation and excitement. Every nerve in Fallon's body was firing, telling her to run.

Despite her instincts, Fallon continued. "I will not be hunted," she started. "I will live among you peacefully. Second, all prisoners in lockup will be freed," she demanded.

Chief Sigurd's brows dropped as he turned to the man beside her. "Are there more prisoners?" he asked with genuine curiosity.

One man simply shrugged.

He waved his hand dismissively. "Easy enough."

Fallon's entire body was quivering, making the chains holding her audibly rattle; they *forgot* about her. If Fallon had not come, Elowen might have been left down there to die. They must have tossed her down there in a drunken mess during the festival and forgotten the next morning. Fallon felt this fury in her bones. Damned fools. All of them. They were no better than the huntsman pouring poison on tree roots, and they were about to learn the consequences.

Because unfortunately for them, Fallon had come to care for the life of one particular Faerie. So, she ignored the heat spreading through her and swallowed down the pressure pushing against her ribcage.

"Lastly," her voice echoed this time, hushing the room. "I will have a place amongst the ranks. Because Beowulf Solveij is *my* kill. And once he is dead, once the northern territory is yours, I promise you will never see me again."

Fallon watched Chief Sigurd's face melt from amusement to fury. She knew everyone else did as well, because no one dared even blink as he adjusted himself on the white throne before he spoke in a low voice.

"You promise?" the chief repeated, standing slowly. He took a few steps forward, sending a wave of nausea crashing over Fallon. Standing was *not* a good sign.

Nothing about this had been a good sign. Fallon should have run when she had the chance.

He slowly descended the steps one by one, his cloak of elk fur dragging behind him. Fallon felt all the words she had spent days preparing tumble to the ground in a useless heap. She might have just wasted her last breaths compromising with a brick wall.

Chief Sigurd adjusted his golden robes and gave her a serpentine grin—a reminder of why Halvar had been such a powerhouse all these years. Sigurd Osmund was not a beast, not like the Wolf of the North or the Boar of the West. He was a scorpion. Waiting, calculating in the shadows until he stuck one, fatal blow. And Fallon had placed herself right in front of his tail.

He pushed the fair hair back behind his ears. "The little girl who betrayed her own people, trespassed into my territory, and openly speaks of treason against a royal house offers *me* a promise?" he asked rhetorically.

Her eyes widened. "I did not *willingly* leave—"

"Enough!" he shouted, stalking back and forth. "Did you know, bastard, that the Osmund Royal House has been breeding the best hunting hounds for centuries? I personally oversee every pup before we send them out. Do you know how we keep our bloodlines so flawless?" he asked dangerously.

She did not care about whatever point he was trying to make. Fallon was too busy trying to stay calm. *No.* Not again. She would not let another chief do this to her. Fallon stood, ready to take out as many people in this room down with her as possible.

But the guard slammed his foot into the back of her legs, sending Fallon's knees slamming into the hard wood. She let out a guttural growl, getting back up. But she was weak. So when the guards knocked her back down a second time, Fallon did not rise again. Because she feared what might rise with her.

Sigurd continued as if nothing happened. "Our bloodlines are never tainted, because we get rid of the useless bitches and their *mutts*." He sneered. "So, why would I wage a war against my dear friend Beowulf Solveij, when all he has done is the exact same thing?"

Her blood became thick, moving through her veins like molten metal. "All he has done?" she whispered it at first, trying to fathom this man's ignorance. "*All he has done?*" Her voice grew with every word. She pulled against her chains, the metal creaking in warning. Fallon could tolerate the insult towards her, but he would live to regret even mentioning her mother.

"You see, we do not actually kill the mutts. Nor do we kill infertile cattle, or the runt of the litter. We simply mark them for what they are, then send them back off into nature—so it can deal with its own creation," he explained.

Fallon's head began to pound. This was all planned. He knew from the beginning what he wanted to do with her, yet he let her come up here and make a *fool* out of herself first.

"If you think your land stands a chance without me …" She seethed through her teeth.

"Oh, but you are only proving my point further." he shook his head at her with fake sadness.

Fallon ripped against her chains, determined to sink her teeth into his thin neck. But Sigurd did not even flinch.

"We set the marked mutts free because we *feel bad* for them. That is the only reason you exist, Barwyn's Bastard: the gods pity your existence too much to kill you."

The scorpion had struck. And the poison in his words seeped into her veins, turning her red-hot with rage. The metal links holding her finally snapped, and Fallon pounced. One chain was still tangled around her wrist, allowing the guard to rip her backwards just before she could tear that grin off his face with her bare hands.

The guard had to put his boot on Fallon's neck to keep her on the ground as she thrashed and screamed. Now, she wanted to ignite. She wanted to melt the skin from their faces. Let him get just a little closer, and he would see what a mutt could really do.

Sigurd tsked at her. "Beowulf got rid of the bitch, but the mutt she produced still barks. The gods sent me a task, and I accept it with honor. Your dirty, illegitimate bloodline ends today," he announced, arms spread wide.

The room erupted in cheers as two more guards came, each of them grabbing one of her limbs. Fallon saw flashes of blood-thirsty faces as the people gathered closer to shout their slander at her. This was not an assembly at all ... it was a mob.

Fallon screamed. No words, no curses, no pleas, or cries. She just had to *scream* from the bottom of her chest.

The gods pity your existence too much to kill you. Fallon did not know if it was the words themselves that hurt so much, or the truth they contained. They hurt so much her mind went numb trying to process it all. She knew if she truly let go, if she gave in to this power, it would kill her and everyone around her. But that day was not today. She had to save it for Beowulf.

She screamed her throat raw until suddenly the sun hit her face—they were outside. At first, Fallon had the terrible thought that they were going to throw her off another cliff. But Sigurd said they don't kill mutts. They mark them.

The sunlight blinded her as she felt her body connect with something flat and hard. It took five men, but one by one each of her limbs were tied down to a plank of wood. Her body was sprawled out into an X, making it impossible to fight her way free.

The guards backed off, and Fallon saw nothing but people and stone surrounding her. They were in the open courtyard.

But Fallon stopped fighting when she saw the man standing next to her. It was not the drooling mob or maniac chief that scared her, but the man covered head to toe in black leather. Even his face was obscured by a leather hood. Only his eyes were visible through two small holes, and Fallon saw no soul behind them.

An Executioner.

The sharp tinge of cowhide bit her nose as the horror set in. Every clan had an Executioner—the chief's bloodied right hand. They were responsible for all the dirty work: beheading, torturing, slaughtering, and cleaning up the mess. When Fallon was young, she heard stories that in order to become one, you must have blue blood: Frost Giant blood. Because only a Frost Giant's soul could be that cold. Only a Frost Giant and Beowulf Solveij. Who had wanted the joy of killing his daughter all to himself.

Fallon smelt her fate before she saw it: the scent of burning metal. She heard the crackling of the embers from the fire and tasted the ash in the air. *We mark the mutts.*

She once again struggled against her restraints as the Executioner approached her. But this time she thrashed and fought out of panic, not anger. He took out a wicked sickle from his belt, and Fallon could do absolutely nothing but shout as he slashed it across her torso. It did not touch her skin, only her clothing. He ripped her shirt clean in half, exposing her pale skin.

Fallon looked down. She watched her stomach rise and fall to shuddering breaths. "What are you doing?" she demanded.

But Executioners did not speak. Fallon followed him with her head as he walked to stand by Chief Sigurd, who stood proudly before the mob around her.

Sigurd's voice filled the courtyard. "This branding iron is used on livestock. Usually, a lord brands his animals with his initials as a way of showing ownership. So when released into the pasture, farmhands can easily sort them. But *these* initials have a special meaning ..."

He turned to speak directly to her now, "This is the nameless mark. It means the animal is *unclaimed*. Unwanted, useless, and unworthy."

She froze. Even Fallon's power stopped buzzing, paralyzed in horror. Now the color of her shirt made sense. It all made sense. It hurt so bad that she could not scream at him that he was wrong, that she did not deserve this. Because he was right.

The look on her face must have said it all, because Sigurd smiled triumphantly. "You have no forebears to name, your birth clan disowned you, and now the Haedilla Clan of Halvar rejects you. If you try to run to Audhild, they will see this mark and turn you away. Even in death this mark will follow you, lest you forget what you truly are: unclaimed."

Everyone stared at her, waiting for more screaming and cursing. But her voice was gone, her muscles were numb, and Fallon was so, so tired. She turned away from him, laying her head back to stare at the clear blue sky above her. Blue, not gray.

Out of the corner of her eye she saw the Executioner pick up the iron rod from the fire pit. It was glowing a harsh red, the air audibly sizzling against its smooth surface. Fallon did not watch—she did not want to know what the mark looked like.

They were taking away her name.

The absolute last thing she had in this life, and they were taking it away from her. The gods took her mother, Beowulf took her home and people, her name was the only thing she had left.

As the Executioner lifted the rod above her, Fallon made a promise to herself. That she would never belong to anything ever again. She would be nothing, have nothing, so no one could take anything from her. After today, all Fallon would be was a beating heart.

Which meant she could no longer own this power, either. She felt it pushing up from under her skin, begging to be set free. As the people around her stomped their feet in excitement, Fallon closed her eyes and gripped her power by the throat.

She imagined herself tossing it into a box and closing the lid. It pounded fiercely in retaliation, but Fallon did not hesitate. She grabbed a chain and wrapped it around the box again, and again, and again, until the glow was completely obscured.

The Executioner was holding the mark right above her stomach, letting it slowly scorch her skin as he lowered it tauntingly. The heat made her skin pop and blister.

She did not hear nor see the world around her anymore, all her brain understood was the pain. Fallon had to escape deep, deep into her mind if she was going to survive this. Her senses dulled down to nearly nothing as she stepped to the ledge of the bottomless chasm that was her soul.

The cage shook in her hands, her power desperate to save her, but Fallon no longer wanted to be saved. The branding iron got close enough that her entire torso spasmed in agony, but she held the cage over the dark abyss. This power did not belong to her, she did need nor want it. In a way, she was protecting it. By keeping it locked away in a place so lost and forgotten even she would never find it. Fallon had lost herself in that darkness. She could lose this, too.

So, she let go.

Fallon watched it plummet into the abyss within her, never to return.

Not even a second later, the Executioner drove the hissing iron home. Fallon did not even get the chance to see the sky one last time before her screams shook the branches of Yggdrasil.

THIRTEEN

Fallon's soul wondered the world between life and death. Floating, sinking, downing in an ice cold lake.

Every so often, there would be a flash of light. Then darkness.

A face or a voice would pull her towards the surface. Then she was dunked back under.

The pain was the only thing telling Fallon she was still alive. It would come in waves, each more excruciating than the last. She would barely get time to suck in a breath before the next one hit. Then numbness would overtake her again.

Fallon did not know how long she was stuck in that storm. After a while the voices faded, the lights left her alone, and all that remained was the agony inside. She used it as a rope to climb towards the light that peeked through her eyelids.

A familiar, cold floor pressed up on her back. The scent of hay, body odor, and piss tickled her nostrils. Fallon started by moving her fingers, then her toes, and finally she was able to blink her eyes open.

The cell. They had put her back in lockup.

Her breath felt hot, as if her insides were still charred from the branding. She did not want to see it, not yet. Not while every movement sent a rush of pain and nausea through her. She practiced breathing with her chest, not her stomach. The smell of her own burnt flesh ... the smell of leather—

She vomited. Rolling onto her side was already unbearable, but her stomach convulsing was so painful it only made her wretch even harder. Fallon made herself take small, quick breaths in and out until the cycle stopped.

Despite the itching burns crawling all over her, she was freezing. Her teeth chattered as she adapted to her body without the crutch of her powers. She just felt so, devastatingly *mortal*. As if her entire existence was nothing more than a feather, waiting to be whisked away by even the gentlest of gales.

As her eyes focused on the world around her, Fallon nearly screamed. Maybe she would have, but she had no air to spare.

Her lips pulled apart, her tongue a dry lump in her mouth. "Elowen?" she barely whispered. "Elowen!" she shouted with all she had.

Across from her, still lying against the bars Fallon had once sat by, the Hulder was on her side. Not moving.

Fallon could not see if she was breathing. She turned on her back and took more short breaths. Using her legs to push her, Fallon slowly inched her way over to the bars. Every movement tore at her wound, fresh blood spilling from the cauterized scabs.

It was only then Fallon noticed the rancid smell of vomit and urine was not only coming from her. Elowen's face and body were drenched in sweat, her white hair damp and sticking to her face and arms. Fallon winced as she reached to place a hand on her shoulder, sighing in relief as she felt it shudder.

"Elowen!" she tried again, shaking her.

The girl's eyelids slowly opened, but only far enough to let a few tears escape. She barely had enough energy to recognize Fallon and process the situation before speaking.

"I just wanted to see the festival," she whispered.

Suddenly Fallon's pain did not seem so bad. She had deserved this, Elowen did not.

"I'm going to get you out," she promised, even though Fallon questioned her ability to even sit up.

Elowen blinked in understanding, her brows furrowing slightly. "What did they do to you?" She licked her cracked lips. "I can't feel you anymore."

"They did what Beowulf couldn't," she explained, adjusting herself to be more comfortable on her back. If this wound did not kill her, infection soon would. She had to get Elowen back before it consumed her. "They broke me, Elowen."

Because the north star her mother had once cherished so dearly was gone. Not a single glowing ember remained.

She kept her hand on Elowen's shivering body while they both pretended they were awake. She could offer nothing but her presence. Not being alone had been enough when Fallon needed it, hopefully it would be enough for her.

They walked that line together for hours. Jostling the other when they started to slip. Fallon was feeling the aftereffects of having her organs boiled inside of her, and it was just about as pleasant as it sounded.

She thought the pain would be quick. That the Executioner would simply press down the screaming metal, and her nerves would die in seconds. But he had been tantalizingly slow, burning his way through her one layer at a time. Her torso was now so tight, she could not bend or distend her stomach. Every time she moved and breathed, another tear that would never heal ripped through her.

Elowen began to shiver so violently, Fallon feared she was seizing. She knew shock when she saw it, but where had it come from? What had been making her so ill?

She reached out and brushed off some grime and tears from Elowen's colorless cheek. What seemed like a lifetime ago, Elowen had sung to comfort her. Fallon took a few minutes to gather some air, then closed her eyes and tried her best to sing a broken song.

It was one that called upon the ancestors to guide you when you did not know the way. It felt appropriate, as they were two souls in the wrong worlds, lost and dying.

Oh Wil-o'-Wisp, please shine your light tonight

as I stand at this crossroad alone
I entrust my fate to the path of glowing light
for I am only blood and bone

As soon as Fallon's throat was too dry to continue, a crash followed by a bright light shook her world. She strained to raise her head, wincing at the pain in her side. Fallon must truly be losing her mind, then. Because as her eyes focused on the blazing torch he was holding, she let out a pathetic sob.

"Jaeger?"

His multicolored eyes were wide as he stared at her. At her blood-soaked shirt, her newly hollowed eyes, and her hand resting on the shoulder of a dying Faerie.

"Help her," Fallon demanded.

He shook his head. "I-I'm *so* sorry—"

"Jaeger," she gasped again. "Please, she's dying. Help her." This time it was not a demand, but a plea.

He hung his torch on the wall behind him and fumbled with the key, trying to unlock Elowen's cell with shaking hands.

"I-I brought my father. He is talking to Sigurd now. That's why I was gone for so long. I r-rode as fast as I could ... I thought I could be back in time but—" finally the lock clicked.

He only glanced at Elowen's tail for a count of three before moving to kneel at her side. His hands were as gentle as ever as he placed the back of his hand on her bare arm.

"Cold," he whispered.

"What?" Fallon moved closer. "What's wrong with her?"

"Shade-poisoning," he mumbled to himself as he got up and ran to check the door. He came back and began opening Fallon's cell. "My father can't distract Sigurd forever. Can you walk? We need to get to the portal."

"Not we," Fallon interrupted.

He ignored her and opened the cell door. He carefully knelt next to her, going to examine the blood on her shirt. She swatted his hand away. "What are you doing? Get her and go!"

"Fallon, don't you see? We need to leave here. The three of us can go through the portal. We can start over and find our mothers."

Fallon seethed. She stared him right in his eyes. "Our mothers are *dead*!" She punched the bars as she screamed the last word, hard enough to feel her knuckles shift. "Get that through your head! Now take her and get to the portal. You alone can't carry us both."

Fallon hated how nasty she sounded; she hated the way Jaeger's face shattered before her with pain and disappointment. But if he hated her, it would be easier to leave her behind.

"He's not alone." A new voice entered the hall.

Jaeger got behind her and slipped his arms under her shoulders as Norman came wheezing down the hall. Fallon was in too much shock to protest. "Norman?" she gasped.

He rested his hands on his knees while he caught his breath. "I heard your screams from the opposite side of the village. Screams I've heard before ... and did nothing to stop." He glanced once at her bleeding torso. "I'm doing something this time."

Emotion kept her from speaking. Even after yesterday, she had yet to shed a single tear. But seeing these two again might be enough to push her over the edge.

"Screams?" Jaeger asked. He tried to push her up into a sitting position, not knowing the damage that had been done.

Fallon let out a helpless howl of pain, and Jaeger immediately placed her back down.

"Fallon—I'm sorry." He winced. While Norman walked over and picked up Elowen with surprising ease, Jaeger reached over to lift her stained shirt before she could stop him.

Fallon squeezed her eyes shut, refusing to look. Seeing it would only make everything worse. She knew it was bad, because neither man made a sound as they stared at her.

Norman's face turned green as all that alcohol surely started to bubble in his stomach. Jaeger gently placed her shirt back. "You need a healer."

"I need to get out of this bloody village. Just help me up," she groaned. Fallon used her legs to stand while Jaeger kept her spine straight. It was enough to make her go cross-eyed in pain, but she stayed standing. Even if Jaeger was carrying most of her weight.

"How do we get out?" she asked as they all headed for the door. Fallon had not actually thought she would get this far, she had yet to plan an escape route.

Norman walked ahead, Elowen still dangling in his arms. "I lied when I said there was only one way out," Jaeger admitted bashfully.

"No shit." Fallon snorted. Without being able to take full breaths, she was quickly becoming lightheaded.

Fallon had to fall within herself, gripping the bonds that held her together with quivering hands. She let Jaeger guide her body through passageways and tunnels she barely processed. Her eyes stayed focused on Elowen's head, her hair cascading like a silver waterfall over Norman's arm. *Just a little farther.*

Her breaths became labored. She made the mistake of coughing once, and it led to a fit of agonizing hacking as she spit up thick, dark blood. Jaeger held her up against a wall to allow her a quick rest, but Fallon was not improving.

"I'm dead weight," she wheezed. "Just go."

But Jaeger grabbed her again, urging them forward. "You think I haven't noticed you're not healing anymore? I don't know what you did, I will never understand the pain you have been through, but I don't give a damn how much you want to die, Fallon. I did not stomach my father for *days* just to leave you here."

For once, she did not want to argue.

Fallon did not know where or how, but after a few more minutes of horror she saw light up ahead. Sunlight.

She let out a sound halfway between a laugh and a sob. "Elowen! Look!"

Shouting was her second mistake. Her first was having hope.

Any chance of escape was ripped from her grasp as the sound of clanking armor came from behind them. Voices preceded by torchlight were quickly approaching.

Jaeger cursed, signaling to Norman, who cursed even more colorfully. He turned to Fallon. "You are going to have to carry her the rest of the way," he said slowly.

Her eyes widened. "I-I can't."

"Yes, you can. Her strength will come back with the sunlight, you just need to get her there. Norman and I will buy you enough time to find somewhere to hide."

He glanced over his shoulder once before turning and grabbing her face with his warm hands. "Get to the portal, Fallon Not-Solveij. And please just … just remember: someone is only truly gone once you forget about them."

Jaeger gently kissed her forehead, giving her a sad smile before turning to run.

Fallon was still shaking her head when Norman dumped Elowen into her arms. "No!" But the men were already halfway back up the stone tunnel, leaving Fallon alone with quivering legs.

He knew. Jaeger *knew* Fallon would not get out of here for herself, but she would do it for Elowen. Fallon gritted her teeth, leaned her shoulder against the wall, and put one leg in front of the other. Because once again, Fallon had to survive.

Her arms were shaking violently, but she carried Elowen through the rest of the tunnel as the shouts behind her only grew louder. Elowen's thin body pressing into her wound was painful enough that even remembering to breathe became difficult.

Fresh air hit her face as they emerged into a secluded meadow. She turned to see the back walls of the Osmund Royal House, the glimmering waters of the moat between her and her enemy. How far did Jaeger drag her?

Fallon hoped Elowen was not awake when she dropped them both onto the ground. She knew she needed to go farther. She knew if Jaeger and Norman failed the guards would come out of this tunnel and see them immediately. But Fallon had nothing left to give. She had finally reached the end of her fire. This was it.

She laid on her back and tried to breathe through the radiating pain as Elowen started to stir. The girl rolled over to face the light like a sunflower, gasping and gulping in the fresh air. Fallon watched it soak into her, the pigment returning to her skin. Jaeger was right: it was healing her somehow.

Before long the Hulder slowly sat up. She wiped the crust from her eyes and took a few long breaths. "We're free," she said gently, running her fingers through the soft grass.

"Not yet," Fallon groaned, surprised her voice still worked. "Please tell me you know the way to the portal."

"Yes." Elowen nodded, pushing her white hair back. It had a fresh shine to it now. "I feel better, but I need our sun."

Fallon nodded, closing her eyes and enjoying the comfort of the soft earth beneath her. "Good. Then get going."

But Elowen reached over and tried helping her up. "No, we are going together," she insisted, weakly tugging on Fallon's arm.

"Get out of here!" Fallon fought, slapping the Hulder off. "Jaeger and Norman might die at any moment, and when the guards come through that tunnel, I will not be able to fight for long. You need to get ahead while you can."

Elowen's arms gave out. She plopped down on the ground next to her, resting her head on Fallon's chest. "No! I am tired of being alone!" she shouted.

Fallon let out an irritated groan. Why were these people taking advantage of her emotions? "We got out so you could go back home and *not* be alone! Go. Get out of here and find your tree."

"I can't get back home," she said quietly. "I cannot open the door ... but you can."

Fallon highly doubted that. But if the sun set before Elowen fully recovered, she might slip back into that illness. Another ten hours without the sun might be the end of them both.

"Fine. Help me up," she mumbled.

They worked together to stand, and now it was Elowen who carried Fallon through the trees. The girl was still fatigued and weak, so they moved at an agonizingly slow pace.

Humming a tune that sounded like the woods at daybreak, Elowen led them south beyond Reinhart. Of course, the portal was as far from Barwyn as possible. Fallon thought they might fall off the edge of the world before they found it. Neither of them spoke much, save for Elowen's constant nagging. Fallon still refused to let the Hulder heal her. Instead, she focused on how sickeningly hungry she was. Fallon realized she didn't even know if her stomach still worked.

After too many minutes, after the sun was nothing more than a faint glow over the hills, Elowen's eyes squinted over Fallon's shoulder, "Light."

"Pardon?"

Elowen pointed. "Light."

Sure enough, when Fallon turned around, she saw what Elowen was talking about. Maybe a mile away, a faint orange glow lit up the tree line. Unfortunately, it was a form of light Fallon knew well.

"Torchlights," she breathed. "They've been following us. Come on, we have to hurry!" She pushed Elowen into a quicker pace.

Fallon felt her heart crack once again. Not because of the pain, not because of the mob following them, but because of the two men who had given them enough time to run. Fallon did not know what would become of them, or if they were still alive at all. All she knew was she never planned to forget the young lord with beautiful eyes who refused to be anything but himself. And the retired warrior who saved them all in the end.

Norman. Jaeger and his mother, Cordelia. They would never die. Because Fallon would never forget.

Elowen pulled her closer and kept running. As the sun fully set over the hills, it was growing more difficult to see where they were going. "We are nearly there! Just find the biggest tree!" she instructed, but they kept tripping over the other's legs. They were a dying, fumbling mess of limbs and hair and blood.

Fallon wanted to argue that they were in fact surrounded by large trees, but she did not have the energy. Not until she slammed into an invisible wall and stopped dead in her tracks.

Something changed. It was barely noticeable; as if she had been swimming in saltwater and suddenly crossed into fresh water. Fallon had to blink a few times to focus her eyes. When she looked back up, she finally saw it.

It was as if it materialized out of thin air. Now before her stood an ash tree so tall and grand, she had to crank her head back to take it all in. It radiated such power and sovereignty, Fallon felt like an ant staring at the world's largest boot.

"Big tree," she confirmed.

A glimmer of mischief twinkled in Elowen's eye. "So, you can see it?"

Fallon shook her head in awe. "Of course I can see it. I don't know how I missed it at first." No other trees or plants grew around it, as if they too stood back in respect.

Shouts sounded from the distance as the orange glow grew closer like a raging wildfire. "Now, Fallon!" Elowen smiled encouragingly. "You can do it!"

There was no door, no handle, no key, or hatch. It was just a tree. Confusion, frustration, and panic all welled inside of her so intensely she wanted to scream. She did not make it this far just to be captured again.

This morning, she did not care if she lived or died. But now she was more than just Fallon. Now, she was the carrier of those names. If she died, so did they.

Fallon's eyes drifted to her right, where a dirt path continued deeper into the woods. They could keep running. Forget this fool's errand of opening an ancient portal. Fallon could keep Elowen safe, and they could run and live another day—

Then, Fallon heard a heartbeat that was not her own. She turned back to the tree and felt a pulse of raw power hit her again and again. She squinted through the night's darkness and saw a faint glow coming from within the tree like a golden heart.

Elowen squeezed her arm anxiously, reminding her of their dire situation. Fallon took a step back, eyes shifting between the tree and the dirt path.

"I entrust my fate to the path of glowing light," she whispered and placed her palm on the trunk of the ash tree.

It hummed with life under her fingertips, sending tingles through her body and scalp. Suddenly, from underneath Fallon's hand, a golden light was born. It spread through the bark as rivers, filling every groove with light. They dropped their heads back and watched it seep into the veins of every leaf until the entire tree was lined with gold. A gale of wind that smelt of wildness rushed through the woods, blowing their hair upwards.

Elowen laughed with joy beside her. It was the first time Fallon saw her smile in days. She too could not help but grin; It was the most beautiful thing she had ever seen. The soul of the sun breathed within the ancient tree.

The light rushed inwards, swirling and dancing as it formed the outline of a lancet doorway. With a loud snap, the wooden double doors opened outwards, revealing a white light more intense than anything Fallon had ever seen.

Elowen took her hand. "Let's go home."

With no hesitation, Barwyn's Bastard escaped into the light.

FOURTEEN

Ronen could tolerate the pesky Anthousai for just a while longer. He could ignore the flirty shouts from Huldra, trip over hopping bunnies and wave back at nymphs if it meant he got to leave Elphyne soon. But an old, weird-smelling female following him was where he crossed the line.

He was *so* close to the Entrance Tree. So close that he was willing to ignore her at first. She appeared about ten minutes ago, after they both emerged from two different tree groves and ended up on the same beaten path.

Ronen glared over his shoulder often enough to signal to her that he was annoyed, but the elderly Fae just kept walking. She wore large, brown robes around her thin frame. Her silver hair was rolled into tight dreads, all piled atop her head. Frankly, she appeared to be homeless. But the gold jewelry covering her neck and fingers said otherwise.

With a large, dramatic sigh, Ronen halted. He gripped the strap of the satchel across his front as he heard her approach.

"Isn't it rude to follow people?" he asked smartly once he knew she was close.

She stopped right next to him. She was shorter than he thought, shrunken with age like a bad fruit. "Isn't it rude to not offer an old female your arm when walking a great distance?" she asked in return.

Ronen turned to face her. Her tan skin was wrinkled, but her eyes were bright and playful. The color of creamed coffee, they scanned Ronen carefully. He patiently waited for her to notice his mismatched eyes, terrible smell, and lack of Fae features. Soon she would be running away in disgust and/or horror, and Ronen could get back to his walk.

But she stayed. She simply grabbed onto his arm and urged them forward, not giving him much of a choice but to walk with her.

"I don't see many travelers on these paths. Are you headed to the Entrance Tree as well?" she asked.

Ronen was in too much shock to really answer, so he just nodded. At first, he was self-conscious about his smell, but this lady smelt even stronger. It was like walking next to a candle laced with herbs and oils.

"How do you plan to get through?" she asked, that mischief still alive in her eyes. "You know only a Fae can open the door."

She knew he wasn't one of them, then. He scratched the back of his neck with his free hand. "Yeah, I—"

"Not to mention the guards," she continued. "Even if an owl has not yet reached them regarding your escape, they will kill you for even trying."

Ronen stopped walking.

"Who are you?" he asked carefully. He looked around but saw no one else approaching. How did she know? Was this a trap?

She let out a cackle and hit his arm. "Boy! I am not going to turn you in, if that is what's troubling you. Though I am curious, why do you want to leave?" she asked, tugging him back into a walk with surprising strength.

But he stopped again. "Look lady, I am not going anywhere until you at least tell me your name."

She rolled her eyes. "Elma. You may call me Elma, for now." She smiled without her teeth. "We still have a walk ahead of us, so tell me your story."

Elma was obviously Fae. Even after hundreds of years her pointed ears, small nose, long canines, and strength remained. If Ronen won her over, she might open the tree for him. Or he could at least throw her at the guards while he escaped. Either way was fine with him.

So, he cleared his throat. "Well, dying in a dirt pit did not sound like any fun. So, I am leaving Elphyne and taking my chances with another realm. Maybe they will try to kill me with some more pizzazz," he said dryly.

She scoffed, slapping his arm once again. "Your terrible story-telling skills will get you hanged before your heritage. Come now, start from the beginning."

If for no other reason than to pass the time, Ronen did as she asked. He told her about growing up in a blacksmith's shop, a childhood without friends, sneaking into houses for food and staying for the bedtime stories.

All the way until weeks ago, when he was taken to face the Lord of Fire himself.

Elma stayed quiet. Only nodding encouragingly and giving sympathetic smiles when appropriate. Ronen realized this was the first time anyone had ever actually *listened* to him. He found himself trailing off into tangents about anything and everything that upset him. It was a nice feeling; being able to speak freely with someone who wasn't going to run away. It felt so nice, he was a bit disappointed when the Entrance Tree finally came into view.

Ronen slowed down. "We should hide."

But Elma urged him onward. "You make a rotten sneak. They already know we are here, might as well go say hello," she said.

"You aren't afraid? What are *you* doing here, anyways?"

Elma gave him a playful wink. "It serves to have friends in high places."

The Entrance Tree was truly something to behold. Twice the size of any other tree around them, it gave off its own, divine energy. A perfect twin of its sister, the Throne Tree. Except its trunk was not curved into a seat, but was wide and strong enough to serve as the doors to their realm.

What the Throne Tree did not have, however, was two Valdyr with massive swords in each hand standing on either side of it. As they got closer, Ronen realized they were not alone. Two more Valdyr and four Barguests were posted around the tree.

Elma approached one of the guards as if they were old friends. Ronen however, stayed back as he foolishly made eye contact with one of the massive dogs. Their golden armor gleamed in the sunlight; the leaf-pattern breastplate molded perfectly to their muscular forms. All Valdyr and Barguests alike bore green and gold; the colors of Elphyne.

Ronen had heard many stories on why the Entrance Tree was sealed years ago. Too many mortals dying at the hands of Sentinels, or other worlds wanting their Fae Gold. It was their densest material, yet it was light as air. Supposedly it existed nowhere else. All he knew for certain was that it all started with Fritjof; who called all Faeries back to Elphyne when Ronen was around five years old, then locked the door. No one in. No one out.

With sagging shoulders, Elma turned and walked back to him. Her voice was quiet and solemn as she spoke, "well, it appears my long walk was all for naught. Go on, boy, they will open the gate as a favor to me," she said, then shuffled past him.

But Ronen was paralyzed in place. And not because of the multitude of sharp teeth around him.

Elma turned around when she heard no signs of him moving. "What is wrong? Don't you want to leave?"

He stared at the Entrance Tree and the guards who had yet to acknowledge him. Elma was right, he did want to leave. Why was he as planted in place as the tree before him?

"You know," Elma stepped towards him slowly. "I had never met a Nøkken until today. I was hoping all those nasty stories were not true."

"They aren't true," Ronen whispered for possibly the ten-thousandth time in his twenty-one years of life.

"Well, here you are! Acting a fool after causing mayhem at the castle and now running away. Is that how you want Elphyne to remember your kind?"

He groaned. "You, Elphyne, and probably these four mute guards have already made up your mind about *my kind*," he sneered. "Why should I care?"

The old Fae stared at him for a long moment. "You very well might be the last Nøkken, half or whole," she said quietly. "Your legacy is in your hands now, Ronen. So I will ask only once," she paused.

Ronen took a step back. In the hours of story-telling, he never once mentioned his name. Who *was* this lady? How did she have the Valdyr in her shabby robe pocket? Why did she smell like a fern threw up another fern?

He opened his mouth to protest, but she cut him off. "Are Nøkken good, or evil?" she asked simply.

"Good," he said, surprised at how quickly the answer came to his mouth.

"Then prove it."

The temperature rose ten degrees as a strong gust of wind nearly knocked him over. Ronen turned, and all of their jaws dropped. The tree—it was opening.

Golden light seeped from its every grove. The Valdyr shouted in alarm, but Ronen could not take his eyes off it as the bark cracked open to reveal a beautiful white haze.

The kindest favor Ronen could give Elphyne was to rid it of his presence. He no longer cared what they thought or what stories they made up in his absence—let them be afraid. They could hold onto whatever delusion suited them best. He just pitied the next sorry species they decided to bully into extinction.

Without even turning back at the strange old woman, Ronen gripped his bag close to his side and got a running start while the guards were still shouting at one another.

He had to shield his eyes as he charged into the blinding light. He did not know what to expect, but the dizziness, his ears popping, and the feeling of weightlessness all seemed normal. Everything was going perfectly, until he slammed into something hard.

That thing grunted back at him as they both went tumbling backwards. Ronen's back collided with the grass as the air was knocked out of him. When his head stopped spinning, he opened his eyes to see the same tree canopy above him. The same blue sky and the same side of the Entrance Tree.

Ronen propped himself up on his elbows and let out a surprised yelp; he had not come out of the tree alone. A girl with hair as red as fire was staring daggers at him, body positioned protectively in front of a smaller form he could not see. Both of them were breathing hard, covered in dirt and blood—a *lot* of blood.

The intensity of her green eyes paralyzed him to the ground. He was glad she spoke first, because he did not know if he could form words.

"Who are you?" she rasped. She spoke with a strange accent Ronen has never heard. "And ... W-where are we?"

He gave his fakest smile. "Welcome to Elphyne. Now, if you don't mind, I'm trying to leave."

Ronen peered around her shoulder and scrambled to his feet in horror. He rushed back to the tree, but it had already closed. There was no more light or wind. All that remained was a strange static in the air that tickled the hair on his arms.

"No! No, no!" he pounded on the bark of the tree with his sore fists. "Damnit!" He turned back around, ready to shout at the girl that this was all her fault, but the Valdyr beat him to it.

Two guards each held the tip of a sword at her neck, but she did not even flinch. Not at the swords and not at the four Barguest's snapping jaws around her. Her skin was a grayish color, and the light was quickly leaving her eyes. The girl was practically dead.

Now, Ronen could see the other form behind her. A Hulder with hair as fair as milk, who was clutching onto the redhead in fear. They were on the ground, unarmed, and wounded. There was no reason to hurt them. He was not sure what possessed him in that moment, but Ronen stepped in front of them with his hands up.

"Woah, everyone calm down for a second! They're Faeries," he said.

"There have been no Faeries outside of Elphyne for over a decade," the guard on the right said.

Ronen snorted. "Oh, so you *can* talk? Well how about you open the tree again, and we will all be on our merry way?" he offered.

"She stays, I will go," the girl with the accent demanded. She had dried blood in the corners of her mouth, and her eyes were glazed over as she stared straight through him. He did not know why, but something about her was oddly familiar.

The Hulder shook her head, clutching onto the half-dead girl and peering up at him with dewy eyes. "Please, she can barely stand," she whimpered.

A horn sounded in the distance. The guard's Fae ears twitched, and suddenly they had their weapons pointed at Ronen.

"They are coming for you," the one on the left said.

"Oh, really? Was that the Nøkken alarm?" he sneered. "Just open the stupid tree."

"They can't." A familiar voice spoke from the trees. Elma, whom Ronen thought was long gone, appeared once again. She was standing back, her hands clasped over her heart. She was staring wide-eyed at the half-dead redhead on the grass.

Ronen clicked his tongue, "I beg your pardon?"

Elma tentatively stepped closer, as if approaching a wild animal. "Opening the tree requires a monumental amount of energy. The Entrance Tree needs twelve hours to recharge," she explained. "Boy, help carry the girl. We need to get moving if we want to stay ahead of the search party."

"And why would I do that?" He laughed.

Elma raised a thin brow at him. "Since you only care about saving yourself: help me get these girls somewhere safe, and you too will have a place to hide until the tree can be used again."

She made a good point. Ronen could never outrun them himself. Plus, he did not trust these guards. Just because Elma asked them to spare him once, he doubted they would do it again.

With a long sigh, Ronen walked over and squatted next to the Hulder. "She's not going to, like, *bite me*, right?"

She smiled uneasily. "Just don't touch her left side," she said quietly, grabbing one arm. Ronen grabbed the other and they helped the girl stand. She was right, the girl could no longer handle her own bodyweight. The short, agonal breaths that escaped her mouth every few seconds was the only sign she was alive at all.

The four Valdyr approached Elma and spoke in quick, hushed tones. Ronen's mortal ears only picked up so much, but he could tell they were worried—fearful even. They kept mentioning Ondorr and another creature that was the last of its kind.

Whatever Elma threatened them with to keep them quiet, it worked. Because every guard (two-legged and four-legged) went back to their posts on either side of the Entrance Tree without another word.

The three of them stumbled west after Elma. For an elderly Fae who needed his arm to walk only hours ago, she sure was hard to keep up with.

"Where exactly are we going?" he shouted after her, wincing as he accidentally let the red-haired girl's ankle smash into a rock.

"To the Longback Knolls."

Ronen could only shake his head in disbelief. He should have run when he had the chance.

FIFTEEN

When Fallon entered that world of white light, she thought she had crossed the Rainbow Bridge. On her way to Valhalla to become one of Odin's Einherjar—warriors who fell valiantly in battle. All celebrating and living together in immortality until the days of Ragnarok, where they would serve as Odin's personal army of the dead.

But there was no Valkyrie on the back of a Pegasus to take her there. Instead, she went stumbling into the void clutching a Hulder to her side—a creature she did not believe was real until days ago. Then they traveled through a portal she did not believe was real until minutes ago.

The next few minutes were a blurry haze of light and searing pain while she caught her breath. She vaguely recalled a boy's face, along with more male voices. As she blinked and swallowed until her wits returned, she noticed she was being carried by strong arms. *Jaeger*? Had he made it after all?

It was now dark and cool, with bright hazes of color in the corners of her vision. As if she were being surrounded by the phantom glow of many Will-o'-Wisps, leading her to her fate. Her mother had warned her about the Wisps: some lead you toward your fate, others lead you to your demise.

Her back was placed against a soft, flat surface. An aroma of peculiar, earthen smells consumed her. Despite the dull pain that still lingered all over her, Fallon felt oddly calm. Comforted.

That was probably why it took only seconds of breathing in that sickly sweet smell for her to fall asleep. Sinking lower and lower, into the depths. Until death was only a fingertip away.

She awoke after what felt like an eternity of rest. Fallon had been in some form of pain for so long, it felt strange to be without it. Her breaths came beautifully easy as she took them one by one, slowly prying her eyes open.

The ceiling above her was made up of rough stone and covered in hanging vines. Their arms hung down like little hands reaching for her, a droplet of milky liquid collected in their grasp. Fallon flinched as one dripped, landing straight on her forehead. She wiped it away, surprised to see her hands scrubbed clean of grime.

Fallon was even able to sit up on her own. The skin on her torso still felt different—tight, sore, and extremely itchy. But at least there was no pain. She wore clothes that were not her own, made of remarkably soft cotton. Where was she? Did Elowen get them through the portal?

Elowen. Fallon scanned the small room, around, but saw nothing but rough stone walls and wooden tables covered in bloody rags, potted plants, and empty glass bottles.

Despite her sore limbs, Fallon hopped off the bed and quickly smashed one of the pots on the table nearest her. She pulled a large piece of broken porcelain from the grips of the tall plant's tangled roots.

There was no door, only a tall archway that led into another empty hallway. Fallon heard rushed footsteps approaching, so she gripped her pathetic weapon and pressed her back against the wall.

An elderly woman turned the corner, shouting in surprise. "By Dagmar's word, child, you nearly scared the soul out of me," she huffed.

Then she took in the broken pot on the floor and the murder in Fallon's eyes. "Why—what are you doing?" she demanded.

She held out her weapon at throat-level. "Where is she?" she asked in return. The elderly woman was small, but beautiful despite her age. Her hair was larger than her head, all nestled in a twisted knot of silver. Fallon's eyes wandered from her face to her ears … tall, *pointed* ears.

Fallon nearly fell over.

The woman let out a sigh through her long nose. "Your friends are fine. I know you must be confused and frightened, but that is no excuse to go around threatening people," she scolded, "come out here at once and allow me to explain."

She was embarrassed at how much her hand was shaking as Fallon took two steps back. "You … You're a—" she could not say it.

"If you will just allow me to explain, this will all come a little easier. But first, you drop that piece of porcelain I spent hours making and remove the shard you think you're hiding between your breasts," she snapped.

Fallon could not help but crack a small smile as she did as she was told, dropping both to the floor.

But the old woman still looked displeased. "Now, apologize to that innocent Burdock you recklessly harmed," she said.

"Who is Burdock?"

The woman rolled her round eyes. "*Arctium lappa*, girl. Its roots are only the reason I managed to purge that infection from your bloodstream." She wiggled her fingers at her.

Fallon looked at the tall plant on the floor, its fuzzy purple flowers lying limp on the floor. "I did not ask to be healed," she said slowly.

The woman let out a noise between a snort and cough. "Oh, I believe you would have sooner welcomed death. Which is precisely why I didn't ask." She gave her a thin smile. "Now, come. That sweet girl is worried sick about you," she said before turning on her heel.

"Elowen? Can I see her?" Fallon asked as she quickly chased after her.

"Of course. You are not prisoners."

The stone walls around them were covered in more vines. These ones had blue budding flowers that gave off a mystical glow. Fallon cautiously poked one, it was no bigger than her fingertip. A flower was *glowing*. They definitely were not in Midgard anymore ... which meant the portal worked.

As they traveled down the hall, the colors changed from purple to pink to an eerie green. There were no torches or lanterns, just flowers. Fallon shook her head in awe, starting to believe that she had actually died in the portal. Fallon was dead and her subconscious was trying to bring her peace by walking her through her favorite memories—her mother's storybooks.

They passed under another archway into a large cavern and Fallon's mouth fell agape. It was four times the size of the room she awoke in. The first thing she saw was a blazing fire pit in the center of the round room. Around it was an entire indoor, alien ecosystem. Just like the flowers in the halls, every shrub, tree, and petal gave off its own bioluminescent glow. The room was alive with shades of purple, blue, green, and pink. She thought her head might explode from the pure *strangeness* of it all. Yes. She had to be dead.

Luckily, she did not get the chance to fall into shock, because she was immediately tackled in a hug.

"You're awake!" Elowen cried with joy.

Fallon smiled; finally, something she was familiar with. Seeing Elowen walking around happy and unharmed calmed Fallon's nerves. She let Elowen's scent of warm jasmine and honeysuckle waft over her.

"You look well," Fallon said.

Elowen was wearing a new dress; a shin-length, simple dress the same shade of green as her soiled one. A white apron was tied around her thin waist and of course there was a slit cut out for her swinging tail. Fallon was shocked at how different the Hulder seemed already: her heart-shaped face was bright, her hair was freshly washed and shining, and her smile ... Elowen was so *alive*. Which meant Fallon was, too. They made it. They were here, they were safe.

They were shooed towards the center of the room. "Go on, by the hearth. I will bring you supper," the old woman said.

Supper? How long was Fallon asleep? Still on guard, she tried to ignore the glow of the flowers around her and find an exit.

As Elowen grabbed her hand and led her over to the fire, Fallon saw they were not alone. A boy around her age sat on one of the three wooden benches around the hearth.

He did not acknowledge them as they sat on the bench across from him. Only his eyes moved to quickly glance at her from over the fire. As their eyes met, she let out a small gasp.

"You."

One blue eye, one brown eye. Fallon had never seen anything like it, so of course she remembered. He had been at the portal. It was one of the few things she remembered since escaping lockup.

He leaned forward to rest his elbows on his knees. Greasy brown hair fell in front of his eyes. "You're welcome," was all he said.

She raised her chin. "I did not say thank you."

"Now you did." He smirked at her.

Fallon bit her tongue. His face and body were covered in dirt, soot, and who knows what. It smelt as if he had not bathed in months. She supposed she could not judge him too harshly, though, as she had no appeared much better herself until someone washed her. She was happy she was unconscious for that part.

He and the old woman both spoke with Elowen's strange yet beautiful accent. Fallon was in a different world, she needed to remember that. Though it was hard to remember something when you could hardly even believe it.

Elowen did not introduce herself. She sat quietly, watching the boy through her hair. She was not the same girl who had danced around her cell when Fallon got sad, not anymore. Elowen had learned the hard way what men are like, and it was a lesson she would unlikely forget.

After a few minutes of awkward silence, the woman returned carrying three stone bowls in her arms. Fallon accepted it hastily, using the wooden spoon to shovel the contents into her mouth. She was so hungry, she did not even care that it was like eating lukewarm, chunky vomit. It was a strange orange color, with random slices of what seemed to be vegetable peels and animal fat.

Elowen slurped hers down just as fast, but seemed to be enjoying it a lot more than Fallon. The boy was a bit pickier and looked to be having a hard time swallowing down a particularly large chunk of mystery meat.

Fallon tried to process everything around her as a means to distract herself. She heard the trickle of water and turned to see all the trees and flower beds drinking from a small stream. It twirled throughout the whole cavern, even running through the white sand that crunched under her boots. It was that same milky-white liquid that had been dripping from the ceiling.

What a strange, strange place.

"So," the woman wiped her hands on her apron and sat on the last vacant bench. "Since we will be spending some time together and I welcomed you into my home, let us do introductions. You may call me Elma. I have watched over this cave for a very long time, so please respect all the plants here. This is *their* home."

Fallon winced. She definitely had not respected that Burdock earlier.

Elma turned to the boy, who had his head down as if she would forget he was there. Fallon knew that feeling. Thinking if you just got small enough, if you flexed every muscle and closed your eyes that you could just disappear and no one would bother you.

So, out of pity, she spoke up first. "My name is Fallon, and this is Elowen," she said, gesturing to them appropriately.

Elma stared at her with misty eyes. Fallon did not trust the way she was looking at her ... or for how long it lasted.

"Fallon," Elma repeated softly.

Elowen dragged her toes through the sand, her short legs barely able to touch the ground. "I have been away for a long time, but I am home now. Thanks to Fallon," she said softly. Too softly. Fallon would have to teach her how to put some power in her voice if she were going to survive out there.

The boy threw his hands up in frustration. "See, I knew you guys weren't Shapeshifters. Those guards can shove—"

"No!" Elma clapped her hands together loud enough to make the three of them jump in their seats. "We do not say those names here, boy," she scolded.

Fallon's interest in the conversation suddenly rose. "This world has Shapeshifters? From the legends I've heard, they don't sound very Faerie-like."

The boy snorted. "Just about as Faerie-like as you," he attempted to mimic her accent, mocking her. "Do all mortals talk that weird?"

"You think I'm the strange one? You should hear you from *my* end," she shot back.

The bonfire between them grew with intensity, its flames turning a bright red. They rose so high she thankfully could no longer see the boy across from her.

"I said, enough!" Elma shouted again. She snapped her fingers, and the fire died back down, returning to a normal orange campfire. "As you will learn, this hearth flame embodies the emotions of the room. While you are here, this fire will remain orange. Every time it changes, I will give you more chores. Am I understood?"

The others nodded and murmured their apologies, but Fallon's eyes were transfixed into the dancing embers. Her hand moved to touch her side, where nothing but ruined flesh met her fingertips. No open wound, no blood, no scab. Just an ugly, rough scar. She could still hear the hissing of the iron as it was pulled from the fire, the way her blood had bubbled …

Fallon had to press the heels of her palms against her eyes to get the memories out. She thought it was just her brain trying to process everything, but she truly had a headache now. Her ears pounded, and even her nose ached with pressure.

Suddenly that goop stew started to move in her stomach. Had it not been for Elowen placing a hand on her back, she would have very unceremoniously put out the fire in front of her.

Elowen continued to rub her back, and the nausea faded. "Fallon, what's wrong?" she asked quietly.

She just shook her head. "Sorry, it's just a lot to take in."

"Your body is adjusting," Elma explained. She turned back to the boy who was eyeing Fallon very carefully. "Your turn."

He sighed through his nose. "My name is Ronen. I was *trying* to leave when you two came through the Entrance Tree. Elma offered me a safe place to stay until the tree can be opened again, with the condition that I help carry your sorry ass here." He pointed at her.

Fallon leaned back in repulsion. "I'm lucky I didn't get a disease."

"Look, red, if anyone in this room is most likely to have rabies, it's definitely you."

The fire between them rose once again, but both Fallon and Ronen calmed back down before it could erupt in red flames. Instead, they just wordlessly glared at each other.

Fallon squinted her eyes. "What, exactly, do you need hiding from?"

"Not what, *who*," Ronen corrected. "The Valdyr are the royal guards, and believe or not they like me even less than you."

Elowen piped up, "We were also being chased, that is why we came through the tree."

"What were you guys in for?" he asked, setting down his half-empty bowl in surrender.

"It does not matter," Fallon quickly interjected. "We made it."

Sensing the tension, Elma stood to her full five feet of height. "It is getting late, and you all need the rest," she said.

Far to her right, down a dirt path through the glowing forest, she could see the mouth of the cave. It was covered by a thick layer of hanging vines, surely an attempt to hide the entrance. Even though there was no need; anyone with a sense of smell would run in the opposite direction of this place.

She tilted her head to the side. "Sleep? But the sun is still out," she said, pointing to the beams of gold breaking through the leaves.

Ronen yawned. "I bet the moon is already halfway to the kiss," he said flatly, as if it made any sense at all.

"The moon? While the sun is still up?"

"The sun never goes *down*. Only the moon does. Is that not how your world works?" he asked in equal curiosity.

Fallon rubbed her temples. A sun that never sets? Having the moon and sun in the sky at the *same time*? Those were signs of the end of the world.

She squeezed her eyes shut. "No. The sun was a spark that came from Muspelheim, set in the sky to illuminate Midgard. The goddess Sol flies it across the sky in her chariot. Her brother, Mani, is what drives the moon after her once the sun has set. Until the day when the sun and moon wolves, Skoll and Hati, devour them and all the stars disappear from the sky. It is to be one of the first signs of Ragnarok," she explained.

Ronen burst out laughing, "There is no way you didn't make up those words."

Elma and Elowen looked at her with strange expressions, and the hearth turned as pink as Fallon's cheeks. "I am telling the truth! The sun sets over the horizon, then the sky turns black. On clear nights, the stars shine bright enough to reflect off the snow. They give direction, they tell stories, and at the very least, they make you feel less alone. But when the clouds take over the sky, your only chance of light is to build a fire. And if you can't find twigs dry enough to burn, it's only you, the cold, and whatever nightmares your imagination makes you see in the shadows."

Elowen cleared her throat. "I remember my first sunset," she said grimly, turning to Ronen. "It is true, the sky turns *black*. I spent the entire night thinking I had wandered into Ondorr," she whispered with a shudder.

"What's Ondorr?"

But Elma has had enough. "I will not repeat myself again: we do not speak those names here. Names have power, and you will do well to remember that. Now, girls, I will show you to your rooms. Ronen, you must bathe before you cause all my buds to close back up."

The boy blanched, obviously taken aback by her words. Elma walked over to the many wooden cabinets along the walls and grabbed him some towels and rags. "I expect you to take no less than an hour. It smells like you have a year's worth of grime," she said, tossing him the pile of rags rather than handing it to him.

Ronen did not move. In fact, it looked like he forgot how to breathe all together. Elma walked over and placed a hand on the boy's shoulder while they shared a quiet conversation.

Fallon turned to Elowen, gesturing to Ronen with her eyes. "I thought all Fae had pointed ears and fangs, like Elma."

The Hulder nodded, stretching her arms. "They do. I think they are very pretty," she said, rubbing her own risen ears. Elowen's drooped slightly, rather than the sharp point Elma's went to.

"Then why doesn't Ronen?"

She shrugged. "Because he is not Fae."

"What is he, then?"

Elowen stared at him for a long moment. Within the halo of her sage green irises, her pupils dilated. "I'm not sure, but he feels like a whirlpool," she said sadly.

Fallon was not sure what that meant, but she had learned to trust the Hulder's peculiar intuition when it came to emotions.

Elma approached them as Ronen disappeared down one of the stone tunnels. "Come."

Walking down the flower-lit hallway, Fallon feared these tiny glowing flowers were the closest thing she would ever see to stars. Did she plan on returning to Midgard alongside Ronen tomorrow? She got Elowen home, just as she promised, so why wouldn't she? Fallon still had a birthright to reclaim and a man to kill. She could not let all of this distract her. No matter how beautiful it was.

They entered the same room Fallon awoke in. The bed of animal furs was freshly made, the bloody bandages were gone, and a new dresser against the wall had appeared. The one thing that remained the same was the broken plant on the ground.

Elma showed Elowen to her own chamber (which was only seven steps away from this one) and returned with hands firmly on her hips.

"Clean it up."

Fallon scoffed. "Why didn't the handmaids clean it?"

The old woman stepped closer, not backing down. "My cave sprites do not clean up after ungrateful little girls. There is a pan and broom in the corner. After you clean it up, you will help me re-pot the burdock," she said.

Fallon has never been bossed around this way before. Usually, Beowulf would make her pick up the broken shards of porcelain by stepping on them.

Seeing no sign of surrender in Elma's eyes, she let out an irritated growl and picked up the broom. As she swept up the soil, Elma paced the room and mumbled to herself, being of very little assistance.

"You warriors are all the same. It's always kill, destroy, and conquer. Do you ever think about the mess you leave behind? Or the lives you affected along the way? If you must pave a road with bone and blood to reach your victory, is it truly a victory at all?"

Fallon's grip tightened on that broom. Not a moment went by that Jaeger and Norman's sacrifice did not cross her mind. She was haunted by the promises she would never be able to fulfill, and their hope in her that had been horrendously misplaced.

Elma left the room and returned shortly, still mumbling. "Well, it won't work here. Everyone in this cave does their part," she said as she plopped another ceramic pot on the table.

Fallon carefully picked up the plant, cradling its roots in one hand. "I know these flowers," she said, examining the pokey-looking purple blossoms. "They exist in my realm, too. I saw them in Halvar."

Elma nodded, taking it from her hands. "Most, if not all, Elphynian plants also grow in the mortal realm."

"But ours don't ... save lives. Not to this extent," she explained, gesturing to her once fatal wound.

The old woman chuckled. "Oh, but they do, child. Their healing properties are just muted. If you were to take this very flower through the Entrance Tree and plant it, it would grow to be an ordinary burdock. *But*, if you took a burdock from there and planted it here, it would absorb the magic that waters our soil and be enriched with power. Does that make sense, Fallon?" She looked at her carefully.

Fallon let out a nervous laugh. "A week ago, it wouldn't have. But after being here, after seeing everything with my own eyes, I'm terrified of how much sense it makes."

"Good. Remember what we spoke about here," she said as she buried the tan roots in their new home. "I will have another assignment for you in the morning. For now, enjoy your rest," she said with a wide smile, revealing two wicked fangs.

"Goodnight," Fallon said quietly as Elma hobbled out. She wondered if all Fae were like this; inherently kind and accepting. Even with the laws of Viking *grio*, Fallon had been dragged by a horse and shot in the shoulder. Not to mention the day her own power tried to consume her.

A power that had been quiet ever since that day in the Royal House courtyard—the day Fallon had laid it to rest in order to save her mortal body.

There was no door to her chamber. Fallon tried to keep quiet as she dragged her bed across the room so her back was no longer facing the open doorway. She hopped on the bed, surprised to see her own reflection staring back at her.

On top of her new dresser were her old clothes, cleaned and folded. Behind them, leaning against the stone wall, was a large frameless mirror.

Fallon got up and slowly stepped closer. She delicately ran her fingers along her face, down her neck and across her collarbones. Skinny. Pasty. Disgusting.

One tooth was still missing from her mouth after that tussle with the Vali. Her green shirt sagged on her once strong shoulders. It was as if someone had stuck a needle in her and sucked out all the gusto and valor—all the things Fallon worked to build up. Even some of her freckles have faded, lost among the valleys of pale scars.

But there was one scar in particular that she was avoiding. Fallon reached under her skirt, feeling the risen skin that now made up her torso. Elma and her magical plants did the best they could, but this wound ran far, far too deep to be healed. That branding rod had burned its way through her skin and onto her soul. A soul that had already been so lost, so alone and dreary.

Elma had plenty of reasons and opportunities to ask about it, but never did. And for that she was thankful. Maybe it was the reason Fallon always caught the old woman staring at her with weepy eyes.

Her heart raced, adrenaline kicking into her system as she stood before the mirror and mentally prepared herself. She had to do it. Before Fallon returned to Midgard, she had to see who she was returning as.

So, with the trembling hands of a coward, Fallon lifted her shirt.

A sob of anguish escaped her mouth as she stumbled backwards, crashing into her bed frame. It was even worse than she imagined; a hideous purple-red color, the scar tissue was thick and uneven like poorly twisted rope. From the bottom of her left breast down to her pant line, the nameless symbol overtook her:

It was a massive letter U, where the peaks slashed downwards and crossed each other.

An X and a U, for unwanted.

Unworthy.

Unclaimed.

She covered her mouth with both hands to hide the sounds of her whimpering. Her entire body shuddered with every breath, unable to contain the horror coursing through her system. She felt claustrophobic: trapped within this ugly, rotten skin of hers.

Livestock. She shared this marking with illegitimate *pigs*. Saliva dripped from her trembling lip as Fallon raked her nails down her stomach in maddened fury, itching and tearing until she bled. She wanted this thing off of her.

Once her nails were packed with blood and flesh, she sank onto the floor and tucked in her knees. *Breathe, you need to breathe.* She prepared for her power to rise, but no warmth filled her chest. There was nothing but pain and void. Good. She never deserved that power.

Beowulf ripped the world from under her feet, and Sigurd Osmund made her a prisoner in her own body. He made sure no matter how far she ran, no matter where she hid or how hard she fought, Fallon could never escape this. Not even death would relieve her of this mark, this damnation of nothingness. Fallon the bastard: chief of misfits, ruler of nothing.

So, death could have her, but she would not walk into those gates empty handed. In one hand she would carry Beowulf Solveij's severed head by the eyelids, and Sigurd Osmund's in the other.

Fallon slowly rose to her feet and approached the large mirror, squaring off with her own reflection. *You will not kneel to Death.*

Repeating that line had gotten her through the darkness of nights, but things were different now. The game had changed. She leaned forward, fogging up the mirror with her breath. "Death will kneel to *me*."

SIXTEEN

For as long as he could remember, Ronen was teased relentlessly about his smell and appearance. But today, when a short cave-woman told him his stench was offending the surrounding plant life, he officially reached an all-time low.

Everything changed when she said the magical word: *bathe*. He had been quick to explain that bathing required water, and water was off the table for him.

But Elma just smiled at him sympathetically as she explained, "I do not fear you nearly as much as you fear yourself. The bathing chamber is down there, one left and two rights. There will be bottles of bath salts in the cabinet, please use three of them." She smiled, giving him a few firm pats of the cheek.

He looked around. Was this some sort of joke? Did Fallon put her up to this? "But I ... don't you—"

"The Little Folk speak highly of you, Ronen," she interrupted, "don't disappoint them."

The Little Folk gossip about me to random witches?

Ronen was so confused and conflicted, he got pretty lost trying to find the right chamber. This cave was a labyrinth, every tunnel split off into two more tunnels. The Longback Knolls stretched for miles, and Ronen began to suspect maybe all those tall hills were connected. All leading back to this very mountain where he was blackmailed into dragging Fallon's limp body.

As he turned yet another corner, Ronen knew he found it at last. For the first time, he saw a door. If any chamber was going to have a locked door built into the stone walls, it was hopefully the bathing one.

Sure enough, as he slowly pulled on the handle, steam poured out at his feet. It was a small, round room. With most of the floor taken up by a bubbling hot spring.

He could not stop the anxiety flooding into his chest as he closed the door behind him. He could not stop his heart from pounding or the wave of guilt from washing over him. Why was he so nervous? There was no one here but him. There was no one to tell him no. Yet he checked every corner anyways. Opened every cabinet and even peered into the hallway one more time.

When he was sure no one was around, Ronen undressed and tossed his disgusting clothes aside. In the wooden cabinets along the wall, he found vials of colored salt rocks and even a new set of night clothes. They were tailored perfectly to his size. Maybe the Little Folk told Elma that, too. He just hoped they left out how he cried himself to sleep most nights, had never kissed a girl, and his indescribable hate for tomatoes.

He approached the edge of the pool, his toes hanging off the edge. Ronen did not know how to swim. What if he drowned? The water was dark and bottomless, save for the shallow edges that bubbled with heat.

He popped the corks off a few bottles of salts. One smelt of vanilla beans and another smelt of freshly hung lavender. Ronen did not know if mixing the scents was a bad idea, but he supposed pretty much anything would be an improvement.

He reached out and poured them into the bath. They fizzed on the surface, turning the water into a pink and purple swirl. He feared he added too much, as a large layer of white bubbles quickly grew to coat its surface.

"Stop stalling," he whispered to himself, bouncing on his heels. But every time he looked down, he just saw the flask of water Munjor had tossed at his feet.

Staring at his own stupid reflection, he watched one memory after another ripple across the surface. He saw little Ronen running through the rain. Pushing himself until he puked, trying to get away from the mob of children chasing him out of the orphanage. And his first day at the shop, when he learned how to spend hours next to a fire and ignore his thirst. He saw Bhaltair's golden eyes, then nothing but the darkness as his earthy coffin was sealed.

Water ruined his life.

So, Ronen put on clean clothes and walked out of that chamber. He walked until he could no longer smell vanilla and flowers. The pool of water remained undisturbed behind a locked door, exactly where it belonged. Exactly how the Fae had trained him.

Ronen walked out into the hearth cave to return his towels to Elma, but found an empty room. Well, empty besides the glow in the dark jungle that lies within. He could just go to sleep, but Ronen was no longer tired. Nothing sounded worse than lying alone inside his head.

The ground under his feet changed from white sand to dark soil as he moved through the cave. He knelt and ran his hands through the stream of white liquid. It was warm, but it made his fingers tingle like his hand was asleep.

Finally, he saw something he knew. He poked a bush of funny-smelling orange blossoms. From their centers sprouted an odd almond that Ronen was familiar with: the anam nut. It was one of the few Elphynian plants that had psychedelic effects. When he was a teenager, he would take them recreationally to stay up for days watching imaginary shapes move across the sky. He never knew they came from flowers.

As he moved closer to the mouth of the cave, Ronen wondered what the mortal realm was going to look like. Listening to Fallon speak about the black sky was as terrifying as it was fascinating. Would he get a job at another blacksmiths? Would he make mortal friends? He supposed he could try anything he wanted. But if it were that easy, why did Fallon come through that tree looking as though she had just been through battle?

He was about to walk back and turn in for the night when something in the dirt caught his eye. Leading inside the cave was a bunch of boot prints and scuffles from when he and Elowen dragged Fallon in yesterday. But there was one trail of prints leading back *out* of the cave, even though no one has left. Or at least, they weren't supposed to.

Given they were too large to be Elma's, and Elowen did not seem to believe in shoes, that left one reckless redhead unaccounted for.

Ronen should let her go. She was honestly more trouble than she was worth. But she knew nothing of Elphyne. She had no idea about the Centaurs lurking in the tall grass, or the Sentinels and Blights that waited for anything that got too close to Ondorr. Plus, if he let her die, Elma might not open the Entrance Tree for him. So, he pushed his way through the wall of vines and into the sunlight.

The moon was past the sun as Ronen hiked farther up to get a better vantage point. The Longback Knolls were on the southwest region of Elphyne, the rest of their hills eventually disappeared into the shadows of Ondorr. The hearth cave was in one of the largest hills—closer to a mountain than a knoll. It had rocky ledges covered in moss and vines, causing Ronen to trip multiple times.

He turned south towards the Entrance Tree, but saw no sign of her. What was she thinking? Even if she managed to force four Valdyr to open the tree (which she most definitely could not) it couldn't even be opened for another few hours.

A breeze swept through the valley, making his hair fly in front of his eyes. He turned around to face it, staring out into Knolls. Anywhere that wasn't a risen hill was covered in tall grass, but not trees. This was the only place in Elphyne where trees don't grow, and there was a good reason for it.

He scanned the valley before him. Not too far ahead, within the six-foot tall grass, a red dot could be seen parting its way through.

Fallon. She was going the wrong way.

Ronen took off in a sprint down the mountain and disappeared into the maze of green. He knew that somewhere, obscured in these hills, tribes of Centaurs were waiting. *Daring* people to step foot into their territory. Even if by some miracle she avoided them, the trail she was on led straight into Ondorr.

He could not see a foot in front of him, but he kept going. Blades of grass sliced his arms and cheeks as he ran and called out her name. It was quite literally like trying to find a needle in a haystack.

Eventually, he heard her call back. "Ronen?"

"Hey, captain foresight! Where are you?" he shouted, turning towards the sound of her voice.

They were close enough he could hear her moving through the grass. "I'm fine, Ronen. I—" *Crash.*

Fallon was only an inch or two shorter than him, so her forehead slammed into his brow bone as they both tumbled to the side.

He rubbed his sore face, "We really have to stop meeting like this," he laughed nervously.

They had fallen into a section of grass that only went up to their knees. But Ronen knew areas of short, jaggedly cut grass was a sign of a much *bigger* problem.

Fallon rubbed her head and scowled at him. "What are you doing?" she demanded.

He threw his hands up in the air. "Oh I don't know, only saving you for a second time."

She stood up and dusted off her pants. "Thank you so much, brave knight, for saving me from that nice walk I was having," she said loudly. Too loud.

"Keep your voice down," he urged.

She scoffed. "Don't tell me what to do."

He was going to rip out his hair. Instead, he walked in a circle and gestured to the chopped grass around them. "Do you know what did this?" he asked.

She raised a brow and shrugged. "A cow?"

"You are being dangerously arrogant, Fallon. A herd of Hempia has been here. They are the only other animals around here, because they are the only creatures who can outrun a Centaur," he explained.

She sized up his words. "Are they aggressive?"

"Wild Hempia are just as large and territorial as Centaurs. Some are bred to help pull farm equipment, but you can't kill them."

Fallon shoved past him, continuing into the grassy field. "I can try."

After taking a few deep breaths, he turned and ran to catch up with her. "I mean you're not *allowed* to kill them. It's illegal. They are sacred to Dag—our god," he explained.

She stopped walking, turning to face him. "Do not engage with big cows or their pony-man friends. Got it. You can go now," Fallon insisted, pushing him away somewhat gently. She continued on once again, and Ronen did not chase after her this time.

"*Do not engage,*" he mumbled mockingly to himself. "So, what? Were you some sort of warrior in the other world? Is that why you don't seem to be afraid of anything?" he shouted. His concern for her safety was quickly waning.

She turned sharp on her heel, hands balled into fists. "I was—" she started, but quickly bit her tongue.

At least he had her attention. "What was your master plan, then? To take that Hulder hostage and barter with the guards to open the Entrance Tree for you?"

Fallon stormed up to him. He was not proud of it, but Ronen ended up taking a few steps back to keep some distance between them.

"You are right. I don't know a damn thing about this world," she sneered, "but let me tell you a few things about *my* world since you seem so keen on getting there. I've seen men pull down the tops of pine trees and pin them to the ground. You tie one arm to one tree, and the other to the next. When you cut the ropes, the trees spring back up: ripping a grown man in twain. All over a simple disagreement. I've seen women have their ribs snapped from their sternums and pulled back into a pair of bloody wings. Then left alone to have their organs fall to the ground. Does that sound like the type of place you run to, or run from?"

She stared deep into his eyes, and once again Ronen was struck with a sense of familiarity. That beautiful meadow of green lined with gold. He just could not figure out where he had seen it before.

When he did nothing but shake his head and gulp, she continued, "I found Elowen tossed away and forgotten in a *prison cell*, Ronen. Dying from some illness caused by lack of sunlight. That is what they do to Faeries. They don't remember the alliance we used to have. Is that really what you want to happen to you?"

"That's exactly what happened to me," he said quietly.

She took another step forward. "What are you anyways, if not Fae? You don't look like anything."

"Then keep thinking that," he shot back. "You're not entirely wrong."

It was nice talking to someone who didn't know. Fallon had no idea what he was, what his father was, and what his kind were known for. She was completely unbiased, so if she ended up hating him, that meant Ronen was the problem all along. And he didn't know if he wanted that answer.

She opened her mouth, but before she could say anything, another female voice rang through the hills. They both turned to see a visibly distraught Hulder emerge from the grass.

"You left me there, alone!" Elowen shouted, pointing directly at Fallon.

Fallon pinched the bridge of her scarred nose and let out a slow breath. "Do all you Faeries have such separation issues?"

Ronen put his hands up in defeat. "Let's all just get back to the cave before we attract something we don't want."

Fallon nodded. "Ronen will take you back, Elowen. I will meet you there by morning," she said. Fallon took one step before Ronen grabbed her wrist, pulling her close enough so Elowen wouldn't hear:

"We both know you're not out here taking a midnight stroll, Fallon. You're out looking for a fight, just like every other bully who wants to feel something," he spat. She pulled against his grip, but he held tight. "I take back what I said before—you aren't brave at all. You just don't care if you get hurt. And I hate to break it to you, red, but dying from a fight *you* started doesn't make you a warrior. It makes you a coward," he said as he finally let go.

He was fully prepared to be punched in the face, but it never came. She just stared at him with those all-too-familiar emerald eyes.

Then, a loud shriek sent a flock of birds fleeing to the sky. Before either of them could register it, a massive form emerged from the grass and grabbed hold of Elowen. The jet-black Centaur tossed her onto his back like a sack of potatoes, then rode off as quickly as he had come.

Ronen turned to flee, knowing very well you do not take a toy from a Centaur, but Fallon started in a dead sprint *towards* the beast. No question in her eyes, no hesitation in her step. Fallon was running before Elowen even got out a shriek.

He had only seconds to decide what to do. Elma might let it slide if Fallon disappeared, but if he lost both girls in one night, she would never forgive him.

So, Ronen took off after them. His arms pinwheeling around him as he shouted after her, "Fallon! This is a *do not engage* situation! DO NOT ENGAGE!"

SEVENTEEN

Fallon's entire body shut down when she saw Elowen being carried away by that *thing*. The world around her dimmed as all sound and smell disappeared. Her vision narrowed down to focus only on the Centaur's black behind. She was not the archer, but the arrow. Hurling towards her target in an unstoppable fury.

Luckily, she felt that strength again. The same one that had allowed her to walk for days on end in Halvar and take an arrow to the shoulder. But the warmth of the light she used to possess never returned. There wasn't even a spark in her as she ran. Just cold, calculated instincts.

Even with her speed back, the sound of hooves thundering into the earth eventually faded into the distance. Ronen was right, these creatures were born to run. She needed time ... she needed to reevaluate and plan. Fallon started to slow down, but not soon enough. Not quick enough.

Suddenly there was a break in the grass, and the earth in front of her vanished. Nothing but a rocky ledge awaited her.

Fallon collapsed to all fours and skidded to a stop, sliding in the grass until her head and shoulders hung over the ledge of a small cliff.

The world around her faded to white. The grass far below disappeared behind a thick white fog, and Fallon felt the snow soak into the knees of her pants and bite at her skin.

Chains weighed down her arms as Hagen pushed her head down, forcing her to look over the snowy peak. It was only her, the swirling gray clouds below, and one fatal fall. A single drop of crimson blood collected on the tip of her nose, and Fallon watched in terror as it fell. Parting its way through the clouds and disappearing into the open maws of the abyss.

Death had gotten a taste of her that day, and it had been chasing her every moment since.

A pair of hands grabbed her shoulders and pulled her back from the edge. Landing hard on her ass, Fallon blinked and shook her head until the white around her melted away, and she was back in the warm grass.

"Do you believe me now?" Ronen panted. How did he catch up with her? How long was she peering over the edge?

Fallon crawled backwards on her hands and knees, getting as far away from the ledge as possible. Through the blood roaring in her ears, she focused on one word: Elowen. She still needed to find Elowen.

Ronen was breathing hard, the sweat dripping from his brow left clear streaks down his dirty face. "Hey, are you alright? You're even paler than usual."

She swallowed down the bile rising to her throat. "I don't do heights," she rasped. Fallon was panting harder than Ronen, but it was not from running.

Fallon waited for whatever joke or snide remark was about to come out of his rotten mouth, but he stayed quiet. He simply nodded and turned to see for himself. Just watching him walk along the edge so carelessly made her lightheaded.

"There!" He pointed down and to the right. "I see her!"

Fallon instantly got to her feet, but made no advance forward. "Is she alone? Is she hurt?"

He shook his head. "No, they still have her. It looks like he took her to the rest of the herd. They are walking east now, they will pass right under us," he explained.

She closed her eyes, trying to formulate a plan. "How many are there? Are they armed?"

"We don't have time for me to paint a picture for you, their walk is faster than my jog. Here," he turned and held out his arms as a human railing. "Come look. I will stay right here, you won't fall," he promised.

His blue eye caught the gleam of the sun above them, and for once Fallon saw no jokes or tricks behind it. They watched each other carefully as Fallon took tiny steps forward. She knew he could make a mockery of her, and Ronen knew she could just as easily push him off the edge. It was a strange test of trust for two people who have only known each other for a day, but they both passed.

Fallon peered over his shoulder, feeling her body start to sway. She had to battle the urge to place a hand on his arm to steady herself. She tried to stay focused on Elowen and not the sickening stench that came with standing so close to Ronen.

Five Centaurs of various shades of brown and black trotted far below. Their top halves—their human halves—were covered with nothing but pure muscle and what Fallon assumed were tribal markings. Their hair was either straggly and wild, or shaved off all together. The one in front carried Elowen on his back, her long hair lifting in the breeze like a white flag.

"What do you think?" Ronen asked.

"That you didn't bathe when Elma told you to." She made a face. Fallon was already used to holding her breath when she was close to him, but luckily the breeze was pushing his odor downwind.

She smiled victoriously as his cheeks turned pink. "And you left the cave when Elma told you not to. We both suck. Now, what's your plan to get Elowen back?"

Fallon looked down again, the beasts already neared the base of the hill she was standing on. She needed to think of something quickly.

But the Centaurs beat her to it.

A large gale of wind swept through the valley, carrying the scent of body odor and mortal blood down the hill and right into the flared nostrils of the lead Centaur.

His head shot straight up. Fallon grabbed Ronen and pulled them down onto their stomachs just in time, but there was no way their presence went unnoticed.

"What?" Ronen yell-whispered. "What happened?"

She gritted her teeth. "Your hygiene is what happened."

"If you really want to play the blame game, it's *your* fault we're in this mess in the first place."

Fallon looked around for anything at all that could help him. "Which is why I'm going to get us out of it. Did they see us?"

He crawled forward on his elbows. "I don't think so, they're standing in a circle. The big one still has Elowen—wait! Fallon, they're running!" He turned over his shoulder. "Fallon?"

But she was not paying attention. Because Fallon's eyes were locked on two massive forms a few yards to their left. It looked like a massive yak had been dipped in silver. If that was not magnificent enough, their curled ivory horns tapered to a deadly point.

Ronen followed her gaze, the blood draining from his face. "That would be a Hempia," he confirmed.

"Sacred indeed," she breathed. She slowly rose to her elbows as a terrifying, stupid plan formed in her head. "Where are they?" she asked with urgency.

Ronen pointed, following them with his finger so Fallon could trace their progress. They were getting close. Close to her and to their one competitor.

"I don't like that look on your face." Ronen groaned.

Her lips curled into a wicked grin. Yes, this was going to be a disaster. "The enemy of my enemy is my friend," she whispered as she leaped to her feet, charging straight for the glistening silver beasts.

She was horrified to see there were actually *seven* Hempia grazing in the grass, but she did not let it slow her down. She could hear Ronen following her, cursing profoundly as Fallon picked up a rock and tossed it right at one of their big noses.

"Hey!"

At first, nothing happened. It simply stared at her with eyes as black as midnight, as if Fallon was the most audacious creature it had ever seen.

Then, more heads turned towards her. Eventually she had the whole herd's attention, all of them snorting and huffing in annoyance. None moved, but all of them watched her carefully with intelligent eyes. Eyes that were pointed down—to her feet.

"Don't you dare!" Ronen shouted from behind her, but she was running out of time. Fallon took one dramatically large step forward, then another. As soon as she crossed the invisible line that marked their personal space, she swore steam started to pour from the Hempia's black nostrils.

With three drags of its hoof, the first one charged.

They were huge, but they were not agile. Fallon jumped to the side and grabbed Ronen's arm as they both raced down the rocky side of another hill. It was so steep, they both quickly lost their footing and half slid, half stumbled down. A stampede of hooves and horns right at their heels.

Beside her, Ronen was shouting with what she thought was fear. But when she caught a glance of him, he was smiling and laughing like a madman.

"Ronen!" she called out nervously. She had not gotten this far in her head yet. Fallon was out of ideas, and the Hempia were closing in.

Before she could scream, Ronen slammed his body into hers and dove them to the right. They slid behind a pile of fallen boulders, and Ronen pulled her in close. They ducked their heads down and pulled their legs in as the Hempia split around them like water.

The world thundered around her as twenty-eight hooves pounded into the ground only inches from her limbs. Dirt was kicked up everywhere, blinding them. They coughed and waved their hands around just in time to see the herd collide with the hollering Centaurs. Shouts, snorts, stomps, and screams echoed in the sky. She timed it perfectly.

The Centaurs scattered as the silver stampede flew into the clearing. The Hempia had gained so much momentum, they couldn't stop if they tried.

Fallon quickly got up and climbed the boulder, trying to squint through all the dust and fur to find Elowen within the chaos.

"There she is." Fallon cupped her hands around her mouth, "Elowen, run!"

The Centaur had tossed her aside in surprise. She stood motionless in the center of it all, her skin ashen and pale. The two groups of wild animals chased each other around her, getting dangerously close.

Fallon jumped down, ready to run straight into the storm before Ronen grabbed her, "Don't! You've pushed our luck far enough. She's in shock. Any Hulder would be," he explained quickly.

She shoved him off of her. "What does that mean? Why did they take her and not us? We were standing there in the open long before she came."

"You really don't want the answer to that question." He laughed nervously. And by the amount of discomfort on his face, Fallon believed him.

Fallon needed to get her out before they realized they lost their prize. She kept shouting and waving her arms in the air, trying to snap Elowen out of her daze.

She turned to curse Ronen for trying to stop her, but he was no longer at her side. "Ronen?" she called out for him, swearing under her breath.

Before Fallon could take another step, a terrifying horn rang through the hills. It pulled up a vague memory, one buried under too much dust to see clearly. Fallon had heard that horn before, after she came through the Entrance Tree.

Apparently, the Centaurs and Hempia were as alarmed as she was, because they all quickly divided and ran in opposite directions. Leaving one trembling Hulder in the middle of a torn-up field.

Fallon looked up to see Ronen standing on the pile of boulders. In his hand was a Hempia horn, pulled from the skeletal remains at his feet. He held out his arms proudly. "The enemy of my enemy is my friend!"

She laughed in disbelief. He *could* listen after all. Fallon turned and jogged over to put her arm around Elowen, who did not so much as blink as they met up with Ronen at the top of the hill.

Elowen wrapped her arms around him and immediately began sobbing into his chest. Ronen was obviously uncomfortable, but patted her back gently. "Hey, it's okay. We wouldn't let you go with them. Now, let's just get back to the cave before Elma notices we're all gone."

Elowen wiped her nose with her apron and turned to Fallon with an empty expression. There wasn't any sparkle in her eyes. As if Elowen had temporarily stepped away from her body, leaving herself in a dazed survival mode. The Hulder walked over and wordlessly hopped on Fallon's back, nestling her face in the crook of her neck.

"That works." Fallon chuckled. She supposed Elowen had enough adventures for today.

By the time the hearth cave was in sight, Elowen was snoring directly into Fallon's ear.

"What was that horn?" Fallon finally asked.

"It's the Valdyr's way of announcing their presence," he explained. "Even Centaurs don't mess with the Castle Guard."

"So, the wall-deer are the warriors in this world?" she asked, the word staggered uncomfortably on her tongue.

"Valdyr," he corrected.

"Not my point." She thought for a moment. "That is why you were trying to run and hide in my realm. They were coming for you, not me."

"There's a lot more to it than that," he snapped. Fallon saw his exterior change as his walls were pulled up.

Always so secretive. "You never answered my question about what you are."

"No. I didn't."

Fallon did not really care what he was. She was not going to dig for his past, just as she expected him to not dig through hers. So she just shrugged, "I cannot judge you for it, if that is what you are afraid of. I am many things, but not a hypocrite. I was running away to your realm just as you were running to mine." She gave him an uneven smile.

"I think you were running for a few more reasons than that," he said quietly, gesturing to Elowen with his chin.

Speaking of which, Fallon made sure Elowen was still snoring (and drooling) soundly, then turned to him. "So, do Centaurs eat Huldra?"

Ronen ran his hands down his face. "This is not a conversation I thought I would have today." He let out a breath. "So, there are only male Centaurs. No females," he started.

"I noticed."

"Well that obviously makes reproduction … complicated. A baby Centaur must be carried by a creature that is used to having both Faerie and animal blood," he explained.

Fallon stopped walking. "They were going to ... so they *kidnap* Huldra and make them—" She gagged. "How does that even work?"

He shrugged. "That's why no trees grow here. Sometimes a Centaur and a Hulder are very happy together, sometimes not."

Fallon shook her head in disgust, tightening her grip on Elowen's legs. "Then how are Huldra convinced?"

Ronen did not seem thrilled about her question. "Do you know how trees work? Their seeds fall to the ground and sometimes grow into new trees and all that? Well, if a Hulder has love in her heart and the help of a Fae, a seed from her tree will drop. It will sprout into another tree in which her Hulder daughter will grow and be born from," he explained begrudgingly.

She had to laugh. "Do you realize how absurd all of this sounds? I'm carrying a Hulder on my back and I am still struggling to comprehend that she is real. I need to find her tree so she can be reunited with her family," she said. "Do all Faeries have these strange ways?"

"No, the rest of us do it the old-fashioned way." He winked.

Fallon rolled her eyes in disgust. They both laughed and walked the rest of the way in silence, save for Elowen's snoring and constant twitching. Fallon swore she was hitting them both with her tail on purpose.

He glanced at Elowen. "If you found her in the mortal realm, that means she has been there since the Entrance

Tree closed fifteen years ago," he said quietly. "We need to get her back to her tree. It's the only reason she survived out there. It gave her the energy from the Elphyne Sun."

"If it's really been that long, I'm not sure if she even knows where it is." Fallon never thought of that. She could only hope that if her tree survived unharmed this long, it could last a little longer.

Once they were hiking up the hill to the cave mouth, they talked strategy about sneaking back in. The moon (which ended up being thrice the size of the moon Fallon was used to) was quickly setting.

Ronen went in first, slipping through the wall of vines. He was supposed to signal to her when he confirmed all was clear, but that signal never came.

She whispered his name a few times, but there was still no response. Was he selling her out to Elma? Taking credit for saving them both and blaming Fallon for the whole ordeal? *Over my dead body.* She gritted her teeth, tightened her grip on Elowen's legs, and stormed into the cave.

She immediately saw Ronen, just standing there like a fool. Fallon was about to go kick him over just for the fun of it, but she saw what he was staring at. Then she too was immediately paralyzed in place.

A wild-looking Elma stared at them with her arms crossed, sandaled foot tapping impatiently. Behind her, the hearth fire was a tall pillar of spitting red flames. It lit up the room in a hellish aura.

"Well?" she finally spoke, glancing between them all.

Ronen pointed behind him. "Elowen sleepwalks!" he announced loudly, voice cracking.

"Is that so?" she said in an unimpressed tone. She clasped her hands behind her back and walked towards them slowly. "You know, I have many eyes in this realm. I have been alive a very long time and have made many friends along the way," she said.

The boy chuckled nervously. "You don't look a day over two-hundred."

Fallon blanched. "*Two-hundred?*"

Elma ignored her. "I could figure out what you three were up to with one letter, so I am giving you one opportunity to tell me the truth yourself."

Ronen turned to her, his brown eye dark and grim. Fallon did not know what to do, she needed to buy them some time.

"Can I please get Elowen to bed? She's drooling down my neck," she begged.

After eyeing them carefully, Elma nodded. "Quickly."

The fire behind her died down to a bright orange as she made her way to their shared chamber. Last night, Elowen had dragged her mattress next to Fallon's bed. Nature followed Elowen everywhere, so now flowers and vines sprouted from the cracks in the stone floor around them.

Fallon knew how to flip someone over her shoulder, she had just never done it in a *gentle* way before. "Come on, work with me," she whispered as she struggled to carefully plop Elowen down on the bed.

She stirred slightly. "Fallon?" she rasped, looking around groggily.

Fallon sat on the edge of the bed, letting the blood flow back into her arms. "Yeah, Elo, I'm here." She laughed nervously.

Propping herself up on her elbows, Elowen sat in confusion. After a moment, her eyes began to water.

"I-I think \ \ I had the worst dream. It felt so real." She shook her head as the tears fell down her cheeks.

Fallon did not want to lie to her, but if this was how her brain coped with the trauma then maybe it was for the best. So she treaded carefully. "Well, you're okay now," she said.

Elowen looked up at her with those pale green eyes. "Not that long ago, I thought I would never make a friend ever again. Then you came along, and now I have three." She smiled sadly, "I was with loneliness for so long, I thought she and I were friends. But now I think her real name was sadness, and I don't need her anymore. I have you."

Her words pierced Fallon's heart like a sword in stone, sending cracks spider-webbing across her soul. Not breaking—but *liberating* her from the armor of her own making. She felt her heart beat once, then twice, in a way she had not felt in fifteen years.

Fallon leaned forward and wrapped her arms around Elowen's thin shoulders. "I can't promise a fair world, but I can promise you will never have to face it alone ever again," she whispered.

EIGHTEEN

When it came to punishment, Fallon endured everything short of Odin being hanged from a tree for nine days with a spear in his side. Beowulf tried something similar once, but Fallon got herself down in a few hours.

That is why she had no fear or apprehension as she headed back to the hearth. Whatever wrath Elma possessed, Fallon could take it. Besides, what could a simple old woman really do to her? She doubted there was anything that could kill her at this point. Sigurd Osmund said it himself—Death pitied her too much to take her. Even that awful power of light failed to destroy her.

Though sometimes at night, if Fallon stayed still as death, she swore she could still feel it rumble deep within her. Not dead, not quite alive, but … slumbering.

The only sound was the white sand crunching under her muddy boots as Fallon approached the hearth fire. Ronen sat on one of the benches with his head in his hands, Elma standing over him with arms crossed impatiently.

He glared up at her. The hearth fire between them was burning low, nothing more than yellow tongues licking the logs. His face was stricken with anxiety, giving her a look with his eyes that said *run!*

From somewhere in the oversized sleeve of her gray robes, Elma pulled out a corked jar. In it was a smashed pile of small-headed mushrooms.

Elma reached in and pulled out a handful of three or four of the long stems, holding them out to Fallon. "Eat."

"I'll pass," she declined. Fallon didn't even fancy the normal mushrooms from her world, let alone ones that *glowed* orange.

Elma approached her slowly. It was clear in her face that she was done with the fun and games. She grabbed Fallon's hand and smacked the wet plants into her palm. "I wasn't asking, girl. Eat, then sit."

Fallon winced as she sniffed the mushrooms. She knew the poisonous plants of her world—lily of the valley, nightshade, foxgloves, hemlock, and wolf's bane alike. She tried to examine its characteristics but found no similarities. Poisoning was a foul way to die, but it sure sounded a lot better than having another iron pressed against her skin.

Taking a deep breath, Fallon tilted her head back and popped them in her mouth. They tasted like sour radishes.

Once she swallowed, Elma nodded in approval and motioned for her to take a seat next to Ronen, who had been uncharacteristically quiet.

"*Malus-lingua luxaeterna*," she said proudly, examining the jar in her hands. "While some have it in their gardens to attract pest-eating insects, I find it has more useful properties. Allow me to demonstrate. Both of you, please say: *my favorite color is yellow*," she asked sweetly.

They watched each other in confusion, but did as they were told. "My favorite color is yellow," they said in unison.

Fallon gasped and nearly fell off the bench. As Ronen spoke, a small glow emitted from his mouth. By the time he finished his sentence, his entire tongue lit up orange like a jack-o-lantern.

She pointed at him in horror. "Your mouth!"

"No, *your* mouth!" he pointed back, laughing.

Fallon clamped both hands over her face, turning back to Elma. "What is this?" she demanded.

"The latex in *Malus-lingua luxaeterna* reacts to deceit. So, as long as it coats your mouth, I will be able to see anytime you lie. Now that we all understand each other." She walked over and sat on the bench adjacent to theirs, "Tell me what happened tonight."

Fallon was impressed. Maybe a world of magic was going to be tricker to navigate than she thought. "But I never lied in the first place," she said defensively. Not yet, at least.

Elma raised a gray brow at Ronen, who shied away from her. "This one tried to feed me a story about him tricking the two of you into getting him to the Entrance Tree, like I was born yesterday!" she scoffed. "Thus, I have no choice but to resort to these measures."

For once, Fallon was speechless. She turned to him, but he kept his eyes fixed on the fire before them. He really tried to take the fall for everything? After she almost got them all killed?

"No." She shook her head slowly. "No, it was my fault. I left, and they followed me. We had an encounter with the Centaurs," she said quietly. Her mouth was dry, but not orange as she went on to explain everything that happened.

Elma rubbed her hands together nervously. "Severely misunderstood creatures, Centaurs. You see, two minds live inside them: the man and the beast. When calm and unprovoked, they are extremely intelligent and rather pleasant to speak to. But all it takes is one wrong word and …" She shook her head. "You three are very fortunate fate was on your side."

"Actually, it was a herd of Hempia that was on our side," Ronen corrected.

The tips of Elma's thin mouth turned upwards. "At least Dag was watching over you in my absence."

Fallon felt a tightness in her chest. She hated this feeling. She hated admitting she was wrong and that she had failed. Usually, Beowulf would just order the Vali to toss her into the frozen lake, or chain her to a stake outside overnight. No one had ever asked how she felt about anything. No one ever gave her the chance to speak her part. She found it rather uncomfortable.

"I am happy to see you all made it back, but this cannot go unpunished," Elma said sternly.

She and Ronen let out a groan and dropped their heads as Elma got up and walked to a large hutch against the wall. Opening its birchwood doors, she rummaged around until she pulled out a tall vase full of dirty, round objects. "Come."

They walked around the cave until Elma spotted a vacant flowerbed. To their left grew a tree with a spiral trunk and purple leaves. Ronen reached to touch it, but Elma quickly slapped his hand away.

She then reached into the jar and pulled out one of the spheres that was no bigger than her palm.

Fallon snorted. "Are you going to throw them at us?"

The old woman tsked at her. "That would teach you nothing. This is the bulb of *Achillea verumcor*. Similar to the mushroom you just ate, it has some unique features due to Elphyne's magic."

"Are we supposed to be taking notes or something?" Ronen asked, clearly annoyed. Fallon knew she could never keep all these names straight. Unable to decipher which plants would heal her and which would kill her, she ultimately decided to just never touch anything.

Elma ignored him. "This beautiful member of the *Asteraceae* family does not need water, sunlight, nor nutrients. The only thing that can make it grow is love, pure energy, and joy. The river that flows from a loving heart can make anything bloom."

"That's lovely. Unrelatable, but lovely. What does it have to do with us?" Ronen asked impatiently.

The smile dropped from Elma's face. "Because of your little nightly crusade, I will not help you open the Entrance Tree until Fallon makes these flowers bloom. Whether that takes a day, a week, or a month, you three will remain here with me," she said sternly.

"*What?*" They both cried.

Ronen raked his hands through his hair, giving her a look of disgust. "In that case, we're all screwed," he hissed.

This had to be some sort of joke. "I thought you said we weren't prisoners?" she asked.

Elma chuckled. "This is not a prison, child, it is your best option. You are more than welcome to leave, but you will never get past the guards, or convince them to help you. And, as you have both experienced firsthand, the creatures of Elphyne never rest." She turned to Ronen. "Eventually, the Valdyr will find you out there. They always do. So, I offer you warm beds, food, and work. It has been so long since I've had youthful hands here to assist me." She smiled.

Ronen got in Fallon's face, his blue eye alight with fury. "Congratulations on getting that fight you wanted, red. I hope it was worth it," he said, then turned and stormed off.

She was speechless. Fallon could hardly believe her luck. "Why? Why this?" She pointed to the jar of unborn flowers.

Elma grabbed Fallon's hands and pressed the flower bulb into her palm. "Because I fear the day you learn you can't punch, scream, and stab your way out of everything, it will be far too late."

Fallon wanted to tell her it was beyond too late, but the woman had a sadness in her eyes she could not define. She always stared at her like she was searching for someone else in Fallon's face.

"Here." Elma squatted down. "You must be the one to plant it," she explained as Fallon helped the old woman settle onto her unsteady knees.

Letting out a sigh of defeat, she reluctantly dug through the damp soil with her fingers, pretending she was clawing Ronen's face off. Elma instructed her on exactly how deep to dig, how to position the bulb, and how much dirt to pack back on top. When she was done, she sat back and examined her work.

To no one's surprise, a sprout did not magically appear instantly. "Well?" Fallon made a face. "How do I *love* it into growing?"

Elma chuckled. "The same way you love anything," she said as she stood and dusted her hands off on her apron.

Fallon pinched the bridge of her nose. This was going to be a long few days. "Can you at least give me somewhere to start?" she asked through clenched teeth.

"Talk to it." Elma patted her shoulder. "Let it know it is not only welcome to this world; but worthy of being in it," she said and slowly shuffled away.

This had to be the most emasculating, mundane, and humiliating task Fallon had ever been given. Surely it was a trick: this was just a rotten bulb. Fallon was going to spend the rest of her life trapped in this cave talking to a pile of dirt. With only a moron boy and an old witch as company. Well, at least she had Elowen.

Her eyes wandered down the stone path. Through the bushes, she could see Ronen standing by the hearth. He and Elma were exchanging some unpleasant words, ending with the woman once again shoving a towel into his hands and walking off.

It seemed his night was going just as good as hers, so she rolled onto her feet and walked back to the fire. He did not look up at her from his spot on the bench as she approached. He might have ignored her all night if she did not say something first.

"Why?" She crossed her arms.

He put on an exaggerated smile. "Why what?" he asked sweetly: sarcastically. Annoyingly.

She rolled her eyes. "Why try to take the blame from me?"

"I don't know." He shrugged, but the faint glow of his mouth was telling a different story.

She snorted. "It looks like you swallowed a Will-o'-Wisp." She noted as she sat down cross-legged in the sand.

He rubbed his eyes with the heel of his palms. "What does that even mean? Your accent was cool at first, but it gets really old, really fast."

Fallon would be offended if she did not feel the exact same way about him. She was tired of his voice, but most of all she was done with his smell. She scooted closer to the fire, hoping the hot hair would burn away the stink.

"In my world, they are ancestral spirits in the form of a blue flame. They can ignite and disappear in a matter of seconds, reappearing wherever they please. Some lead you to your destiny, others lead you to your demise."

"How do you tell the difference?"

She shrugged. "Don't be foolish enough to follow a spirit into the woods." She paused. "Not that long ago, I believed magic was long gone from my world—everyone did. Everyone but my mother. She never stopped believing," she said.

He watched her carefully. "So, there are really no good people in the mortal realm?" he asked quietly.

"There were two." She smiled sadly. Her voice caught in her throat, "But they are gone now. Trust me, Ronen, Elphyne is your best chance."

He tilted his head to the side, "Yet that realm is your best chance?"

Fallon was tired. Of Ronen and his questions. She stood up, dusting off her trousers. "Some of us are all out of chances," she said quietly. Fallon turned and left the hearth before he could say anything else.

She checked on Elowen one last time before climbing into her own fur-covered bed. Perhaps she could ask the Hulder to make the flowers grow. Because Ronen was right; if it was up to Fallon to get them all out of here, they were royally screwed.

Fallon was stuck. She could not venture out on her own, not yet. There were still too many unknowns. She had to learn more about the Castle Guard, predators, and this Ondorr that everyone always whispered about.

Until then, she could play along. This place was inarguably better than the stone walls of the Solveij House or any cell she could be tossed into. She has waited nineteen years to get her throne back, she could wait a few more days. Besides, this gave her more time to help Elowen find her tree.

As she laid on her back, Fallon raised her hands to her face. She examined her pale palms, scarred from years of pulling ropes. Each knuckle had been broken at least once, some ended up healing slightly crooked. Fallon could see her hand pressed against the Entrance Tree's warm bark, watching the golden ichor seep through its cracks.

She reached in herself, rummaging around for any sign of the power that had nearly killed her. She shuddered at the memory—the feeling of being ripped apart only to be put back together. If Jaeger had not been there to calm her down, she would have been trapped inside a storm of her own creation forever. A dying star, abandoned on earth. She was better off without it.

We can go on that journey together, he had said. He wanted to be here, not her. Jaeger was supposed to make it here and find his mother. Gods, Fallon told him his mother was dead. She screamed it in his face. Yet he ran to his own death, still believing in his mother and in Fallon.

Her hand moved to itch her side, the same way she always did when she thought about him. He and Norman. When she went back, Fallon would learn what became of them. She hoped they died quickly, and a Valkyrie took their hand when she couldn't.

All of this was her father's fault. Fallon could not wait to spit on Beowulf's grave. To sit upon that throne of iron. Her fantasies consumed her as she fell asleep, taking her into dreams of red skies and dancing skeletons.

After what felt like only minutes of slumber, Fallon was rudely awoken by vegetable peels being tossed at her head.

She groaned as she slowly sat up, stepping over multiple carrot tips and potato skins. Elma was shouting up and down the cavern for them all to get up for breakfast. Fallon supposed she was going to have to get used to a farmer's sleep schedule.

Somehow, another new set of clothes was already on her dresser. Once again tailored perfectly to her size. Fallon changed into the neutral-colored clothing and did not make it one step out of her chamber before Elowen found her.

"Good morning!" she chirped, snagging a rogue potato skin from the tangle of Fallon's hair, and popping it into her mouth.

"Did you sleep alright?" Fallon asked, worried the memories of last night would come back.

But Elowen just shrugged. "I think I was stressed. But I am excited for today," she assured her.

They walked out to the hearth to find a half-asleep Ronen sitting at his place by the fire. Based on his haggard appearance, he once again refused to bathe. Fallon did not understand why he was boycotting personal hygiene, but she just hoped it would end soon.

Elma walked over with two ceramic plates in her hands, handing one to Elowen and Ronen. She could smell the cooked eggs and wilted greens from where she sat, and her mouth watered with anticipation.

But Elma approached her empty-handed. "You, girl, only get to eat if you spend at least five minutes in your garden." She smiled, her round eyes unwavering. Elma's oversized, cascading robes were a light blue color today.

Fallon pressed her lips tightly together and crossed her legs. Signaling she had absolutely no intentions of getting up, let alone talking to dirt. She would not be trained like a dog, doing party tricks for her next meal.

"Stubborn, ungrateful, cowardly." Elma shook her head.

Fallon's lips turned up into a grin. "I've heard worse."

"Come on, Fallon, I will go with you," Elowen whispered, nudging her arm.

But Elma raised her hand. "That is kind of you, dear, but this is a decision Fallon needs to make on her own."

The old woman snapped her fingers, and they all gasped in surprise as a third plate of food *floated* towards them.

Elma accepted the plate from the air with a simple. "Thank you." And sat down on her bench to eat.

"What magic was that?" Ronen asked, crumbs tumbling down his chin.

"None. My cave sprites have been in servitude to me for many years," she explained, taking a bite of her eggs.

Cave sprites. That explains why things kept magically appearing. "Why can't we see them?" Fallon asked.

Elma looked around, as if to make sure none of them were listening. "Sprites who have lost their way usually end up in caves such as this one. They wander, losing their memories and even their forms. I offer them purpose and knowledge to keep them distracted while their very existence slowly fades away."

"Ghost butlers," Ronen clarified. "You have a ghost butler."

"No matter how big or small, visible or invisible, all life deserves a chance," Elma said. She snapped her fingers again, and three small bread loaves were carried by invisible hands and presented to everyone but Fallon. She did not care. She had gone much longer without food and in much harsher conditions.

So that was exactly how the next four days went. They did more dusting, sweeping, weed picking, and harvesting than she thought possible. Every morning they were each given a list, though Fallon's was usually doubled, as she had to help Elowen with many of her tasks. But Fallon quickly learned Elowen was not one to complain. She simply did as she was told and to the best of her ability. It made Fallon put her own attitude in check—if Elowen was happy to do something, Fallon could be too.

It took two days for Elowen to warm up to Ronen. After what happened to her, it was no wonder why the Hulder was so weary of men. She broke the ice by offering him a pile of dirt (her favorite snack) to which he awkwardly accepted.

Elowen did not care if her hands got dirty or if her dress tore. Fallon swore she was doing it on purpose, because every time it did Elma would simply sew her a new one. Each with more color and ruffles than the last. The old woman did not seem to mind, either.

"I was never blessed with a daughter of my own," she explained to Fallon one morning as she was spinning more yarn. "I could barely handle two boys, trying for a girl just wasn't written in my fate." She laughed.

Fallon watched her tan hands work the spindles. Elma was old, but her pointy cheekbones and chestnut eyes were still beautiful. Above her Fae ears, her hair was the same—gray dreads rolled into a massive bun atop her head. Fallon could never get her hair to achieve that. She just restored to braiding off some portions to help remove some thickness.

One evening after Fallon restocked Elma's wheel with wool, she walked back out to the hearth to find Elowen. The Hulder was off somewhere else, probably admiring her reflection as Fallon often found her doing, leaving no one to talk to but Ronen.

It turned out the boy was good with his hands. For days she had watched him build shelf after shelf, cabinets, watering systems, and he even fixed the stubborn drawer in her dresser.

Fallon walked over to help hold a plank of wood level as he hammered it into the wall. "Where did you learn to do this?" she asked, trying to keep her arms steady above her head.

He removed the nail from between his teeth. "I grew up in a blacksmith shop," He explained. "Where did you learn to be so bitter?"

"I grew up in an ice fortress." She gave him a smile as cold as the frost in her veins.

He stopped hammering. "What? Like a castle?"

Their faces were only a few inches apart, so she turned to speak into the wall. "On Midgard there are three Viking clans: the Blodvingers, Haedilla, and the Avvore. Each is led by a Chief and represented by the Royal House. I was once considered a Blodvinger," she added spitefully.

He nodded along. "It's okay, I got kicked out of my home too."

She snorted. "Why do you assume I was kicked out?"

He closed his eyes in frustration. "Because you said you were *once* a blood-winger, and you are about as forgiving as this wall I've been trying to nail through," he spat.

Fallon dropped her arms. One side of the shelf fell to the ground, a crack spreading up the middle of the wood. "*Blodvinger*," she corrected.

"Really?" he exclaimed, throwing up his hands.

She rolled her eyes, "Calm down, it is just a piece of wood," she said. But Ronen paced back and forth, running his hands through his greasy hair.

A small amount of guilt trickled through her as she stared at the janky, half-up shelf. She only felt worse when she saw Ronen's face as he stared at the broken plank of wood. At first, she thought it was just grime on his face, but now she saw the dark circles under his eyes were all too real. Eyes that were far too tired to be twenty-one.

"I'm sorry, Ronen. I can help you fix it," she said quietly. When he still said nothing, she waved a hand in front of his face. "Ronen?"

He finally looked up at her, "I know it's just a piece of wood, Fallon, but it's also all I can do to feel ... useful. This is all I have to offer. It wasn't enough to convince the only person who ever cared about me to let me stay, so it *must* be enough to convince Elma," he said, "but you broke it."

Through the dirt on his skin and past the walls he put up, Fallon could see glimpses of the man that hid behind all those jokes and jabs. See why he had been wordlessly working these past few days without rest.

She turned to face him, powering through the smell. "You were right. I was banished from my home, from my clan and my village. I wasn't enough, either. But maybe our combined efforts will be enough this time; two halves equal a whole, right?"

He stared at her long enough to count each freckle on her face. "Right," he said at last.

She grabbed the nail from his hand and put it between her own teeth. "Good. Then show me how to build a cabinet."

PART TWO
Chief of Misfits

NINETEEN

Over the course of a week, Ronen slowly faded into one of the cave sprites. Passing time by carrying out tasks, quiet and unseen. One day everyone would forget his name, and eventually he would too. That did not seem like a terrible death. To dissolve back into the universe he came from, the footprints of his existence whisked away by the wind.

It sounded better than being a spectacle. Everyone cheering as his kind was finally eradicated once and for all. So, until the day they came for him, Ronen would be here. Building pathetic furniture and eating more greens than anyone ever should.

Fallon stopped him from leaving Elphyne for a reason. He just wished the gods had sent someone a little nicer to steer him back on track. Ronen had been chasing after nothing when he tried to run away, and he still was. Still searching for a light he would never find. A moth cast in darkness.

On the nights he was too tired to throw a pity party for himself, he would enter the untouched bathing chamber. Fully clothed, with tears dripping down his cheeks like the condensation on the stone walls.

Every time he even considered getting in, he felt rods being slammed down on his knuckles. The hot breath of people shouting in his ear, and the guilt that crumpled him up from the inside. Eventually, he could no longer stomach the sight of his own reflection. The door to that bathing chamber did not open again.

When the morning finally came, he accepted his breakfast and to-do list from Elma with a fake smile. Ronen enjoyed listening to the girls laugh while he worked. They collected leaves to propagate and wrote labels for jars. He will admit, it was nice to see Fallon start to loosen up, as their future depended on it. He was reminded of that with every meal as he watched her stubbornly refuse to talk to her flower buds. How could she do that? After a full day of sanding down tree scraps and sorting nails, he was famished.

Which was why whenever he could sneak it, Ronen kept one of his dinner rolls in his pocket. If he set it on his bed and politely asked the ghost butler to take it to her chamber, it was usually gone when he came back. He hoped it was working and they were not just stealing it for themselves. But Ronen didn't think ghosts had stomachs.

Why was he doing it? He had no clue. Ronen had no clue why he ran after Fallon with the Centaurs, or why he even helped them from the Entrance Tree in the first place.

Ronen has spent too much time in his own head lately. He did not want to kick off his shoes and get comfortable in there, not yet. Because yes, he was frustrated and upset, but above everything Ronen felt *lost*. How could he be mad he couldn't leave the cave, when he had nowhere to go anyways?

At least he knew how to do this one thing. He could build as many cabinets as Elma threw at him. So, he kept hammering until the bad thoughts were too far away to hear.

When Fallon approached him one evening offering help, he was afraid she was going to ask him about the appearing rolls. Luckily, she had little to say as she held the shelf up for him.

Ronen took his time just to see how long she could hold it. But Fallon's broad shoulders never faltered, and she never once asked for a break or complained. One thing he quickly picked up about Fallon: she could endure.

What she did have to say, though, made him want to punch her right on that scar across her nose. But by the end it was all worth a broken shelf. Because he got something he had not received for as long as he could remember:

A smile from someone who understood.

Not a look of fear, of disgust or pity, but empathy. Ronen peered into her emerald eyes and felt *seen*. Part of him was ashamed for craving that validation, which was why she could never know how much that one smile meant to him. Fallon was not traditionally beautiful, but a regal woman indeed. He had never seen anyone like her before, yet he was still struck with déjà vu every time he looked at her for too long.

He saw in her eyes that she was telling the truth about her past. With the pure intensity that came with talking to Fallon, you would have to be a fool to think she has not been through a lot. He saw it when she came through the tree, and he saw it when she got too close to that cliff out in the knolls. She had turned white as a ghost, her eyes empty and cold.

Ronen wanted to ask about it, but right now was not the right time. Because for once, he got to boss *her* around. And he planned to enjoy every second of it.

She wasn't useless at handiwork. At least, not as useless as Ronen was when he first started. Fallon just got frustrated easily. Yes, she threw around tools and cursed at inanimate objects in a language he did not understand, but she was strong. Really strong. Together they were able to flip over a large table with a squeaky leg Elma had been complaining about.

It was in a room Ronen had never been in before. All around them were crates upon crates full of pressed papyrus. It was slightly unsettling in a way, to be in a library of empty pages. Maybe this is how the gods felt when they were born into this world: a blank canvas that was theirs to paint, a story that was theirs to tell.

He even got Fallon to laugh a few times as they bantered about this strange place and Elma's hoarding tendencies. It was the first time she smiled long enough to show a missing top canine. She probably lost it in a fight, or in some cool Viking ritual. Ronen had never done anything cool in his life.

It was easier to talk when they did not have to look at each other. With both their hands busy, he asked her more about the mortal realm she kept calling Midgard. She returned the favor with her own assortment of questions. While she asked about the Valdyr, the dead royal family, and Ondorr, Ronen just wanted to know about the stars.

"So, what makes the sky black again?" he asked, cursing as he pulled a nail from its striped socket. No wonder the table had been wobbling.

Fallon let out an irritated sigh and walked over to grab one of the chambersticks off the ground. One by one, she snuffed out every other wick with her bare fingers until the candle in her hands was the only thing illuminating the room.

Ronen kept quiet. Something about the way the fire lit up the golden flecks in her eyes made his heart begin to pound. The shadows around them kept creeping closer, tickling the back of his neck. He kept his eyes focused on the dancing flame and on the dangerous girl who mirrored its wickedness.

For once, she sat directly in front of him. She gestured to the flame in its brass chamberstick. "Sun." She then pointed to the blank wall beside them. "Sky."

She let out one sharp breath and the flame went out. She pointed to the black wall that now melted into the shadows. "Night."

"Just because I'm an orphan doesn't mean you have to talk to me like I'm stupid," he joked. Why did he always say stupid things when he was nervous?

"Now, look," she said as she scooted closer. She cupped her hand around the wick and blew gently, giving it just enough oxygen to come back to life. Hot orange embers bounced off and floated around their faces.

"Stars," Fallon said proudly.

They both watched in silence as each ember found its way to the ground. Ronen tried to calm his racing heartbeat. It wasn't even because he was in a nearly pitch-black room with a stranger, it was because she wasn't really a stranger anymore. Not her, or Elowen.

He had to remind himself this was all her fault. If he had just been five seconds quicker, or she was five seconds slower, they could have all gone their separate ways. And most of all; she didn't know he was a Nøkken. She might never look at him this way ever again, and it was probably for the best.

She set down the chamberstick. "Do you understand now?"

"I understand perfectly," he nodded, face falling grim. She was the reason he wasn't free right now.

Suddenly Fallon's eyes widened. She leaned forward and put her hands out in concern. "Wait—I'm sorry. You can't be in darkness." she stammered as she aggressively pulled him up to his feet.

Ronen laughed, pushing off her callused hands. "Relax, it takes a bit longer than that," he explained. He, Elma, and Elowen all stood at the cave mouth every morning to bathe in the sunlight. Drinking it in like morning tea.

"It's true, then? What I watched happen to Elowen—shade-poisoning—it happened to you?" she asked.

He shrugged it off. "I lived. I guess there is one advantage to having some mortal blood," he said. She did not need to know the details of his imprisonment. She didn't deserve to.

"Well, there's no point in risking it," she said and hurriedly went to find a match. Together they relit all the candles, finished up the table, and put everything back in place in time for supper.

He nodded at her awkwardly in thanks. Now that their task was done, there wasn't a reason to stay together. "Well, I will see you at the hearth."

She put her hands on her defined hips. "What, are you going to go freshen up before supper?" she smirked.

He tried to hold in his smile. "Careful, red, that was almost funny."

Fallon stuck her tongue out and shoved past him. As she stepped out of the room, she turned her chin over her shoulder. "We're all homeless, Ronen. A rightful Clan of Misfits. I don't speak to you bluntly because I think you're a fool, I do so because I know you'll understand," she said, then disappeared down the hall.

Ronen considered her words as he picked up his tools and walked back to his own chamber. He was an orphan, but he had not been completely alone. He always had Urg and the Little Folk taking care of him. They told him what to do, where to go, who to trust and how to live. For that he was thankful, but it had all been taken away so suddenly. Ronen oversaw his own choices now, but he was a blind man drowning at sea.

A ruckus from outside his chamber drew him from his thoughts. Ronen quickly walked to the hearth to see Fallon and Elma shouting at each other, and it seemed to be far more than their usual bickering before every meal.

"I'm tired of this!" The old woman was shouting as Ronen approached.

Elowen's body was stiff and rigid as she watched the two chase each other around. Ronen knew Elowen always hated this part. The fire was burning dark red, a shade so deep and hot it scorched him from four feet away.

Elma waved her hands at Fallon, "This little show you've been putting on is nothing but a pathetic attempt to control the situation. What, my dear, are you so afraid of?"

Fallon opened her mouth to argue, but closed it again before answering, "I'm not afraid," she said in the least convincing tone Ronen had ever heard.

Some of the anger dropped from Elma's features as she let out a long breath. "If I asked anyone else to make those flowers grow, it would be done in a day. I'm sure even Ronen could muster up the affection needed to nurture the plants," she said.

He snorted. "Thanks?"

"But obviously that is not the case with you," she continued, clasping her hands behind her back. "Clearly the problem is not the nature of being told what to do. For days now you have been scrubbing floors and emptying chamber pots at my request with little to no retaliation. And you are not one to shy away from a challenge, we saw plenty of that on your first night here. So, am I truly left to believe that a sprout is more intimidating to you than a Centaur?" she cooed, peering down her nose at Fallon.

Everyone stayed very still, not sure how she was going to react. Ronen was ready to pick up Elowen and run, but Fallon's eyes kept trailing back to the Hulder who looked like she was trying to melt into the bushes.

Fallon clicked her square jaw a few times before she spoke. "Why is all the focus on me? The boy can't bathe, and Elowen can't stand the sight of her own shadow let alone a dark room," she protested.

Elma stepped forward and grabbed Fallon's hands in her own. "Dear, I am asking you to *be* an example, not be made an example of," she spoke barely louder than a whisper.

He watched the words wash away Fallon's anger like a cleansing rain. He did not understand women. How could they just switch their emotions in the flip of a coin? They changed their moods more than Ronen changed his socks.

At that, Elowen finally ran over to hug Fallon. They were all shocked to learn Elowen was the oldest out of the three of them, but their height difference made her appear much younger. Her arms wrapped around Fallon; she barely reached the girl's chin.

"I bet your flowers are going to be white." Elowen grinned excitedly.

Fallon laughed nervously. "Let's not get ahead of ourselves."

"Orange." Ronen put his hands in his pockets awkwardly. "I bet they're going to be orange."

"Why's that?" she asked, gently pushing Elowen's face off her chest.

He shrugged. "It was the first one to come to my head. And it's my favorite."

Elma clapped her hands together excitedly. She looked between them all with pride. "Elowen, come with me. We will need to make food for four tonight. Let's give Fallon a moment," she said gently as the two women scurried off excitedly.

No one invited him to help in the kitchen or talk to flowers, so he assumed he was being dismissed. As usual.

But this was the first time he had seen Fallon appear uncertain about something. She was still planted firmly in place, shifting her jaw back and forth as she always did when that absent look took over her eyes.

"Do you want to be alone?" he asked. Even though he would pay a lot of money to see Fallon sing a lullaby to a pile of dirt.

She nodded, raising her chin. "I can do it alone."

"That doesn't mean you have to," he reminded her.

Her head fell to the side like a doll as she gave him a long stare. Suddenly Ronen was acutely aware of how gross he was. He crossed his arms and turned his head away, feeling the sudden need to be anywhere else but in front of her.

"But I get that's not really your style," he stammered before walking off.

Coward. Moron. How could he face the mortal realm if he could not even face one mortal girl without succumbing to shame? He thought he had gotten over caring about his appearance long ago. But that was around the Fae—people he despised. He enjoyed the thought of them hating him. He loved that they avoided him. But that wasn't going to work anymore.

As he entered his chamber, he saw another towel folded and ready on his nightstand. Maybe tonight was the night. Maybe Elma was right; if Fallon could face her demons, so could he.

TWENTY

The first time a blade was put in Fallon's hands, she was five years old.

She could string her own bow when she was six and saddle her own horse at eight. Fallon understood the tasks that were presented to her then, they came like second nature. Nothing more than lacing up her boots.

So why couldn't she understand this?

Fallon sat on her knees before the empty flower bed, her body rigid and uncomfortable. She could still see where her nails had raked through the dark dirt. Fallon picked at her calluses and braided her hair, desperate for any sense of familiarity in this unknown territory. But was it truly unknown? Had she never spoken with kindness in her entire life?

No. Because Fallon had the most beautiful mother in all the realms.

Asta's voice could summon the rain from the sky. She could reach into the sunlight and strum the bonds of the universe as harp strings. Fallon still remembered the way her mother's red hair spilled onto the book pages she read from. She was time, beauty, and joy all wrapped up in a honeysuckle and elderberry scent.

They fed the magpies on the windowsill together and snuck into the kitchens to make fruit tarts. It was them against the world, against Beowulf and the Solveij House. They might have even had a chance, had Asta not met her untimely end and left Fallon to feed those magpies alone every spring.

Fallon wondered what she would have been like if Asta finished raising her. Would she be as kind as Elowen? Would she have been taught how to fight? Would Fallon have *needed* to fight?

The world would never know. Because Fallon was never given that opportunity. Her mother was dead, and despite what Elowen thought, Fallon was destined to be alone. Unwanted. Unclaimed.

But that did not mean this flower had to have the same fate. If nothing else, Fallon would give it the chance she never had. *What did Elma say?*

"Tell it it's not only welcome in this world, but worthy of being in it," she said quietly to herself. Perhaps this little bud was worthy. She didn't see why not.

What a world it would be if Fallon ever heard those words herself. Maybe she, too, would have bloomed. Never the matter. Fallon sat back on her haunches and crossed her legs. She had nothing to say from her own heart, not yet. Maybe the song her mother used to sing in hard times would be enough for now.

"Oh Wil-o'-Wisp, please shine your light tonight as I stand at this crossroad alone …"

Fallon awoke the next morning to a wave of hot pain rushing around her face, from the tip of each ear down to her jaw. She tried to rub it out as she stepped over Elowen, nearly slipping on the girl's endless waves of hair.

Fallon suspected her friend was behind the rolls of bread that kept magically appearing, but every time she brought it up the Hulder acted clueless. It was strange because Elowen was a terrible liar. Yet she seemed to genuinely not know what Fallon was talking about. She even seemed a bit frightened at the idea of bread spawning in their room.

Ronen wasn't sitting on his bench as the girls walked out for breakfast. Nor did he appear when the food was served. This was Fallon's first breakfast in over a week, so she scarfed down every bit of egg and greens on her plate. Elowen had to remind her to come up for air. The handmaidens at the Royal House would have tied her shoulders to the chair to keep her posture straight, and then broken her knuckles for eating so hastily.

Not anymore, and never again.

While Fallon collected everyone's plates, Elma encouraged Elowen to go and see what was keeping the boy. She got up but stared hesitantly at the dim hallway before her.

Fallon put her hands on her hips. "What do we say to our fears?"

Elowen took a deep breath. "Screw you, I'm not afraid."

"Good," Fallon nodded in approval. "Now go, warriors don't dawdle."

Wringing her hands together nervously, Elowen repeated that phrase as she disappeared down the stone corridor. If she called for help, Fallon would be at her side in an instant. There was nowhere that Hulder could go that Fallon would not follow.

Elma turned to give Fallon a look of approval. "Just a week ago, I had to put a glowing *Dracaena trifasciata* by the chamber pot so she would use it. Does she know where she is going?" Elma asked, scrunching her gray brows.

Fallon took a long sip of her tea and sat back down. "No."

"Well, that gives us some time then." She turned to face Fallon; her knees hidden under waves of brown robes. "How did things go last night? You were quiet at supper."

She shrugged. "I tried, Elma."

"I know, I believe you."

"But what if," Fallon shook her head. "What if I'm just not the right person to do it?" Jaeger's words echoed in her mind: *all you know is the feeling of an empty heart.*

Elma pulled Fallon to her feet. "My dear, I have been alive a long time and met many people. And I have come to one simple conclusion: people are good when given the chance to be. It is clear to me now that you were never given that chance," she said, her thin neck bobbling. "It is safe to say you have become a master at surviving, but now is your time to start *living*."

Fallon took a step back. "Is that what this is supposed to be? A chance to be benevolent when life has been nothing but a cruel master to me?" She let out a low laugh, an omen of certain death. "They put a leash around my neck, and I bit it off. *I* did that. I had to save myself. Over, and over, and over again. There was no one there to save me. So what do you expect of me now?"

Quiet. Elma was unnaturally, impossibly quiet as she stared at Fallon's face. Her anger sang a song in her blood, invoking the muse of whatever ancient heart thrummed deep within her. *I'm here,* it seemed to say, *I remain.*

And Fallon, too, remained

They heard footsteps approaching. Elma wiped her damp eyes and turned to Fallon. The glow of the plants around them eerily reflected in the whites of her eyes.

"A circle has no beginning and no end. The only way to escape a cycle is to break it," she said.

It was too late for Fallon to ask questions as Ronen and Elowen finally emerged into the cave. The boy obviously had a long night: his hair was matted to one side, and a thick glaze coated his mismatching eyes. Ronen always looked like he just left a screaming match, yet she had never once heard the boy raise his voice. It made her wonder what sort of chaos went on inside his head to make him so exhausted all the time.

Elowen, on the other hand, was smiling. She whispered something in Ronen's ear, and to his credit he gave a pretty convincing smile in return. Fallon knew the Hulder enjoyed him as a person, she said he reminded her of a lotus pond. Fallon had come to trust Elowen's judgment. If she said Ronen was good, she believed her. Despite how aggravating he was.

"Can we tell them now, Elma?" Elowen begged excitedly. Her waist-length hair was tangle-free, as always. Oh, how nice it must be to have that seductress magic. Fallon spent ten minutes trying to comb through hers, then just braided it to the side in defeat.

Elma nodded. "As a reward for everyone's hard work, I decided you all can join me on an errand today," she announced.

The three of them eyed each other carefully. "You mean we get to leave the cave?" Ronen asked.

She nodded. "So long as you behave. Tending to this garden is not my only responsibility. I have favors to fulfill and an old friend to see."

As they all got ready, Fallon wondered if Elma was rewarding them, or if she just didn't trust them enough to be left here alone. Fortunately, she quickly learned it was neither:

Elma needed pack mules.

They parted their way through the vines of the cave mouth and trotted down the mountain. Fallon and Ronen each carried two bags slung over their shoulders. They followed behind Elma and Elowen, who gossiped excitedly ahead.

Elma had neglected to tell them where they were going, but Ronen was quick to cantankerously remind her that it didn't matter. Because even if she had, Fallon didn't know where anything was anyways.

Rather than turning right into the hills called the Longback Knolls, they continued southwest onto more even ground. Fallon was elated to hear she would get to see more of Elphyne, and after only twenty minutes she was not disappointed. The sky was clear with only a few lingering clouds, but the sun did not burn her. Not the way the Halvar sun did. She felt it melt into her skin, instantly lifting her spirits.

Ronen only spoke when she bombarded him with questions. Like why the mushrooms here were so large and how the birds sang more beautifully than a choir of sirens. They even passed a field of clovers that went up to her ankles. She searched the ground for one with four leaves; her mother used to say they brought good fortune.

"Do Hempia only live in the Longback Knolls?" she asked, curious as to why they had not seen many animals yet save for a few rabbits, deer, and birds.

"Yes, they don't have to fight anyone over for grass there," Ronen explained in a bored tone.

She thought for a few moments. "Why are they so sacred?"

He let out a long breath. The bags they carried were heavy, and Elma kept a surprisingly good pace, but the boy easily kept up.

"Hempia used to be small and tan, like normal cows. Until a farmer went into Dag's temple and sacrificed one to him, asking for help with that year's harvest. Instead of taking the animal's life, Dag blessed it with strength and build," he explained.

"And he turned them silver?"

"He is the moon god, so if you are capable of having an imagination, you can see why that is," he said testily.

Fallon resisted the urge to wrap the strap of her bag around his neck. "And the others?"

"Other what?"

"Gods."

"There are only two gods: Dag and Dagmar, the moon god and sun goddess. He holds our hand as we enter Twiloh, the afterlife in the sea. And she provides for us in life here on Elphyne. Her sacred animal is the Peryton, but you'll probably never see one of those. No one does."

She nearly stopped dead in her tracks. "You only have *two* gods in your entire pantheon? That must be nice." She whistled.

"How many do you have?" he asked defensively.

Fallon did not even know if there was an answer to that question. "Too many to memorize. I pray and make my offerings, but I was never interested in divinity. I know the basics: there are two groups of gods, the Aesir and Vanir. The Aesir are led by Odin, the All-Father …" she trailed off. Ronen was not even listening.

If she cared, she might ask what was wrong. Being an ass was not out of character for him, but this was a bitterness she had yet to see. He was not sad, but almost spiteful with her.

She shook her head. "Forget it. I suppose it's not important here."

"Keep talking."

"What?"

"Keep going. Your weird words are a nice distraction," he said.

She did not know what he needed to be distracted from, as there was nothing before them but green fields and tree groves, but she did not ask questions. "Well, did you know there are more realms than yours and mine?" she asked.

That seemed to get his attention. "I do, but I never knew how many. Can we get there?" he asked.

She shook her head. "From what I understand, the Entrance Tree only connects our two worlds, like a bedroom with an attached bathing chamber," she explained. The memory of Jaeger and Mimir's Lake pained her heart. Watching the childish light in his hazel eyes as he unknowingly explained the world his mother was from.

"And that bedroom is in a house, with other rooms," she finished, swallowing down the stinging pain in her throat. "I used to believe there were nine rooms—nine realms. Though if each of them has their own connection like this one, who knows how many there could be."

Ronen kept his gaze straight, locked on the back of Elowen's white head. "What are the eight others? What lives there?"

She strained to recall the information she had been taught so long ago. "The first two realms to be created from the Ginnungagap were Niflheim and Muspelheim; one made of fog and ice, the other a burning hellhole. They are at the top and bottom of the World Tree, Yggdrasil. Then on that tree is Asgard, where Odin leads the Aesir gods. Then Midgard, where I am from, is home to the mortals."

She counted on her fingers as she went on. "All frost giants are from Jotunheim, and light elves are from Alfheim, while dwarves are from Svartalfheim. The Vanir gods live in Vanaheim, and finally the dishonorable dead all end up in—"

"Dead-heim?" Ronen guessed.

She smiled. "Close. Helheim."

He shook his head. "Eight other realms. What other species are out there that you know of?" he pressed.

She clenched her jaw in frustration. "I'm not an expert, Ronen. We can ask—"

"No, it's fine," he snapped.

She watched him for a moment. They passed through another grove of trees that were littered with sweet-smelling flowers, yet he seemed to enjoy none of it. It was as if he wasn't even here.

So, she somewhat harshly pushed him into a tree, and got into his face as he had once dared get into hers. "What is your problem today?"

He grit his teeth as the back of his head made contact with the hard bark. She was expecting him to push her back, she even planted her feet in preparation. But Ronen was in no mood to fight. He took some long, deep breaths through his flared nostrils.

"If I tell you something, do you promise not to stab me? Or run away, or not let me around Elowen?" he asked.

He stared at her with eyes wasted and worn. A broken down, tired man whispering a final plea. Fallon knew the look of farewell; she had seen it too many times in her mother's face. Why did Ronen have it now? What was he saying goodbye to?

Fallon put her posture in check, eliminating the aggression from her stance. "I once tried to hide something from someone I should have trusted from the start. When it was revealed, I told him he could turn his back on me. I wanted him to abandon me because I couldn't run from myself. But he didn't. So, in respect for him, I swear to do the same for you." she said.

"He sounds like a good person." Ronen said quietly, not meeting her eyes.

Fallon nodded. "He was."

"What was his name?"

She shifted her gaze between his two eyes, still not sure which to look into. "You are avoiding my question."

Ronen gave her a weak smirk; it was the most emotion he had shown all day. "Humor me."

She tried to shrug, but the weight of her emotions heaved down on her as she spoke, "His name was Jaeger. I only knew him for a few days. He was the one who told me about Elphyne. Up until then, I thought all of this only existed in my mother's storybooks," she said.

"Your mother read you Faerietales?"

She nodded. "I think ... I think she might have come here before. When she was alive," she said quietly.

"When did she die?" he asked casually. She supposed to another orphan, it was casual.

"Fifteen years ago," she answered.

Finally, some warmth returned to his face. "Fal, the Entrance Tree closed fifteen years ago. What if she just got stuck on this side? We could find her—"

"Stop," Fallon said softly. "Please."

"Stop what?"

The excitement in his words crushed her. She wished she felt that same. She wished she felt anything at all. "Hope is a needle, Ronen, threatening to unravel every part of me I stitched back together. I mourned for years. She's gone," she said.

The glimmer faded from Ronen's eyes. "Well, you were old enough to remember her telling you stories. That is more than most can say."

Swallowing nervously, and in an unnecessarily quiet voice, he asked her, "did she ... did she ever read to you about Nøkken?" he wheezed the last word as if he had to force it from his lungs.

Fallon's arms fell limp to her sides. Her eyes went wide as she looked at Ronen for what felt like the first time. *Of course.*

His strange affiliation with water finally made sense. The blue eye ... being orphaned as a baby ...

"That's what you are? Half *Nøkken*?" she asked in disbelief. Her mother had indeed read to her about the water monsters. They were seductors, like Huldra, who lived in ponds or lakes. It is said they lured women into bodies of water with their beautiful music. The women were so enchanted, they hardly noticed the crunch of bones under their feet as the water rose higher and higher.

Ronen stood deadly still, waiting. She pulled up a map of events in her head, finally able to see where all the dots connected. "Nøkken are feared here, that's why the Castle Guard were after you," she said.

He nodded.

"And that's where you got shade-poisoning," she added. "They locked you away."

He nodded again.

Her heart dropped into her stomach. "You aren't trusted around water. That's why you ..." *smell like an outhouse* she didn't finish.

Ronen had yet to meet her eyes. His head was almost fully turned to the side in shame, chin-length hair falling in front of his blue eye. Fallon tried to step into his line of sight, but he turned again.

"Why won't you look at me?" she asked, strangely offended.

"Because I don't want to see you look at me differently. I don't want to see the apprehension everyone else has. Not from you, too," he said gently.

She couldn't help but laugh. "You don't scare me, Nøkken. I remember all the stories, yes, but those stories also paint Huldra to be wicked. As we both have seen, not all Huldra are bad. So why would all Nøkken be?" she asked, and she meant it.

Plus, even if he were evil, Fallon was confident she could easily take him down.

So, she bent down and picked up his bags, holding them out to him. He cautiously took them from her hands, finally raising his eyes to search her face for any signs of trickery.

She laughed again, "If you don't believe me, I will eat another one of those orange mushrooms when we get back."

The boy grinned, and some of the fog cleared from his eyes. "Sorry I find it hard to believe that there could be a rational person in this realm. I could kiss you."

She made a face. "Please don't. But if you ever get over your fear of water, I'll reconsider," she joked.

Luckily, he did not take offense. He joked back. "And if you ever get those flowers to grow, we'll go dancing."

They shared a light, comfortable laugh as they turned back to continue following their friends, but Elowen's bobbing head was no longer in sight. Nor was the silver knot of dreads atop Elma's head. They both cursed, starting into a light jog through the trees.

The bags slowed Ronen down, but Fallon could go on for miles. Even though her eyes hurt from focusing on every leaf on every tree, and her sinuses burned with smells she never knew before.

It was starting to become too much. Fallon stopped and rubbed her hands on her face. She had to plug her ears so she would stop hearing the sound of her own blinking.

"What's wrong?" Ronen asked between breaths.

"Nothing." She squeezed her eyes shut. She just wanted to stop feeling every pulse bounce off the tips of her fingers and toes. This realm was meant for Fae, so it left her mortal body struggling to keep up.

After a moment of silence, he tapped her again. "Uh, red?"

Fallon took a breath of air, tasting every spec of pollen in it. "What?" she rasped.

"Whatever you're doing, I'm sorry but we have bigger problems." He pointed ahead. Fallon followed his gaze through the trees and up a tall incline. From here she could see a shining light. No, reflecting light — a waterfall. Yet this one was far grander than the one she climbed in Midgard.

Then, she squinted. "What is that?"

It looked like a blanket of darkness had been tossed over a dead forest. The sunlight just seemed to *stop*, leaving the crooked and tangled trees cast in darkness. The line too perfect to be natural went up the side of the waterfall, , but the water remained glistening.

Ronen swallowed. "That is where I'm willing to bet our senile caretaker is headed. The waterfall is Merrow Cove. It used to be a popular, beautiful place to visit and swim. But every year since the royals died out, Ondorr has spread. It has grown the most here, seeping into the waters," he explained.

The back of the waterfall disappeared into a misty, black haze. As they got closer, Fallon felt invisible hands were pushing her backwards. Pushing her away from that dark, dark place that felt all too familiar.

"Ondorr is a place?" she asked.

He hesitated. "You explained your night and day to me, now let me explain mine to you. Ondorr was created when the gods killed the first Shapeshifter. When they did, some sort of explosion caused a shadow to spread. It grew and grew, giving birth to more monsters and hybrids, each more malicious than the last. When the Sentinels—shadow men—and Shapeshifters began coming into Lysserah to spread plagues, we went to war. It has been at bay ever since, but there is a rumor that one Shapeshifter survived. That's why it's growing again," he explained.

"Do you think the rumor is true?"

"I think nothing is perfect. Everything has an opposite … a bad side. Dark; light, wet; dry, warm; cold, right; wrong. And that right there is Elphyne's dirty little secret. You can't have a perfect realm," he said between breaths. "Everyone thinks Nøkken fought on Ondorr's side during the war."

She punched his arm. "Not all of them. Now let's hurry, I want Elowen in sight."

As they approached Merrow Cove, Fallon had to slow down to take in all its grandeur. Not one, but three waterfalls in a semicircle plunged into a shimmering basin. The water was a stunning green, like the tears of an emerald. This close, she had to crank her head back to see the top.

"There you two are!" an angry voice called out.

Fallon could not help but sigh in relief to see Elowen twirling around in her ruffled dress. Sometimes, Fallon still dreamed of the gaunt, pale girl on the other side of the bars. The one who held Fallon's hand while she pulled off bits of clothing melted into her skin.

Fallon turned to see if Ronen was armed with another excuse for their absence, but his face was as green as the water. "What's wrong now?" she whispered.

He swallowed. "You don't do heights, I don't do water," he sputtered.

"Stay back then."

Despite the reeking forest behind it, the only tree around was one planted on a small island in the middle of the massive plunge pool. It had a short trunk, its bright green leaves erupted into a cloud-like shape. Within it were yellow dots … fruit.

She tilted her head to the side. "A fruit tree? In the middle of a waterfall?" Just when she thought she was used to the peculiarity of this realm, it outdid itself.

She turned to Ronen for an explanation, but he just shrugged at her. Elowen picked up on Ronen's distress and was gently rubbing his back, his cheeks quickly changing from green to red.

"Why are we so close to Ondorr?" Fallon asked as Elma approached them.

Everyone turned to her in surprise. "Well, you don't have to shout," Elma huffed.

"What?" Fallon strained her ears. All she could hear was the cacophonous crashing of water, making her friends sound very far away. She placed her hands over her ears, trying to block out some sound so she could focus.

"Let me guess," Fallon went on, trying not to yell. "This is some sort of challenge. That is a magical fruit you want us to cross this dangerous water to retrieve?"

Elma chuckled. "If you count something being delicious as being magical, then yes. It is a lemon tree."

"Oh." Fallon felt her ears get warm as the others snickered at her.

Elma continued, "I planted it there myself, many years ago. Its roots drink from the waters below. The health of the tree shows me the purity of the water," she explained.

Fallon tilted her head back to see razor sharp thorns growing like skeletal hands down to the rocky ledge. "You worry Ondorr will seep into the water?"

She nodded solemnly. "It already has. Many Merrows have died of an incurable illness due to it," she said.

Fallon turned. "What's a Merrow?"

She heard Ronen laugh humorlessly. "You're really in for a treat this time if you thought the Centaurs were bad," he said from behind her.

"Don't you have some business to attend to?" she asked impatiently.

He eyed her curiously, then caught on. "Oh—yeah, Elma I'm going to go take a leak." He turned on his heel.

"I do not think it is wise for us to split up again!"

Ronen turned and held out his arms. "Well then, does anyone care to come watch?"

The three women stood motionless.

"That's what I thought," he said and continued back into the trees.

TWENTY-ONE

Luckily, Elma did not make her go babysit Ronen.

Instead, she pulled them forward to the rocky brink of Merrow Cove. She squinted across the water, "My eyesight is not what it used to be. Fallon, dear, can you spot if any lemons are rotten?"

She was about to say *absolutely not*; the tree was nearly forty meters away. Yet as Fallon squinted her eyes, they focused on many yellow dots. Some of which were not yellow ... but dark and wrinkled.

"There's a handful of bad ones," she said. "Maybe five."

Elma gave her a cheeky smile. Fallon did not like that smile one bit. She also did not like the fact she could see, hear, and smell nearly everything here. Fallon didn't like it. She gave up magic in Halvar for a reason. She was a mortal, heading back to conquer and claim her mortal homeland.

Elma then reached into the bags Fallon carried, rummaging through the contents. "Even one is too many.

I might have waited too long this time …" She continued to mumble to herself about rationing out her supply.

Elowen, however, was three steps behind them. She wrung her apron in her hands and looked over her shoulder again and again. Fallon carefully set down the bags and walked up to her friend.

"Elo, what's wrong?" she asked.

The Hulder shifted from foot to foot. "I don't like being this close to Ondorr. It smells funny," she whispered.

Indeed, Fallon also picked up on a scent that sent a chill through her. It was like someone tossed rotting meat into a pool of sulfur. "It's alright, an entire waterfall separates us. Elma will hurry, won't you?" she asked over her shoulder. The old woman was setting up groups of multiple jars and burlap sacks.

"The more hands the better. If we want to get this done quickly, I will need your help," she said. She reached into the heaviest bag and pulled out a miniature cauldron.

They watched Elma grind, pour, and stir together a batch of yellow liquid. While she worked, Fallon walked along the water's edge. She peered into the crisp turquoise water, but saw no fish. Or Merrows. Maybe they were invisible.

"I wouldn't get too close to the edge, dear," Elma warned. "The Merrows hold a bit of a grudge against the surface. They felt abandoned after the war and left to be consumed by Ondorr. I alone cannot stop the shadow from spreading, but Mother Merrow asked me to help in any way I can."

Fallon threw up her arms. "Maybe if I knew what a Mother Merrow was, I would be better at avoiding them," she exclaimed.

Elma stood and wiped the grass from the bottom of her brown robes. "There is only one Mother. She gives birth to all Merrows. She has given me the honor of calling her by her name, Agnetha."

"One mother? Like ants and bees?" Fallon turned to Elowen. "Please tell me you have ants and bees here."

"Bees don't want to be touched," she confirmed.

Fallon snuck a glance over the water once again, tilting her head to the side. "Bees and ants," she whispered to herself. Her head dropped to stare at the ground beneath her feet. If the Merrows were not here, then where were they?

"This is the entrance to a colony, isn't it?" she asked at last. There must be an entire aquatic ecosystem under her own boots.

"You are clever." Elma smiled proudly, gesturing to the bubbling cauldron. "But more importantly, you are strong. All I need now are three lemons." She smiled at her expectantly.

Fallon glanced back and forth between the crashing water and the old woman. "You mean from that specific tree?"

"Yes."

"No other lemon will do?"

"No."

"What exactly are you making?" she asked suspiciously.

Elma tentatively packed away her empty bottles. "A special kind of purifier. You see, Ondorr has two weaknesses: sunlight and saltwater. All Faeries, Merrows included, are freshwater folk. If I were to simply pour saltwater into the cove, it would only add to the damage. So, I made a recipe for artificial sunlight," she said.

A wave of anxiety rushed through Fallon. Artificial light? Is that what Fallon had been doing all those weeks ago? She and Jaeger thought her powers of light were foreign ... but maybe Elma knew something others did not.

Elowen bent down and sniffed the cauldron. "Does it truly work like sunlight?" she asked.

Elma shook her head sadly. "It is not nearly as potent, but it is all I can do. And I fear I will not be able to do it for much longer—radiation is not easy to come by. Only certain rocks found deep in the Boudevijn Mines contain enough to grind up. It is an extremely dangerous task only an Orculli can do." She placed her hands on her hips. Elma wore such large and abundant robes; Fallon forgot the woman was actually quite petite.

Sun rocks? "Where are the mines? Can we go get more?" she asked. Maybe the secret to Fallon's old powers lay there as well.

"Boudevijn is on the other side of Elphyne. If you think the Longback Knolls are tall, the eastern mountains are monumental. They must be to house the Orculli, the three-legged giants of the east," Elma explained.

Fallon pressed her knuckles into her eyes. "My brain has no more room for this information," she groaned.

Elma laughed lightly. "It will all come with time, dear. Let's just focus on today. Now, back to those lemons." She pointed again.

They all turned to the lone tree. Fallon could not deny the beauty in front of her, but she was too on edge to really enjoy it. Something did not feel completely right. Maybe it was just Ondorr whispering to her, but she was just about ready to pick up Elowen and leave.

"I am not swimming anywhere before you tell me more about Merrows," Fallon said. She knew she could make it to the little island in ordinary waters, but she did not want any surprises.

Elma sighed impatiently. "Much like Centaurs, the Merfolk of this realm are misunderstood. They are playful and curious, they just sometimes forget that surface creatures can't breathe underwater," she said nonchalantly.

"Then it will not be my fault if I have to give them a quick reminder," she grumbled as she knelt to remove her boots.

Elma rolled her eyes. "Just pocket three lemons, then swim back. There is no need to fret; the Merrows will only come to the surface when I pour in the potion."

Fallon desperately wanted to complain, but this was far better than being asked to climb. She knew of Merfolk, her mother told her to stay away from sirens and mermaids. The half fish, half woman hybrids had charmspeak. Much like her Hulder friend. That would also make Ronen half seductor. Fallon almost laughed out loud, that boy had about as much charmspeak as a toad.

Would Ronen call himself her friend? Fallon was still not sure what qualified as friendship. She did wish the Nøkken was here, though. He could probably just walk across the water's surface if he wasn't so traumatized. Never the matter, she could do this. Hopefully.

Elowen rummaged through a few bags until she came up with a thin, but long bundle of rope. "Here," she said, tying it around Fallon's waist. "Now you can't drown." She gave her an encouraging smile. Elowen clutched the other end of the rope so tightly her tan knuckles turned white.

Fallon grabbed Elowen's hands. "I will be fine, Elo. I will grab an extra lemon for you," she whispered. That got a real smile out of her.

Making sure her hair was tightly secured in a braid, Fallon took two deep breaths before diving in.

Fallon braced for the skin-biting cold she was used to, but this water was pleasantly warm. It was soft against her skin, like rolling in satin sheets. She breached the surface and started kicking, keeping her breath in rhythm with her strokes.

The farther she went, the louder it got. Fallon could feel the currents tugging her every which way, but she kept her pace consistent. Fallon had to keep her head straight. The last thing she needed was to veer off track and exhaust herself.

Elowen cheered from the shore, but soon enough even her voice was drowned out by the crashing of water.

Fallon stopped to tread water for a moment and catch her breath. Thankfully, she was nearly halfway there. She flipped onto her back and circled her arms to use different muscles.

This, however, was a mistake. Because now, Fallon couldn't see the depths below her. Nor what lurks within them.

She kept seeing flashes out of the corner of her eyes. She told herself it was just the waterfall splashing, but waterfalls weren't *purple*.

Merrows.

Her adrenaline kicked in, making her heart race and her feet kick faster and faster. When she flipped back around, it suddenly dawned on her how deep this cove was. Fallon could not see the bottom, only the tunnel that appeared to go all the way to the center of the world.

Panting heavily, Fallon realized she might have overestimated herself. Her body became heavy, and her feet began to drag. She felt a dull pain on her waist and realized it was not the water she was fighting—it was the rope.

It must be too short. And Fallon knew Elowen would never let go of it.

She was a lot closer to the island than to the shore, so she made the quick decision to untie the rope around her.

Once Fallon felt it drop, she immediately went back to paddling. The back of her neck tingled in sickening anticipation. She felt like something was about to grab her any second, but then her hand smashed into something hard. Fallon swore she felt something graze her ankles as she pulled herself up onto the grass and rolled as if her life depended on it.

She made it. Fallon only felt safe when her entire body lay flat on dry land. As she caught her breath, she stared up into a sky full of leaves and lemons. The tree was bigger than she expected, though she supposed this was no ordinary lemon tree. *Nothing* in Elphyne was ordinary.

Her clothes stuck uncomfortably to her skin as Fallon sat up to look for her friends. They were waving their arms and jumping up and down, so she waved back to show she was alright. She wished she could hear them, but now Fallon was surrounded by a waterfall on three sides. The sheer volume of it was maddening.

The island was about the size of her chamber back in the hearth cave. There was grass, some rocks here and there, but what caught her eye were the many decomposing lemons on the ground. They were mushed in and brown, fertilizing the tree with their lives. Fallon had not seen these before. She needed to tell Elma this was worse than they thought.

The smell of the rotting fruit was enough to make her gag as she plucked three good lemons from the tree. Stuffing them into her pockets, she caught sight of a bad one just out of arm's reach.

Fallon took a hesitant step forward. The lemon was not moldy or brown—it was turning black. Inky veins spread across its pale, dry surface. She examined the ones at her feet; they were as dry and shriveled as raisins. The very life sucked out of them. This was *much* worse than they thought.

She turned back to the shore, trying to signal to her friends she was headed back. But Elma and Elowen were still waving their arms wildly … and Elowen was still clutching that rope tight in her hands.

Something was wrong.

Fallon should have trusted her gut. She spun in a circle, watching the water carefully. Hidden within the ripples, flashes of purple broke the surface; fins. There was one to her left—then her right. Then both.

She was surrounded.

Fallon had to think. Saltwater and sunlight. They hate saltwater and sunlight—

Then, the noise around her slowly faded into the background. The pressure lifting from her eardrums was enough to make her sigh in relief. Soon after, she heard the softest, most sumptuous sound lazily dance down her ears. It was like someone ran a feather down a harp. It was so gentle on her sore ears she was nearly brought to tears. Where was it coming from?

She got on her knees, practically crawling to the water's edge and peered into the glassy surface. Fallon saw her own reflection staring up at her, eyes unfocused and hollow. She had to know where it was coming from. She wanted to go there and never hear the horrors of the world ever again.

When the noise suddenly stopped and she remembered her name, it was already too late. Fallon heard Elowen's horrified shriek all the way from the shore as two webbed hands grabbed onto her wrists. All she saw was purple scales and sharp teeth as she was pulled into the depths.

TWENTY-TWO

Emotions were the cruelest gift the gods ever gave. Men begged for the ability to create and destroy worlds, so they gave him the ability to create and destroy himself instead.

So after one of the worst nights of his life, the absolute last thing Ronen wanted to do was *go for a walk*.

Then it got even worse when two bags were tossed on his shoulders and he got stuck walking with the human question mark. Every time Fallon asked him something, a small part of him was tempted to just make up an answer horrifying enough that she would stop. Why not? She was not staying long enough for it to matter.

He tried to bathe again last night. After that failed, he lowered his standards to just washing his hands.

Ronen touched the water, stared at it until his eyes hurt, and he felt nothing. Absolutely nothing. No connection or magical bond. He was just a mortal washing his hands. On the inside, Ronen always knew he had no powers. Confirming it just hurt worse than he expected. That little speck of hope was gone. Maybe Fallon was right; hope was dangerous.

Then why was he here? Why did the Little Folk save him and not just let the Nøkken die out? Maybe the only reason they let him live was because he *was* so useless. If the only good kind of Nøkken was a dead one, maybe the best kind was a powerless one.

If he *could* control water, would Ronen be the same person? Would he still be here, right now, pretending to take the world's longest piss while his companions chatted with Merfolk? Maybe he could have earned the respect of the Fae. Or maybe they would have just killed him a lot sooner.

And then there was her.

Why couldn't she just hate him like everybody else? Ronen had spent the better part of their journey to Merrow Cove mentally preparing to tell her and Elowen. And then when she shoved him, something in him snapped. He was done. He was done lying, done trying, done hoping he could pretend to be anything other than what he was.

But then she wasn't afraid of what he was, and he didn't know how to feel about it.

Ronen was quite certain he did not *like* Fallon. She was a little too … fiery. Not the kind of fire that warmed up the room, but the kind that burned your house down if left unattended. It was probably more of the fact she was the first woman to ever give him the time of day. Plus, after seeing her in action, she was the kind of person he wanted on his side. She was doubtlessly crazy and lacked most manners, but you would be a fool to go against her.

Elowen was a completely different story. Once she warmed up to him, she was what Ronen imagined a sister would be. At first it appeared like she preferred to stay in the background, but Ronen learned she just blended with the natural world so seamlessly you forgot she wasn't a flower. She floated as a breeze through the cave, putting out all the fires Fallon started. He knew there was so much more to her than just a beautiful face. But Fallon protected her so fiercely, Ronen feared she would unintentionally shield her from all the good parts of the world, too.

It actually frightened him how often Elowen just seemed to appear when he was upset. Even this morning, she had walked in on him staring absently into the mirror on his desk. Well, it had been a mirror before Ronen put his fist through it. The ghost servants cleaned up the shards on the ground, but there was no putting it back together. With all the cracks and missing pieces, all that stared back at Ronen was a frown and one blue eye.

Elowen tapped lightly on the wall, making him jump in surprise. "Ronen? Your breakfast is getting cold," she said gently from the doorway.

"It's morning already?" he asked, shaking the thoughts from his head.

She timidly entered the room and sat down on the opposite end of his bed, holding her hands in her lap. "Did you have trouble sleeping?" she asked. Her bare feet swung nervously, toes barely grazing the floor.

Ronen did not want to bother her with his thoughts. "I guess so, but that's normal for me."

"Is lying normal for you, too?" she asked quietly.

He could not help but chuckle at her bluntness. "It wasn't always. I think I've changed. Or maybe I've always felt this way and was just too distracted to notice," he said.

"I changed too," she said after a moment. "I get nightmares sometimes. It all started when I woke up after Fallon saved me from shade-poisoning. I think there's a little black dot still inside of me," she said, placing a hand over her heart.

When he said nothing, Elowen scooted closer and placed her hand on his heart. "I think you have a little black dot too. Have you ever been poisoned?"

His skin erupted in goosebumps where her hand touched. "Yes."

She nodded. "It must be a marking of some kind, like a scar on the skin. I'm sorry that happened to you, Ronen. You didn't deserve it, you don't belong there," she said. A single sentence, but it touched his lifelong deprivation of sympathy.

Ronen caught a glimpse of his eye in the mirror. Cold, solid blue. "How do you know?"

"Because it hurt you," she said simply. "And the sun healed you, just like me and every other Lysserah Faerie. I think you have been spending too much time with that black dot." she said, jabbing her finger into the center of his chest.

"Alright, you might have a point." He laughed. "What about you? What are you going to do with your black dot?" he asked in return.

She thought for a moment, squeezing her eyes shut in concentration. Elowen must have been around six or seven when the Entrance Tree was locked. How had a young Hulder ended up on the wrong side?

"Fallon says warriors slay their demons," she said quietly.

"Well, what does Elowen say?"

She finally looked at him. She truly was the most stunning Hulder he had ever seen. "I think … I think I'm going to take care of mine," she said at last.

Even now as he walked through the trees, Ronen was still thinking of her words. The darkness had left a permanent fingerprint on her soul, and she wanted to keep it safe. Treat it as her own. Perhaps Ronen had done himself a disservice by tossing away and hating every broken part of him. No one wanted to help that little boy at the orphanage; the fangless one with mismatched eyes and round ears. Maybe he could hold his own hand. The older, somewhat-wiser Ronen had plenty of advice for that boy.

He was on his third lap around a small grove of trees, swatting away Anthousai as they flew around his head and through his hair. The pesky flower Faeries giggled like bells, whispering among themselves.

The flashes of color and the buzzing of their insect-like wings was giving him a headache. Ronen was just about ready to take off his boot and—

A loud scream echoed through the valley, sending the Faeries zipping into the trees.

Elowen.

Ronen ran. Luckily, he had not strayed too far. As he neared, he saw Elowen and Elma standing at the shoreline. They seemed unharmed but when he got closer, he saw one unoccupied pair of brown boots lying in the grass. Of course she was the problem.

"What happened?" he asked, whipping his head in every direction. There were no Centaurs, no Merrows, no Valdyr or any sign of danger. It was actually quite pretty.

Elowen went to her knees, frantically splashing her arms around in the water. "Let her go!" she shrieked.

Ronen had to pull her back so she did not fall in. He turned to Elma, but the old woman was consumed by shock. "Elma! What happened?" he asked again.

But her eyes were transfixed at her feet, where a travel-sized black cauldron had appeared. "I don't understand, it's as if they thought she was …" she trailed off, staring at the yellow liquid.

Ronen was officially irritated at the lack of explanation going on. He grabbed Elowen's shoulders and made her look at him, her pale green eyes were wide with fear. "Where is Fallon?" he asked, taking time to enunciate each word.

Snot dripped down her nose as Elowen gulped down her sobs. "I can't swim," she whispered.

He turned back to the cove, his blood running cold. Far out, he could see bubbles erupting on the surface — they took her. Fallon was going to drown. He was going to watch her die. No, Ronen was going to *let* her die if he didn't do something.

The water seemed to stare back up at him in challenge. Ronen had no powers, no magic, and no advantage. He wanted to spit in the water and walk away. Walk far, far away from that useless Nøkken inside of him.

I think I'm going to take care of it.

Maybe he was done bullying himself into submission. Maybe he was done shattering the already broken pieces just to feel sorry for himself.

Ronen carefully set down a screaming Elowen. He did not think, care, or consider the consequences before he dived in.

As it turned out, Ronen also did not know how to swim. Luckily it was a lot easier than he thought. In fact, pushing his way through the water was even easier than running as he made his way towards the disturbance in the water.

At first, all he could see was a tornado of bubbles, seaweed, and fins. Merrows were much larger than Fae, mostly because of their long tails. From the waist down was a fish's tail covered in purple scales, and from the waist up they were somewhat human. They each had different lengths of green hair, but they all had those angular, pure white eyes with no pupils or mercy.

He saw her. She was surrounded with four Merrows pulling her down with their webbed hands. Fallon was putting up an admirable fight, kicking and thrashing with all she had. Ronen rose to take one last breath before diving down.

They were deep enough that the pressure on his body made his eyes start to bulge. Fallon's movements became slower, as the last bit of air must be leaving her lungs. Ronen mentally called out to her, begging her to look up as he clawed his way through the water toward her.

By some miracle, she did. Strings of blood floated around her from where the Merrows had scratched at her skin and bit her with their mouth full of fangs. The sight angered him, enough to waste at least thirty seconds of air by shouting, "*Stop!*" into the water.

To everyone's surprise, the Merrows let go. They turned to him and made a strange hissing noise. He watched the gills on their necks open and close twice before they darted off, waving their long bodies through the water with unnerving speed.

He was almost there. He kicked and kicked, now completely upside down as he dived for her.

Fallon reached her hand up towards him, but her legs stopped kicking. The world around them moved in slow motion. It seemed as if the closer he got, the farther she sank. Her chest began to heave, taking in water.

Fallon's hair rose around her face like a fiery halo as she locked eyes with him. From above, sunlight broke through the water sending fractals of light across her freckled face. He was only a hand's length away as a beam caught her eye, illuminating the golden fibers in her iris so they glowed.

The water around him iced over, freezing them in time.

His mind flashed back and forth between the face before him, and the face he had seen weeks ago in the throne room: the queen made of stained glass. *That's* why Fallon always seemed so familiar to him—they were practically twins.

Finally, his hand closed on hers and time started again. Ronen's body was on autopilot as he pulled them up. His heart pushed against his chest so powerfully he thought it might burst.

They broke the surface. Ronen pulled her in and used his arm to squeeze Fallon until she started to cough. She was a useless lump of soggy hair and muscle as he paddled them towards the sound of Elowen's shouts.

The Hulder was waist-deep in the water waiting for them. She let out a sob as she helped him drag Fallon onto the shore. They were both gasping for air as they flopped onto the grass. Elowen held back Fallon's hair as she spent a good minute hacking up water, but Ronen was motionless. He just stared at her. How had he not seen it earlier? And more importantly, what on Ondorr did it mean?

Fallon wiped her mouth with the back of her hand and turned to Elma, seething with rage. "Is that what you call *curiosity*, witch?" she screamed, her voice raw. Ronen swore he saw steam rising from her head.

Elma smiled nervously. "Did you get the lemons?"

Fallon made a face of disbelief. She rummaged through her pockets, angrily tossing one at the ground with each word: "Damn. You. All."

She took a few full breaths, and some of the color returned to her lips. Fallon turned towards him, giving him a low nod.

"But not you," she corrected.

Every time she looked at him, all Ronen could see was those glowing eyes …

"Ronen?" Fallon slowly got to her feet. "What's wrong?"

She took a few steps forward, but Ronen crawled backwards in fright. It didn't make any sense. It was impossible.

"Fal … Fallon, you look *exactly* like the dead queen: Asta Alfrothul."

TWENTY-THREE

One name, and Fallon was drowning again.

Her chest collapsed at the sound of the name she thought only existed in her mind. Fallon felt like they were all moving impossibly slow, each breath lasting an eternity longer than the last.

Ronen just stared at her. His face was slack with fear and surprise—fear of *her*. Little did he know, she was just as terrified of him in this moment. Elowen and Elma went quiet, why was everyone so quiet? It left room for the word to echo through her soul: *Asta, Asta, Asta.*

Fallon approached him tentatively, and thankfully Ronen did not run away this time. He only flinched as Fallon reached forward and wrapped her arms around him in a tight embrace, ignoring their soggy clothes slapping together and the smell of fish.

"I cannot remember the last time I heard another person say my mother's name," she whispered. Then, she laughed. She laughed as her body quivered with emotion. Asta had truly existed.

"Uh, Elma …" he patted her back gently. "I think I broke Fallon."

Everyone laughed as the tension drained from around them. Ronen turned pink as a radish as she pulled away. She used her thumb to move the brown hair sticking to his face so she could see his eyes: striking blue and chestnut brown.

Yes, it should be impossible for Ronen to know her name. She should be questioning why he put *queen* in front of it. But Fallon did not want to worry about that right now. For just one, ephemeral breath, she wanted to savor the fact that she was not the sole carrier of her mother's memory.

But Ronen did not share her endearment. "Your *mother*? The one you told me was dead? But that … that means you—you're Elphyne's lost princess," he whispered in awe. Then, his face iced over. "That means you're Fae."

A month ago, when Jaeger had told her just about the same thing, Fallon denied it. A part of her still wanted to. Fallon always knew her mother had been special, so hearing she was Fae made sense. But a queen of an entire realm …

Fallon felt all her blood pool at her feet. "But that can't be true." She shook her head. Fallon turned to Elma. "It must be a coincidence. My mother would have told me if she were a bloody queen! She would have taken me here. She—Asta would *never* leave me with Beowulf all this time! Her name was Asta Solveij, and I was Fallon

Solveij. Not Alfrothul," she insisted, struggling to even say the strange surname.

Fallon refused to believe it, but her heart broke with every word. All the comfort and glee she felt only moments ago melted off of her, exposing her raw, untreated wounds.

The grim expression Elma gave her only made Fallon feel worse. "Alfrothul was her maiden name, child. Before she married your father."

"No!" Fallon shouted, loud enough to make Elowen jump. "I don't believe you."

Fallon had to sit down. She rubbed her eyes and chewed on her knuckles as it all came together. Fallon might have finally found the missing part of the puzzle; the reason behind all of Asta's strange behaviors.

Elma's bottom lip wobbled. "I must finish my work here, then we will go back to the cave and speak. I didn't wish it to happen this way," she said in a distressed tone.

"You knew?" Fallon asked dangerously. She began to tremble so violently the water was shaken from her hair. "Since the Entrance Tree you knew, didn't you? That's why you've always treated me differently?"

The old woman with heartbroken eyes nodded slowly. She turned to Ronen, who had been standing back quietly. "Please, help me pour this so we can go," Elma asked.

He was staring daggers at Fallon. He needed to be careful, she was really in the mood to hit something. Ronen walked past her with a cold shoulder as he and

Elma lifted the cauldron and poured the contents into the water.

Elowen sat down in front of Fallon and grabbed her hands. "You can talk to me," she said.

She did not know where to start. She rocked back and forth, blinking away every tear that came, never letting one touch her cheek. "I only saw my mother for weeks at a time. Then, she would leave for a month or two. She said she was taking care of foreign business, as was her duty. But if she was here … if she truly came to Elphyne during that time, that means she chose to leave me behind."

After an entire winter came and went when Fallon was nearing the age of five, she knew something was wrong. Her mother missed many parts of her life, but she never missed one of her birthdays. Yet she did that time and every year after.

Fallon came to accept that Asta had died. Maybe in an enemy clan ambush or a tragedy in travel. Asta *must* have died, because Fallon refused to believe her mother would just leave her with Beowulf when she knew damn well how he treated her.

But she did. "If my own mother left me to die when she could have saved me, how am I supposed to live with that?" she muttered. Fallon squeezed her legs and pulled her hair. She was too aware of the grass under her, too aware of the drop of water sliding down her calf and the saliva in her mouth. Fallon needed to leave. She wanted to turn all her senses off and just take a break from existing.

Elowen scooted closer and shook her head. "There's always more to the story, Fallon."

"No." Fallon stood up. "No. She didn't want me here. If she left me with Beowulf, then that was her final wish," she said coldly. Fallon started off towards the cave. She needed to grab what little things she had and pack a bag for her trip back to the Entrance Tree.

Luckily, no one bothered to stop her. The path they took here was simple enough to trace back, and soon the Longback Knolls came into view. Her fingers cramped from being clenched into fists for so long, and her skin was raw and sensitive from being rubbed against her damp clothes. But the pain and discomfort were the only thing keeping her present in the moment, otherwise Fallon would be spiraling down, down, down. Towards all the ruins inside of her. Where she would find nothing but ashes, rust, and a forbidden power chained inside a box.

The harder she tried to run away from the truth, the closer it became. But why Beowulf? Why Barwyn? It was as if she was trying to escape everything Elphyne was. Escape being queen …

Fallon felt so trapped in her own mind and body, she might have walked straight into the ocean and never noticed. But something caught her attention. Something that tugged on her instincts, making her stop at the base of the mountain.

"Fallon?" Elowen asked as they caught up with her. "What's the matter?"

She turned to Elma. "Someone else is here." She didn't know how she knew it, but she could smell the past. Someone had walked right here, not that long ago.

Surprisingly, a long smile spread on the woman's face. She hiked up her robes and hurried up the trail like a giddy young girl.

Fallon held her arm up to her friends. "Stay here, I'm going to check—"

Ronen forcefully shoved past her. "You're not in charge of me."

She reached out and grabbed the back of his collar, pulling him back behind her. He tried to fight, but she kept her grip and pressed her forearm into his neck. "But I'm in charge of her. You *stay behind me*, Nøkken, so at least she can run while they're busy breaking your bones," she hissed.

He slapped her arm off, his eyes two tones of blazing fury. Fallon walked off before he could say anything else, but at least he stayed by Elowen. Petty, petty men.

Men. That was what she smelled. It was not necessarily a bad smell, it just seemed to carry every masculine trait within it. Fallon followed it all the way into the cave mouth where Elma had already disappeared into. Slowly, she parted the vines. Peeking just enough to see—

"Oh."

Males. Positively males.

Two large figures stood on either side of Elma, who was smiling bigger than Fallon had ever seen. The larger one had tan skin and dark, braided hair. While his companion was slim and fair, with blond hair almost as long as Elowen's.

As soon as she let out a breath, their heads snapped to her. Fallon might as well have announced her presence with trumpets and banners. Sighing through her nose, she stepped into the hearth cave and slowly approached.

The man with a thin face grinned at her, eyes green and misty. His friend, however, was stone-faced as he stared her down. Fallon took in their pointed ears and felt the magnitude of their presence. They both wore a leaf-shaped chest plate made of what might be gold, over a finely stitched green uniform—warriors. Fae warriors.

Fallon was about to say something, but unfortunately for them all, Ronen beat her to it.

"No!" he cried as he dragged Elowen through the vines, "Elma, you turned us in?"

Angry, and quite frankly embarrassed, Fallon turned to him with wide eyes. "Were you dropped on your head as an infant?" she asked through her teeth. He was going to get them all killed.

"You don't understand, Fallon. We need to get out of here!" he urged. Elowen was peeking over his shoulder and making heart eyes at the blond.

A gruff voice interrupted them. "Shall we leave so you two can continue to argue loudly in private?" the taller one asked.

She bit the inside of her cheek. This was *not* how Fallon wanted to handle this situation. The stupid boy was throwing her off her game. She tried to start over, rolling her shoulders back and acting like she did not just crawl out of a lake. "Elma, what—"

"Fallon ... there's *really* something you should know."

She whipped around, ready to wring his neck. "Interrupt me one more time and so help me Odin—"

"*Fallon!*" It was only the genuine fear in his eyes that stopped her from using one of those vines to hang him. "That walking sack of meat is Bhaltair Herleif, General of the Valdyr. And Fritjof's right hand man," he whispered.

She looked back and forth between them. The grim male was glaring at Ronen with just about as much disdain as she was. "You two know each other, I presume?" she asked.

"Oh yeah, we go way back," Ronen snapped.

He gave an unimpressed huff. "I don't imagine I'm getting that thank you I deserve," Bhaltair said. His voice was rough as granite. He had a predatory gaze that made Fallon straighten her spine. With one glimpse she felt like he knew all her weaknesses. She wouldn't be surprised if he knew what she had for breakfast this morning.

Ronen took her by surprise by stepping in front of her. Maybe he had a death wish after all. "Thank you, general generosity, for abducting me from my home and throwing me into a pit to die. I really couldn't have done it without you." He bowed his head with enough disrespect that made even Fallon want to punch him.

Bhaltair stalked forward, and every hair on Fallon's body stood up. She instantly pulled Ronen back, even though she should let him learn where that smart mouth of his could get him.

The general halted, only inches from her. Gods above, Fallon barely reached his chin. From here she could see his pointed ears, dark stubble, and wicked fangs he bared in warning. The man's eyes were a glowing, feline yellow. She could not lean back, stand down, or so much as blink as he sized her up. Just as Hagen had taught her.

He flicked his eyes once towards Elowen, and suddenly Fallon didn't care how massive he was. She bared her teeth back, giving him a single warning: *mine*. Ronen and Elowen were hers. To touch them was to declare war on Fallon and her army of inner demons.

"Your name is Fallon?" he asked. He had no lines on his rugged face, as if he had never smiled in his life.

Fallon gave a low nod. She could not expose her neck. Her hips were turned slightly to keep her left side—where the more important organs were—farther from reach.

Then, Bhaltair turned his back to her.

Fallon scoffed, trying to keep her face from being visibly offended. Absolute dismissal. He apparently decided Fallon was no threat at all if he so carelessly exposed his back to her.

He walked back to his comrade. "It is true. You can see it clear as day. She has her mother's eyes."

An angry, estranged noise left Fallon's mouth. She was starting to unravel. For years she longed for someone to talk about her mother, but this wasn't what she wanted to hear. This is not what she has been imagining for the past nineteen years.

Bhaltair's back was still turned. She planned to land a kick right in between those wide shoulders, but Fallon only got three steps in before her feet suddenly got stuck to the ground.

She cursed, looking down to see two vines wrapped tightly around her ankles. Fallon was too amazed to be angry. Magic was real, and it was terrifying.

Elowen quickly pattered up, and as soon as her hands touched the vines, they relaxed enough for Fallon to slip through. The Hulder had trembling hands and wide eyes as she observed the towering males before them.

Elma finally spoke up. "I believe some introductions are in order." she said as calmly as possible.

Now Ronen stepped up, and the tension in the room became palpable. "No offense Elma, but I don't think sitting around the campfire and sharing stories is going to work this time. Besides, I know everything I need to know," Ronen said, crossing his arms.

Bhaltair's brow twitched slightly. "Do you?" he asked testily. He stood with his hands clasped behind his back. Nothing about his immaculate posture showed he even cared any of them were there.

"Who do you think showed the Little Folk where to find you in the first place, boy? And who has kept the Valdyr off your tail ever since? This place has done well to mask your scent, but it will not last forever," he said with a sour tone.

Ronen dropped his arms and turned to Fallon for help, but she only shrugged.

"How did you know I would be headed for the Entrance Tree?" he asked.

For the first time, the slightest shadow of a smile crossed the general's face. "Cowards always run."

Fallon put her hands up. "You two can finish this later. I want to know what business the General of the Valdyr has knowing what my mother's eyes looked like," she said, a little grossed out.

Elma grabbed her hands. "Fallon, dear, if you have any trust for me at all, you can trust him. He is my son," she said with a smile. If it were not for that grin on her face, that gleam of a mother's pride, Fallon would never believe her.

"*What?*" She and Ronen cried in unison.

Elowen smiled back and forth at them. "Oh, I see the resemblance! You must be so proud," she said, taking a single step forward.

But Fallon quickly pulled Elowen away, still not trusting Bhaltair and his quiet friend. Ronen, however, appeared more confused than any of them. He pointed to them respectively, "How did *that* come out of *that*?" he blanched.

The blond man let out a soft chuckle. Bhaltair shot his comrade a look saying *don't encourage him*.

Fallon leaned down and picked up the biggest rock she could find. "Alright, the next person to tell me a lie is getting their mouths rearranged."

Elowen immediately ripped the rock from Fallon's hand and gave her a disciplinary point. "No!"

Then, the quiet man with soft features began to move his hands. He made various, smooth gestures with his slender fingers. Fallon flinched at first, expecting some sort of strange magic to appear in front of her. But after a moment, Bhaltair just let out a huff of a laugh. "I was thinking precisely the same thing."

Still on edge, Fallon tensed. "What was that?"

"Oh, I'm sorry, is it finally my turn to speak?" The general sneered. "This is my second, Captain Enok Ellwood," he said.

Enok gave them all a warm, close-lipped smile. He had the eyes of a deep forest, and with one glance at her feet the vines crawled back into the ground. He was the one who commanded them.

"Did you rip out his tongue or something?" Ronen asked.

Bhaltair did not even blink. "He does not speak."

"Yeah? You should take some lessons."

The Fae warrior took one step forward, and once again Fallon had to place herself between the two haughty men. Bhaltair peered down at her with a raised brow. His nostrils flared delicately—he was scenting her.

"Enok said that though you may resemble her, you are nothing like Asta," Bhaltair translated.

"I'm nothing like a woman who left her child to die in a frozen wasteland? I will take that as a compliment."

"Fallon!" Elma cried.

"What?" she cried back. Fallon felt the last few strings holding her together finally snap. "What could you possibly say to defend her? I was *alone* there, Elma! Do you have any idea what Beowulf did to me? I was marked as a bastard because of her absence. Every single day was just torment and trial like the swinging of a pendulum. And you know what? I stitched *myself* back together. I don't need her because she made me learn to live without her!"

Silence.

Enok shook his head sadly and turned to his friend, but Bhaltair's eyes were glued to the wall behind her.

Fallon let out the breath she hadn't noticed she was holding and turned to Elowen, but the Hulder wilted away. Pressing her back against Ronen's chest and dropping her head.

Elma stepped forward. "Please, Fallon, come with me. There is so much I want to tell you—so much I *need* to tell you," She pleaded.

Fallon clenched her jaw so hard she felt her teeth shift. "You have twenty minutes. Then I'm leaving Elphyne."

The old woman pulled Fallon through the cave. They went down dark halls Fallon had never seen before. Elowen ran up and clung to her arm, and the scuffle of footsteps let her know the others followed close behind.

They walked in silence for so long she began to think this was a joke. Or a trap. How far did this cave go? She wouldn't be surprised if they walked out of the other side of the mountain. It was so dark, Fallon could only see the whites of everyone's eyes as Elowen shook violently beside her whispering, "I am not afraid. I am not afraid."

Fallon left her boots at Merrow Cove and was starting to regret that decision. The cave floors were cold on her damp feet as they approached a dead end.

"What is this?" she demanded.

Elma held up a silencing hand as she stared at the stone wall before them. Slowly, she traced her finger against the stone. She made short dashes like tally marks downwards, until she made one long line up connecting them all. She felt Ronen tense up behind her, narrowing his eyes at the invisible markings on the wall.

Poof.

Fallon shielded her face as a cloud of dust rushed into them. Everyone coughed as it settled, revealing an open doorway where an impenetrable stone wall had once stood.

"Come," Elma instructed, walking through the threshold.

"Fallon …" Ronen said unsteadily from behind her.

She should tell him to piss off. After how he acted, he deserved it. But he was also the person who once told her she didn't have to face everything alone. So, she pulled Elowen close with one arm and offered Ronen the other. "It's alright. We go together."

He acted unhappy about it, but his grip was strong as he linked his arm through hers. "You just want to push me in front of you if something bad happens." He mumbled.

"Don't be daft, I could easily outrun you. I would push Bhaltair," she explained. At least that got a smirk out of him.

As soon as her foot crossed the threshold, a ring of torches ignited. The flames were green—peculiar, yes—but not as peculiar as the walls they illuminated. The large, circular room was completely comprised of bookshelves. Millions of colorful spines surrounded them and even more lie on wooden tables. Scrolls, papers, dry quills, and magnifying glasses were haphazardly scattered everywhere.

Everyone let out a breath of wonder as they collectively looked up in awe: the shelves never ended. They went up and up until they faded into the darkness. Everyone but Bhaltair and Enok seemed impressed. Bhaltair took in a large breath, as if taking in the comforts of home.

"What is this place?" Ronen asked, reaching for one of the papers on the table nearest him.

Elma walked over and snatched them out of his hands. "Unless you want the burden of knowing how everyone will die, I recommend putting that down," she scolded and smacked him upside the head with the roll of paper. "Do not read or touch anything!"

Fallon peeked out the corner of her eye, trying to see the title of the book beside her. Alas, it was written in a language she too did not understand. Those symbols … they were the same strange, messy tally marks Elma used to open the door. They reminded Fallon of sutures.

Elma herded them all towards a long rectangular table, where she stood at the head. Fallon placed herself on one side of the table as Elowen and Ronen flanked her, while the captain and general took the other.

"As it would seem, I have not been entirely transparent with you three," Elma announced, her voice echoing through the endless void above them.

Ronen snorted. "That's a fancy way of saying *lied*."

Bhaltair growled across the table in warning, and Ronen pressed his lips together.

"My name is Wilhelmina Griselda Herleif, and you three are the first outsiders to enter the Shrine of Gilocas in over three-hundred years," she announced, her eyes twinkled playfully.

She pushed up the long sleeves of her robes to reveal thin, tan arms covered in scars. Not battle scars—but *letters* in the same ancient language that filled the books around them. As if Elma– Wilhelmina—was one of the magical texts come to life.

"That's what this is?" Fallon breathed, "This mountain is a shrine?"

Elma chuckled playfully, the green torches around them cast a ghostly light on her face. "Not quite. This *room* is a shrine to one of the greatest minds of all time: Gilocas Archumen. He was the very first Overseer of this mountain, known as the Temple of Wisdom. Now, a millennia later, the position has fallen upon me," she said. A breeze rolled through the chamber, rustling the papers on the table before her.

"I have been searching for you for nineteen years, Fallon. And even I did not foresee that it would be you who would be the one to find me," she said, her voice cracking with emotion. "I wish I had been more prepared, but your return was unexpected. I did not know how much your mother managed to tell you."

"She told me nothing."

"So it seems. Thus, I think it's appropriate to start from the very beginning." Elma walked over to one of the many shelves and pulled out a book that appeared as old as time itself. Its yellowed pages were crumpled, and there was more dust than ink.

The old woman slapped the book down on the table. "Does anyone know the story of Elphyne's creation?"

Elowen chirped to life beside her. "Oh! I know!" She took a deep breath in and clasped her hands together. "Long, long ago, before the time of creatures and men, there was the Sky, the Sun, and the Sea. The Sky was all alone, far above the other two. In a fit of terrible loneliness, she shed a single tear. The tear fell for many years, hardening until it was black and hollow."

"At last, the Sun saw the seed of her sister's heartache falling through the air. So, the Sun used the winds to whisper its secrets into the hollow vessel. After many more years, it finally reached the Sea. When it struck the water's surface, it began to sink deep into darkness. In fear of it getting lost and forgotten, the Sea pushed up an island to protect the seed—the island we now call home. Finally, the seed broke open, and the Sun's secrets seeped into the ground. Born of the Sky, blessed by the Sun, and nurtured by the Sea, the seed's roots grew and grew until it gripped the entirety of Elphyne within its grasp. From them sprouted the first ash trees, our Throne Tree and Entrance Tree," she said.

Elowen's voice trailed off until she stood quietly, head dropping to hide her pink cheeks. It appeared that the Hulder's memory only went so far. Given she must have learned this when she was young, it was impressive she remembered this much detail.

"At the very same moment, but so far apart, the first male and female Fae were born from their trees," Ronen said quietly. He kept his head low but finished the story as if he had recited it a hundred times before.

"Dag was his name, and he followed the sun for twelve days until he finally found his wife—Dagmar. No two beings had ever loved each other so intensely. Every breath, every heartbeat, every touch was a language that only they understood. Two souls collided at the dawning of the world, and together they gave birth to their first of the Fae. Then, using the Sun's secret that had been scribed onto their hearts, they created all life on Elphyne: the Anso, Centaurs, Orculli, Merrows, and everything in between was shaped by their hands. All because the Sun whispered the secret of life into a hollow seed."

Fallon spent the moment of silence that followed deciding if she should bring up how her world started with the giant, primeval cow licking a rock of ice. She decided it was not the right time.

Elma smiled at them proudly, but Fallon could not stop staring at the woman's arms. She had heard of scarification before, but never seen it in practice. The symbols wrapped from her collar bones down to her wrists. That must have taken many pain-filled days.

"When Dag and Dagmar welcomed their first four children into this world, they gave them each a gift just as the Sun had gifted them. Two boys and two girls each received a power that would allow them to not only assist in the prosperity of Elphyne but create a deeper bond with their world. Any guesses as to what they were?" Elma asked.

Fallon thought for a moment, her eyes drifting to Enok. "The control over the four elements."

"Correct," Elma said. She flipped through a few pages in her book and ran her finger along the lines. "The power of earth, fire, water, and air were given to the first four Fae children. They were able to pass on this gift to their own children. Sometimes it skips a generation, sometimes it is lost completely in a bloodline. It is rather unpredictable," she explained. "And as the centuries have passed, we have seen fewer and fewer Fae inherit the gifts."

Bhaltair cleared his throat. "Fritjof Aodh takes bloodlines and powers very seriously. You see, in a group of thirty Fae, only two or three have elemental gifts. He and many others believe this is the god's way of choosing superiors through natural selection. Those who are worthy enough to handle the god's power shall receive it, and those who aren't shall not. To them, it is the gifted who should be lords, leaders, and even kings. Not descendants of the fifth born," he illustrated.

"That is ridiculous," Fallon scoffed.

He shrugged. "That is religion."

Fallon shook her head, "And what about this fifth born?" she asked. "If the four elements were taken, what was their gift?"

"The youngest child was given a different kind of gift—royalty and the Ash Throne itself. You will find, Fallon, that everything in Elphyne comes back down to balance. Being a ruler with an elemental gift was just too much power for one Fae, so the gods separated them. The four elder siblings were meant to *protect* the youngest. Because the royal bloodline had this protection, it is the only one that has survived all this time. The Alfrothuls are the only true descendants of the gods," he explained.

Fallon nodded along. It did make sense. This Fritjof they spoke of was a perfect example of why power-happy people should not rule. "So why does Fritjof have so much influence if he is only a lord? One of my mother's relatives leads as king or queen, right?" she asked.

Everyone in the room seemed like they wanted to melt into the walls. They avoided making eye contact with her as Ronen and Elowen suddenly became very interested in the papers on the table.

Elma was the one who broke the awkward silence. "After your mother died, dear, there were no more royals. Your grandparents passed away three years prior, and Asta was an only child. It was so unexpected, no measures had been taken to decide who would replace her. At the time, the King's Court and I thought it best to let the General of the Valdyr take a temporary position as High Lord," she explained.

Fallon raised her brows at Bhaltair. "You?"

He shook his head. "Not quite. I was promoted to general *after* Fritjof was given the status of High Lord. It was supposed to be temporary, someone to keep the peace until we found a new king. Then one year turned into five, five turned into ten and so on. Once he got it, no one was able to take that power away from him."

Enok snapped for attention. He once again made signs and gestures with his hands, and Fallon wished she could interpret them. She focused on breaking up his movements. She caught him pinching his thumbs between his index and middle fingers then flicking his wrists outwards, then he seemed to pat the empty air before him.

"Like taking a toy away from a child," Bhaltair translated.

"All the royals are gone?" she whispered. That left the throne ripe for the picking. How had someone not come to conquer the castle? If a territory was left unguarded for one bloody hour in Barwyn, someone would come to claim it as their own.

Elma nodded. "All ... but you. Very few knew about your birth, Fallon, and even fewer believe you made it past infancy. You have been nothing more than a story in the homes of people who wish for change. Stories that one day, the long-lost princess will return and lead Elphyne back to its former glory."

Fallon gulped. "*Former* glory?" Elphyne was the most glorious place she had ever seen. Confusing, yes, but spectacular.

"As my son said, everything in Elphyne was created in perfect harmony. This balance is what keeps the darkness at bay. But since the Alfrothuls are gone, since Fritjof has taken over, entropy has slowly crept its way into our land. Something out there is throwing us off course. It will only grow until it tips the scale and the Elphyne we know is lost forever." Elma's eyes went wide. "We *must* protect the balance."

Everyone looked at her expectantly, but Fallon shook her head. "I already have a throne to claim, and it's not this one. Besides, this place seems to be doing just fine. I've seen anarchy, I've seen revolts and chaos. This isn't it," she said, a bit harsher than she wanted to.

Bhaltair leaned forward, and Fallon was thankful for the table separating them. "Ondorr is spreading, the King's Court is a menagerie of chaos, a tyrant sits on the Ash Throne, and yet you still wish to return to your deplorable little snow pile of a kingdom?" he balked.

Fallon smashed her fists onto the table, causing dust to fall from the shelves around them. "Your world wasn't the only one affected by my mother's death. My father didn't have the son he needed. I was only four, I was small with red hair. Someone like that is pretty easy to forget about. My father remarried the same year and started his real family. I was nothing more than the chief's bastard daughter living in the Royal House until the day he decided he was done with me."

"Fallon—" Elma raised her hands to sooth the situation.

"No, it's alright. We're all sharing, aren't we? My execution was ordered by my own father. I was thrown off a cliff in front of my entire village. I survived, escaped to another clan, and was betrayed once again by another man who believed I was nothing," she hissed. "I plan to return and take back everything they took from me. If you want to stop me, you're going to have to bury me six feet under the ground and pray I don't find my way out."

Ronen turned to her in disgust. "So this place means nothing to you? Just like that? You would turn down your birthright for the sake of revenge?" he asked incredulously.

"Revenge? I just want to *sleep—*" she stopped to swallow down the ball rising in her throat.

Her whole life Fallon had fought for a throne, and now she had two. She looked at Bhaltair and Enok and it dawned on her; she had more than a throne here ... Fallon had an army. An army of enhanced Fae warriors that could plow through Barwyn like reaping wheat from the field.

She thought long and hard about how she was going to handle this. "Why has no one fought Fritjof for the throne in fifteen years?" she asked, jutting her chin at Bhaltair. "You seem like you could take him."

Ronen snorted. "I thought you didn't care."

"Humor me."

"He is one of the last Fire Fae, and I am not gifted," Bhaltair said. If the male before her was no match, then who could be?

"But there are more somewhere?" she asked, crossing her arms in thought. Even ten Fire Fae would be enough to melt Barwyn off the map.

Bhaltair thought for a moment. "Perhaps. All the recorded ones have mysteriously disappeared or turned up dead," he said in a tone that implied there was no mystery to it.

"We might need one to kill one," she said quietly. "If Fire Fae have a weakness, only they would know what it was."

Enok smiled, nudging Bhaltair and nodding in excitement. If Fallon truly was a princess, that meant these men would have no choice but to follow her. She could conquer all of Valdimir, then maybe return here one day when she was done spending her days bathing in tubs of blood.

Elma turned to her, "This is your chance to get something greater than revenge. Lead these people, and you'll have the kingdom you always searched for. So, what do you think?" Elma asked, that twinkle back in her eyes.

A princess. Not a chieftess, not a lady, but the soon-to-be Queen of Elphyne. Jaeger would have fainted at the sound of it.

So, she put on her most bloodthirsty smile. The one that let everyone know the wolf had emerged from its cave. "I think I'm sick and tired of men sitting on my throne."

TWENTY-FOUR

As they were all walking out of the cave, something in the corner caught Fallon's eye.

There was a painting on the table adjacent to her. Frameless, wilting at the edges, and faded in color. It felt out of place, like a red rose blooming on a naked bush. Fallon approached it slowly and gently blew off some of the dust. She worried if she touched it, it might crumble apart completely.

It was stunning. There was a woman in golden armor, flying across the sky with a pair of magnificent white wings. Her chocolate brown hair floated behind her, and she had a smile of raw freedom. It was just her, the sun, and the open sky. It made Fallon think of the Valkyries, Odin's twelve handmaidens that selected fallen warriors to take back to Valhalla. They flew on the backs of pegasi … but this woman had wings of her own.

"Talia Alfrothul. The last of the Winged Queens," Elma spoke softly behind her.

Fallon whipped around, startled and slightly embarrassed for her absentmindedness. "Alfrothul?" She still struggled to say the name.

"Yes. Your ancestor, Queen Talia, died fighting in the Elphynian War one-thousand and seventy-nine years ago," Elma said solemnly.

Fallon felt her heart flutter with childish wonder. "They let the queen fight on the front lines?"

"Oh, Fallon, the queens were our *guardians*. Kings and soldiers are honorable and fearless men, but only mother with divine femininity has the unshakable instinct to protect her own. She is born with a shield sewn into her soul. And when that crown is placed upon her brow, the needs of her people is what summons the wings to breach from her back." she explained.

Words evaded her as Fallon tried to imagine it. "But you said she was the last?"

Elma nodded, smiling fondly at the painting. "After Queen Talia succumbed to her injuries, her son—the new king—was ridden with grief. He swore to never let his daughter die the same death his mother did. With the threat of Ondorr now contained, and the kingdom thriving once again, little Princess Bianca never bore the armor her grandmother did. Do not be misled—Bianca grew up to become a fine queen. The need for protection was absent, and so even on her coronation day her wings were never summoned. Since then, with every passing queen, the shield that once saved our land has long fallen off," she illustrated.

Fallon smiled, Pity. Maybe she would have stayed if she got some wings out of it.

Elma placed a hand on her shoulder and led them from the Shrine of Gilocas. "Someone will need to pick up that shield again one day. I don't think it will be in my lifetime, but I must pray the gods will send us someone strong enough to yield it."

A small part of Fallon hoped so too. If Elma did not live to see the day, then Fallon certainly would not.

As they stepped out into the hearth cave, they were met with shouting and cursing. Fallon ran out to the fire, where she saw the General of the Valdyr holding her senseless friend by the throat.

"Bhaltair! Drop him!" she shouted. She tried to shove him off, but the Fae warrior's golden eyes were locked on Ronen's grinning face.

He growled. "Why should I? I'm doing nature a favor."

Her attempts at dislodging him were futile. "I am only trying to save you from the pain I've endured for weeks. Look at him, Bhaltair—he is *enjoying* this."

Sure enough, as his face started to pale and the veins popped from his eyes, Ronen was still smiling. He probably loved the thrill of provoking Bhaltair. His feet were off the ground, becoming limper with each passing second.

Seeing she was right, Bhaltair opened his hand. Ronen dropped to the ground, gasping and coughing. Fallon could have helped him up and seen if he was alright, but she had done more than she needed to already.

Enok and Elowen came running up after hearing the noise. Enok began to sign, this time his hands moved quickly and sharply. She supposed that was his equivalent to an angry tone.

Bhaltair raised a hand to him. "Silence," he grumbled.

Enok rolled his eyes and dropped his arms.

"We must get going," Bhaltair said, wiping off his hand on the green sleeve of his uniform. "My absence from the castle is very rare," he said, running a hand over his face. For a split second he rubbed off his mask, and Fallon saw the soul-deep exhaustion in his eyes.

Elowen was holding some leaves in one hand and healing the bruises and broken vessels on Ronen's neck with the other. "Well, I know I'll miss you," Ronen said.

Fallon shot him a harsh glance. "Why did you come at all, then?" she asked in a bored tone, picking at her nails.

Bhaltair seemed just as hesitant to answer as she had been to ask. "Fritjof thinks I am out planning for the meeting he is having in five days. All the King's Court has been summoned to attend. I came to see if it was true: if the Little Folk had brought us a princess ready to claim her kingdom," he said.

Enok slapped Bhaltair's muscular arm and gave a hurt look.

"Pardon me, *we* came to see if it were true," Bhaltair corrected.

Fallon's palms felt clammy. "And your conclusion?"

Bhaltair stepped forward, towering over her. "They were mistaken. They found a little girl, angry and lost in her own made-up world where she is mighty. Even if we could convince them you were Asta's daughter, most of the King's Court is under Fritjof's control. He threatens their villages, their farms, and their families. You would have to bring a strong case in order for them to take that chance on you," he said. Not cruelly, not personally, just an assessment from a general.

Fallon should be happy. This was perfect: the King's Court would never recognize her as princess anyways, so there was no point in trying. She could go back to Midgard and take the throne she knew she could get.

But Fallon needed that army first.

"Let me speak to them," she said at last. Everyone turned to her in surprise.

"Not so fast." Bhaltair held up a hand the size of her face. "I never said you were worth *my* time. I still must go to Boudevijn to retrieve more uranium for Wilhelmina. Merrow Cove must not perish, and I am not spending the four days I have left trying to teach a brat how to run a kingdom."

She clicked her tongue. "I may not have been raised as an heir, but my father was still chief of the most violent clan in Valdimir. I attended every council meeting, just from under the floorboards. I watched every ambush from inside of a crate and read every war plan using only a candlelight. I've never met a king in my life, but I know a thing or two about leading." She hissed.

He stared at her, face as hard and cold as a rock. He would give Hagen a run for his money in a groveling contest.

"I'll make you a deal," he said in a tone that shook the room like thunder. "I am a busy male. If you go to

Boudevijn for me, get into the mines, and make it back alive with the uranium in *three days* ... I will take you with me to the castle. If you want to be a princess, start by getting to know your people," he said. He crossed his massive arms, the plates of his golden armor soundlessly gliding into place.

Ronen stood back up. "Bad deal, Fal. You can't go to Boudevijn."

"Yes, I can." Her left eyelid twitched.

"No, you can't. The Orculli no longer favor the Fae. Allied with the Merrows, they feel left out and forgotten. None of them will even cooperate with you," he explained.

"One might," a soft voice spoke. Elma had been quiet since leaving the Shrine of Gilocas. She sat on the bench by herself, staring into the orange flames.

They all turned to her, and Fallon hardly had time to blink before Bhaltair was across the room and sitting at her side.

Enok stepped beside her and gave her the same smile Elma always did: the smile that was not meant for Fallon. She now understood it was for Asta, for the friend they had lost.

"There is an Orculli named Eerikki. He is a master builder in Boudevijn and has helped me many times before. If you can find him, there is a chance he will assist you. But be prepared: an Orculli always has a price." She warned.

This was sounding worse and worse by the minute. Three days to get somewhere she did not know, find a giant in a land of giants, and make it through the mines and back. It was a fool's errand, that is why Bhaltair offered it. He knew she could never do it. He just wanted her out of the way while the King's Court met.

But Fallon could show no hesitation in front of him. "And if I fail?"

"Or die," Ronen added.

She rolled her eyes. "Or die?"

Bhaltair shrugged, "Then you can go back to your realm with one ludicrous story to tell."

"And if I succeed," she smiled, "you swear to take me to the castle to win over the court?"

"You have my word," he said. There were a lot of things Fallon already disliked about Bhaltair, but he seemed to be a man of his word.

Ronen's voice still had a slight rasp to it from being crushed as he spoke. "I hate to break it to you, gentlemen, but your long-lost princess isn't exactly adept at making friends."

The general nodded his head at Ronen. "*You* are a bigger problem than her social skills. I cannot allow you to travel anywhere with her until you properly bathe. You will be tracked and killed in a matter of hours."

Fallon laughed. "You assume he's coming with me."

"Oh, he is." Bhaltair grinned. What an ass. He was going to make this as hard as possible for her. "You don't know the way, you don't know Elphyne, and you don't know when to stop. If you attempted to go alone, then you would be naive *and* moronic."

Fallon sucked on her teeth, refusing to say he was right. He gave an amused huff at her silent defeat.

Bhaltair clapped his comrade on the shoulder. "Enok and I have one last errand. We will return tomorrow morning so I can say goodbye to my mother." He then stepped dangerously close, and Fallon caught his scent of moss and cloves. His golden eyes were a weapon in their own right.

"If you choose to be a princess, if you choose Elphyne and your people, then wait right here for me. We will escort you as far as possible to Boudevijn on our way back to the castle. If you are not here, I will never speak of this interaction. The King's Court will never know of your existence. Hope is cruel, Fallon, and I will not put the people through it. If you are not willing to fight to the end, don't even bother picking up the sword." He finished.

Bhaltair Herleif brushed past her without another glance. Enok quickly followed, but not before giving her one last kind smile.

"Wait!" she shouted, jogging after them. The warriors had already reached the cave mouth by the time she caught up.

"You knew about Barwyn."

Bhaltair turned over his shoulder. "What?"

"My *deplorable little snow pile* of a kingdom? You already knew about ... me. You must have known her too, didn't you? That's why Elma called for you."

The general and captain stared at one another for a moment, having a conversation Fallon could not hear nor see. Enok gave his friend a few lethargic signs, then walked out of the cave with his head down low.

But Bhaltair stayed. "Long before you three were born, I joined the Valdyr. I made friends with a farmer's boy who was just as out of place as I was, and we got through training together. By my first year I was elected Captain of the Guard. Then on my third, your grandfather, King Ramses, appointed me as the princess's personal guard." And suddenly that face he gave her made sense; that look somewhere between hate and lust.

"Enok and I never went a day without talking to Asta," he explained, "not until she met Beowulf. So yes, we knew about your birth. Which made her death an even bigger tragedy; because we lost any chance of finding you."

Fallon raised her chin. "You loved her?"

"I was supposed to protect her," he answered instead, turning and swiftly parting his way through the cave mouth.

She swallowed. "Protect her from what? How did she die?" she demanded, but Bhaltair was already out of sight by the time she stepped outside. "How did she die?" she screamed again.

A pair of hands grabbed her wrist to keep her back. "He's gone, Fal," Ronen said.

She pulled her hand free and rubbed her face. It was only then she noticed her fingers shaking and how weak her knees felt.

Elowen was at her side in an instant. "I think you need something to eat," she said.

Fallon nodded. "Would you mind helping Elma in the kitchen? I need some air," she said, not letting her emotions show on her tongue, for her friend's sake.

"Of course." Elowen smiled. She grabbed Fallon's hand and kissed her knuckles, running back inside.

She turned to Ronen, who seemed to be lost in a daze of his own. "I supposed I never properly thanked you for what you did at Merrow Cove," she said begrudgingly, swaying on her feet.

Ronen said nothing.

She spoke up. "Thank you," she said louder. "I know it probably wasn't easy."

"It was," he said quietly. "That's the worst part. I wasn't afraid at all—swimming came as easy as walking."

She punched his shoulder. "That's a good thing, Ronen. One step closer to figuring out your potential."

"Yeah, well, not all of us get our fate laid out for us," he said bitterly.

The smile dropped from her face. "I beg your pardon?" she asked in a tone that sent most men running.

He held out his arms in false grandeur, speaking to the stone walls around them. "The long-lost princess is home, everyone! She has come to overthrow Fritjof with the help of her Fae warrior husband!" His voice echoed.

Fallon stayed very, very still.

"You will get a castle and throne and everything you ever wanted. Just by showing up." He laughed humorlessly.

Fallon was so taken aback, she forgot how to move. She now understood what people meant by killing calm.

Fallon saw past the flames of anger and entered a new, cold chamber from the likes of which she had never seen.

She took an unsteady step forward. "I had everything *taken* from me. Down to my basic human rights. I don't owe you a single gods-damned explanation about why I do what I do, Ronen. Besides, why should I care about the words of a man who can't even stand himself?"

They stared each other down. If Ronen saw the death in her eyes, he welcomed it with open arms.

"I don't care where you go, Fallon. I don't care what you do. But you are not taking Elowen with you. She stays here with us."

Fallon grinned, "Choose your next words very carefully," she warned. Maybe she would take that blue eye for herself and carry it around in a jar.

He lowered his voice, knowing Elma and Elowen could possibly hear. "You are talking about waging a war. Do you really want to bring her into that? What kind of friend are you?" He beheld her with a face of absolute disgust. Which was saying a lot from someone who made Fallon's eyes water every time she neared him.

"I will keep her safe," she said flatly.

Ronen shook his head slowly. "It isn't the war she needs protecting from."

"How dare you—"

"Look at yourself! All you want is power and revenge. Is that the example you want to be for her? For your people? Fae or mortal, you are no better than the leaders you hate. You represent the worst of both worlds," he hissed.

Fae. His eyes burned every time he said the word. She laughed bitterly as it dawned on her, "You think I won the world figuring out I was Fae, don't you? Well guess what, Nøkken: I didn't ask for this!"

"*But I did!*" he shouted back with even more animosity.

Ronen never raised his voice at her before.

It shocked Fallon enough to keep her quiet while he composed himself. He took a few breaths, "I did. Every single day, for twenty-one years. If I could just have those stupid ears and teeth, everyone would leave me alone. I let myself think you understood that. I let myself think that it was possible for someone to like me. And you know what, red, I even started to think we could be friends. But now you're one of them, and soon you are going to forget all about Elowen and me. Even if you stay in Elphyne, we'll never see you again. So just go." He waved a hand.

"Being half-Fae doesn't change who I am," she retorted.

He laughed. "That's the best part; I have no idea who you are. One moment you're smiling and picking clovers, and the next you're screaming about vikings and revenge. You denied your throne yet you volunteered for a suicide mission to save the Merrows. I don't think even *you* know who you are," he said.

Fallon opened her mouth, but she had nothing to say to defend herself.

"You bitch and moan about how you hate your mother for what she did. But if you really did hate her so much, then why did you stay?" he demanded.

She swallowed, her mouth dry. "What?"

"Why did you stay with your father? You are nineteen, you are strong and smart. You could have ran away any time you wanted, but you stayed until the day they kicked you out. Why?"

Fallon knew the answer, she just did not want to say it out loud. The words had circled her as carrion birds for many years.

By the look in Ronen's eyes, he knew the answer too. He wanted to hear her say it. Ronen wanted her to stand there and bleed before him.

She shook her head. "I'm not entertaining this."

Fallon stormed off. She knew it looked like she was running away, but maybe she was. To Helheim with it. This one day had felt longer than her entire life, and she was ready for it to be over.

Fallon sat on a rock not far from the cave, she did not need Elma ostracizing her for leaving again. She felt ... cold. Insulting Ronen had brought her no joy or satisfaction. Fallon needed to let the sun soak back into her skin and blood. She hated the cold. Hated it.

Ronen was right. The first thing she noticed about Elowen was that she did not belong in Midgard; a swan amongst geese. She could not take Elowen back to Barwyn, but she couldn't abandon her and break her promise. So, where did she go now?

After a few minutes of staring into the valley before her, Fallon heard the soft sound of crunching grass. Footsteps too light and graceful to be Ronen's. Fallon felt a small amount of relief as Elowen sat down adjacent to her on the rocks.

The Hulder smiled and gently head-butted Fallon's shoulder. "Are you alright?"

"By your empty hands, I'm assuming Elma said I can't eat until I tend to the flowers?"

Elowen cupped her empty hands together, holding them out to Fallon. "You said you wanted some air, so I got you some." She smiled cheekily.

She forced a laugh, "Thank you."

The sunlight cast a golden glow on Elowen's perfect skin. She was unrealistically beautiful. In body and spirit. Fallon was not worthy enough to call her a friend, yet there she was, always at her side. Maybe it had been Elowen who saved Fallon that day in Halvar. And every day since.

Elowen scooted back and gently raised her hands to Fallon's head. Fallon instinctively flinched; every muscle of her neck flexed in panic. She had been thrown around, yanked, and lifted by the hair too many times to allow anyone to touch it anymore.

Anyone but her mother, who used to brush and oil Fallon's hair every evening by the fire.

Elowen moved impossibly slow, letting Fallon adjust as she lightly raked her fingers through her hair. She took a deep breath and let the tingles rush down her spine, purging out all the tension she held there. Elowen hummed softly as she sectioned out strands, fingers snaking over and through like the hands of a master seamstress. Never once was a strand pulled, plucked, or tugged. Not once.

"Ronen thinks I don't know who I am," Fallon said softly.

"Do you know who you are?"

Fallon kept her eyes fixed on the rolling knolls before them, too relaxed to be upset. "Back in Midgard, there is a lake in Halvar said to be blessed with answers. Jaeger and Norman took me there. As we left, I asked the lake the same question."

Elowen's hands froze in anticipation. "What did it tell you?"

"It spoke to me through one of the bravest men I've ever met, but I wasn't listening. Jaeger told me about Elphyne, he said our mothers were here. He said my power—" she stopped herself.

Elowen tied off her hair with a blade of grass. Fallon reached up, feeling the twists and curls leading to the braid made of braids.

She thought of the last thing Jaeger said to her, right before he ran straight to his death to protect them.

"We are friends, Elowen," she started. "Does that mean I can ask a favor of you?"

Elowen grinned, perfect rosebud lips blooming into a smile. "Of course, anything."

"Jaeger, Norman, Cordelia, Asta … and Fallon. Can you remember those names?" she asked carefully.

"Remember them, and keep them close so they are never lost."

Elowen nodded, listing them out loud but stopping at Fallon's name. "Why yours? You are right here," she said, giving Fallon's nose a firm poke of conformation.

Her voice was barely audible. "A girl died at the bottom of that cliff. That I know for certain. She might still be there now, preserved in ice and blood." She said.

They sat for a few minutes, just holding each other's hands as the warm breeze licked her skin. Elowen scooted forward slightly, "Do you remember the law of nature?" she asked.

Fallon nodded. "Life demands life." It was how Elowen's healing powers worked.

"Maybe that Fallon had to die, so another could be born. Like a mushroom growing on the side of a fallen log," she said.

Emotion gripped Fallon by the throat as she nodded in understanding. It was true, then. Barwyn's Bastard was laid to rest six feet under the snow.

And Ronen had seen it. He saw the ghost of Fallon Solveij trying to possess Fallon Alfrothul's body. A *Fae* body ... oh the things Fallon Solveij would have done with a Fae body. Amory would have been one bloody, bloody graveyard.

"Would you like to say goodbye to your friends?" Elowen asked, standing them both up.

"Goodbye?"

"Yes, you always have to say goodbye. Don't be nervous, I will be right here with you," she said, turning them to face the sun above them.

Elowen closed her eyes and bowed her head as she began to pray, "May Dag welcome you into the moonlit waters of Twiloh: Jaeger, Norman, Cordelia, Asta, and Fallon. Where your soul may run forever and never tire. You can go on, knowing your legacy will be safe within our hearts."

She watched Elowen wave to the ocean, blowing a kiss to the line of blue peeking over the horizon.

Take care of them, she silently prayed. Take care of Fallon Solveij, because nobody else had. At long last, that girl's torment was finally over. Just as she always wished for. She didn't get her throne, she didn't clear her name or get her revenge, but she fought until the bitter end. She fought so hard for so long.

Fallon closed her eyes and pictured the snow at the bottom of that cliff melting away. Where a young, broken girl was free to stand back up and run to the stars that called her home.

Fallon Alfrothul opened her eyes to see the sun smiling down at her, and she smiled back. Waving goodbye to every part of her she wanted to forget.

TWENTY-FIVE

"She is an unstable, self-serving, psychotic brat!" Ronen shouted at a very unamused Elma.

She had been standing with her arms crossed, listening as he ranted about Fallon. After overhearing his and her royal highness's pissing match, Elma and Elowen came running from the kitchens to put out the fire growing between them.

Ronen still had plenty he wanted to say when Fallon went storming off with Elowen chasing after her. Seeing his frustration, Elma pulled him deeper into the cave to talk.

Ronen cursed about the surprise visit by General Ballhair the Great. He cursed about Elma hiding her cool scars from him, and about every decision that had gotten him here. Ronen was tired, he didn't know how to feel about what happened at Merrow Cove, and most of all he was hurt. He felt lied to.

When he was done, Elma adjusted her billowing sleeves and calmly motioned him into the kitchen. Fine.

Maybe she would let him punch the bread dough or something.

The kitchen was a simple, square room with lots of counter space. The brick oven was lit, comfortably warming the stone floors. The orange glow of a slumbering fire, and the trace of ash in the air made him think of the shop.

She shoved a knife and a platter of mushy squash into his hands. "Despite your colorful tongue, I am proud of you," Elma said. She leaned up against the counter, grinding today's collection of greens with her pedestal and mortar.

Her words caught him off guard, and suddenly Ronen forgot how to hold a knife. Even Urg had never claimed to be proud of him. "I-uh, thanks."

"Do you know why?"

Ronen quickly became uncomfortable—he hated any kind of compliment or praise. He awkwardly sliced the yellow squash with fumbling fingers. "No," he said quietly.

Elma reached for the cupboard, and Ronen helped her grab some handmade plates. He knew exactly where they were, because he had been the one to wash them almost every night. He always kept Elowen's favorite blue one to the left.

"I asked you to prove yourself, and you did. You have been a true gift to those girls," she explained.

He snorted. "Could have fooled me."

"Pay no mind to Fallon, she has had a long day," she said with a dismissive wave of the hand.

He's had something on his mind ever since he figured out she was the princess. Something that might get him executed or banished, but someone had to say it.

"You can't let her be queen," he said softly.

Elma turned to him with a glare that made him grateful he was the one with the knife. "Fallon may very well be our only chance of regaining balance."

"Is it really saving Elphyne if you are just replacing one dictator for another?" he asked.

She shook her head in disappointment. "You need to be easier on that girl. The road of grief is a long and painful path, and one she had to walk alone," she chided. "Stop judging her for what she has become, and start to sympathize with all she had to endure to become it. You might realize you two have more in common than you think."

Ronen stopped cutting. "So what, she's strong? That does not qualify her to run an entire kingdom," he mumbled.

"I have seen nearly four queens in my lifetime. All of them taught from birth how to lead. Etiquette classes, speech lessons, and history studies every single day. All they knew was a just, fair life. Fallon did not get any of that. Who knows the true *value* of peace better than someone who was born into war?" she challenged, scraping all his vegetable slices into a large bowl.

"Fallon has never known peace."

"But she has seen it in her dreams. That makes it all the more precious, all the more worth fighting for." She smiled warmly.

Ronen felt her words scatter across his skin and crawl down his back. "You really think she can do this?"

"Not alone. She will need people to guide her in the right direction. Because one day soon, the Ash Throne will test her. As it always does before an Alfrothul's coronation."

He snorted. "A *tree* is going to ask her a math equation?"

But Elma's face was absent of humor. "The Ash Throne is the most powerful being in Elphyne, rivaled only by its sister born of the same seed. The Alfrothul family and the Ash have an arcane, ancient bond. On their twentieth birthday, a prince or princess will prick their finger on the branches. Upon the taste of Alfrothul blood—the Sun's blood—the throne will design and construct a crown, made from its own branches. Each crown is unique to the ruler, symbolizing their unity with the Ash Throne and the gods who were born from it." She explained.

Ronen whistled. "I never knew that was real."

"As real as you and I," she mused, "Fallon is not yet twenty and has a lot of learning to do. The Ash knows this. All we can do is help her and pray she passes the test. Even when she tries to push us away." She gave him a playful wink.

"Yeah, if by push away you mean forcefully exile." He laughed.

Elma shrugged "She will come around. The gods blessed her with that Hulder. Even I did not see that one coming," she added quietly, rushing to place a tray of risen dough into the oven.

Ronen was right at her heels. "What was that? How much did you see coming? Did you know about me?"

"I am the Overseer of the Temple of *Wisdom*, dear, not the temple of foresight." She chuckled. "My oracle days were long ago. Fallon chose to save that girl all on her own. That alone should tell you all you need to know about her heart, despite the cage she keeps around it."

Fallon did save her, and more than once. Elowen told him the story. Looking back, she probably saved him, too. He learned enough about the mortal realm to know he wants nothing to do with it. If Fallon had not blocked him from leaving, he might have gotten killed already. Or worse.

He and Elma finished preparing lunch in silence. It was the first time he got to make food for everyone, and it felt nice. Working side by side with an elderly Fae that occasionally insulted him warmed his little Nøkken heart. A heart that had been broken and misused for too long.

A princess. Ronen had managed to get on the Princess of Elphyne's every last nerve. For that, he was proud.

He was, however, ashamed of how he spoke to her. Ronen had been at his breaking point. Every moment in that magical library was full of resentment and envy. He was so focused on hating her, Ronen barely heard her confess to a life of isolation and abuse. If Ronen had been treated like that, he would want revenge too.

He should have never raised his voice at her. Because Fallon raced after a Centaur not even knowing what it was, but when she almost slid off that ledge, all the life had drained from her eyes. He saw that same fractured look when he yelled at her.

If all of that wasn't bad enough, he now had to deal with the fact he might see more of the general. *That* had been a sick surprise. Elowen was right, though, he did see the resemblance between him and Elma. The general had his mother's dark skin, short chin, and high cheekbones. Though it appeared that kindness, nurturement, and personality skipped a generation.

"My son was right, you know," Elma said as the two of them walked out of the kitchen, a full plate in each hand.

Ronen shuddered, getting the weird feeling that she could read his mind. "About what?"

"It would be unsafe for the girls if you left the cave so … traceable," she said sweetly.

Pungent. She meant pungent.

Ronen snorted. "I don't recall agreeing to go to Boudevijn."

She gave him that all-knowing smile that made him want to break a table. If she was so smart, couldn't she just tell them how to stop Fritjof?

Elowen, famished as always, ran up and took one of the plates. Two weeks ago, she would hide behind Fallon when he was around. But now she talked on and on to him. Elowen laughed at his jokes, listened to him rant, and occasionally offered him flowers she picked.

He peeked through the glowing foliage, but didn't see Fallon. Elma handed him one of the plates in her hands and nodded her head up the dirt path. "There. Go."

"She's the princess now. Can you still make her do this?" he asked, alluding to the flowers she had yet to coax into growing.

"I can, and I will. Though I have hope tonight might be different. Maybe there will be someone to hold a lantern while she walks that long, steep path," she said, as more of an order than a suggestion.

Well, at least he had a peace offering.

It took him a minute of walking to remember where her flower bed was. Her back was turned to him as he sat down in the dirt, making sure to stay out of fist-throwing range.

He knew she noticed him. Her nostrils flared at the plate in his hands, but her eyes stayed fixed on the hoed dirt in front of them. Her jaw was jut out to the side—as it always was when she was thinking—full lips pursed in concentration. From here he could only see half of the long scar across her nose, and for the first time he wondered where it was from. He cared where it was from. How many fights had she seen, knowing it would never be the last?

"I was waiting for her to come back."

Ronen blinked. He wasn't expecting her to speak.

"That is why I never left Amory. If there was even the smallest chance she was alive, she knew where to find me. If I ran, I would only be putting more distance between us," she explained quietly.

It was her gentle, defeated tone that helped Ronen relax. Fallon pulled her legs in and rested her chin on her knees. It was such foreign body language for Fallon; off-guard and forlorn. Her hair was done up, surely the work of a happy Hulder.

"I knew you didn't hate her. Because I never hated my parents, either," he said, playing with the food on his plate.

"I thought I could. Especially after everything I've learned about her today. But no matter what you tell yourself, you can't hate someone who you would burn down the entire world for, just to see again," she said.

He looked up from his plate. A curl had escaped its braid, falling to caress the side of her face. It cast a shadow on her already defined jaw. Ronen had to force himself to turn away.

He cleared his throat, "I don't have a place here. In Elphyne, I mean. No one wants to be around me, and even the nice ones only trust me as far as they can throw me." He swallowed. "Not long ago, a crazy old lady asked me if Nøkken were good or evil."

"I've seen a little of both," she said, peering at him out of the corner of her eye.

Ronen felt his cheeks heat up. "I said good. Because that's all I've ever wanted to be—the exception. But to be honest, I haven't been doing a very good job. I let my bitterness for the Fae shape who I was until I didn't even recognize myself. I was lost for a long time. But then ... you appeared. Everything isn't hopeless anymore; Fritjof can be stopped. Maybe with a new princess and a fresh

Elphyne, there will be a place for people like me." He turned to her and was happy to see she was looking back at him. "If you can kill a fire-breathing lord with a god complex, then I can end a thousand-year cycle of fearing the unknown. But we can't do one without the other."

Fallon nodded, so he took that as a good sign. He scooted as close as he dared. "It ends with me," he said sternly. "It can end with you too, when you're queen. Everything your father did to you, everything he stood for, you don't have to repeat it. Maybe the best type of revenge is to be nothing like your enemy," he offered.

Her back straightened. Fallon turned to him, eyes so green and round they swallowed him whole. "*When* I'm queen?"

He scoffed. "How typical of you to pass over my beautiful speech and jump on the complement. Yes, Fal. Despite your many, many, *many*—"

"I get it." She laughed.

"—many faults, you're the type of person who stands back up. You survive. Elphyne needs a survivor. So, if you don't mind me tagging along on this little royal-revenge escapade, I'll help you to Boudevijn. Then to the castle. Thanks to Bhaltair, I know a few ways in and out," he said, sticking out his hand.

She looked him over for a second. Without anger seeping from her every pore, Fallon was actually ... pretty. He could see the freckles dusted across her cheeks and nose, and there was another scar cut across the tip of her left eyebrow. Those eyes; they were queen's eyes alright. A single thread of gold melted into an emerald.

Her hand was callused and warm as it clasped onto his. Her wrist and knuckles were a maze of pale scars. Every inch of her was a story—a tragedy written in her own blood. And one day, Ronen planned to read it. Word by word, scar by scar. He would get to know his princess.

Gripping his hand hard enough to make him wince, Fallon gave him that feral, unyielding grin that summoned blood and carnage. "It ends with me."

TWENTY-SIX

Fallon once thought her enmity was untouchable. That the bottomless sea of anger inside of her would never run dry. Yet with just four, simple words, the dam broke.

"It ends with me."

The sentence reverberated inside of her, sending a strong wind through the chasm of her soul. It whisked away the dust, revealing parts of her that had been long forgotten. The parts that dared to hope, to feel and dream.

Find something that sets your soul on fire, and follow it.

For the first time in her life, Fallon felt that something. It was not the stale, cold air in her chest when she thought of Barwyn. Or the icy daggers that pierced her heart when she fantasized about slitting Beowulf's throat. This was a rooted, ancient warmth that slowly began to stir. Not awake, but yawning.

Her stomach audibly growled, and Ronen let out a small chuckle as he moved the plate of food out of her reach. "You may be the princess, but Elma made me the king of this plate. And I'm holding it hostage until I see some bloomage," he said, raising a brow.

She laughed. "Already drunk with power, I see."

"Oh I'm going to enjoy every second."

But Fallon was not enjoying this. The boy made no move to get up, and Fallon knew she was too embarrassed to say anything in front of him. She felt too exposed already. She would rather strip naked before him than sing.

Seeing her apprehension, Ronen let out a dramatic sigh and swiveled around on his rear. With his back now to her, he secretly nibbled at the food as if she could not see.

The flowing river of a loving heart can make anything bloom. Well, Fallon would be lucky if she were able to summon a single drop. She was about to quietly sneak away while he was distracted, but then he started to whistle.

It was probably just an attempt to kill the awkward silence, but it crashed into Fallon as a sonic wave. That song. Fallon knew that song.

It was soft, leaping through the air like the gleeful feet of dancers. Ronen's notes spun around her, unraveling the tight wrap she kept around herself. Right on entrance, Fallon softly sang the lyrics she had only heard once before.

When she was young and could not sleep, she snuck out of bed. Her mother was brushing her long hair in the mirror, and Fallon listened as she sang softly to herself.

The words were a delicate letter to a lover, promising the life of a rose-scented dream. She got to the last line of the chorus; it was her favorite part:

"No storm, no peril, no monsters of legends old, could take us from our own little eternity."

Ronen slowly turned as a last note escaped his lips. His eyes were wide, brimmed with silver. "How do you know that song?"

"How do *you* know that song?"

"It's an Elphynian wedding song. It-it was just the first thing that came to my head."

She smiled. Her mother had been singing her wedding song that night in front of the mirror.

Fallon has been so focused on all the time she never got with Asta, she started to neglect the memories she did have. The two of them playing knights and ladies on the bed, birthing the foals, and sneaking past the Vali to stargaze on the roof of the Royal House.

Luckily, Ronen seemed just as mortified as her when she asked, "Can you keep going?"

He took a large breath, then picked up where they left off. The second verse was meant for dancing, where the two souls intertwined as one. It enchanted her feet as the words poured down on her.

Not able to sit still any longer, Fallon grabbed his hands and stood them up. Their world's might be impossibly different, but they managed to find the one thing they shared in this moment.

Their forearms raised and pressed together as they danced in circles. Ronen's voice joined hers, and his smile was contagious as they became breathless and free.

The world was not fair. Even though Fallon should have gotten longer with her mother, even though Asta did not need to die so young, the two of them had created their own perfect little eternity. And Fallon would carry it with her forever.

When they reached a decrescendo, Elowen came running. She was upset at first for being left out, but quickly recovered once Ronen offered his hand. Behind them, Elma clapped along with tears in her eyes as the three of them started all over again and spun each other around like fools.

Ronen was brilliant. He lifted Elowen, dipped Fallon, and sang along all without missing a beat. She rested her hands on her knees for a moment to catch her breath, but when she turned around the man was gone.

She was about to shout for him, but Elowen grabbed her by the waist and danced them around some more. It was not even singing anymore; they were just belting the lyrics to set the savage parts of their hearts free. Aimless, unstoppable, and beautifully obnoxious.

As she glanced over her shoulder, Fallon did not acknowledge the patch of white peace lilies that blossomed from her flowerbed. She did not care about the brand on her stomach, or the color of her hair. Because in this moment, in this new little eternity she was creating, Fallon was happy.

And somewhere deep within the crumbled ruins of her soul, peeking out from beneath the rubble, a light began to flicker.

PART THREE
The Light Queen

TWENTY-SEVEN

Bhaltair Herleif thought he would have to enter Dag's sea of souls before he ever saw those eyes again.

He remembered the first time he ever saw them. Bhaltair was fourteen, standing in line with all the other children to receive his daily bowl of stew. At lunchtime, the castle kitchens would hand out leftovers to the poor families of Castletowne. His mother sent him and his older brother here every day—to the round door on the east side of the wall that separated the Golden Castle from the surrounding town.

His brother was busy chatting with a young woman around the corner, leaving Bhaltair in charge of getting both of their rations. When it was finally his turn, he rushed forward to the sullen-faced woman handing out a bowl to him.

"Next," she called.

Bhaltair gulped, staring down at the single bowl in his hands. "Miss, my brother—"

"Next!" she repeated, glaring at him harshly. The man behind him shoved forward and took the next bowl.

Valdyr were posted on either side of the doorway, making sure no one came around twice. Bhaltair was frozen in place, trying to figure out what to do. He was supposed to grab one for both of them. His brother would be furious, as he so often was. Which meant Bhaltair would be going home hungry and bloody.

Then, a slim figure slipped through the doorway as if she were nothing more than a gentle breeze. Were it not for her rust-colored hair, he might have not even noticed her. She was around his age, perhaps younger, with a face that looked like it had been carved from ivory. *She's a living statue of an angel,* he remembered thinking.

Those emerald eyes drizzled with gold met his own, and suddenly Bhaltair didn't care about how badly his brother was going to beat him.

"Here," she spoke in a soft, hurried voice. "For your brother. I see you two here every day, I know you are not sneaking seconds."

She pressed another bowl into his hands, her skin felt like sun-soaked velvet. He did not even have time to mutter a thank you before the guards noticed her.

"Princess," one said sternly, an order within itself.

It was only then Bhaltair noticed her fine clothing, glittering yet simple jewelry, and dainty tiara tucked away in her red waves. Princess ... *this* was the young heir to the Ash Throne his mother always talked about?

She gave him a warm smile before rushing back through the door, behind those castle walls. Where she watched him and all the other poor families get their rations every day. Not the snotty, spoiled hellion he had imagined.

It was on that day Bhaltair knew he had to get on the other side of those walls. Where the girl that moved like a spring's gale was, and where his brother wasn't. The problem was: Bhaltair wasn't special. He was giftless. Known only to his peers as the witch's son who was born in a cave. Or the golden-eyed brothers who wore tattered clothes—the elder having a violent reputation.

Bhaltair could not be a servant, he could not work in the kitchens, he had no royal blood or musical talent, but he was smart. He was strong and ended up outgrowing even his brother that same year. So, every day for two years, he woke up with one goal on his mind: to protect and feed the other young boys with no fathers. And to see the princess on the other side of the wall again.

On his sixteenth birthday, he enlisted for the Valdyr.

He always wondered if Asta recognized him. Even after he joined, after he was appointed her personal guard, she never mentioned the bowl of soup that introduced them.

Ten years. Bhaltair only had ten short years with Asta Alfrothul. The most selfless, genuine, and gentle person he had ever met. Now, more than ever, he was grateful for those ten years. Because her own daughter only got four.

Fallon. Asta wanted to name her daughter Fallon since the day she discovered she was pregnant. Were it not for that and the uncanny resemblance, Bhaltair would have never believed they were of the same blood. This girl was brash, cruel, and cold. They were a dove and a raven, somehow from the same nest.

When Wilhelmina wrote to him weeks ago explaining the situation, Bhaltair was elated. Finally, something good was happening. He thought saving her daughter was a way he could make things up to Asta, but the only thing this girl needed saving from was herself. He could smell the anger on her, it coated her skin and hair.

It took him all of thirty seconds to decide. Ever since Asta died, that was all Bhaltair ever did: make the decisions no one else wanted to. The King's Court was a ring of seemingly random people Fritjof called for, but they had survival instincts. They would never agree to put Fallon's stubborn ass on the Ash Throne. She could not protect their villages, grow their foods, manage trade and money, or keep peace between the peoples of Elphyne. As a matter of fact, her very existence threatened all those things.

Yet despite the world of differences between them, there was one thing this princess and his old friend had in common: they were relentless.

When Asta wanted something, or gods forbid she wanted to see an end to something, there was not a force alive that could stop her. It was when the cunning side of that pretty little smile came to play that Bhaltair always had the hardest time saying no. Those were the times when having Enok was imperative. Luckily, he still spoke back then. He *had* to speak, a lot, to reason with Asta and Bhaltair. The three of them got into more trouble than he would ever admit, but nothing ever went wrong. Not until the day everything went wrong.

Today, Fallon gave him that same wicked smile her mother sometimes wore. When the gold in their eyes came to life, playfully swimming circles around their irises like koi fish. It was only that light, that shimmer of sheer will that made him compromise with Fallon. As he would have compromised with Asta.

Did he think she could do it? Probably not. With only a Nøkken boy and Hulder girl as company, he imagined they would fail within the first few hours. He and Enok could only escort them as far as Dewdenn Village before they must make their way back to the castle.

But did he *hope* she could do it? More than anything.

Because Bhaltair had a horrible feeling about this meeting. Nothing was adding up, and every day Bhaltair lost more and more of his Valdyr to Fritjof's influence. More families threatened, more livestock burned. He had all his gifted warriors under close watch, knowing they would be Fritjof's first target.

As awful as she was, Fallon was still Asta's daughter. She was a Fae who belonged in Elphyne. Whether that was on a throne or on the streets was yet to be seen, but she was a princess by blood. A royal. Which meant it was still Bhaltair's duty to protect her, but how could he? How could he pledge his allegiance when they both knew he failed her family already?

He remembered collapsing into Enok's arms, screaming and wailing like a child as he released the tidal wave of agony ripping away at his heart. *I wasn't fast enough!*

The image was permanently branded into the back of his mind: A beautiful woman in a white dress, lying motionless on the shadow-soaked earth. A fallen angel, with her cold hand still reaching out for the saving grasp that never came.

I wasn't fast enough.

TWENTY-EIGHT

Ronen Nøkken vomited so violently, he felt like a Shapeshifter morphing into a savage beast.

He tried to get as far away as possible first, but bile and horror forced their way out of his mouth before he even reached his chambers. Still shaking, Ronen crawled on his hands and knees to his bed. *Oh gods. Oh gods oh gods ...*

He could still hear the girls singing and laughing, so he covered his ears to block it out. Ronen was pretty sure that was what caused it. The girls, the singing, the music, it made him *feel*—

"Oh gods," he groaned out loud, pressing even harder on his ears.

It was as if for a split second during that song, Ronen grew a third arm. Another extremity suddenly at his will. Except this one did not feel with touch, but with sound. And what it felt with those phantom fingers made his insides squirm.

Ronen wanted to melt into the floor. He wanted to fade away into the shadows under his bed and never be seen or spoken to ever again. Unfortunately for him, he had made friends with the one girl that would never let that happen.

Just as she had done a hundred times before, Elowen appeared to place a hand on his shoulder and pull him back from the shadows that called him.

With his ears covered, he did not hear her or Fallon approach. He yelped at her touch, which only added to his embarrassment. They had surely followed the trail of vomit and tears to find him, and no one seemed impressed about it.

"Ronen?" Fallon knelt beside them. The way she always rolled the *R* in his name did not help him stop shaking.

He swallowed. "I think I'm freaking out."

"What happened?" Elowen asked gently, placing a hand on his sweat-soaked forehead. She was too close. They were both too close for him to even breathe. Ronen had to push them aside and walk around until the nervous energy in his legs started to ease.

Fallon walked alongside him, trying to keep up. "Use your words, Ronen. What happened?"

He did not even know how to answer that question. "I ... I felt it. The music, the-the voices they all mixed until for a second, I could *feel* it," he croaked.

She grabbed his arm. "Feel what?"

"Water."

The three of them became motionless. Elowen was the first to remember how to breathe, taking three careful steps towards him. "Water? Like … the wet kind?" she asked.

"That's the one." He laughed nervously.

Fallon's face stayed emotionless with trained neutrality, but her shoulders stopped moving with her breaths. "How do you feel?"

He rolled his eyes. "Relax, princess—I've had the urge to drown you since the day we met. I've learned to control it."

"You know what I meant. Tell me exactly what happened."

He reluctantly told them about the third arm that came to life when they were lost in song, and how it seemed to play with the water around him. It felt the water in the cup across the room, the stream round them, his bathing chamber, and many others he did not even know about. This cave, temple, whatever it was—it was larger than they could have imagined.

Elowen worriedly assessed him for damage. Oddly enough, her hand lingered over the center of his chest where he pictured the arm sprouting from. "You don't feel any different," she noted.

"That's because he's not," Fallon said flatly. "It's always been there. He just woke it up."

The memory of feeling water he was not touching replayed in his mind again and again. It was foreign, uncomfortable, and sickening.

"Well, I would like to put it back to sleep," he moaned, feeling his stomach churn.

Fallon watched him for a moment, her eyes lost in thought. He ended up having to turn away from her intense gaze. Elowen assisted him back onto the bed, where she rubbed his back until the nausea faded and his head began to clear.

Ronen felt guilty as he answered more of their questions. He felt ashamed and embarrassed, as if he was confessing he had a terrible disease.

Then, Fallon snorted. They turned to her in surprise, but she continued to snicker until it evolved into a full-on cackle.

For once, Ronen was not amused in the slightest. "Care to share with the group?" he hissed.

She slowly composed herself and walked over to grab him on the shoulders. "Nøkken, you were right all along. Everyone *did* have the wrong idea about your kind. All the stories were missing one single detail. You don't control water—not the same way Fae do. Just like healing doesn't come from Elowen directly. It's not you."

"You are rotten at comforting people, do you know that?" He raised a brow.

Her eyes gleamed. "Music, Ronen. In every story I ever read, Nøkken were musicians. They always had instruments. Not to enchant women's *minds*, but to enchant—"

"The water," Elowen gasped.

It all made sense. It made so much sense it hurt. "How did I not realize ..." he shook his head.

The girls were smiling wildly at him. "Ronen, we figured it out! You *do* have powers!" Elowen squealed, aggressively shaking him.

"Do you have a lyre? Or flute or snare?" Fallon asked excitedly.

"I'm an orphan, remember?" he snorted, "I was more focused on finding shoes, not instruments." He has never even touched a musical instrument before.

She smiled. "You had your powers this whole time, you just didn't know how to use them. Captain Enok is also gifted, perhaps tomorrow he can help you."

"Woah, woah, woah," Ronen stood. "Are we sure this is the right choice? I never knew about any of this because there wasn't another Nøkken to teach me. Which also means there's no one to *warn* me. What if there is more to it that we don't know about?" he insisted.

Fallon crossed her arms. "You're afraid."

"You bet I'm afraid! I could flood this place. I could kill you guys."

Elowen smiled. "You won't," she said it with so much confidence, Ronen almost believed her.

Fallon nodded. "If you start to get out of control, I will break you. Then Elowen can put you back together." She smiled.

He laughed. "Thanks."

They smiled awkwardly at each other for a moment. This was new to them all ... friendship. Fallon called them something once—a clan of misfits. Three half-blooded, beautiful misfits against the world.

"Does this mean you will actually bathe like Bhaltair told you to?" Elowen asked sheepishly.

He shook his head. "Not because lardass told me to, but because he told me *not* to for twenty-one years."

The three of them laughed and chatted in his chamber until the moon consumed the sky. Fallon was being a little too quiet, only laughing along or adding small comments. Ronen knew what it was like to put your body on autopilot while your thoughts wandered through every corner of your mind. His friend was not currently behind those emerald eyes as they spoke. Not when Elma called for them to make supper, or as they sat by the fire to eat.

This time, Fallon sat with a plate already full of food. He turned to Elma, but the old woman was just smiling. Not at Fallon—but behind her. Where peeking through the glowing bushes was a patch of freshly bloomed white flowers.

After dinner, everyone retired to their rooms for the night. While Fallon simply gave him a firm nod wishing him luck, the Hulder—a master at subtlety—kept giving him exaggerated winks all night. It must have worked, though. Because Ronen felt little to no fear as he stood tall, naked, and unwavering before the bubbling bathing pool.

Luckily the bath salts had been restocked, and this time he poured in all four vials. The scent was so strong it stung his nose. If Ronen just made no noise, he should be fine. The water wouldn't hurt him. It didn't at Merrow

Cove. There were no guards, no villagers, no music, and no red-headed banshee to stop him.

One foot at a time, Ronen Nøkken lowered himself into the steaming water.

A cloud of filth grew around him but was quickly lost in the endless pool below. Ronen lifted his arm and watched all the muck melt away. He laughed and splashed until he no longer knew if it was water or tears on his face. Ronen was losing a layer of skin, one that had restrained him to his community's standards. But it held him no more.

TWENTY-NINE

Fallon paced back and forth in her room, trying to run away from her own thoughts.

"Please, lay down," Elowen whispered again. She was laying on her makeshift bed on the floor, pulling her tail back every time Fallon nearly stepped on it.

But Fallon's blood was roaring in her ears. Over dinner, she asked Elma about the members of the King's Court. They were all Fae—all *gifted* Fae. Who were more likely to have gifted children. Even better than that, none of them were Fire Fae. If there is truly only a handful of them left …

Fallon finally stopped pacing. She plopped down next to Elowen and quickly kicked her legs under the blanket. "I know what he wants," she said.

"What who wants?" Elowen asked hesitantly.

"Fritjof. He wants to be the leader of the leaders; the blessed amongst the gifted. If he becomes the sole Fire Fae, he could convince everyone the gods chose him." Her face went slack, "He could convince everyone to make him king."

Reaching up, Elowen slowly started to undo all the small braids Fallon had nervously tied all day. "But you're the *princess*, Fallon. You heard what Elma said: your ancestor was the youngest Firstborn. You are the last living descendant of Dag and Dagmar."

Fallon let out an irritated sigh, but Elowen's fingers combing through her hair slowly coaxed the beast to sleep. "Even if the King's Court believes me, even if they follow me, an army of Fae wouldn't stand a chance against an army of element-wielding worshippers. Bhaltair was right: I would be leading them to their deaths." It would be a massacre, led by an inferno-blooded messiah.

Elowen's hands paused. "The Fae aren't the only ones with powers, you know."

A grin crossed Fallon's face as she turned to her clever, clever friend. "Elo … you are a genius. Nymphs control the weather. Centaurs are wise, and Orculli are strong."

Elowen's sagebrush eyes glimmered. "The Anso people can fly, my people heal, and the Merrows can swim. We have the last Nøkken alive on our side, and a princess to lead them all." She let out a breath of wonder.

"Then it will not be a battle between Fritjof and I after all." Fallon whispered, "Nor one between Fae and Faeries; but a *war* between two of the most influential forces in all the realms."

"Love and hate?"

"Worse: faith and fear."

Ronen shielded his face from her gaze for the third time this morning. "I did not wake up at the ass-crack of dawn to go to Boudevijn just so you could all stare at me," he growled, "Knock it off!"

But Fallon could not help it. Ronen was *clean*.

His skin was a shade lighter than she expected, while his hair was a shade darker. Face scrubbed clean, she could now see his sunken cheeks, cleft chin, and red-tipped ears.

Elma nearly had a heart attack when she saw him. "My, you smell wonderful, dear!" she cried, grabbing his face and kissing each cheek.

Admittedly, Fallon felt quite proud of him. She would never tell him that, of course. All this female attention was already getting to his head. Elma was right, though, he did smell nice. But not like bath salts or oils.

She picked up on it as they sat together by the hearth. With the muck gone, she could detect his true scent. The one that was unique to each individual, as if a drop of their essence was bottled into a perfume.

Ronen smelt of pond mist and burnt vanilla. It was deep and robust, but refreshing in a way that made her want to keep breathing it. Fallon locked it into her memory, just as she had done with the others.

Ronen was drawing her a map of Elphyne in the sand while she filled him in on her thoughts from last night. He had some colorful words to say about Fritjof but seemed to agree with her theory. On their map, Elowen made piles of sand to represent the mountains surrounding Boudevijn and found small ferns to use as trees.

"Bhaltair should be here by now," Elma said worriedly from beside them. She had been keeping one eye on the cave mouth all morning. "He is not one to be tardy. I raised him better than that."

Ronen shrugged. "Maybe he's busy arm-wrestling a Centaur or something."

Elowen, still busy at work, sat back on her heels and looked around. "I need some rocks for the villages. Fallon, can you find me some pointy rocks?" she asked with a smile that erased the word *no* from your vocabulary.

"Only the pointiest, my lady." Fallon bowed.

She walked around the cave, collecting large and small stones in hand. When none of them were good enough, it quickly became a contest between her and Ronen to see who could find the most perfect house-shaped rock. It was a nice distraction from the weight in her gut that only got heavier with each passing minute.

Noon came and went, and still no sign of the general or captain. While Elowen and Ronen took a nap on the sand, she and Elma sat at the hearth. Elowen's hand was outstretched towards Fallon, as it always was when she slept. Some nights, when the Hulder thrashed or whimpered, she grabbed it. To remind them both that they weren't alone anymore.

When evening fell, a storm of uneasy energy blew through the cave. Everyone was on edge, but no one was eager to talk about it. No one wanted to be the one to say the general wasn't coming. Fallon did not care either way—she had been looking forward to a fight all day. It had been a long time since she hit something. Her bones jittered together in anticipation, and eventually she could wait no longer.

While Elowen assisted Elma with supper, she and Ronen retreated into the glowing gardens to discuss their next move.

"We need to go *now*. We are only wasting time sitting around and waiting," she pushed.

But Ronen did not agree. "As much as I hate to say it: we need them, Fal. They are going to explain to us where to find Eerikki and the mines. Not to mention, we wouldn't get far without Bhaltair's knowledge on Valdyr patrols. In case you forgot, they still hate us."

"They still hate *you*," she corrected, "they have no idea how much they hate me yet. Three days have already turned into two, Ronen. Is it even possible anymore? I think the general sent us a red herring." She sighed through her nose.

Ronen snorted. "A what?"

"A distraction. He wanted us to think we're heroes and focus on Boudevijn while he and Enok went back to the castle. I bet the meeting is going on as we speak." She sneered, glancing over her shoulder at the cave mouth.

He grabbed her face to turn her back to him. "Hey, cut it out. I know that look: you want a fight. But maybe *that* is what Bhaltair wanted; for you to march up to the castle all pissy and make a fool out of yourself in front of the King's Court. He called you a little girl, don't prove him right," Ronen warned.

She pushed his hand away, but he grabbed her chin again, "Hold on, did you do something to your face?"

Well, he certainly knew how to make a woman feel pretty. "What?" she reached up and touched her face in horror. All seemed normal until she felt her nose. The cartilage was stiffer, coming up to a point. She gasped, instantly reaching to her ears—Fae ears. It must have happened in her sleep. Fallon had almost gotten used to her senses being dialed up since arriving in Elphyne, but she never expected to look the part. Even after learning she was half-Fae.

Fallon slowly turned back to Ronen, waiting for that fire in his eyes to ignite. He has said some rather distasteful things to her about her heritage. Would he have even more resentment towards her now that she resembled the people he hated?

But Ronen swallowed down whatever emotion he felt. He nodded his head, even trying his best for a smile. "Fae looks good on you, halfling."

"It appears Elphyne's magic has finally taken a hold of you," a happy voice chided from up the dirt path. Elma walked towards them; pale blue robes illuminated by the flowers.

Fallon tried to repress a smile. "A normal Burdock planted in Elphynian soil."

Elma winked. "Who said it was born normal?"

The old woman handed them each a bowl of dark violet stew (why could it never be a normal color?) and jerked her head towards the hearth. "Come. And whatever you were conspiring to do, don't do it."

"Relax, we haven't gotten that far yet," Ronen admitted as they trudged along.

He may not have gotten that far, but Fallon did. She has been plotting in the background all day long. If Bhaltair truly lied to her, then he could not be trusted. She did not know why he still worked for Fritjof, why the Lord of Fire trusted him even though he was not gifted, or what truly happened to her mother.

Which meant her backup plan was still in the air. If there was really no one on her side here, then fighting Fritjof would be meaningless. Perhaps striking a deal with him was an even better option. One hundred gifted warriors in exchange for her silent leave. He had no one to oppose him, and she had what she needed to take back Barwyn.

The choice should have been simple. Any Solveij would not hesitate to take the lesser risk and greater reward. So why was doubt biting at her heels like a snapping dog?

Fallon sat quietly for the rest of the meal feeling like a traitor for her intrusive thoughts. It did not bother her weeks ago when she planned to spill her guts to the Haedilla in order to save her own skin. Honestly, she had been excited to do it. Why? Because Barwyn's Bastard *was* a traitor there. But not here, not yet.

Her brand itched as she climbed into bed that night. The scar sometimes burned while she slept, as if the memories were still trapped under her skin. It was as if her own body was screaming at her: *Remember!*

As if she could forget. Her life so far had been nothing more than a beast chewing her up then spitting her back out, each time with more scars and demons than the last. But things have changed. If nothing else, this entire journey had gifted Fallon one thing: perspective. From here, she could look back and decide if she would go running back into the maws of the beast.

Fallon always thought she needed her anger. She thought maybe rage could help her stand, make her breathe and make her run. If she let go, was there even anything left of her that the wildfire did not consume?

Yes, there was. No matter how hard she tried to dismiss it, there was that wild heartbeat that thrummed when the sun touched her skin. Fallon feared if she returned to Barwyn, if she gave up her Fae magic and life here—she would never feel that warmth ever again.

The next morning started a little more chaotic than usual. Fallon had only just shuffled into the main cavern, her vision still cloudy with sleep, when a loud rustle echoed through the cave. Two large forms burst from the bushes before Fallon could even make a fist.

"Well, glad you could make it," Ronen said sardonically. He barely got out the last word before Bhaltair Herleif shoved him to the ground.

The general and captain had finally arrived, but not in good spirits. Bhaltair's golden eyes were ablaze as he locked onto her. "You."

Every hair on her arms stood on end as he approached her. Everything about him—his body, the way he moved, the armor that clung to him as second skin, it was all nothing short of lethal. Fallon did not step back, but swiveled on her heel as he circled her.

"The last man who used that tone with me before breakfast did not make it to lunch," she warned, "Just get to the point. Why are you late?"

He bared his fangs. "The point, your highness, is the male I've been tracking down for months was found dead near the Ondorr border. There was barely enough left of him for his mate to identify."

Her heart stopped beating. "What?"

"Enok spent hours reading through old archives, trying to find any record of a Valdyr with the gift of fire enlisted within the past century. There was *one* left alive. It took weeks to track him down, but we were too late." He stopped moving, and Fallon feared he was readying to pounce. "Were it not for you, we would have never stopped here. We could have reached Geralt a day earlier when we were meant to. We could have saved a life and had a Fire Fae on our side."

Fallon felt his words slice across her abdomen. She felt her guts hit the floor, but she masked it. "So what? Are you telling me this to make me feel bad?" Because she did, she truly did. But any emotions, even good ones, were weaknesses. Especially in front of a warrior like Bhaltair.

Irritation was clear on his rugged face. "You asked me a question, and I answered it: I was late because I had to arrange a funeral," he spat the words at her feet.

The only person brave enough to move was Enok, who stepped between them and began to sign calmingly, to his comrade.

Fallon checked on her friends. Elowen was hugging Ronen's arm tightly. Surprisingly, Elma was nowhere to be seen.

So, Fallon had been right after all. Fritjof was now the last living Fire Fae. He was a step closer to becoming king, and Fallon was ten steps farther from stopping him.

Enok turned to them, signing while Bhaltair watched and translated. "I have watched Fritjof for a long time. He used to be just a—" Bhaltair choked, "Enok, they are children. I'm not saying that."

Enok rolled his eyes and rephrased. Fallon once again tried to assign movements to words as Bhaltair spoke, but it was hard to keep up. "He was only a bully who loved being in power. But he has changed over the past fifteen years. A darkness has awoken inside of him, I can see it in his eyes. So little of the General Aodh we once knew remains. Now he is just …"

Enok's hands froze in midair; she supposed that was the physical equivalent to being at a loss for words. He looked to Bhaltair, making a thumbs-up with one hand and hitting it on the open palm of the other.

"An empty shell," Bhaltair finished, turning back to Fallon. "He has never made a move like this. Fritjof is by no means a saint, but he has never been so uncalculated and bold," he said.

"You mean to say I scared him?" Fallon raised a brow.

Bhaltair gave her a sidelong glance that said *don't flatter yourself.* "We mean you changed things. Your arrival has started the game, forcing him to move after years of happily mooching off the castle and playing king."

Fallon raised her hand. "I have only left this cave twice. How does he even know who I am?"

"That may be my fault," Ronen said sheepishly from behind her. "The Valdyr found a letter from the Little Folk a few days before you came through the Entrance Tree saying they found you."

"And you translated it for them?" Fallon demanded.

He put up his hands in surrender, "Do I really have to explain that I don't do well under pressure?"

"That letter was meant for me," a steady voice said. Finally, Elma slowly descended the steps to where they all stood arguing in the sand. Bhaltair offered his arm, and together they all migrated towards the hearth.

Her aging face was more taught than usual. Her apron was a crumpled mess, surly victim to her anxious hands. She squinted her eyes at Ronen, "The Little Folk taught you how to read Ogham? How did they do it?"

Ronen made a face. "*Ohm,* what?"

"*Ogham*; the language of the trees."

He shrugged sheepishly, "They taught me that language along with English when I was young. I always thought it was just how they communicated," he explained. "Rightward dashes are taps, left are pops, diagonal ones are clicks, and straight is snaps," he said casually.

Fallon was bewildered on many levels as she shouted, "The shrine, Elma's arms, you could read it all along and you didn't—"

The Overseer clapped her hands together harshly. "We will speak more on this later. I fear I must bear some bad news first. I have received another letter. Whatever plans we had for Merrow Cove must be postponed. Bhal is right, the game has officially started," she said grimly.

Elowen scooted closer to Fallon. "Who did you hear from?"

She licked her dry lips. "Arlo Fartre, a trusted member of the King's Court. He owns and runs the largest greenhouse in Elphyne, specializing in the realm's supply of healing herbs," she explained, "He is just as hesitant about this meeting as we are. In fact, he does not think it is a council meeting at all—but an election. Trapped within the Golden Castle, and surrounded by hundreds of Valdyr, they will be forced to choose between giving their lives or their vote. If the majority rules, Fritjof could be crowned king in less than a fortnight."

It made sense. If Fallon were in his position, she could not say she wouldn't do the same. "In a few simple moves, Fritjof has put Elphyne in check," she groaned.

"But not checkmate," Ronen interjected. While everyone else had taken a seat, he remained standing. "It's our move now, and we have something he doesn't."

Elowen smiled, "A queen."

"Exactly. So, let's play our queen." He gestured to Fallon. "Send her to the election. The choice is obvious. Sure, she's a stab-happy, mannerless halfling, but she's better than him," he said, smiling contently.

"Thank you, Nøkken," she snarled.

Bhaltair was not ready to celebrate victory quite yet. "There are two things wrong with your plan. First, we do not have the numbers to pull that off. I only fully trust Arlo Fartre and Lady Honeymaren Larue of the King's Court. That leaves us two to seven."

Enok moved his hand down from his chin in a way that resembled stroking a long beard, then pointed to Fallon.

"Enok brings me to my next point," Bhaltair nodded towards her. "You do not turn twenty for another four months. Even if it was a unanimous vote, you are not old enough to be queen. Our entire mission would be redundant."

"You remember my birthday?" she asked quietly.

He nodded. "Yours is on the tenth of April, Asta's was on the tenth of July. It was easy to remember."

If only it were. All her life, Beowulf never remembered her birthdays. It was only Asta and Hagen, up until the past few years when even Fallon started to forget to care.

She dropped her head into her hands, letting out a growl that had been building in her throat. "We need more time."

"We have forty-two hours."

"I know how to count." She snapped.

They all sat in deep thought, the only sound was grumbling stomachs and impatient sighs. This was all a disaster. Maybe she would have better chances in Barwyn after all.

That was, until the deceptively clever Nøkken opened his mouth. "Princess, have you ever been invited to a party?"

She snorted. "No."

"Me neither," he shrugged. "So, when you see one, what do you want to do?"

A sickly smile spread across her face like dripping oil. "Ruin it."

He nodded, "We obviously can't kill him, we can't stop him yet, we're outnumbered and outmatched—so, let's just ruin his day in order to give us another one," Ronen offered.

Fallon nodded along. "If we flip the board onto his lap, then at least we'll *both* be scrambling to get our pieces back into place."

The hearth fire rose and hissed into a bright yellow as they all turned to Bhaltair. His face was as unreadable as ever, but the firelight danced in his golden eyes. "That might be so horrifically imprudent, he would not see it coming. We just need to show them Fallon, show them another option before the next vote."

Enok snapped for attention. He signed to Bhaltair, who nodded in agreement. "Enok warns how Fritjof does not take disrespect lightly, and he is obviously not above murdering innocents in cold blood. Anyone who sides with us will be in great danger. Fear is a powerful influence—and one they have been under for many years. They will need a lot of convincing to take that risk," he said sternly.

But Fallon's excitement did not waver. "Leave that to me. But we will need a war camp for the new court. A safe haven to bring anyone who sides with us. We can train, speak without fear, and plan for the future." She turned to Elma, "not that I don't love the cave, but even the six of us are crammed in here. The more people that join us, the more room we will need."

Elma rubbed her hands together. "I will have something arranged for when you return. We stay within the Longback Knolls, where my magic can reach and where the Centaurs can protect us," she said.

They all looked each other over. They were really doing this. It took her a moment to realize when they were all staring at *her* expectantly.

Fallon always knew she was born to rule. She was the product of two mighty leaders, after all. But as fate would have it, she would not simply inherit the throne. Nothing was that easy. Before she could rule, Fallon had to lead.

The general must have seen the determination in her eyes. "Are you certain this is how you want to introduce yourself to your people? Forever remembered as the young, reckless princess who runs off risks and luck?" he asked carefully.

She raised her chin, "If I were to show them anything else, it would be a lie. They will have to take me for what I am: a young, reckless, bandit princess ready to do whatever it takes," Fallon said proudly.

Elowen took her hands. "So, what is it called?" she asked, biting her bottom lip in anticipation.

"What is what called?" Fallon laughed.

"You said we need somewhere for the *new* court. We don't have a king, not yet anyways." She winked, "We need a new name. For everyone in this room and whoever comes with us to follow Princess Fallon Alfrothul."

Fallon thought for a moment. This was not for her, but for Asta. For her mother's legacy and the hope she left behind in the hearts of her kingdom. Fallon was going to need every drop of it to make this work.

It was a physical effort to restrain her smile so her face did not rip in half. "I suppose this commences the first meeting of the Light Court," she announced.

Elma clapped, her eyes beaming with pride as everyone joined in. Enok placed an arm low across his waist and bowed deeply. This time, Ronen translated:

"Long live the queen!"

THIRTY

Ronen thought his ravenous thirst for acceptance and purpose would forever go unquenched. Yet here he was: part of a group planning to break into the Golden Castle with the Princess of Elphyne and the General of the Valdyr.

Well, *they* were planning. The two of them had disappeared into an empty room with a table and a map hours ago. Ronen could hear them yelling from where he sat with Enok and Elowen in an adjacent chamber, packing all their bags for the journey. Yet he did not feel any less included, or any less childishly excited to do something he was not supposed to do.

Despite the harsh tones and sharp words, Fallon was having the time of her life. Somehow, war plans and head-smashing were calming to the princess. They all listened as Bhaltair and Fallon discussed entries, targets, back up plans, where and who to avoid, and everything else Ronen would never think to consider. He has never even been in a real fight before. Not one where he hit back, at least.

Not surprisingly, Enok was a great listener. Elowen went on and on about Fallon, trying to get Enok up to speed on the life of Asta's daughter. He had a thin, kind smile and patient eyes. Ronen exercised that patience by constantly asking how to sign every word he could think of.

When even Elowen was running low on things to talk about (which was not often) Enok gently tapped him on the shoulder. He raised three fingers as a *W* up to his chin, tapping it once.

"I don't know that one, sorry," Ronen admitted.

Enok picked up a skin of water, sloshing it around until Ronen understood. "Right. Water. You want to know about my powers," he said as casually as he could.

The captain raised a playful brow: *I never said anything about powers*.

Ronen took a deep breath. "I feel like I'm starting life from scratch again. I have to relearn how to walk, talk, and think with this new … thing," he stammered.

"Have you tried it again since that night?" Elowen asked.

He shook his head. "No, and I haven't felt it since."

Enok raised his palms up and lightly shook his wrists, a common sign that was easy to guess: what. *Felt what since?*

If anyone would understand the strangeness that was controlling something outside of yourself, it was the experienced Earth Fae before him. "When I heard the music, it was like I had another pair of hands. Ones that could feel what my mortal ones can't. I think it's because

I'm only half Nøkken that I can't sense the water all the time, I need a doorway," he explained.

"Maybe that door should stay closed," Bhaltair called from the other room. Stupid Fae hearing.

He and the princess walked over with grim faces and crossed arms. "The last thing we need is even more unpredictability. If you're smart, you'll lock that door and throw away the key. Do you really want to taint this court's image even further? You are lucky Fallon has decided to even take you with us. Stay back, stay quiet, and no Nøkken nonsense," he ordered.

A week ago, that sentence would have left a black bruise on his already sore soul. Blow after blow, Ronen would have taken it and convinced himself he deserved it. But Fallon pressed her lips together and watched him carefully. She wanted him to stand his own ground this time ... she believed he *could* stand his own ground.

Because Ronen was not a punching bag anymore.

It ends with me.

"No," he said quietly.

Everyone turned to him in surprise as Bhaltair became impossibly still. His dark skin blended into the cave walls, leaving only two golden eyes swallowing him whole. Ronen knew as soon as the general got one word out, it was game over. He had to keep going.

"No," he said more assertively this time, "You can't tell me, or anyone, how to use their powers. And if you're *smart*, you'll let the only one of us who can counter a Fire Fae be in that castle with Fallon. Because as all-mighty as you are, General Herleif, that sword of yours can melt. Trust me—I made it," he hissed.

The silence that followed threatened to burst Ronen's eardrums. Then, all too slowly, Bhaltair stood to his full height and glared down his wide nose. "It's about time the nineteen-year-old mortal girl wasn't the only one with a spine." He grinned coyly.

"Half mortal!" Fallon corrected from behind them.

"Half weak, half fragile, half slow …" Bhaltair turned over his shoulder. "Shall I keep going?"

"As much as I know you would enjoy that, we all have work to do." Fallon addressed them all with a stoic expression, "We leave as soon as the moon rises. We will travel through the night and hopefully arrive in Castletowne by evening tomorrow. Once the three of us make it inside the wall, we hide out until the election. We decided that Bhaltair and Enok's positions are too valuable to compromise this early in the game. So once we get inside, we will be on our own."

Ronen shrugged "Yeah, what else is new?"

Fallon smiled—actually *smiled*—at his comment. Who knew it took planning a hostile takeover to put her in a good mood.

She continued, "We leave in roughly twelve hours, so use them wisely. Ronen and Elo, you should practice your powers. We'll need them," she encouraged.

The general turned on his heel to face her. "You, meet me back here in thirty minutes. You might have been a fighter in the mortal realm, but you are Fae now. It's time to learn to fight as one," Bhaltair ordered.

She strutted past him. "Make it twenty-five minutes." Fallon grabbed Ronen and Elowen's arms, quickly dragging them into another room.

Ronen's mortal ears heard Bhaltair grumble some words to his mother before his and Enok's footsteps faded down the hall. Fallon remained silent, resting her elbows on the table and staring at the map until she knew the general and captain were out of Fae earshot.

"You don't have to do this." She said at last, taking a moment to look them each in the eyes. "I know I have put us in dangerous situations before, but this is different. You heard what happened with that Fire Fae; every mistake could have a fatal consequence."

He snorted. "What? Being chased by a herd of Hempia or swimming a few laps with the Merrows *didn't* have fatal consequences?"

Elowen put a silencing hand on his arm. Apparently, it was obvious to everyone but him it was no time for jokes.

The Hulder's small, angular face was ageless as she looked up to Fallon, "My whole life I've dreamed of castles and princesses. When I was alone for all those years, I used to pretend I was walking through the royal gardens. I had a dress made of flowers, and a group of beautiful maidens as my friends." Her smile grew with every word, "But now, it doesn't have to be a dream. There really is a princess, and she is more amazing than I could have imagined. So, of course I'm going to help in any way I can. One day, I want to be one of those maidens walking with a princess in the gardens."

The girls interlocked hands, as they often did, and Ronen watched the exchange of silent thanks between them. Their friendship was the truest mystery of all. But Ronen would never forget that day at the Entrance Tree, when Fallon was ready to use her dying breath to protect Elowen. He had never seen that kind of love before.

Elowen's words had a surprising impact on him, too. Not that he was keen to stroll around the castle in a frilly dress, but he wanted to help this vision come to life. The way he used to live, the way he used to feel every single day … he never wanted to go back to that. Somewhere out there, there were even more twenty-one-year-old outcasts still as lost as he was. But hope was finally here. And as it just so happened—so was he.

Ronen cleared his throat. "I have been tired for a long time. I always thought it was because I had done too much … been through too much. But now, I can see it's because I haven't actually *done* anything at all. I've never done something that mattered or made me feel that spark of life everyone always talks about. Please, Fal, don't try to take this away from us. I know you're just trying to protect us but keeping me back would kill me more than any blade could," he explained.

Fallon shook her head in dismay. "I thought this would be easy. My whole life, I watched my father order armies into a slaughter with a smile on his face. I thought it would be a joy, an honor, to escort hundreds into the gates of Valhalla. But now … even asking the five of you to help me seems like asking too much. Does that make me weak?" she asked quietly.

"It's what makes you strong," Elowen assured her. "I think that is why your father feared you so much: in a land of iced over hearts, yours was beating."

Fallon let out a dark, humorless laugh. "Beowulf Solveij fears nothing—he feels nothing."

"He felt threatened by you," Elowen explained gently.

"How could you possibly know that?"

Elowen placed a hand on Fallon's twitching hand. "Because happy people don't hurt people."

Beowulf. Ronen only knew a sliver of what he did to Fallon, and it was enough to make him want to risk the mortal world. Just so Ronen could find him and make him pay. "Your father was the weak one, not you." He assured her.

Fallon shook her head, "you don't understand—"

"How much *strength* does it take for a grown man to toss around a little girl?" he demanded.

She grit her teeth together. "None."

"How much strength did it take for you to survive it?"

Fallon went quiet. If the princess truly grew up in a place where the ability to feel compassion was seen as a threat, it was a miracle the girl could even smile.

"Whatever kept your heart from freezing over for nineteen years—it's the same thing that made those flowers grow. It made you save Elowen that day. Now, you need to use it to save us all," he said.

Fallon rolled her shoulders back and leveled her gaze in an art Ronen could never master. Steady, calculated, strong. The girl who should be broken into a thousand pieces stood taller than he ever could. Because Fallon was a dangerous type of crazy; she did not run from pain, she burned it as fuel.

"I feel confident in this plan, but plans go wrong," Fallon said sternly. "Things change and mistakes happen. So, if all else fails, you get back to this cave. Promise me."

Elowen and Ronen smiled. "We promise."

Hopefully Fallon didn't see his fingers crossed behind his back as he said, "So, let's hear this master plan."

"These are for you."

Bhaltair shoved a heavy, lumpy bag into Ronen's chest. He untied it with a huff and peered inside. At first, it just looked like a bunch of junk. Then his eyes focused on the strings, the pipes, and the brass—

"Instruments," he said in disbelief.

"If you want to be a Nøkken, you might as well be a good one. I can teach Fallon how to use a sword, but I cannot teach you how to use *this*," he gestured to Ronen's pathetic form. "So get some practice in while Enok shows Elowen how to advance her healing skills, Dag forbid we need them."

Ronen could not tell if the intense itching under his skin was from excitement or sheer terror. Before he could muster up a thank you or even ask where on Elphyne the general acquired these, Bhaltair was gone.

Ronen walked over to the wooden bench by the hearth and dumped out the bag's contents in one loud crash. A lyre, a flute, an ancient-looking fiddle, and a single drumhead. How was he supposed to learn to play these in just a few hours? Did it not take years upon years and a strict regime to master an instrument?

The hearth fire flicked a deep orange behind him, and something caught Ronen's eye under the bench. One instrument, smaller than the others, had dropped in the sand. He picked it up and twirled it in his hand: seven hollow reeds were tied side by side, ordered from shortest to longest. A simple pan flute.

Ronen blew off some sand, his breath accidentally catching a few of the holes. The single note echoed through the silent chamber, sending a rush up Ronen's spine so strong it nearly knocked him on his ass. He laughed to himself as he tried it again, this time sweeping his lips across all seven reeds. It was ancient and calling— more of a voice than a sound. Oh yes, he liked this one.

"Here." Elma appeared out of the shadows (as always) and placed a bucket of sloshing water before him, as well as an empty bucket beside it. "Get the water from one bucket to the other," she said simply.

Ronen choked on his own spit. He glanced nervously back and forth between the pan and the bucket. "Can you turn around or something?" he asked, feeling a little power-shy.

Elma chuckled, adjusting her robes as she sat down on the bench across from him. "If you don't mind, I want to observe. That way I can write down our findings and leave it here for the next Overseer as part of my contributions to the Temple of Wisdom. You see, people fear what they do not understand, and the more we can teach others about you, the less they will fear you," she said.

The pan became a heavy weight in his hands. "They made an enemy of me before they even knew my name," he said coldly, watching the water before him ripple.

"What name?"

He rolled his eyes, "Ronen."

"Ronen who?"

"Ronen Nøkken." He mumbled.

She walked up and slapped his back. "Hold your head up when you say it! And don't drawl your words. If you cannot say your own name with even an ounce of pride, how do you expect anyone else to?" she demanded.

"What about me should I be *proud* of, Elma?" he shot back, "The part of me that got kicked out of my only home, or the part that got me buried alive?"

Elma grabbed his hands, wrapping them tightly around the flute. Her thin fingers trembled as she held him close. "*This.*" She whispered, "The gods called them gifts for a reason, child. I fear people like Fritjof are making us lose sight of that. They are not weapons, or curses, or prizes presented to only the brave. These gifts are our connection to the gods and the world they created for us. That includes you."

Ronen had indeed lost all faith that the gods knew Nøkken still existed. Maybe if he could do this, if he could help the princess save Elphyne, they would see him.

"Maybe they were all evil." He said quietly, "My ancestors, I mean. Maybe all the stories were true, and they died fighting for Ondorr. But obviously some survived. They must have escaped from this realm and made a home elsewhere. That would make me a product of those who chose not to fight. Of a Nøkken who wed a woman and didn't drown her. This is for them, too. Of course I want to fight for Fallon, but I'm here for all the Nøkken who didn't get to see a fair Elphyne." he said in a voice he didn't recognize. A voice that didn't mutter or stutter or crack.

Elma stepped back and looked up at him with silver-rimmed eyes. "There you are," she whispered.

Ronen knelt by the buckets, raising the pan to his lips. A bridge—he needed to make the water a bridge. An arc of sound: up, over, down.

"Concentrate," Elma probed.

"Since when has saying *concentrate* ever helped anyone concentrate?"

He released an unsteady breath, trying not to cringe as that phantom hand breached from his chest. His mouth moved across the hollow reeds without a second thought, and the door to a world where water and sound were one opened before him.

The water in the bucket slowly rose in a slim, wobbling tower. *Holy shit. Holy shit—*

The tower fell, and the door slammed in his face.

"Damnit," he cursed.

Elma shook her head as she sat back down, pulling a piece of parchment from the sleeve of her robes and scribbling down some notes. "Stop being afraid of it," she chided.

"I'm not afraid of it."

"Yes, you are."

"It feels gross!"

"It feels *different*," Elma corrected, "And different is not wrong."

Ronen tried again, keeping his breath steadier. The tower stayed up this time, but now he had to move it over. He visualized it, and his hands automatically moved to meet his needs. One gentle decrescendo later, and the sound of splashing water overpowered his flute.

He stepped back, "I did it."

Elma clapped, the ball of twisted dreads on her head bobbing in excitement. "Well done, boy! Now, again."

Now more excited than terrified, Ronen did it again. And again. And again. He sat on his haunches in front of the two buckets and cycled through the instruments, trying to make sense of the madness. The flute moved the water so fast, it knocked over him and the buckets. While it took him twenty minutes of brain-melting drumming to even get a drop up.

Elowen and Enok came by after overhearing his strange—and probably dreadful—symphony. Ronen always wondered why Fallon fought so hard to protect a random, helpless Faerie in the mortal world. Now, after seeing how hard Elowen laughed when he made some water drops fall into her mouth—he understood. He would destroy kingdoms for her, too.

"We have to show Fallon!" she cried, "She will love it!"

The Hulder's tail was swinging wildly in excitement as she practically dragged him down the corridors. It wasn't that he didn't want to show Fallon, he just felt … lame. She was a warrior, a princess, and a survivor. Why would she be amused, let alone impressed by his party tricks?

They followed the sound of swords clanging until they entered a large, empty chamber. The floor was sanded down and smooth, and the flickering torches on the walls made it one of the brightest rooms he has seen. Perfect for sparring.

Bhaltair and Fallon had their backs turned, both shirtless and gleaming with sweat. She was breathing heavily, while the general seemed only slightly disgruntled. It wasn't until she turned around that Ronen realized the labored breaths were not from fighting—Fallon was crying.

His entire world came to a crashing halt. Ronen forgot about music and powers and Fae. He forgot what sound even was as his eyes trailed down her exposed torso.

"Fallon … what is that?"

THIRTY-ONE

Fallon never used swords.

Well, her wrists did not allow her to. She had broken them too many times trying to get out of chains or throwing poor punches. Thus, the weak ligaments and inflamed scar tissue made it nearly impossible to parry Bhaltair's endless stream of attacks.

He was throwing her on her ass as if she were a novice. All those hours spent training with Hagen seemed worthless now. Her old mentor pushed her to her absolute limits, breaking her down in order to build her up into something stronger. Hagen used to say pain was just the weakness inside of us dying, thus it was something to yearn for.

Hagen *killed* Fallon Solveij. She trusted him, and he killed her.

Wielding her sword with both hands, Fallon barely got it up in time to block Bhaltair's downward blow to her face.

He drew back his sword, the sound of metal slicing metal rang in her ears. "Where are you right now?" he asked, "You are looking right at me, yet you don't see me."

She gulped down as many breaths as she could while his sword was down. Her body was weak after over a month of being on the run, locked up, and put on a cave-dweller's diet. But she refused to ask for a break, even as the hours passed. Bhaltair had discarded his armor so it would be a *fair* fight. But it only made her feel worse for not landing a single nick on his perfectly honed, tan chest.

What was the point of all that pain if she could not even make one Fae warrior flinch? If she could not do this, Fallon Solveij died for nothing.

"I am in a stuffy cave, fighting you, with a worthless sword," she grumbled, wiping the sweat from her nose.

He examined her for a moment. She must have looked as terrible as she felt, because Bhaltair took another step back. "You are not ready," he said flatly. "If you cannot see past your own anger to fight the enemy before you instead of the one in your head, there is nothing for me to teach you."

Little did he know, her anger was currently the only thing keeping her standing. "I'm not done," she rolled out her wrists, "Again."

"I said we are done."

Fallon spun, throwing her momentum into her hips as she swung with everything she had. Bhaltair not only blocked her, but disarmed her and got his arm around her neck in seconds.

She let out a scream of frustration, clawing at the impossibly strong arm pressing against her windpipe. The scar on her side stretched and ached from all the movement—a burning reminder of just how useless she was.

Bhaltair leaned close to her ear. "Tell me where you are. Tell me what you see."

Red. Fallon saw red as she kicked and tossed her weight around while she still had the strength. "I see the pole he chained me to, stuck in the frozen ground." She screamed through clenched teeth, "I smell the leather, see the iron—"

Bhaltair squeezed harder, cutting off her voice. "Why do you hold onto that anger so tightly? What does it do for you?" he demanded.

Her head already buzzed from lack of air. She tried to tap out, but he did not let go. He could kill her right now if he wanted to.

Fallon started to see stars as she finally lost the ability to fight back. He wrapped his other arm across her shoulders, helping her stand as he slowly released the pressure on her throat. "Let go, Alfrothul," he said with surprising gentleness.

"I can't," she gasped.

"Why?"

Fallon could not stop her chin from wobbling. She was helpless against the tears gathering in her eyes. "He hurt me."

The oxygen flooded back into her head like a pounding wave, purging out the fog that had lingered there for decades. She kept repeating those three words; the answer to every question that ever plagued her. "*He hurt me,*" she blubbered again and again.

Bhaltair kept her close. "That pain is yours to bear. No enemy, friend, or death can relieve you from that burden. I know your anger feels like the only thing keeping you afloat. But if you just *let go* for one goddamn second, you will see your feet can touch the ground," he said, letting go of her at last.

Fallon wobbled on her feet, but then stood still as the world reformed around her. With every blink came a teardrop, but her vision had never been sharper.

"Let go," he repeated, "And walk back to shore."

She turned to face him. He did not discipline her for crying. He patiently waited as she hiccupped and sniffed until she trusted herself to speak again. Fallon could not remember the last time she cried like this in front of someone.

"After my mother died, how long did it take you to find your way back?" she asked. If he could do it, so could she.

"I was dragged back," he said solemnly, "by my duties and responsibilities as general. But I found myself trapped in a place I did not recognize. I was lost, trying to navigate a world where she did not exist," he said.

"It felt like the entire world was mocking you, didn't it?" Her voice was barely audible. "How the sun still *dared* to shine, how time still dared to move on without her. My entire world was shattered, yet the one around me didn't care. Didn't even blink."

He gave her three slow, firm nods.

Beowulf never said her mother's name ever again. But Bhaltair was proof that someone else had felt the world end. He saw the sky fall that day, too. So Beowulf could rot in Helheim.

Fallon had to pull off her sweat-soaked shirt to cool down, feeling sticky and overwhelmed. Bhaltair was right; fair or not, this pain was hers. If Fallon was going to stop this cycle, she was going to have to destroy it — before it destroyed her.

She was still lost in thought when her friends came bursting into the chamber, giggling like children. Ronen's cheeks were pink as he stumbled towards her with Elowen and Enok right on his heels.

But then he paused, and his smile dropped so fast Fallon heard it crash on the floor. By the time she realized her mistake, it was too late: she was so eager to wipe the tears off her face, she forgot to put her shirt back on.

Ronen stopped breathing entirely. "Fallon … what is that?"

She did not have to look to know where he was pointing. She felt four pairs of eyes staring right at her exposed stomach, their gaze burned more than the iron did. Fallon did not look. She did not want to see that ugly, uneven *U* and *X* that followed her everywhere.

She swallowed a few times, refusing to take her eyes off the stone wall to her right. "A farewell gift from Midgard," she croaked, "A permanent reminder of what I am."

"What. Is. That," Ronen asked again, each word an obvious effort.

Elowen covered her mouth with trembling hands, burying her face in Enok's chest. Fallon never let Elowen see the whole thing. She never let anyone see how broken she was. How could they look at her if they knew she was falling apart at the seams? How could they trust her to protect them if they knew she failed to save herself?

Fallon knew her raised chin was a lie. The confident boast in her voice, her posture … it was all a lie. So for once, she dropped the act. Because friends did not lie. If they were going to love her, they had to love all the broken, ugly parts of her, too.

Nineteen years' worth of agony poured into her voice. Shards of her broken soul sliced her throat on the way out, so speaking felt more like bleeding as she forced her mouth to move. "It's er … it's a brand that they put—that they put on livestock. It means unclaimed, Ronen. Unclaimed, Unwanted." She gulped, "Unworthy."

Bhaltair left the room without a word, taking Enok with him. Good. She wished the others would have followed, because Fallon could hardly stomach the sight of Elowen's silent tears. Fallon was handing them her pain on a platter, and she had no choice but to trust they wouldn't throw it back at her feet.

Ronen moved for the first time since entering the room. He did not cry or run away. Untamed *fury* boiled in his eyes as he stepped closer to her than ever before, his nose nearly touching hers. "Well like it or not, Fallon Alfrothul: *I* claim you. You are *my* friend. Today, tomorrow, crown on your head or shackles on your ankles, you are my friend. So as long as Elowen and I are alive, you don't get to use that word anymore," he said in a voice she had never heard from him.

A wave of relief washed over her. She wanted to tell him she claimed him, too. That she would rip the moon from the sky if he or Elowen asked her to. But Fallon could do nothing but nod and bite the insides of her cheek as Elowen ran up to hug her.

They saw her broken pieces, and they didn't run away. *That* is what friendship was. And Fallon finally found it.

She offered her hand to Ronen, but he shook his head. "I'll pass. You smell worse than I did a week ago."

Somehow, a laugh escaped her. A small, genuine laugh that she did not even know she could produce. It seemed that whenever she misplaced it, Ronen was always there to hand her back her heart—and Elowen reminded it how to beat.

Not that long ago, Fallon swore to never belong again. The wounds left by those who were supposed to love her still gushed blood every single day, but these two made her see healing was possible. They made her *want* to heal.

So Fallon grabbed him by the collar and forced him into an embrace. She felt so warm with them, she started to believe there was a cure to a frostbitten soul.

"If the three of you are finished," Bhaltair grumbled from the doorway. "We leave in five hours. You should get some sleep while you can."

Fallon and her friends made beds around the hearth fire. Ronen and Elowen were exhausted, so it did not take long for their breaths to turn into hushed snores. Fallon was wide awake, staring at the stone ceiling high above.

Because tomorrow, this entire realm was going to learn her name.

It would carry across mountains and send ripples through the surrounding ocean. Like the metallic taste in the air after lightning struck, Asta's daughter would leave her mark.

Fallon Alfrothul had a body full of scars she would use as a map to lead her people. Lead them *away* from every ounce of pain she had ever endured. She could retrace her steps back to where she came from, but the horizon ahead was so, so beautiful.

The ancient, whispering heartbeat inside of her hummed in response, aroused by her thoughts. But something told Fallon not to touch it, not yet. It was still in that cage at the bottom of her soul. Pacing, flickering — waiting. Until the moment their two hearts beat as one.

Boom. Boom. Boom.

A long-lost princess with red hair and her mother's eyes stood on a hilltop, staring in awe at her homeland.

As she and the newly established Light Court made their way across the land, Fallon felt as though she was seeing Elphyne for the first time. Sounds were no longer just sounds; they were whispers in a language she had known since birth. Every color had a scent, and each scent carried a taste she ravished in. Now, in her Fae body, Elphyne was nothing short of an experience. She understood why this realm was not for mortals—they would never understand nor appreciate the art they were surrounded by.

Fallon could see Dag and Dagmar join hands as they painted this land with nothing but seawater and divinity. She could imagine Dagmar's gold-stained fingertips brush across the soil, leaving meadows and groves in her wake. Dag traced a single line across the ground, creating valleys and rivers for all their creations.

Unfortunately, her enjoyment kept getting interrupted by Ronen's complaining, Elowen's awful habit of wandering off, and the two crankiest Fae in the Valdyr nagging her about queenly duties.

The Longback Knolls were still in sight, but the hearth cave she had come to love and trust was at her back. They traveled north, over lush green hills and through dense tree groves. Fallon saw more birds, rabbits, and deer in six hours than she had seen in her entire life. Not to mention the Faeries that flew around as native as the squirrels.

"Woah," she breathed for possibly the hundredth time. Fallon pointed to a stunning butterfly warming its wings on a tree trunk. It was the palest shade of blue, the body so white it nearly glowed.

Enok placed a gentle hand on her back, pointing to the elegant creature. He then made a sideways V with his index and middle finger, moving from one shoulder to the other then down to his side. With the same index finger, he trailed a straight line from his eye to his jaw.

"Of course." Bhaltair rolled his eyes.

Fallon grinned. "What is it? What did he say?"

"Crying!" Ronen shouted, as if they were playing a game of charades. "Teardrop! Sad!"

Elowen clapped her hands excitedly. "The first one was a shirt! Or maybe—dress! Um … sad dress!" she guessed.

Bhaltair massaged his temples. "Princess's Teardrop. The butterfly is called a Princess's Teardrop."

She could not contain her smile as her little friend flapped to life, seeming to respond to its name. It made a full circle around them before disappearing into the blue sky.

It felt wrong to be tired while the sun was still out, but she supposed that was something her body would have to adapt to. It did not appear to be midnight at all, but the massive moon stacked right under the sun said otherwise.

Enok chuckled, rustling Ronen's hair as if to say *better luck next time*. His laugh was the closest thing Fallon would ever hear to his real voice. It was soft, but masculine. Like the smooth coat of a wolf.

The Captain of the Valdyr walked ahead with her friends, occasionally steering Elowen's shoulders back in the right direction. Bhaltair had not spoken to her much in the hours they spent walking side by side. Even less had he looked at her. Yet no matter how fast Fallon sped up or slowed down, he stayed right at her side. An old habit of shadowing Asta as her appointed knight.

"Do you remember what he sounds like?" Fallon asked quietly, staring at the back of Enok's blond head.

To her surprise, Bhaltair managed a smile. "Unfortunately, I do. Nearly twenty-five years' worth of nagging, worrying, and scolding is permanently burned into my memory."

She did some math in her head, trying not to make a face as she realized how old the general and captain must be. But thanks to their Fae blood, Fallon was sure they appeared the same as they did the last time Asta saw them.

"How long?" She asked, her voice no louder than the Princess's Teardrop's wing flap.

He hesitated. "It has been almost five years since I heard my brother's voice," he explained at last. Fallon instantly felt bad for asking. It was none of her business, but that answer did not satisfy her curiosity. She wanted to know what could make a man abandon his own tongue.

Instead of asking, she settled on just staring at Enok's back, hypnotized by the shifting plates of his golden armor. The sun should be reflecting into her eyes, but the metal seemed to absorb the sunlight. It pooled into the golden cast like running honey; Fae gold, Ronen had called it.

Ronen slowed down and fell into step beside her, leaving Enok to keep track of Elowen. He pointed east, over a dense forest of tall, lean trees. "Right through there is Athol Village," he said.

"Your home?"

He shrugged. "I guess you could call it that. The orphanage where the Little Folk dropped me off is there. I only ever left going on deliveries with Urg. Well," He shot a sour glance over his shoulder, "Until recently."

"I had a job to do. Nothing personal." Bhaltair shrugged.

"Maybe not the first punch to the face, but the third felt a *little* personal."

The general had not so much as broken a sweat after walking for hours on end. He seemed anxious to speed up, but he stayed at the rear.

He peered over their heads, eyes glazed and distance. "Believe me, boy, I was just as disappointed as you that day. I thought I finally found her," he mumbled.

"The Shapeshifter?" Fallon asked.

"Lower your voice," he snapped.

She rolled her eyes. "You're just as bad as your mother."

"The Nøkken of Athol Village was my last lead. Now, I must start from scratch again." He shook his head in frustration.

Fallon peered west, where she knew the dark shadow of Ondorr stood looming over her green lands. "Why are you the only one who seems to care about her? As far as I can see, she's causing a lot less problems than Fritjof."

He made a sound that might have been a laugh. "I am the only one who seems to care about many things. You see, Elphyne was not always as safe as it is now. Before we secured the border during the Elphynian War, the children of Ondorr would often cross into Lysserah. They spread plagues and death to anything and anyone they touched. Why do you think the Golden Castle was built directly under the Sun, surrounded by waterfalls fed by the ocean?"

She cursed under her breath. "Ondorr's only weaknesses."

"When even that was not enough to keep the royal family safe, a wall was erected. Made by Orculli master builders and the Overseer, it still stands today: separating the castle grounds from the surrounding village. But, if that Shapeshifter is still out there, she threatens all of that. She could have offspring and raise another dark army," he explained.

Ronen was breathing heavily, and she no longer believed it was from the physical exertion. He had felt the touch of Ondorr—as had Elowen. If the agony they described was from mere darkness, what kinds of horrors could be inflicted when that darkness was given form? Sentinels, Blights, Fodden … shadows, nightmares, and plagues.

"What do they want?" she asked. "To kill the royal family?"

Ronen visibly shivered. "They don't *want* anything, Fal. They are soulless, mindless, and heartless. All they understand—if it even counts as understanding—is spreading misery."

But that did not make sense to Fallon. Everything had a purpose. Perhaps whatever—or whoever—created Ondorr in the first place was responsible for sending armies after the Fae. Shapeshifters seemed to be the most sentient ones, maybe they ruled Ondorr as kings. Still, the question remained: why?

For now, Fritjof was their biggest enemy. Maybe once Fallon sat on the Ash Throne with the Lord of Fire's head in her lap, she could go Shapeshifter hunting.

Dewdenn Village was about half the size of Amory, but far nicer than any village Fallon had ever come across. The roads were made of stone blocks, allowing the multitude of wagons smooth passage through the busy streets. Flower baskets hung at every corner, and pen animals walked freely with their owners.

"First Fae village?" Ronen joked, laughing at the look on her face as they all crouched behind some hedges. "Don't worry, you get used to it."

He did not mean the hundreds of pointed ears and deadly canines before them. He meant the obscene *beauty* that was the Fae people. They were all perfect—even the children. The story books did not do them justice. Fallon was suddenly bitter that she had missed out on that part of her Fae genetics.

Suddenly, her gawking was cut off. The hedge she knelt behind grew to obscure her view. She snapped around to see Enok and Bhaltair with their heads perked up and eyes dilated. "I made sure to put Valdyr I trust on rotation to any villages we might cross through. You three rest while I speak with them, they might have updates from the castle," Bhaltair ordered.

He stood, Enok parting the hedge so he could pass through soundlessly. As the bush closed behind him, it grew to cover them in a semicircle, away from prying eyes. Enok had done so without even lifting a finger.

Ronen immediately grabbed his bag, took some apples from Fallon's pack, and walked off into the trees. He has been practicing his powers nonstop. No one seemed to mind, though, as each of their breaks was filled with gentle music.

After a quiet midnight snack, Elowen rested her head on Fallon's lap and almost immediately fell asleep. Fallon knew she was more exhausted than she let on. For the last few hours her tail hung low at her side, and she rubbed her eyes so much the tan skin around them turned pink. Fallon tried not to shift her legs as she gently moved strand after strand of white hair from her snoring face.

Silence was a comfortable thing with Enok. For much of her life, it had been a bad omen. The moment the owls stopped hooting before the war horn sounded ... the suction of air as the chamber door swung open. But not here. Enok said enough with the way his long and lean body was positioned comfortably.

He examined her for a moment, the gentle breeze lifting his long hair. She knew he wanted to say something, he just couldn't. Not without Bhaltair around. Instead, Enok hovered his hand above the ground, and she watched in awe as a small sprout erupted from the grass. It grew and grew, weeks of development happening in seconds. Its bud unfurled into hundreds of petals all hugging one another, a shade of pink so light it was nearly white.

Slowly, almost painfully, Enok plucked it. He held it so tight that his fingernails turned white, but he eventually offered it to her. Fallon smiled in thanks, "It's breathtaking. There were few flowers in Barwyn, but my mother sometimes brought me some. I had to hide them from my father, so they never lasted long," she explained quietly. Fallon wondered if the chest full of dead flower petals was still there, crammed under a broken bed long outgrown.

She was just starting to doze off when Bhaltair returned. Fallon was a bit proud of herself when she heard him coming, even though he was doing nothing to mask his steps. Then she caught the heady, medicinal musk that was his scent as he rounded the corner.

"Any updates?" Fallon asked urgently as the general took a seat in the grass across from her.

Bhaltair seemed deep in thought. "The location of the meeting has finally been disclosed. It will take place in the Castle Sanctum. It is a religious, sacred place directly below the throne room. Why would he …" He looked up and blanched at the sight of the flower placed behind her ear. "Where did you get that?"

His head snapped to Enok before she even gave her answer. The two shared a silent conversation that left both men with shattered expressions.

Upon hearing Bhaltair's return, Ronen came staggering back to the group and pushed Elowen's legs out of the way to sit by Fallon. "Is everything alright?" he asked tentatively.

She could smell the metal from the flute on his lips as he spoke. Fallon had to force her eyes, nose, and ears away from him.

For the first time, it was Bhaltair who signed to Enok. Fallon's shoulders dropped as they both kept pointing at her.

"You heard me," she groaned to Enok. "When I asked ..." She was too embarrassed to finish the sentence. If she had wanted to know why Enok did not speak, she should have gone to him. Not Bhaltair.

Enok leaned over and plucked the flower from her hair. He spun it in his fingers for a moment, glancing once at his friend. *Translate?*

Then, he started to sign in a way Fallon had never seen. His fingers danced through the air, as if he was a composer of an orchestra where the instruments were words, and their music was anguish.

Bhaltair took a deep breath. "Fae are not like mortals when it comes to marriage. We have mates, not husbands and wives. Every one of us is born with a part of our soul residing in another, and we spend our lives searching for the person to complete us. I found the other part of me when I was nineteen, her name was Aine." He signed her name delicately, like he was holding cracked porcelain in his palm.

"She was the youngest of seven sisters, all of them working as servants in the castle. They tried to sabotage her dreams of being a healer by reporting missing herbs from the kitchen. I was the one tasked with confronting her about it. But when I entered the healer's quarters, all I saw was a young woman with raven hair and green-stained fingertips, clutching a pink peony to her chest."

Fallon's heart struggled to beat. Even Ronen had gone slightly pale as they both listened and watched intently. "I grew whatever herb or plant she asked for, so she didn't have to steal anymore. Soon our meetings in that healer's room became nightly. As the years passed and our vows were spoken, my new position as captain demanded more of me. If I was ever gone or occupied, I could still feel that room. I could feel her, no matter how far away I was. So I grew a flower to remind her I was still there," he smiled at the flower in his lap, "And that she was still my perfect peony."

"I loved her in silence, I loved her so loudly I feared the sky would crack and fall if I dared to even whisper her name. The gods may have given me the power of nature, but *she* was my gift. When we wed, I gave her everything I was. My soul, my hands, the very air in the lungs … it all belonged to her. But the day our daughter was born, her womb ruptured. Nothing could stop the bleeding. I could not give my mate my last breath, but I could give her my last words. I told my sweet Aine I loved her, and there is nothing left for me to say until the day I see her again," Bhaltair translated.

Never before had someone's words gripped Fallon's heart so tightly; it felt like someone was trying to rip it straight from her chest. She turned to Ronen, but found him already watching her. Fallon wordlessly asked him to speak. She did not have it in her. Not when her leg was becoming damp from Elowen's tears dripping down.

"And your daughter?" Ronen asked carefully.

Enok somehow smiled, "Her name is Nara. Nara Peony Ellwood." He finger-spelled her name proudly, "She lives with my father on my family's farm north of Castletowne."

A part of Enok's mate remains in this life. She must be coming up on five years old now. Fallon understood what it was like to grow up without a mother, and some days it was worse than any shadow soldier or fire lord. For Enok, she would give this little girl her best chance.

Ronen raised his fingertips to his chin then lowered his arm palm-up. He then made a fist and rubbed small circles onto the center of his chest. *Thank you, I'm sorry.*

Enok placed a hand over his heart, politely excusing himself as he walked off into the trees beyond. Leaving behind a single pink peony in the grass.

She turned to Bhaltair, who refused to look in their direction. He had spoken those words about soul bound love as if they were his own. As if he understood the torture of a broken heart all too well.

THIRTY-TWO

It took a solid hour for Fallon to process the Golden Castle.

From afar, it looked like the most beautiful oil painting in the world. Then, when she was up close (even if it was from under a hood and hiding within the shadows of Castletowne) it felt like a dream. A mirage. Something too beautiful to bear. She once read that if the Asgardians ever showed their true godly form to a mortal, they would combust on the spot. And right now, Fallon was at major risk of combusting.

Those hours of studying the map of this town had paid off, because Fallon was having a hard time leading Ronen and Elowen through the busy streets without getting sidetracked. The afternoon rush had just started as they found a good place behind some crates to gather their wits.

Castletowne was even more breathtaking than Dewdenn. Obviously a wealthy community, the red-tiled roofs and lines of storefronts made the Solveij Royal House seem like nothing more than a shack in the woods.

They separated from the general and captain upon arriving. They needed to get back to the castle before Fritjof noticed their extended absence. Fallon was to meet them at a round door on the east side of the ten-foot wall as soon as possible. Bhaltair warned her that Valdyr were posted every fifty feet along the wall, and it was important to not seem suspicious.

She snagged some empty crates from the back of a wagon and handed one to each of her friends. "Here, carry these. We need to look like we have a purpose."

"We do have a purpose, they just won't like it," Ronen shrugged.

Would they? How many of them were on Bhaltair's side? Only the general himself could tell. Fritjof had records of each soldier's name, where he lived, and his family members. That slip of paper was the ball at the end of their chain.

She urged her friends forward, holding the wooden crates in their arms as if they had produce for delivery. While Fallon navigated, Ronen was in charge of keeping Elowen's cloak over her hair and tail. Huldra lived at their trees, so they rarely walked around the villages. Not to mention, Elowen's face tended to draw a crowd.

As they entered the eastern district, the stone path under her feet turned into compact dirt. Round, glass windows were replaced by crooked wooden planks, and suddenly she and her friends were not the only hooded figures loitering about. Perfect.

They ditched their crates on a random doorstep as Fallon scanned the solid stone wall. The castle was built onto the side of a mountain, and they were now close enough that Fallon could squint and see the dots of gold positioned on the cliffs. Next to them was another, much larger form—their war dogs, Barguests. Ronen had pestered Bhaltair about his own companion (a massive female named Thetis) for the majority of their journey.

Finally, she found the door. It was larger than a typical door, round and made of dark wood. Unfortunately, she was not the only one interested in it. A mass of people lingered around, kicking the dirt and tapping their fingers impatiently. What were they waiting for?

As if on cue, the door slowly creaked open. Two Valdyr stepped out and stood at attention. Standing at the threshold was an elderly woman in servant's clothing, holding a steaming bowl in each hand.

Everyone immediately ran to get in line. There was shoving, cursing, and bickering as everyone fought for the front. Fallon understood that hunger in their eyes: it meant there were many drooling mouths, but only one carcass to feed on.

"A lunch line?" Elowen whispered. "Are you sure this is where we are supposed to be?"

Fallon nodded. "Bhaltair said to find the door, and I'll know how to get in. He said I just have to be myself."

"Do princesses get first dibs or something?" Ronen snorted, eyeing the crowd.

Fallon followed his gaze, where people were still throwing elbows. Ronen once told her that there was no such thing as a perfect realm. Despite all the glamor and beauty they walked through to get here, Castletowne still had its slums. Just like Amory, Dewdenn, and Penswallow.

She might be a princess, but right here in the dirt is where she belonged. Thieves, beggars, and bastards they were. Scarred and beautiful.

Ronen eyed her wearily, "Your highness?"

A long, nearly animalistic smile crossed her face. "Wrong Fallon."

His head dropped. "Dag help us."

"Keep Elowen close," she ordered, then pulled down the tip of her hood and walked straight for the front of the line.

It did not take long for someone to notice her. A gangly, yet attractive teenager with blonde hair threw out his arm. "Back of the line, girl!"

Fallon easily shoved past him. Ronen was right on her heels, one arm around Elowen's shoulders. "We're with her!"

"Hey!" the boy shouted up ahead, "There's a girl cutting!"

This caught the Valdyr's attention. Their long hair swayed as they stalked towards her, golden lances in hand. This was not enough … she had to get them through that door. Not escorted to the back of the line.

Fallon turned to the closest man pointing at her and punched him in the face.

Forgetting to reel back her Fae strength, the man instantly collapsed to the ground. Ronen cursed loudly behind her, but Fallon was too busy marveling at the fact her hand didn't even hurt.

She heard a *whoosh* of air to her left and ducked just in time to dodge a blow from the unconscious man's friend. Soon enough, she was caught in a tornado of fists and fangs. She heard shouts that the food ran out, that someone passed out, and people were cutting in line. Fallon kept swinging, just for the fun of it. Her feet danced in the dirt to a song she thought was long forgotten. Now that Bhaltair helped her to see again, she could feel again. The numbing fog was gone.

A massive gust of wind knocked almost thirty people on their ass, including her. Every voice died out as a third Valdyr stood in the doorway. His wavy hair was icy blond, blue eyes so pale they blended into the whites of his eyes.

"Enough," he ordered. "Turn in whoever started this shitshow, or this door will close for the rest of the day."

With no hesitation, every dirty little finger pointed at her and her friends. It was an effort not to smile as she helped Ronen and Elowen to their feet. Fallon copied Ronen: hunching her shoulders and dropping her chin submissively as the beautifully pale guard approached.

He grabbed her arm in a bone-crushing grip, then seized her friends by the backs of their cloaks and dragged them all forward. No one breathed, no one even dared to stand back up as they watched three stupid children get escorted through the round door and onto castle grounds.

The first thing Fallon noticed was the vaguely familiar smell—the air after fresh rain; clear and earthy. It was the scent that always clung to her mother's dresses when she visited.

From here, she had to crank her head back to see the tops of the golden towers and arches. There were three massive bridges, just as Bhaltair had described. Though he left out all the magnificent gardens and fountains that made up the castle grounds themselves.

The man hurriedly pulled them behind one of the ivory fountains, water spouting from the pursed lips of three stunning nymphs. He pulled off all their hoods, his eyes instantly locking onto Fallon's.

He paused. "It's true, then," he said quietly.

Fallon stared right back. "I don't know what you're talking about," she said in a low tone.

"My name is Ivan, but everyone calls me Ghost. I was in the same platoon as General Herleif when we were recruits. I spent many nights getting him and your mother out of trouble," he said, a small glimmer in those pale eyes. "You have her eyes."

Ronen rolled his eyes. "I have a feeling this will not be the last time we hear that sentence today."

But Fallon did not stand down. "Is that supposed to make me trust you?" She was told it was Bhaltair who would fetch them.

She felt a gentle breeze rush across her neck and tickle her scalp. Those eyes … the nickname …

"You're an Air Fae," she breathed.

Ghost nodded. "That is why General Herleif asked me to help. I've been keeping away your scents since I spotted you."

The fountain was on their right. Ghost purposefully positioned them out of sight from the guards on the mountain. If he were with Fritjof, he would have left them out in the open where backup could easily find them.

Fallon turned to her friends, giving them a small nod.

"Now, then." Ghost went on, "All Valdyr were accounted for this morning. Only those who we know walk behind Fritjof were assigned to guard the meeting. The rest of us remain here and on village patrol," he explained.

Elowen pulled the flaps of her cloak tightly around herself mimicking a bat. "Well, at least all of our friends are here."

"Yeah, that's what the pig said when he walked into the slaughterhouse," Ronen mumbled.

Fallon jabbed him in the side. She gestured with her chin to the golden bridge behind him. "Is that the east bridge?"

Ghost nodded, "The bridge is mostly used by servants traveling from their quarters to the main tower. You should have a clear walk to the Throne Room level of the main tower. It is traveling down to the Sanctum that will prove a challenge."

Little did he know, that was her favorite part of the plan. "Let's not be late, then."

"Here," Ronen placed an arm around her shoulders, bending one knee and giving himself a dramatic limp. Ghost *should* be taking them to the west tower for lockup, so they needed an excuse to go to the healer's tower. No wandering eyes from the mountain would be surprised to see one of them got injured during that brawl.

Fallon reached her arm across his waist to offer more support, feeling his entire torso flex at her touch. "You don't really have to put all your weight on me," she grunted. At least he didn't smell awful anymore.

"Are you calling me fat?"

"We're homeless orphans, we can't get fat."

Elowen came forward, taking Ronen's other arm around her own slim shoulders to take some stress off. "Don't use that word," she said quietly.

"What word?" Fallon did not recall cussing.

"The *O* word. We have a family now. That's why we're here," Elowen insisted.

She felt Ronen's heart pounding. "That's exactly why we're here, Elo," he assured her.

Ghost offered no assistance. He did not even look at her as she asked, "how many Valdyr answer to Fritjof?"

"About forty percent," he whispered into the air as if he used the wind to carry his words. "They take their orders from Latrell—a lieutenant who worships the ground Fritjof walks on. He too remains in the castle."

She cursed. That was nearly *half* of the castle guard. "How many are gifted?"

"All of them."

They walked in silence for the rest of the way. She tried to stay calm as they passed Valdyr after Valdyr; all with long hair, gold and green uniforms, and carrying an entire armory on their person.

Fallon struggled to keep her head down. They walked along a trimmed path, winding through one magnificent nature display after another.

Ronen must have sensed her internal struggle. Or maybe she was just squeezing him too hard. "How are you feeling?" he asked, keeping his head low.

Fallon had not really thought about it. "I'm too busy to feel."

"Liar." Elowen giggled from the other side of him.

Fallon gritted her teeth. "A little angry, I suppose."

"With you, that's a given."

"I mean I should know exactly where the throne room is. I should know where everything is. I was supposed to be raised here, but I'm a stranger," she admitted. Even Ronen had been here before.

They eventually reached the base of the east tower. Instantly, Fallon caught the scent of fresh linen and herbs. But there was more to it than that ... mildew and body odor stained the wooden door as they approached. Ghost walked up the small stone steps and rapped his knuckle on it a few times.

The door opened just a crack, and a jaded woman peeked through at them. "Are you in need of service?" she said in an unnaturally rough voice.

Ghost gestured to the three of them awkwardly holding onto each other. "The boy got hurt. Can you tend to his leg before I take them to lockup?" he asked with more respect than Fallon ever heard her father give to servants.

The woman seemed weary, but opened the door and ushered them in. She and Elowen helped Ronen up the stairs and into the stuffy room full of stained cots and full wash bins. It was not until the door shut behind her that she noticed the other occupants—six women of varying ages. All with raven black hair and chestnut eyes.

Given Fallon's fangless smile, Elowen's cascading white hair, and Ronen's two-colored eyes, it did not take long for the alarm bells to start ringing. The eldest woman, outwardly appearing into her forties, gave them a stare cold as ice. "What is the meaning of this?" she demanded. Her voice was strained and raw, as if she screamed her lungs out only minutes ago.

As she spoke, a scar on her pale neck stretched and bobbed. It was a burn, no doubt—in the shape of a handprint gripping her throat.

"You are Aine's sisters," Ronen blurted.

The room instantly became hostile. Even the bin of hot water in the corner stopped steaming as Fallon picked up on six racing heartbeats.

It was not exactly the way she wanted to start things, but it was too late now. All she could do was shoot Ronen an irritated glance as she raised her hands, instructing her friends to do the same. "We are friends of Captain Enok. We don't want any trouble ... not with you, at least. We plan to stop whatever Fritjof is planning today. So please, just pretend we are not here. We only need to hide for a few hours," she said, trying to empty as much compassion into her words as possible.

The scarred woman watched her with harsh, feline eyes. It was like being in a room full of panthers. Not the little kittens that servants are portrayed to be. "If he told you about our Aine, you must mean a great deal to him," she cooed in that ruined voice. Notably ignoring everything Fallon said. She was not satisfied—not impressed or convinced in the slightest.

Elowen dropped her hood, stepping forward delicately. "I am very sorry for your pain. We will keep her name close. Aine was more than a servant or a healer, she was a mother. A kindred spirit."

"A sister," another woman interjected. Her raven hair was tossed up in a messy braid, falling apart after hours of work. "She was our baby sister."

Everyone nodded in agreement. Everyone but the eldest, who was still staring the three of them down. Elowen's tactic was good, but not good enough. Not with women such as her—women like Fallon.

She pulled up her shirt ever so slightly, enough to reveal half of the brand on her side. Even that much was enough to make Ronen visibly wince beside her. "Where did you get yours?"

"From a man who thought he could silence a lion," she purred, a small smile playing on her lips. "Where did you get yours?"

Everyone in the room stopped breathing as both women smiled knowingly at each other. "From a man who tried to leash a wolf."

Some of the hostility cleared from her eyes. "What is your name?"

"I am Fallon. This is Elowen and Ronen."

"What makes you think you can succeed where others have failed, Fallon? Why should I believe any girl who comes stomping into my quarters can defeat Fritjof Aodh? Especially one who is obviously not from here?" she asked. Alluding to Fallon's unshakable accent.

Fallon tried not to let her frustration show on her face. "Because Nara may have six beautiful aunts to help guide her, but you will *all* be lost in a world turned to flame. Help us today, so we have a fighting chance tomorrow. I may just be a girl, but I carry a name strong enough to put Fritjof in his place," she assured them.

The women fell silent. Another older sister, with her hair chopped at the shoulders, placed a hand on her sister's arm. "Look at her, Hedda. Who do you see standing before you?"

"Impossible," another voice whispered.

"She should be dead."

Hedda pressed her lips into a thin line. "I suppose when Queen Asta told us she lost you, she did not mean to the grave. You have her eyes."

Ronen snorted. "What did I say?"

Fallon ignored him. "She told you the truth. But I'm here now. So, I will ask you one more time: will you help us hide?"

Hedda nodded to her sisters. "We are at your service, princess."

After answering a lot of questions, scarfing down a tasteless meal, and a quick nap, Fallon and her friends quietly went over their plan once again.

Ghost excused himself after the servants accepted them, promising to update Bhaltair. Hedda and the other sisters—Marin, Lana, Cyrus, Celeste, and Rochelle—made sure the three of them had everything they needed. More servants entered and left the tall chamber, but none even raised a brow.

"Some servants bring their children in here while they work if their mate is away or busy," Cyrus, the second youngest, had explained. She washed some tunics in a bin of fresh ammonia and lavender, trying to cover up their mortal scents.

While Elowen was being fitted in a servant's gown and apron, Fallon and Ronen went through the contents of their bags. Thanks to Bhaltair, they knew that any sign of threat or invasion would send the castle into lockdown. So, they needed to create a crime scene. Preferably as close to the meeting as possible, so danger seemed imminent. Bhaltair would lead the members of the King's Court to a designated safe location, where Fallon would be waiting.

Ronen peeked out of the tall stained-glass window for the tenth time. If there was one thing this castle was not short on, it was windows. She supposed for a people who thrived on sunlight, it made sense. She had even found herself joining Elma and the others when they stepped outside of the cave every so often to shake the shadows off.

"We should leave soon," Ronen said, more to himself than anyone else. "The election starts in less than an hour." His right leg would not stop bouncing, and he had not put down his pan flute since they arrived.

Her own heart was heavy with dread as she adjusted the short sword tucked into her belt loop. "Do your people pray?" she asked.

"Like, to the gods? I guess some do. Elma would know more about that stuff than I do," he admitted. It was clear by his face Ronen was not a fan of the topic, but at least his leg stopped bouncing. The sun from the window illuminated half of his face, flickering across the glistening lake of his blue eye. Fallon finally decided she did like that eye better.

She reached out and grabbed his wrist as he pushed back the hair from his face. "Don't be nervous."

"I'm not nervous," he said defensively, shaking off her hand.

She pointed, "You do that with your hair when you're nervous, and that was the seventh time within the past ten minutes." She laughed.

He let his hair fall once again to cover his reddening face. It was longer now that it was clean, almost touching his shoulders. He bathed so much now it might be cleaner than hers.

"I used to pray to gods," she went on, trying to ease the tension in the air. "But they never answered me. I just assumed they thought I was as useless as everyone else did."

He shook his head. "It's because they weren't your gods."

"What?"

"They weren't your gods. You are a direct descendant of the Sun Goddess, Fal. I'm sure they could sense that. Maybe they were a little scared by it, too," he mused.

Fallon snorted at the thought of it, "No god would fear me. They probably thought I was just … strange."

"Well, you are the strangest person I've ever met."

"Thank you."

Elowen came bouncing over, twirling so they could get a good view of her new dress. It was brown, plain, and unseamed at the edges. Yet even the yellow-stained apron could do nothing to mask Elowen's beauty. "Isn't it perfect!" she squealed, sticking out her rear to show there was not a tail in sight.

Fallon laughed, patting the creaking cot beside her. "Come sit. We need to hide your hair."

The Hulder had the very important job of reporting the staged break-in to a nearby guard. With a criminal at large, the Valdyr will be too busy finding a man that doesn't exist to pay much heed to terrified servant girls. She was to spread the word to everyone she saw, leaving breadcrumbs of panic until Ronen retrieved her.

Fallon twisted her white hair in high braids, knotting them together at the nape of her neck. "Give us thirty minutes. As soon as the clock hits eight, the meeting will start. Just cross the bridge and enter the main tower. You will see it right away," she explained.

Elowen nodded. "I know, Fallon. I can do it," she reassured her.

But Fallon's heart was being poked with needles of doubt. She even considered dressing up Ronen as a girl to replace her, but they needed Elowen's healing powers in that room in case anything went wrong. After seeing Fallon in so much dismay, Hedda volunteered to go with her. She said servants always went in pairs.

When it was time to leave, Fallon tied a white bonnet on Elowen's head. She then took her friend into a tight embrace. The last time they were in a castle, everything went wrong. And Jaeger and Norman were not here to save them this time.

"You can let go of her now." Ronen chuckled.

She did not realize how tightly she had been gripping Elowen's shoulders. "Be smart. Don't do anything I would do." She laughed nervously.

"I could never do the things you do," she whispered.

Hedda pulled Elowen in close. "She won't be alone."

Ronen had to physically pull Fallon from that room. From her best friend she was throwing to the wolves.

"I'll find her, I promise," Ronen said as they ascended the spiral staircase. "She needs to do this. She needs to be someone more than the forgotten Hulder in the cell. I will take her to the safe room myself."

Fallon knew he was right, but she still felt nauseous. "Do you remember where it is?"

He had his back to her, but she could feel him rolling his eyes. "I have been here once before, you know. I remember the hall to the throne room. There is a framed painting of some guy with a lot of medals—"

"Sir General Montan Agnello, first General of the Valdyr."

"—the painting is a door, but it opens right to left. I remember."

They reached the top of the stairwell and paused to make sure no guards were on the other side. Bhaltair said the castle would be an unorganized mess in his absence. It made sense they were understaffed up here while so many Valdyr guarded the meeting. She would have to thank Fritjof sometime for being such a worthless leader.

Ronen was watching her carefully. He noticed she was staring right at the ivory doorknob, but made no move for it. Fallon hardly moved at all. Because she knew what was on the other side—a bridge, with a stomach-twisting drop to either side.

"Which side do you want me on?" he asked gently.

She was so thankful Ronen had a mortal nose. Otherwise he would be able to smell the sweat pooling in every crevice of her body and the bile bubbling in her throat. "My left." Her weaker side.

They tossed on their new, fine-made cloaks they borrowed from the piles of laundry in the servant's chambers. A deep red and purple, stitched with silver thread. The plan was to pass as two lords crossing the bridge.

For the first time in years, Fallon prayed. To the goddess that might actually listen: please let Dagmar be watching over her young, strange descendant.

Willing her hands into stillness, Fallon pushed open the door. The bridge was large enough that a full carriage could ride across with ease. Beautiful, winding bands of gold made a protective railing on each side. She could see all of Castletowne from here. She could see the Longback Knolls and smell the waterfalls and rivers running beneath them. Then, as her eyes trailed down to the straight plumet under them, she began to go cross-eyed and dizzy.

"Lords don't loiter," Ronen nagged, tugging on her sleeve.

She winced. "Sorry."

They each carried a bag of ropes, a grappling hook, and a bottle of blood (thanks to Elma and her strange collection of everything organic and peculiar) at their sides. Fallon used it as an anchor, focusing on the weight in her hand to keep her steady.

"Just keep your eyes on the door," Ronen suggested. But it only seemed to get farther away with every step she took. Fallon swore the entire bridge started to lean to one side, like a dog trying to shake the fleas from its back.

This high up, the wind was strong enough to force them to hold their hoods in place. Which did nothing to help Fallon's growing unsteadiness. Ronen pressed his shoulder against hers, steering her back to the center of the bridge as her knees wobbled uselessly. Fallon felt as pathetic as a newborn deer; weak and unable to stand.

"We're almost there," he assured her.

"I'm sorry," she stammered. Her brain forgot how to breathe and walk at the same time.

But Ronen laughed. "You knew how this would go, yet you put it in the plan anyways. I just can't decide if that makes you brave or crazy."

Not a second too soon, Ronen shoved open the door and practically threw her inside. Before she could check for danger, before she could even grab her blade, Fallon pressed her brow against the nearest wall and breathed deeply.

Ronen's footsteps echoed in the empty hallway. "This is eerie. It's like the castle is abandoned," he whispered.

"Our lives would be a lot easier if it were," she panted.

Fallon eventually peeled herself off the wall. Ronen gave her a nervous smile, spreading his arms wide. "Welcome home, princess."

He was right ... this was hers. The fine green and silver rug, the wisteria flowers raining down from the ceiling, and every pane of painted glass lining the walls. In another life, she could have been raised within these walls. She could have spent her younger years chasing the echo of violins through the sun-soaked halls, not hiding in every dark corner she could find.

She was not sure if it was anger or heartbreak on her face, but Ronen stayed clear of her. "Since it is your castle, I'll let you choose which window we break," he added wearily.

Fallon quietly scanned the walls. If only she had known. If only Barwyn's Bastard had known this place existed outside of that stone prison …

"Fal," he called out to her, but his voice was pushed to the back of her mind. A deep, sharp pain erupted across her chest as Fallon peered down the long hallway. This feeling … like someone was trying to pull her soul from her body … she has felt it before. Over a month ago, when she first met Elowen. Though now it was clear that the golden string of fate was not pulling her towards the Hulder—it had been pulling her *here*.

It was not the loud crash that snapped Fallon out of her trance, but the metallic scent of blood that followed. Her head snapped around, where Ronen was clutching his bleeding elbow to his chest as he stared at the shattered window at his feet. "This is the best day of my life," he said to himself with a smile.

"Ronen, I—"

"No time. Come on." He ripped the bag from her hands, pulling out every ring of rope they had. Fallon's fingers were fumbling as they tied the ends together, trying to make it as long as possible.

Ronen did everything—hooking the grappling hook onto the windowpanes and tossing down the slack. He splattered the vials of blood, leaving a dripping trail down the hall. All while Fallon tried to rub away the burning ache on her sternum. Then, she gasped as she felt one sharp tug upon that invisible string so strong it nearly pulled her out of her boots.

Danger.

Forcing her ears to open and her brain to work, Fallon heard voices coming around the corner. She grabbed the back of Ronen's cloak, pulling him behind her. "Someone is coming."

"Where are the stairs?" he whispered.

She cringed. "They're using them."

"Can we just ... knock them out?" he asked desperately.

Four. Fallon heard four sets of footsteps. "I'm good, Nøkken, but not that good." Not right now. Not against Fae.

Too late. The Valdyr rounded the corner and instantly froze. Their eyes snapped from the broken window to the rope, then to the blood dripping down Ronen's arm.

"Stay right there!" one guard ordered as they all reached for their swords.

"Run!" Ronen urged, shoving her back towards the bridge. They threw themselves through the door, stumbling over their cloaks as the men shouted from behind them.

Think. "Any ideas?" she shouted, her nausea instantly returning.

"None you will enjoy," Ronen panted, peering over the railing.

She turned over her shoulder and immediately regretted it. Their plan worked a little too well—now the castle knew there *really* was an intruder. At least the meeting would still go on lockdown. Bhaltair and Elowen would still have time.

Ronen grabbed onto her arm. "Keep running. And … and just don't scream."

"What?"

"Don't scream. It will mess me up."

As they neared the center of the bridge, Ronen stopped. "What are you doing?" she demanded.

He grabbed her shoulders. "They never listened to us, Fal. We never had a chance those days we were chained and mocked before kings. But you are free this time, so make it count. For both of us."

"Ronen, I—" But she never got the chance to tell him thank you. She still needed to tell him that she claimed him.

The last thing she felt was Ronen's arms wrapping around her waist in what she thought was an embrace. Then, he hauled her over his shoulder with surprising strength. Using her weight to send them both toppling over the railing.

For the second time in her short life, Fallon fell to her death.

THIRTY-THREE

Bhaltair knew his entire life had gone to shit the moment he heard the order to carry a dining table into the Castle Sanctum.

Everyone was running around the castle like mice when he and Enok returned at last. Servants and guards alike carried furniture, plates, and table liners through the halls as members of the King's Court arrived one by one. It was so much madness, no one even asked him where he had been the past three days. No one seemed to care about his presence at all.

Ghost had given him a quick report before leaving to find the children, but Bhaltair already knew. He noticed right away these men were not his; he felt like a salmon in a school of trout walking down these halls. It was also abundantly clear someone had taken it upon themselves to change Bhaltair's orders.

But right now, the fact that every guard in sight would not even look him in the eyes was not even the worst part.

It was that iron wardrobe.

Bhaltair felt it the second he entered the Sanctum. The windowless, dome-shaped room was the only underground part of the castle (at least, until Fritjof ordered the excavation and creation of the pits). The brown roots of the Ash Throne directly above grew down to completely encapsulate the room. It was a highly sacred place, where a Fae could return to the grasp of the great tree from which their goddess was created.

The last time he entered this room was four years ago, when Aine passed away. Enok came here to pray, to beg the gods to take him instead and give Nara back her mother. Aine had been a thing of sweet, gentle beauty. Bhaltair missed her big smile and famous lavender thyme lemonade.

Unable to curse the gods aloud, Enok had simply sunk to his knees in this very dirt and screamed. And screamed. And screamed.

The room was usually empty, save for a massive altar and piles of offering stones. Even the floors were left untouched, upturned soil squashing under his boots. The point was to keep it as natural as possible, just as it had been the day the gods were born. But now, against the far wall, rested a large wardrobe made completely out of iron.

It must have taken three Fae to carry it down here. Multiple torches lined the room, but the firelight did not seem to touch it. In fact, Bhaltair could hardly get his eyes to focus on it at all. The lines of every drawer seemed to blur together. Every instinct he had was telling him to stay far, far away. He could smell nothing inside of it. The iron was a wall, blocking out every one of his Fae senses.

He stopped the next Valdyr who was unfortunate enough to cross his path. "Where did that come from?" he demanded, pointing to the strange cabinet.

The male, much younger than Bhaltair, simply shrugged. "It was already there when we brought the table in," he answered in a far too casual tone.

Bhaltair declined his chin, keeping his eyes low and locked on the young guard's throat. Waiting.

"Uh—sir," he finished with a gulp.

He kept waiting, leaning closer to the boy's pulsing jugular.

"General, sir," he corrected.

Unbelievable. Bhaltair dismissed him with the simple jerk of the chin, watching as a few servants set the long dining table. There were ten chairs. Enough for the King's Court and Fritjof—but not him. Whoever changed orders did not want Bhaltair in attendance.

Turning on his heel, Bhaltair followed the young guard back up the stairs. His scent was easy to track: body odor (common with the younger guards) and twine-tied acorns. Bhaltair knew a young male desperate to prove himself to his master would be in a hurry to tell him all about Bhaltair's question. Thus leading Bhaltair straight to whoever thought he was in charge here. And he had a feeling he knew exactly who it was.

With all of his men on village patrol or guarding and castle grounds, Bhaltair was on his own. He was not anxious, just … irritated. He had spent a long, long time dealing with Latrell. Bhaltair was a patient man, but he was reaching a breaking point.

He followed the young male back up to the main level of the central tower. Only a handful of men bowed to him as they passed. But Bhaltair spent decades earning the respect of his comrades. He could do it again.

Finally, he rounded a corner to a scent he recognized all too well. Latrell stood listening as the boy gave his report, that oily smile on his bearded face. As soon as Bhaltair approached, all eyes were on them. Whenever he and Latrell were in the same room, the tension was palpable. Young and old guards alike flocked to it like moths to flame.

The guard bowed—*bowed*—to Latrell before making his leave. Bhaltair took his place, standing right in front of the ex-general. Shock and surprise were visible on Latrell's face for only a second, but it was quickly replaced by that smug grin.

They stood eye-to-eye, "You are now assigned to the castle gates. Tell Marlo you are replacing him," Bhaltair said simply.

Latrell let out a hot breath right into his face. "Welcome back, Bhaltair. I have orders from the High Lord—"

"And I just gave you new ones." *He* was the general. The Castle Guard answered to *him* and the king. Not Fritjof, or any other lord.

The men around them did not even try to hide their stares. Latrell's eyes scanned their surroundings once, mouth visibly tightening as he refused to be submissive in front of his men. "And who is to replace me at the High Lord's side tonight, then?"

He wanted to smile, but Bhaltair kept his expression as flat as possible. "I am."

Latrell had always been a coward. It was no surprise when his first instinct was to run away. "I don't take orders from you anymore," he muttered, turning to walk away.

But Bhaltair grabbed his elbow, feeling the golden armor creak under his grip. "I will give you one more opportunity to address me properly." He let the words seep from his lips like drops of venom.

Latrell took the bait. Anger flashed in his dull gold eyes. "Your days as a general are coming to an end, little brother. Enjoy them while you can," he hissed.

Bhaltair has not heard the word *brother* come out of Latrell's mouth in years. It was so secret amongst the guards, but everyone knew they were far from family. Bhaltair did not even consider his elder brother a friend.

Coming to an end. Tonight's events might be even more influential than he thought. He smiled playfully. "Are you refusing an order from a superior?" he asked.

Latrell's face morphed into one of pure hatred. Such malice should not even be possible for a Fae, but Latrell never recovered from their father abandoning them. Now, he sought the love and approval of yet another unstable male figure.

"You can shove your superiority—"

With one arm already secured, it was simple enough for Bhaltair to take his brother to the ground. Older or not, they were equal in build now. Latrell was not strong, brave, or loyal. He was exactly like their father: pathetic.

Latrell did not give up right away—maybe he had grown up a little after all. He landed a weak headbutt, so Bhaltair returned the favor tenfold. Latrell crashed back down, dazed enough that Bhaltair could get both arms behind his back.

"You are dismissed for the rest of the day without pay for disrespecting a superior," Bhaltair announced, pressing his boot onto the side of Latrell's face. He could escort him to the barracks himself, but there was no fun in that.

"Neil, Murphy, make sure he finds his way to his rooms," Bhaltair ordered. The men who ignored him only minutes ago now obeyed his order without question.

Bhaltair turned to the rest of the men who were frozen in place. "Anyone else feeling tough today?" he demanded, folding his arms behind his back as he slowly paced around the hall.

"You are welcome to join him. None of you are being forced to be here—you *chose* to be. You enlisted, just like I did, the day you turned sixteen." He turned to a short, curly-haired guard with skin as dark as night, "Espen, you followed in your father's footsteps by enlisting."

He nodded, "And his father's father."

Bhaltair turned to his right, where a man stood so tall, everyone had to look up. "And you, Jesper, came here to keep an eye on your younger sisters who work in the kitchens. How old are they now?"

Jesper swallowed. "Twenty-two and nineteen, sir."

"They are lucky to have you as a brother. As are all of you," he gestured around him. "All of *us*. Because on that day when you were sixteen, you chose to become a brother. Not a king, not a lord or a merchant ... but a Valdyr. You did not know what was in store for the kingdom, yet you gave your oath. You did not know what challenges the gods might throw at your faith, yet you put on that golden armor. So don't abandon it now just because things get hard."

An older man popped out his chest in challenge. "What if we want to be more than a guard? What if we are tired of staring at the boots of kings, when the gods gave us more power than them?" a susurrus of agreements echoed in the halls.

Bhaltair shrugged. "Then I wish you the best of luck."

The man, Khaol, twisted his face in confusion. "You aren't going to stop us?" He asked, his hand firm on the hilt of his sword.

"No, I'm not. Because standing behind that king you loathe so badly, will be me." Bhaltair finally released his grin, exposing the fangs that had ripped the heads from Sentinels.

"And me," Jesper called, standing at attention and slamming the butt of his spear into the ground.

Espen was next, and many more followed. Their staffs pounded onto the golden floor; one unit, one guard, one heartbeat. The heart of the kingdom.

Only four men walked away to follow Latrell, offering Bhaltair nothing but loathing glances. It was not much, but it was a start to getting his Valdyr back.

Because if it came down to it, Bhaltair did not know if he could kill them. They were not evil, they were just ... misguided.

As Bhaltair walked back to the Sanctum, the empty gap in his heart felt wider than ever before. Asta could have solved this all in an hour. She would have told him what to do. He did not know if it was her brilliance that he missed so much in moments like these, or just the companionship. Someone *else* to make these choices and carry these burdens. He was supposed to be her appointed knight, but most days it had felt the other way around.

Then he remembered Fallon, and suddenly the weight on his shoulders felt a little lighter. A little more bearable.

That child should not be alive. A scar like that ran so much deeper than flesh and bone. Those mortal men stitched an eternal exile onto her very skin and set her free. That was worse than any death Bhaltair could think of.

Fallon's mother was torn from her, then she was raised to feel worthless in a world she did not belong in. How? How could Asta leave her there? How could she not see where this would end?

He would never forget the day he stopped asking her that question. Bhaltair was waiting at the Entrance Tree, just as she always ordered him to do. She was tired from her journey back from Barwyn—a journey she should not even be able to survive—and he should not have pushed her. But he did anyway. Demanding why the child was hidden, and why they could not raise her in the castle.

It was on that day he noticed the haunted, dark veil behind her emerald eyes for the first time. It was something he had never seen before, as if she was afraid of the world around them. Like she could see something there that he couldn't. She had told him off harder than ever before, even cursing at him a few times.

"You don't understand, Bhal. I'm giving my daughter her best chance." She nearly sobbed, "You must trust me. Once it is safe, I will bring her home."

So he did. Because every day after that, the dark shadow behind her eyes never left. She was still his Asta, still the brightest light the world had ever been gifted, just … scared. All the time.

Bhaltair worked endlessly. Hunting Shapeshifters, training with the best of the best, cooling any dispute, and assuring peace amongst the tribes of Elphyne. Yet it was never enough to make her feel safe. He stayed by the Entrance Tree when Asta went into labor on the other side. The mortal sun was not strong enough to fuel their magic. If anything had gone wrong during that labor, they both would have died.

All the preparations in the Sanctum were ready, and the King's Court were on their way. For just this moment, though, Bhaltair was alone with the gods. It was just him, the altar, and the iron wardrobe in the corner.

He looked up, where the roots of the Ash Throne reached down for him. "What could make the woman who never raised her voice run straight into the depths of Ondorr?"

THIRTY-FOUR

To her credit, Fallon didn't scream.

Instead, she let out the most graphic display of curse words Ronen had ever heard as the air ripped at their ears and eyelids. They fell straight down for what felt like an eternity. Fighting against the wind, he clawed for the pan flute tied onto a necklace under his shirt.

The way he saw it: either the Valdyr killed them up there, or they survived this fall and Fallon killed him once they reached the ground. She only had herself to blame ... *she* was the one who told him to believe in himself. Here he was, doing just that, at the worst possible time.

Suddenly the shouting stopped, and Ronen forced himself to look over at her. Fallon wasn't moving at all anymore. Her body was completely limp. Ronen made Fallon Alfrothul pass out from fear. Oh gods, she was *so* going to kill him.

As the ground drew closer and closer, Ronen flipped onto his back. The cape folded around him, creating a safe bubble where the wind was not tearing away at his skin. Weightless, mortified, and under a lot of pressure, Ronen began to play.

He immediately felt the river running directly below them. It was running south, and it was strong. Something about it was different, though. This water was *heavier*—denser than anything he had yet touched.

Ronen thought about Elowen. He thought about the way Fallon had hugged them both so tightly, her arms shaking as if afraid to crush them. That's exactly what they needed right now. Ronen squeezed his eyes shut and played like their lives depended on it. Which it did.

He summoned the water towards them, its arms open wide just as Fallon's had been. When they collided at last, the impact wasn't bad, but he would surely have a bruise in the morning. He heard a second *smack* as the river rose to consume Fallon as well, both cuddled in water like a half-hatched baby bird.

Too out of breath and mortified to continue, Ronen stopped playing. But the second he did, the water dropped them another fifteen feet straight down into the pounding current. But falling fifteen feet was better than falling a thousand feet.

Ronen tried his best to swim, but most of his remaining energy went towards screaming and searching for Fallon. He couldn't see her red hair anywhere. He might have drowned trying to find her, but a glove-covered hand clamped down on his arm. Ronen was pulled from the river, his soaked clothes sticking to him uncomfortably. He did not care who it was, nor did he care if a sword was about to come down onto his neck. He had to find her.

A panicked Enok ripped off Ronen's bag and cloak, grabbing his face to make sure he was conscious. "Captain!" Ronen gasped.

Enok kept pointing to his own eyes, then the bridge, then Ronen—he had watched them fall. Unable to scream for help or grow anything soft enough to break their landing.

"Fallon." Ronen spit the dry taste of saltwater from his mouth. "I lost her." His skin felt hot, but his insides were ice cold. Panic. Ronen was officially panicking.

The captain shook his head, tapping his wrist like an imaginary watch was there. *No time.*

He helped him up, but Ronen needed to get back to the river. "No!" he shouted, fighting back. "She was unconscious! She could drown!"

Enok tugged on him hard enough to let Ronen know he was serious: they needed to get out of sight. Who knew how many guards had seen everything unfold. If he ran along the riverbank, he could end up leading the guards straight to her.

"I'm sorry," he gasped, letting Enok drag his shaking body to cover. He had to believe she was strong and smart enough to find the safe room by herself. "I'm so sorry!"

Ronen felt the water catch her safely, he knew it. Ronen *had* her … if he just hadn't let go so fast …

Suddenly the familiar scent of lavender and ammonia rushed over him. Enok threw open the door to the servants tower and pushed him in. His green eyes were wide and his skin still ashen pale as he kept signing the same word over and over: He circled his right fist around, coming back for his left hand to cover it.

"Hide!" One of the sisters, Cyrus, translated as she grabbed Ronen's arm. Then Rochelle quickly closed and locked the door, leaving the captain on the other side all before Ronen could even get in a breath. Just as quickly as he had come, Enok was gone. Fallon was gone. This plan had gone so, so wrong.

"What happened?" Cyrus asked.

Ronen scanned the room. His heart had never beat this fast for this long before, the pain in his chest was getting unbearable. "Where's Elowen?" he demanded.

"She and Hedda left only a minute ago, why—"

He was already moving. He crossed the room and raced up the spiral staircase, taking the steps three at a time. The girls didn't know the guards sounded the alarm early. The castle was about to be on lockdown, and they needed to be in that saferoom before it happened. "Elowen, stop!"

Fortunately, he found them right outside the doors leading onto the bridge. Unfortunately, he was not the only one.

Three Valdyr had them at sword point as Ronen came flying around the corner. Still dripping wet and breathing embarrassingly hard, he could not appear more suspicious if he tried. Everyone froze, staring at one another in confusion.

He watched all the Valdyr's nostrils flare. Their wide eyes snapped to his arm, where a line of crimson blood dripped from his elbow to his fingertip—the same blood on the glass shards of that broken window.

If Ronen started running now, he could lose them at the river. Alas, Elowen Middlemist's heart was too big for her own good.

She did not even acknowledge the blades pointed at her. Elowen ran to his side, grabbing his arm in her trembling hands. "Ronen, what happened? I need a flower—"

"Stop, both of you!" a guard ordered.

Ronen got the sense they were not in the mood for bargaining, but Elowen put out her hands calmingly. "I'm just going to heal him."

"Elo…" he groaned. He wanted to be frustrated with her. He wanted to shake her shoulders and demand what she was thinking, but how could he? This is just who she was.

The tallest guard with dark skin lowered his even darker eyes. "Jakes said there was a male and a female. Inform Latrell we found them."

One guard turned and sprinted down the bridge while the remaining two closed in on them. Elowen kept insisting they help her find a flower or vine. The brown-haired guard snatched her by the wrist, causing her to yelp in surprise.

Ronen's vision turned red.

He was not sure where it came from, but Ronen stepped forward and ripped off the guard's grip. He didn't deserve to touch her. He didn't deserve to even be around her.

The man immediately swung at him, landing a solid hit to Ronen's nose. He almost forgot how bad it hurt to be punched, and the hot rush of blood that followed. In the two seconds it took him to recover, Ronen decided he never wanted to feel this way ever again.

So for the first time in his life, Ronen punched back.

His first thought was: *why did no one tell me hitting someone hurt your fist*? His second thought was: *oh shit*.

The Valdyr—who was just as shocked as he was—glared at Ronen with fire in his eyes. "Get the girl," he growled to his partner.

"No!" Ronen screamed. He tried. He tried so hard to keep them away from her. Kicking, punching, cursing, he threw his entire bodyweight against the Valdyr but it wasn't enough. Because they were Fae, and Ronen was not. It did not take them long to overpower him, but he never stopped fighting back. All the way across the bridge, down the stairs, and into the main hall. Ronen lost track of how many times they hit him.

He made a promise to himself as they dragged him and Elowen down the hall: he would not go back into that pit. Even if it meant he had to end his own life to avoid it.

A new man, stockier than the others, approached them with an excited smile. Something about him was vaguely familiar, but Ronen's vision was now obscured. He could feel his heartbeat in his eyelids.

"These are the terrorists?" the man asked in surprise, his eyes trailing over Ronen's beaten form.

"Try not to cower in fear." Ronen spat, blood spurting from between his teeth.

The man turned to the guards holding them. "Come. We must get to the High Lord immediately."

"But sir, the meeting—"

"Will continue after I show him what a useless general Bhaltair Herleif is. While he was lounging in a seat next to the High Lord, I found two terrorists breaking into the castle," he said smugly.

Ronen wanted to roll his eyes, but it was no longer physically possible. "The only thing you found was the worst haircut on Elphyne."

"Who are you?" Elowen asked, voice quivering.

The man had an ugly, sickly smile. "General Latrell."

General? He and Elowen had to hide their confusion as they were dragged down another golden hallway. Ronen tried his best to make eye contact with her, to show her she was going to be fine, but he must not have seemed very reassuring. She shook so violently the bonnet fell off her head, and strands of her stark hair were falling down. Huldra could make people sick … she could compromise all three Valdyr right now and they could run.

But it was not his place to ask that of her. Huldra were a tipping scale, trying to keep balance between harming and healing. Ronen knew that little black dot had thrown her off. Experiencing that kind of darkness makes you question yourself. Maybe Elowen was still finding her balance, so he was not going to mess with it.

They were taken down a wide set of ivory stairs. His knees throbbed with every step. Ronen had to keep reminding himself that at least Latrell was taking them to Bhaltair. He would help them.

Being underground again made every nerve in his body fire. He did not know this part of the castle even existed. It was just as beautiful and ornate, only with torches and chandeliers instead of windows. The artwork around them seemed more holy than the rest of the castle. It matched the set of double doors at the end of the hall, carved and painted in the likeness of the Sun goddess and Moon god.

There were so, so many Valdyr. Some were standing like statues, others were collaborating with one another, and some even appeared quite stressed. Regardless, each one bowed at the waist to Latrell as they passed. One that appeared around Ronen's age stepped forward. "We are preparing to move the King's Court, sir. Three units—"

"No need." Latrell waved a hand dismissively, nearly hitting the young guard in the face as they passed. With one nod, Latrell had four guards pulling open the doors before them. What Ronen saw on the other side, however, was somewhat underwhelming.

Nine people were standing around a large, mahogany table in a mostly empty room. The food on their plates was untouched, and none of them seemed happy to be there. Even more guards in gold flooded the round room.

"What is the meaning of this?" the voice that haunted his nightmares demanded. Fritjof Aodh strode over from his place at the head of the table, empty chalice in hand.

Latrell took a knee, bowing low before the inebriated Fire Fae. "My lord, there is no need for alarm. The terrorists responsible for breaking into the castle have been captured. You may continue with your meeting."

"Wait!" a voice shouted from the crowd. A lanky guard stepped forward, "My lord, this is that Nøkken from Athol we locked up weeks ago! He has returned seeking revenge."

"Or to avenge his kind!" someone else shouted.

The room was filled with dramatic gasps. As stupid as it sounded, it was actually a perfect cover story. No one needed to know about the long-lost princess assisting him. Not yet.

Fritjof turned his head. "I thought you disposed of him?" he whined.

Finally, the big loveable brute himself came into view. Bhaltair rounded the table, as unamused as ever. He did not even look at Ronen. "He must have somehow survived, sir. Allow me to finish the job myself," he said. Sir, not lord.

Latrell hissed, "He obviously failed the first time, my lord. Please, let me carry out this simple task for you."

Fritjof folded his red robes tighter as he stared at them. "And her? The seductress?" he said, bobbing his too-small head at Elowen.

"An accomplice, my lord. Surely her powers were the reason they made it as far as they did."

Enok and Bhaltair were right. Even since the last time Ronen had seen him, Fritjof was ... different. He was skinnier, the flesh of his face and wrists clung tightly to his bones. His hair was thin and absent of pigment, falling loosely to his back.

Bored, drunk, and overall incompetent, Fritjof shrugged. "I see no threat. So, I will use them in tonight's demonstration. At least it will save me two good guards." He laughed, "Bring them here."

Demonstration? Ronen immediately turned to Bhaltair, but he did not acknowledge him. All the relief he once felt quickly washed away. Would Bhaltair let Fritjof kill them if it meant giving Fallon time?

Elowen began to cry as they were pulled next to the dining table and forced to their knees. Nine fearful faces examined them. Seven men and two women, all pale and gaunt, took their seats once again. Latrell stood directly behind them, sword drawn and ready to smite them if they tried to run.

Ronen was able to scoot over just enough to press his shoulder against Elowen's. She kept whispering, "Screw you, screw you," to herself with wobbling lips.

Being underground was hard for her, too. Ronen already felt suffocated and claustrophobic. He slowly raised his hand, circling his fist around his heart to sign *I'm sorry*. Bhaltair was watching them carefully, so Ronen circled his fist again, telling the general he was sorry for messing up.

"Now, where was I?" Fritjof announced, his voice echoing around the round chamber. "Too long, my friends. Too long have we lived in fear of the darkness on the other side of our land. The shadows of Ondorr have plagued our people since the birth of the gods. Yet no king, despite his *mighty blood*, has been able to do a thing about it. You see, that is the problem with monarchies — they are unpredictable. What if all the sons are weak? What if they are giftless? What if a king died and a child was the only one left to rule? We have seen all of that before. Because in all honesty, that system is flawed."

A woman at the table with dark skin and piercing blue eyes cleared her throat. "That system was given to us by the gods when they gave their fifth child the Ash Throne. It is not your place to question that," she said sternly. Ronen hoped she was on their side.

Fritjof smiled without his eyes. "Was it? You will find, Lady Honeymaren, that I am well versed in our history. The way I remember it — and feel free to correct me — the gods gave the gift of power to their first four children. The fifth was left with a tree," he sneered. A few people laughed.

He circled the table like a cat toying with its prey. "I was reminded of this nearly twenty years ago, when I led my unit into Ondorr after a Sentinel sighting. Ten men went in, three came back out. The only reason the three of us survived is because the gods spoke to me that day. They told me another war was coming, one that would make the first Elphynian War feel like child's play. And that I, Fritjof Aodh, would have a major role to play in it." He announced.

"Yeah, the tyrant that sacrifices us all to Ondorr," Ronen hissed.

Latrell smacked the pummel of his sword into the back of Ronen's head, causing him to see stars. Elowen helped keep him steady, pressing her brow into his shoulder as if she could take away his pain with nothing but sheer will.

Fritjof tsked in his direction but moved on. "They explained to me how in the beginning, the four firstborns used their powers to seal and contain the darkness. Their powers were straight from the gods—raw and fresh. Over the millennia, as the gifted have mated with the average, our powers became weak. That, court members, is why Ondorr is once again rising. It senses our weakness," he insisted, his lips and teeth still stained red from the wine.

No ... he was wrong. None of the elements could even stop a Sentinel. Only seawater and sunlight—the power of the *gods*—would destroy them. Fritjof was lying right to their faces. Ronen turned, hoping to see a table full of suspicious glances, but everyone seemed ... afraid. They would do or say anything just to get away from the man in front of them.

"But," Fritjof smiled, resuming his place at the head of the table across from Ronen. "Some of our families kept true to the god's blessing. Generation after generation, every child born gifted without fail. Isn't that right, Larue? How old is your daughter now?" he asked.

All life drained from Honeymaren's aged face. She wore a fine, turquoise gown matching the cosmetics smeared on her upturned eyes. "She turns twenty in three days," she said dryly.

"Is it right to say she is just as fine of a Water Fae as you are? And as all your family has been?" Fritjof asked simply. Playful, dangerous embers danced in his crimson eyes.

The lady only nodded.

"And Lord Arlo, your family has been running the castle's medicinal greenhouse for how many years now?" Fritjof asked.

A thin, raven-haired man with a bad mustache shivered as Fritjof said his name. "As long as anyone can remember."

Ronen's eyes slowly scanned the table. Oh gods ... they were all purebloods. Now this strange ensemble of a court made sense. Fritjof did not care if they owned land or worked on a farm, they just had to come from a gifted line. He just needed their strength and influence. Fritjof was going to rally up the purebloods and dispose of the rest—*a fresh beginning*. No more mating with the non-gifted, and no more mating with mortals.

In that case, Fritjof was going to really, really hate Fallon.

Fallon Alfrothul ... the last true descendant. Ronen couldn't take this anymore. If these people forgot about their history, they would never see Fallon as the rightful ruler she was. "The elder siblings were given gifts to *protect* the youngest who sat on the throne! You all know that! There is a reason why only someone with Alfrothul blood can even put their ass on it! None of you could. Pureblood or not. Don't listen to him!" he insisted.

Elowen spoke up despite her shaking voice. Just as Fallon taught her. "The royal bloodline is the last one remaining from the Firstborns." She turned to Fritjof, "s-screw you. We are not afraid."

Latrell knocked them both forward, and Elowen let out a cry as her chin smacked the dirt. He raised his sword high above them, but Fritjof held out a hand. "Wait. Out of pure curiosity: where did a *Nøkken* learn Fae genealogy?"

"The Little Folk of the forest!" Elowen interjected, "They are his family, they love him!"

This got a reaction out of the court. Everyone turned to one another, looking at Ronen as if he had just gotten there. Apparently, having invisible babysitters was a good omen. To Ronen, it was simply a lifetime of being paranoid he was being watched every time he went to the bathroom.

Everyone but Fritjof seemed impressed. He slowly waltzed his way around the table to kneel in front of him. To be honest, Ronen would have rather taken his chances with the sword still above his head. He wished Latrell had just skewered him as all the moisture in the air was sucked away.

Ronen's head was still spinning as he investigated Fritjof's eyes. There was no light behind them. No life. The crooked smile on his face, the amusement in his voice ... it was as if someone else was speaking through him entirely.

"Where are your Alfrothuls then, boy?" he whispered. He asked again, but Ronen just pressed his lips tightly together. If only he knew who may or may not be fighting her way through the halls above. Even Elowen darted her eyes upwards, as if Fallon would magically descend from the ceiling to save them all.

Fritjof stood to his full height. The torches mounted along the walls doubled in heat and intensity, lighting up the room in a hellish glow. "The Alfrothuls are *dead*! Your precious royals are *gone*! In their place, the gods sent me. But I come not empty handed, allow me to demonstrate," he said with a maniacal chirp in his voice. He gestured to the far wall, where a strange object stood.

Three guards approached the weird piece of furniture hesitantly, like it was a wild animal about to bite them. Fritjof raised his arms excitedly, scooting everyone forward, "Come, now! Everyone gather round, don't be afraid!"

Personally, Ronen felt pretty afraid.

The odd wardrobe shook something inside of him. It gave off a dark wave of energy, and the black dot on Ronen's soul jumped in response. He turned to Elowen, who gave him a grave nod. She felt it too.

Latrell kicked his side. "On your feet."

"No thanks. I never liked show and tell."

"Too bad. You're the main act." He laughed, picking up Ronen by the shirt and dropping him onto his feet. Elowen was slowly getting up, rubbing the dirt from her face and elbows. Latrell pressed his sword into her side.

Elowen crossed her tan arms in defiance. "My best friend is going to *kill* you," she said.

Ronen chuckled, feeling his diaphragm rub against his bruised ribs. "Yeah, I really wouldn't do that if I were you."

Latrell looked confused but had the better sense to listen as he herded them to the front of the group. They walked past Bhaltair, but their friend did not even cast them a glance. How was he doing that? Ronen just wanted one sign to show it was all an act, and the general cared about their lives. Just one nod. But it never came. Ronen supposed Bhaltair has had the last fifteen years to practice being the general everyone needed. Did the appointed knight that proudly guarded Asta Alfrothul's every step even exist anymore?

Fritjof approached the weird armoire. This close, Ronen could now see the smooth, hammered material—iron. Every knob and hinge were made of pure iron, something Ronen understood well.

This was a project that would have taken his entire shop many months to complete. It must be Orculli made. Those giants could shape and bend most metals with their bare hands.

"Brothers and sisters, I wish to show you not my gift from the gods, but my gift to you. As we all know, fire is useless against the shades of Ondorr. The inky darkness simply absorbs it. Sucks it up like a sponge tossed in water. That is why, for the coming war, Dag and Dagmar have given me what will be known as the Godflame." He smiled, lifting his hand as it burst into nothing but a small, normal-looking ball of fire.

Ronen started a slow clap. "The Fire Fae can make fire, everybody." He snorted. Lady Larue and a few other court members had to turn away to hide their grins.

Fritjof bared his fangs. "What appears normal to you is beyond your comprehension. See for yourselves," he hissed, then turned around and threw open the iron doors.

Ronen felt it before he saw it. Everyone screamed in horror as a wave of blackness poured out from the armoire, coating the floor as tar.

No.

Ronen instantly grabbed Elowen, shoving her behind him as his eyes focused on a form within the shadows. It had to crawl out, extending its long limbs until it could stand to its full height—a terrifying nine feet. It had no features, no definition, no soul. Just a solid shadow that reeked of decay. It roared in their faces, causing people to faint, piss themselves, or some combination of both.

Everyone tried to run, but the Valdyr made a wall behind them, pushing them back. Every Valdyr but Bhaltair, who kept blinking at the creature. So this was a surprise to him, too.

Honeymaren pointed a shaking finger at him. "You have gone too far, Aodh! Stop this at once!"

A wave of heat smacked Ronen in the face as a line of flame was drawn at his feet. It rose as a protective wall, separating them from the Sentinel. Fritjof stood fearlessly, that ball of flame still in hand. He reached out, and the Sentinel stepped back with an ear-piercing shriek. Impossible ... it was avoiding the flames.

"Your god-sent is right here!" Fritjof laughed, toying with the monster as if it were nothing more than a stray dog. Ronen did not want to believe it, but no darkness spread beyond the line of flame. Fritjof's fire *was* different. But how?

Fritjof smiled triumphantly, crossing his arms behind his back. "Now, we may begin the second part of our evening. I chose you all in hopes your judgment was as pure as your blood. The second age of Elphyne is coming, and you must choose which side of it you will be on. If you join me and make me your king, this power could be yours! We can start again and get back the power we once had." He waved his hand and the flames grew higher, causing the Sentinel to cry out and slam back into the iron armoire.

"Or …" he continued, "you can be on your own and take your chances on the other side of that line."

Everyone was paralyzed in fear. Ronen wondered if they even heard Fritjof's voice over the smell of soot, sweat, and rotten eggs filling the room. Fritjof rolled his eyes, "I only need five of your votes. So, the first five to take their rightful seats at the dining table will stay on the King's Court. All their families, land, and assets will be under my protection when the second war comes," he offered.

Four people—three men and one woman—shoved their way through the wall of Valdyr and practically threw themselves into their seats. Ronen, Elowen, Honeymaren, Arlo, an elderly man, and two other men remained. One spot left.

Elowen had once again fallen into her trance-like state of shock, her arms stiff and locked around Ronen's chest. Where was Fallon? Was she still waiting for them in the safe room? Or was she dead at the end of that river? Ronen had to buy her time.

He turned to the remaining members of the King's Court, "The Alfrothul bloodline is the only one who gets the throne," he repeated slowly, trying to make eye contact with everyone one at a time.

"Maybe you need a reminder of what you are up against. You are all old enough to have possibly *seen* a soldier from the dark woods, but have you ever seen one suck the life out of a Faerie?" Fritjof asked, tilting his head innocently at him.

Ronen tried to back up, but he slammed into an impenetrable wall of muscle and gold. "No!" Ronen shouted as all eyes turned to them. "No—not her!" he already failed Fallon; he couldn't fail Elowen too.

There was a ruckus coming from the other side of the doors, surely someone had noticed there was a god's damned *Sentinel* in the castle. Someone would stop this.

Honeymaren stepped forward, the fire casting a yellow glow on her dark skin. "No matter what happens to me, my daughter will know what happened here today. She will spread the word, and you will never get the followers you desire," she spat. The lady hiked up her flowing cyan skirts and walked over to stand beside Ronen.

This time, when Ronen faced the darkness, he could say he stood for something. He fought back. Maybe that's why he wasn't afraid as Honeymaren rested a hand on his shoulder, as defiant and brave as the princess she did not even know existed.

Fritjof looked disappointed, but not worried. "There is one more seat at the table. Declare me as your king, and you will never have to fret about Ondorr ever again. Don't you want your families to be free? Your children?" he reminded the four men remaining.

Arlo and the other three men glanced at each other sadly. The Sentinel was still screeching and fighting against the flames as Arlo offered his arm to the elderly man. Together, they both walked over to stand beside Ronen.

Death didn't seem so scary when you weren't alone. More and more of his fear melted away as he saw the determination in the court's eyes. They were not here for Fallon. They were not here for the Light Court or any rebellion. They just understood Fritjof was wrong. It was the first time Ronen considered that maybe being an outcast was a good thing. If following evil was the only path to belonging, then his soul would join Fallon's in the land of the unclaimed.

Fritjof shook his head in disappointment. "Such a waste of good blood." All it took was one flick of his wrist, and the Godflame vanished.

Shadows darker than anything Ronen had ever seen poured towards them. Elowen's screams of terror broke his heart and soul. But Ronen could do nothing but squeeze her close as the Sentinel stepped over the charred line burnt into the dirt.

THIRTY-FIVE

Plan, fail, improvise. That was all Fallon's life had become.

When her friend threw her off a bridge, she decided to never make a plan ever again. Because for some reason, all her plans were doomed to fail. Maybe the gods couldn't kill her, but a dumb Nøkken could certainly try his best.

She did not remember a lot from the fall. Fallon saw the world spin around her as Ronen tossed her over the railing. The feeling of being weightless once again was too much to bear. She had to travel inward, into that safe space in the back of her mind behind the blazing fire of her soul, and there she remained until the voice returned.

The same voice that woke her at the bottom of the cliff and told her to run. Soft and feminine, but urgent: *get up, north star.*

It was only this time, when the voice called out to her again and again, Fallon knew without a shadow of a doubt who it belonged to.

"Mother!" she gasped, sitting up and instantly regurgitating salty water onto the ground. Fallon sputtered, wiping away the hair sticking to her face. She frantically spun around, half expecting to find herself in the afterlife with Asta ready to greet her.

But she was still here; face down in the grass, the bottom half of her body still in a river. River ... Ronen. Ronen had caught them. Fallon laughed, hauling herself onto shore. "I don't know if I should stab you or kiss you first—"

But Fallon was alone.

"Ronen?" She called out. She was still on castle grounds, but the main tower was far upstream. Suddenly the reality of the situation struck her, and Fallon felt exposed. There was a small, ivory bridge crossing over the river to her left. Fallon ran for it, having to crouch down to fit underneath. Where was Ronen? How did they get separated? Would he try to find her, or meet in the safe room?

Fallon rubbed her face, taking a few breaths to calm her rapid heart as she tilted her head back to the sky. "Mother, you know this place. I don't," she whispered. "I need to get to them."

Even with her Fae ears, their footsteps were barely audible. As always, they were gone in a flash. Leaving nothing behind but an arrow tip and a single orange berry in the grass beside her.

She felt the Little Folk watching her as Fallon slowly picked up the stone triangle, a ball rising to her throat— Jaeger. Norman. She examined the cloudberry further and found a single nibble taken out of it. Fallon had to cover her mouth to muffle the sounds of her laughs and sobs; they were alive. Jaeger survived.

Fallon squeezed the arrow tip in her hand so tightly she felt it slice through her palm. "I made it, Jaeger," she whispered, blinking away the tears collecting in her eyes. "You were right. It's real, and you're going to see it one day. I promise."

She crawled around the corner, making sure there was no one watching as she plucked the most unique flower she could find. It was a beautiful orange, with tall, leaning pistils covered in pollen. Nothing like this grew in Halvar.

Fallon used her thumb to coat one of the petals with the fresh blood from her palm—a blood oath. She was alive, and she would come back for him.

"Never yield, Jaeger Hulderson." She smiled, picturing Jaeger's face: the other side of her tarnished coin. "Tell the stars I miss them."

She gently set the flower down in the grass, slipping the stone arrowhead into her pocket. Fallon checked her surroundings one last time, then took off into a run towards the next ivory bridge. When she glanced over her shoulder, the Elphynian flower with a blood-soaked petal was already gone.

Her mother knew that was exactly what she needed today. Moving with more diligence than Fallon had ever displayed in her life, she made her way towards the massive main tower. Valdyr passed her left and right, but there was always a convenient hedge nearby. As soon as one sprouted from the ground, she sprinted or rolled behind it with a smile on her face. The wind blew west, then east or north. They never once scented her. Ghost and Enok were watching her.

The closer she got, the stronger she felt that bond again. Soon, the pressure on her chest was agonizing. Fallon supposed that meant she needed to hurry. She picked up her pace until she could see the details of the golden doors before her.

Fallon took shelter under the looming branches of a weeping willow tree. Bhaltair had warned them that once the lockdown commences, there is no getting in or out of the castle. So where were the guards?

A soft wind blew through the trees, and within the susurrus of tiny leaves brushing together, Fallon heard a voice once more: *Go, Fallon.* This voice was not her mother's, but it was not a stranger, either.

Fallon saw no one under the tree with her. Just a voice at the end of the wind. "Go where? It's too risky to just walk in," she whispered back a little harshly.

With another sweet-smelling gale, the branches parted for her and exposed the main doors once more. This time, though, they were wide open. Elphyne still baffled her every waking moment. Maybe a realm ripe with magic was not so bad after all.

She slowly stepped into the open, and suddenly there was not a guard to be seen. Actually … there was no life to be seen at all. Birds no longer chirped, Anthousai no longer buzzed in her ear, and even the mighty rivers seemed to hold still.

In a land where night was a place and not a time, anything was possible. Because somewhere, somehow, Asta was holding the gates of time shut for her.

Go, the voice said again. This time it was a plea.

Others might have ignorantly sauntered in those doors, but Fallon knew better. Despite the rush, Fallon put her back against the door before peeking inside: greenery grew wild and free along the golden walls, flowers dripping from the ceiling like stalactites. Her eyes followed the beautiful, mosaic tile floor all the way to the end of the hall. Where two open doors revealed a majestic, regal figure staring right back at her.

"You," Fallon gasped. A powerful surge of energy crashed into her as if to say, *you*! Finally, after all this time, Fallon found the other end of that golden string. Since Halvar—perhaps even since Barwyn—the Ash Throne had been calling out to her.

Fallon fell in love with every star she ever saw. She longed for the days when the clouds gave mercy to the skies, and beams of sunlight skidded across the frozen lakes. But this tree ... it made all that look like the bottom of a chamber pot. Its trunk was curved into a seat, branches going so wide and high she could not even see the top. She did not even notice she was walking towards it until she was halfway down the hall. Closer. Fallon wanted to get closer and meet—

Slam.

The doors behind her snapped shut, making her jump and snap out of her daze. A second later, the doors to the throne room followed suit. One by one, the other wooden doors lining the hall slammed shut by some invisible force.

"No, no, no!" Fallon ran for the nearest one, but it shut right in her face. The entire hallway fell into an even deeper, eerie silence. Leaving Fallon trapped and alone.

Her heartbeat was so loud in her ears, and her small breaths were crashing waves. She slowly creeped forward, calling upon all her training to silence her feet. Lockdown. This must be the castle on lockdown. Which meant the King's Court was safely secured somewhere. Her eyes scanned the walls, desperately searching for the painting she knew acted as the safe room entrance. If she could find it quickly, her friends might be right behind—

"Fallon."

All sense of time and space left her body as Fallon forgot how to breathe. The golden walls melted around her like candle wax. It took every single ounce of courage she had to turn her head towards the sound of her father's voice.

Standing there, where she had been only moments ago, was a ghostly apparition of Beowulf Solveij.

Fallon stumbled back, falling on her rear and crawling backwards. She was too terrified and baffled to even scream. He was made of shimmering blue flame, eyes just as endless and hollow as she remembered. He towered over her; a bear hide draped over his shoulders. Fallon felt the fear of a broken child seep back into her, taking control of her body. Fight. Endure. Survive.

Then, from somewhere that sounded so far away, she heard her name again. But not from Beowulf. Fallon knew better than to turn away from her father when he was angry, so she crawled backwards into the wall. Taking deep, haggard breaths, she turned her head ever so slightly.

"Fallon!"

On the other end of the hall stood another glowing form: *Ronen*. She let out a gutted sob that might have been his name. The blue flames he was made of danced and twirled as he smiled back at her.

"How ... I-I don't understand ..." she gasped, taking in their transparent forms. "Oh gods. Wisps! You're wisps." Fallon shook her head, dropping her face into her hands. It was worse than her first day in Elphyne. This was all so strange, so *impossible* ...

The blue glow of the Ronen Will-o'-Wisp intensified. He was pointing behind him, where Fallon felt the Ash Throne send another wave of magic at her. This time it was sharp, slicing through her ears like a knife. Reminding her that it—and all Elphyne—was in distress.

But Fallon had been in distress for a long, long time. Her body gave out as she turned back to Beowulf, her fingers and toes going completely numb. He pointed over his shoulder, the order all too familiar: *get out*. Leave this castle, leave Elphyne. He wanted her to come face him, with or without her army. Because Fallon had sworn to their gods she would get her revenge, she swore legends would be made.

All those years of being ripped apart piece by piece ... an entire childhood stolen from her. *Stolen*, by hands that were supposed to love her. Fallon would never get those years back. Her skin would never be clear of scars. And it was his fault.

Her borrowed time was over. Fallon had to pick right now: would she sit upon a throne of ice and iron, or a throne of ash and sunlight?

All it took was seeing her father's ugly, ugly smile one more time for her to finally make her choice. There were no more excuses. No more hesitation. Now, clear as day, her heart pulled her towards her true north.

Fallon slowly got to her feet, stumbling a few times before she got her footing. Her knees were made of clay as she unsheathed her blade. She never even raised a weapon to Beowulf before—she never got that far. But that changed today. Everything changed today.

She squared her shoulders, facing her father head on. He declined his chin, smiling down at his prey as it climbed into its trap. The last time she saw that monstrous grin was the day she died.

Fallon Alfrothul raised her sword high and used all her new strength to drive it straight into the floor between them.

As the steel sank through tile and earth, she felt it slice through the links of a chain she never realized was shackled to her ankle. A rusted, bloody chain covered in ice and snow.

"My heart is no longer yours to bleed," Fallon exclaimed. The power of her voice surprised her, causing the windows to rattle in their panes. "You stay away from me, and you *stay away* from my family. I may not have gotten to watch the life leave your eyes, father, but you are dead to me."

For the first time in nineteen years, Fallon turned her back on her father. She focused ahead on the boy smiling proudly at her. And she knew that far, far away, Fallon Solveij was proud of her, too.

She heard a snap of air behind her as the Beowulf Will-o'-Wisp disappeared, taking that broken chain with it. Fallon sprinted for Ronen, but he too melted into the air as she tried to throw her arms around him. She had to blink the blue flames from her eyes, looking back up to find the doors to the throne room wide open.

Then, Elphyne woke back up.

The moment Fallon crossed the threshold, time started again. She could hear the wind outside, smell the wool rugs, and feel the sunlight pouring in from the stained-glass artwork all around them. Everything was back to normal—including the guards.

"Stop right there!" someone shouted. Fallon ducked just in time to avoid being knocked in the head. She rolled, trying to distance herself from the two Valdyr while she regained her wits. The castle was not on lockdown after all ... which meant her friends were still somewhere in the castle.

The men, both brown-haired and handsome in their golden armor, pointed their spears at her. "Where did you come from?" he demanded. Both men seemed a bit dazed and lethargic, as if they just woke up from a long nap.

Fallon smiled, angling her feet in a defensive stance. "You wouldn't believe me if I told you."

They both made a face, confused more by her accent than her statement. "We did a full sweep after the two terrorists were captured. Where were you hiding?" one demanded.

Her blood ran still. "Two? Where are they?"

The guard grinned, fangs gleaming. "So you are with them, then? Are there more of you?"

She did not have time for this. "Take me to them and I will answer all of your questions," she pressed.

More footsteps echoed down the hall, and four more men came running towards them. "You are in no place to be giving orders. Now, on your knees," He said, waving in backup.

They were lucky Fallon left her only weapon in the hallway. These must be the men Ghost told her about—the ones who follow Fritjof and Latrell. They had her cornered in moments.

"Hold on," a tall one held up a hand as his nostrils flared. "What are you?"

"A mortal!" Another sneered.

Fallon grit her teeth. "*Half*-mortal." And lunged. Not at the men, but at their spears.

It was why Fallon never cared for them—they were easy to lose track of and oh so easy to redirect. She grabbed one by the shaft, kicking the wind out of the Valdyr behind it. Fallon spun like a fresh spring storm, knocking down everything and everyone in her wake.

Freedom.

It was *freedom* that now danced with the violence in her veins. This is what Bhaltair had been waiting to see. The black veil that vengeance had cast over her was gone, and for the first time ever, Fallon moved as a Fae. Ducking, swiping, parrying. Her Viking roots ran long and deep, but now paired with the new skills Bhaltair taught her, she felt unstoppable.

Even when a sword sliced through the shoulder of her shirt, and when a punch to the gut left her wheezing, Fallon never wanted to stop. Walking backwards up the stairs, she kept dodging the swing of their best fighter. He was even bigger than Bhaltair, with eyes as black as night.

Fallon tripped on the last stair, falling backwards only inches from the throne. This guard was the only one who dared to ascend the staircase with her. The others waited at the bottom, watching them hesitantly. Fallon saw this as a sign they still had respect for the Ash Throne.

All except the brute trying to behead her in her own castle. He swung down his sword, and Fallon clamored back. She gripped onto the arm of the throne to help her stand. There was a loud hissing noise, and everybody froze as Fallon cursed and pulled her hand back.

There, where her hand had just been, was a small puddle of golden liquid. A single drop slid down the side, leaving a shimmering trail down the wood. Fallon held up her hand—it was still bleeding from where Jaeger's arrow tip had dug into her skin. But when her blood touched the ancient tree …

Everyone watched in awe as the Ash Throne began to *move*. Wood creaked and leaves rustled as new branches grew and weaved together, right on the seat of the throne. At first, she thought the tree was forming a rod. Then it grew outwards, each tiny branch coming to a deadly point, creating the sharp edge of a—

Fallon's jaw dropped. An axe.

Right before her, the tree wove her a double-sided axe out of its own branches. As if it used her blood to taste her every need and desire. A stunning weapon, made of immortal wood.

She slowly reached out, yanking it free from the branches as if only picking an apple. It fit perfectly in her hand—light enough to swing with one arm, but heavy enough to gain momentum.

Without even turning around, Fallon swung. The familiar sound of cleaving bone sang in her ears as the obsidian-eyed man fell to his knees. His head hit the ground a second later.

Fallon arched her back and roared. "*I love magic!*"

She leaped down the entire flight of stairs, landing in a roll and coming up swinging. She never left a fatal blow, just enough to incapacitate the remaining men. Their Fae bodies would heal soon enough, and hopefully so would their minds.

Right as she faced the last of them, the world swirled around her in slow motion. Fallon collapsed with a scream, placing both hands over her heart. A sickening, twisting pain made her vision go black for a few seconds. This foul feeling in her gut ... Fallon got it every time she laid eyes on Ondorr. But this time it was like the darkness was trying to climb its way down her throat and out her nose.

She turned back to the Ash Throne, who only looked back down on her and bristled its leaves impatiently.

"Taking orders from a tree instead of getting the iron throne," she grumbled to herself, slowly getting back on her feet. "Brilliant choice, Fallon."

"You—" a quiet voice made her whip around, axe at the ready. But all she saw was a young man, clutching his leg as dark blood spilled from between his fingers. "You touched the throne, and you're still alive?" he whispered. He was pale faced, obviously in shock, and so ... young. He barely fit into his armor.

Fallon knelt beside him, "Aye. This is all as surprising to me as it is to you, so can we help each other out?" she asked, trying to lower her voice the way Elowen did when she spoke to Ronen.

He nodded, watching her with wide eyes as Fallon used her axe to cut a strip from the bottom of his green cloak. She placed it above his wound and tied a knot, but hesitated before pulling it taut.

"Where are the prisoners they caught today?" she asked slowly.

The boy gulped. "I was in the hall when Latrell took them to the Sanctum to face Fritjof. No one has come out since," he winced. "More guards will be here any second."

Fallon felt her heart squeeze into a ball. She pulled the fabric as tight as she could, making the boy groan in pain until the bleeding stopped.

Wiping off her hands on the sides of her pants, Fallon stood and grabbed her weapon. "How old are you?" she asked, quickly tending to her own wounds.

"Sixteen."

She nodded, "I was seven."

"When you became a guard?"

"When I had to choose. Between faith and fear. I wish I could say I made the right choice, but I didn't. I like to think that if … if I only … if I just had a single drop of *hope* back then, maybe things would have gone differently for me. So don't make my mistake," she said and turned for the door.

The boy tried to get up but fell back down. "Wait! Who are you? How are you alive?" he repeated desperately.

Fallon turned over her shoulder, smiling up at the stained-glass window before them. Where a beautiful, red-haired woman smiled back down at her. "You can call me hope."

His eyes shifted back and forth between them. Then he fainted.

Fallon sprinted down the hall, using her memory of the map Bhaltair drew to find her way. She heard the thunderous steps of more guards approaching from every direction. In only minutes, she had an entire mob chasing after her. Arrows whizzed past her, missing her head by only a hair. But Fallon never stopped running. She had no time. A sense of impending doom hung over her like a dark cloud, and it got worse with every step towards the Sanctum.

Soon the throbbing in her temples made her go cross-eyed with pain. She was close. Her boots screeched against the tile as she came to a sudden halt, so fast she felt her organs slam into her gut. Taking in a long breath in, Fallon's head shot down. On the ground between her feet, lie five drops of crimson blood.

Blood that smelt of campfire on the riverbank. Like the fog that curled around a pond at dawn.

Fallon slowly turned her head, where at least fifty Valdyr guarding a single hallway raised their weapons. There was another forty coming around the corner behind her, but Fallon grinned as she stepped towards the large doors where she could smell even more of his blood.

Rage was no longer her soft-lipped lover, but it was still her dear, dear friend.

Fallon's vision was a blur of red and gold. The Valdyr came in waves of blades, wind, and fangs, but Fallon was the storm itself. Her axe was just as much a part of her as her head. It never splintered, never dulled, and never relented no matter how many of them they cleaved through. It was at that moment its name was born into her mind, as if whispered by the axe itself: *Himintelgya*. Heaven-Scraper. A weapon that could rip the stars from the sky.

The black cloud around her was growing, and Fallon knew she was running out of time. The second nothing was left in her way, she threw open the doors.

The darkness struck her so intensely, she felt frostbite forming on her fingertips as pulsing waves of night poured from the room. No one even noticed her. They all had their eyes locked on—

No.

At the other end of the room loomed a demon more grotesque and terrifying than anything she had ever seen. She almost vomited at the stench of it. A nine-foot man but hollowed out and filled with decay and darkness.

A Sentinel. In Lysserah. And it was walking towards her friends.

Fallon moved so quickly, she felt her bones bend and her muscles tear. In one blink she was halfway across the room. Then she was on top of a grand dining table, plates and drinks shattering around her as she pushed her body to its limits. She watched Elowen and Ronen hold each other and duck in horror. She saw predator and prey; a snow squall rolling towards a little girl on a hill with no one to save her.

It ends with me.

Fallon felt her soul ignite as she took one mighty leap from the table. She landed mere feet from her friends. Fallon's heart beat so fast until it no longer beat at all— replaced by an ancient hum that no longer scared her.

A taloned, black hand dripping with shadows reached in for the kill. Fallon hurled herself in front of Ronen, throwing out her arms to protect them. From her hands a brilliant light was born, bursting from her open arms and expanding into a shimmering dome around them.

Pure, bone-warming sunlight filled the room as the Sentinel shrieked in horror, clamoring back into a dark cabinet. It hissed at her, watching with wide eyes as its shadows melted away anytime they got close to her light. A light that had lived within the deepest, most haunted parts of her soul, and still knew how to shine.

Because a star must collapse before it is born.

Fallon claimed it, just as it claimed her—a light born from the darkness. And together they would bring death to its knees.

THIRTY-SIX

For the first time in his life, Ronen got to experience a sunrise.

The cold, stale darkness around him was banished back into the shadows—just as Fallon said it would. A brilliant light blinded him through his eyelids, warming his frozen body down to the bone. *The sunrise is a sign, a promise; that the terrors of yesterday are over,* she once said.

When he opened his eyes at last, he saw those red waves, that wolf's smile, and emerald eyes laced with gold. Fallon Alfrothul was her own kind of sunrise: where wild was a color, and she was the sky.

Every cut, bruise, and broken bone in his body slowly mended until there was nothing left but the crusted blood on his skin. He could not help but laugh as tears of joy poured down his cheeks. Ronen was so utterly confused, but he didn't even care. All that mattered to him was that he *didn't* kill the Princess of Elphyne after all.

Although … the blood smeared all over her face, the axe made of twisted tree branches, and the new sun-wielding power did raise some questions. But he decided to worry about that later.

He watched as Fallon flexed her hands, and the glistening dome expanded outwards until every single court member and guard was safely inside. With a cry that sounded like glass being scraped against stone, the Sentinel pressed itself back into the iron armoire, shrinking in size and howling in pain. Now only Fritjof stood just outside the wall, staring at them through the transparent dome in unhinged fury.

Most people were on their knees, staring at Fallon as if she were some sort of god. Others, like Latrell and his men, quickly moved to stand beside Fritjof. Even though he was the last to do so, Bhaltair stepped on the Lord of Fire's side.

Elowen had a hand clutched over her heart, extending the other to Fallon as if she were a warm campfire. Indeed, Ronen wanted to bathe in her light. It was everything right about the world. Yet it had been trapped within a girl who had experienced only the worst.

Fallon turned to face the room. Her hands shook, but her voice was solid as stone. "My name is Fallon, but my mother called me north star," she started. Her voice ... it was a leader's voice. Not the angry girl he once called a coward.

"I am the last living descendant of Dag and Dagmar, and the daughter of Asta Alfrothul, blood of the fifth born. I have traveled very far to claim my throne." The way she said *my throne* invited no question or challenge.

She turned to the Lord of Fire who seethed at her. "It does not matter how many elections you hold, Fritjof Aodh. It doesn't matter how many guards you manipulate, or how many gifted Fae you collect. Because I am going to take each broken, discarded piece of this realm and forge them into something glorious," she declared.

The dying Merrows, the misunderstood Centaurs, the secluded Anso and Orculli … all forgotten by the Golden Castle. Fallon was going to summon them all. An army of the unclaimed.

Fritjof was nearly foaming at the mouth. His face contorted, more animalistic than human. "*Sunblood*! How did a rotten mutt like you come to possess this?" he demanded, tossing up flames left and right. Panic sparked in the red pools of his eyes. Panic and *fear*. Fritjof thought this would be a display of his powers, but Fallon made it a display of hers.

She clenched her fists, and flares of light erupted across her skin and through her hair. She never backed down, but Ronen saw her knees wobble. He saw her sucking in her bottom lip, the way she did when she was unsure. If this power was as new to her as it was to him, this could go very badly. And fast.

Fritjof, of course, was not helping. He kept shouting at the court, calling them traitors. He summoned the flames from every torch in the room, throwing them against Fallon's dome in an explosive show of orange and gold. He nearly torched his own men, but he did not even blink.

A column of fire erupted behind him, but not in front of him. As if ... as if he were *protecting* the—

"Enough!" Fallon shouted, her breaths now becoming labored. "Unless you want to kill your leverage." She jerked her chin at the the King's Court still hiding under the dining table. Elowen and Ronen rushed to their side, making sure everyone was alright.

Fritjof paced back and forth like a caged animal. "So, you have come to kill me and take your throne? I'm afraid I cannot let that happen." He hissed. Ronen did not think it was possible, but a Fire Fae was sweating.

"No." Fallon shook her head. "You do not die today. I came only to collect my court and to give you your one and only warning."

She slowly approached the wall of light. Fritjof met her, creating his own wall of flame between them. Ronen did not know how she was tolerating it—he could feel his eyelids burning from where he stood ten feet back.

Fallon bared her teeth, and to everyone's surprise, a Fae fang now protruded from her once empty socket. "I am the Sun's walking heir, yet I have seen everything the darkness has to offer. So don't ever assume you know what I'm capable of." She spat.

Fritjof smiled back at her. He tilted his head to the side as if the flames whispered sweet things in his ear. "Take whatever traitors you want. Go build your kingdom of sticks and stones, little girl. Because I'm going to be right here, ready to take it all away from you when it will hurt the most," he whispered gently.

"You're not the first to try, but you will be the last." She turned to walk away, but smiled sweetly over her shoulder. "Your move, *Lord of Fire*."

Ronen quickly gathered Honeymaren, Arlo, and the three other men who had been willing to die for them. "Are you coming with us?" he asked hurriedly.

"Until the bitter end," Honeymaren assured him, her sapphire eyes were transfixed on the princess stumbling towards them.

Ronen went to ask the remaining four court members, but Elowen grabbed his shoulder tightly. "No," she whispered. She was pale and shaken, as if someone had just dupped a bucked of ice water on her head.

That's all he needed to hear. "Let's get out of here."

"My lord!" a familiar, measly voice objected. "We cannot let them just walk out! We can lock up the girl, kill the rest—"

"I said *get them out!*" Fritjof screamed. All his flames died out, all except the ones encircling the armoire.

Latrell smartly shut his mouth, glaring daggers at his brother. But Bhaltair simply shrugged, rounding up his men. "As you wish."

Elowen ran to Fallon, just in time for them to catch each other as both of their knees gave out. The light around them slowly faded, and Ronen's eyes had to adjust to the now dim room.

Fallon was drenched in sweat, her cheeks and nose as red as her hair. "How was I?" she rasped, her dry lips sticking together.

He laughed. "You made it count, red."

"This is not the end!" Latrell shouted, visibly shaking with restraint, "Enjoy your last days on Elphyne!"

The two younger lords helped Fallon walk. She was pretty out of it, not even raising her head as she answered the many questions flung at her. Ronen not-so-politely told everyone now was not the time for an interrogation. He grabbed Elowen's hand, and the Light Court made their way out of the Castle Sanctum.

Every guard stared them down as they passed. Ronen kept glancing over his shoulder the entire walk out of the castle, too on edge to even enjoy their victory. Why would Fritjof just let them go? Why did he *want* them to go?

Not them ... Fallon. He wanted Fallon out of that room, even more than he wanted all of them dead. And what was that word he called her ...

Finally, fresh air brushed across his cheeks, and all his worries seemed to melt away. Once they were off castle grounds, Fallon collected enough energy to approach him. Ronen tensed. Oh gods. She remembered the bridge after all.

He held up his hands, "I know, Fal, I know. In retrospect, maybe there was an easier way off—"

She suffocated him in a hug. His cheeks heated up as he became keenly aware of the rest of the court staring at them.

"I claim you, too," she breathed into his neck.

He tried to hug her back. He tried to laugh, or to speak, but nothing was working. "I know," he managed. "You saved us, Fallon. Again."

Fallon pulled back, brushing her thumb across the skin under his left eye. Her touch sent chills scattering down his spine. "Actually, I think it was you who saved me." She smiled.

Arlo Fartre cleared his throat from behind them. "Your highness, surely we are being followed," he said worriedly. Arlo was a string bean of a Fae; scarily long and thin. He appeared older than Bhaltair, his black hair trimmed in short coils.

Fallon grinned, looking south towards the Longback Knolls. "I sure hope so. I have a few people I need to thank."

The court all wore concerned expressions, but Ronen and Elowen broke out in matching grins. All Fritjof's men were in the castle ... and all of Bhaltair's men were out here. Ronen had a funny feeling any search party would be led to a dead end, with no reported sightings of a red-haired princess and her peculiar court.

Ronen made this walk once before, so he took the lead with Fallon. She made him tell her everything from the moment they were separated at the river. He tried to sound impressive, but none of it compared to her side of the story. She told him about the throne room and the way her blood had turned into golden tree sap once it touched the Ash Throne.

Ronen demanded to see the axe while she confessed to knowing about her powers. How she had not used or thought about them since Midgard. He wanted to be mad that she once again lied to them, but he was too busy gawking over her new weapon. That tree had better craftsmanship than everyone in his old shop combined. Fallon actually gave it its own name—which he could not pronounce—and spoke about it as if it were a person. It was kind of sweet; to see a Viking and her weapon like a little girl with her doll.

Everyone was tired, and rather traumatized, so the walk back to the Longback Knolls ended up taking double the amount of time it took Ronen. During their many breaks, they did introductions and gave their stories. The Light Court now consisted of: himself, Princess Fallon, Elowen, Lady Honeymaren, Arlo Fartre, Lord Conall of Briarden, Frans Holger, and Lord Jerrick of Enia. Each had their own reasons for hating Fritjof. Arlo and Frans were not lords, they were just unfortunate enough to hail from the pureblood families Fritjof had his eyes on.

They all gathered under a thick canopy of trees, munching on whatever vegetables and berries Arlo and Jerrick could grow. Which was not much, since Arlo specializes in herbs and Jerrick was too busy trying to save a dying village to care about advancing his powers.

Elowen left with Honeymaren to find water for Frans. The old man was struggling to keep up. He was still tall and broadly built despite his age, but his lungs and heart have seen better days.

"It was my mother's side of the family," he explained between breaths, "that maintained the gift of Air through all generations. When she became pregnant with twin boys, our family was overjoyed to welcome two more."

His eyes were a slate gray, matching the silver hair neatly combed on his head.

Ronen sat forward. "You are a twin?" he asked.

The look on Frans's face let Ronen know he asked the wrong question. "I am. Or rather, I was. My brother Dara was born giftless. We were so young when my mother sent him away because of it. These days I … why, I hardly remember him," he said sadly.

Fallon's jaw flexed a few times before asking, "Your mother gave up one of her children because they weren't gifted?" she asked.

"She was embarrassed. She thought she had just broken the bloodline. So, she told everyone Dara died of an ailment his small body could not overcome." He shook his head in frustration. "So when I hear that awful Fritjof speak, all I hear is my mother's voice. He wants to send all of them away, just like Dara," he said.

He turned to face Fallon, taking her hands in his own. "But when I saw you, young miss, I saw the younger version of myself fighting for him. I would have loved and welcomed him all the same. Gifts or not. But by the time I found out the truth, it was far too late. He was gone." Those gray eyes welled up, decades of pain and longing wrinkled on his face.

Jerrick placed a hand on the elder's shoulder. The lord was only seven years into his twenties, yet seemed as old as Frans. His forest eyes were sunken in, lined with dark circles. Ronen liked him. He had wordlessly taken responsibility over Frans, helping him walk and carefully sit when it was time to rest. Though Elowen had pointed out maybe it was his tendency to always help others that caused those sad, tired eyes half-hidden under blonde curls.

Conall, however, was a different story. He was a Water Fae, like Honeymaren, yet he stayed put every day while the lady went to collect water. He was quiet, keeping to himself and only ever speaking when spoken to. He had the same caramel skin as Elowen, but where her hair was stark white, his was chocolate brown. Ronen knew his village, Briarden. Urg often traded with their shops, as it was another production village, akin to Athol. But Briarden made chains, locks, bars, and—

And perhaps ... perhaps iron armoires.

As they trudged down the next hill, Ronen nearly fell to his knees with relief. He never thought he would be *happy* to see the Longback Knolls. But no one was happier than Fallon. Everyone constantly nagged her about her powers, her mother, and her plans. Maybe that was why she walked so far ahead this morning, barely within eyesight.

"She's afraid," Elowen said from beside him, causing Ronen to jump in surprise. Elowen had been uncharacteristically quiet since they left this castle. This was the first time she has approached him.

He snorted. "What does she have to be afraid of? She's a walking sunbeam."

Elowen thought for a moment. "She didn't feel loved by anything in Barwyn. She *liked* the snow, the magpies, and the stars, but she never felt loved by them. It was easy to make mistakes because she didn't care. She only wanted to be Chief because people told her she couldn't be." She explained.

"Now, she's a princess because we *need* her to be," he sighed.

Elowen nodded in confirmation. That was a lot for one person to take. Indeed, Ronen often found himself always going to her for answers, for a plan and for a friend. Fallon didn't have anyone to turn to.

Ronen knew he could never bear the weight she carried, and she would never let him try. But he could be someone to lean onto when she needed to take a breath. He would continue to hold that lantern while she walked the unknown path ahead, for however long it took.

He was so lost in thought, he didn't notice when everyone else stopped walking. It took him a moment to even realize Elowen was no longer at his side. When he finally turned around, everyone was staring at him. Honeymaren had both hands over her heart, and everyone else's mouths were agape.

"Guys?" he asked dumbly. He followed their eyes—not at him, but beyond him. Ronen whipped back around, and his jaw dropped so fast he felt it pop.

Fallon stood ahead, but she was not alone.

Everyone moved impossibly slow, taking tentative steps towards the princess. Before her, in all its regal glory, stood a fully grown Peryton: the sacred animal of Dagmar.

Twice the size of a normal stag, it stood nearly three feet above her. Even taller were its glistening golden antlers, wide and deadly. No one saw Perytons anymore—*ever*. They were hunted to near extinction for those golden antlers and hooves. Luckily, their massive wings made it easy to flock somewhere safe. The green, red, and blue feathers were so shiny he swore they were cast in silver. This was likely the first and last time any of them would get to see one.

Despite all of that, the most bewildering part was that Fallon was *petting* it.

She ran her hand up and down its nose, and it let her. All of them watched with a mixture of wonder and horror as it nuzzled up against her like a housecat. Its grand wings were folded at its side, but he could still see all the muscle that made up its body. This was perhaps the third life-changing moment that Ronen experienced today, and he was not sure how much more his brain could handle.

"Well, if that isn't proof, I don't know what is," Arlo said quietly.

"Proof of what, exactly?" Conall asked, speaking for the first time today.

Ronen smiled. "Dagmar's last heir. No one can deny it now."

As soon as they got too close, the Peryton stepped back with a huff. It appears that not all was forgiven between Fae and Peryton, and Ronen did not blame it.

Fallon beamed, the scar across her nose stretched with her smile. "It's magnificent. Are all your bucks this way?" she asked.

It sniffed Fallon's head one more time, then turned down the hill. It took only four steps before it spread its massive wings and took off into the sky, back into hiding.

Ronen felt like a giddy little kid. He just saw a Peryton. He could not wait to hold this over every Fae's head for the rest of his life.

Everyone rushed to Fallon, explaining to her the significance of what had just transpired. If the people knew about this, they would not even look in Fritjof's direction. Frans kept saying it was a sign from the gods, but Honeymaren and Jerrick thought it was the Peryton's own free will. It must have felt Fallon's power surge at the castle and came to investigate.

Fallon raised her hand, and everyone instantly halted. Her eyebrows scrunched. "Do you feel that?" she asked quietly.

Arlo stuck out his hand, "Magic," he confirmed, scanning the ground. "A combination of smokey quartz, malachite, *Pimpinella anisum,* Balm of Gilead, Bloodroot, and carnations if I were to guess," he said casually.

"That's an awfully specific guess," Ronen said.

His full lips turned into a smile, "Because I'm the one who wrote the spell." He winked.

Fallon reached down for her axe she kept tucked into her belt loop. "What kind of spell?" She asked.

"A modified protection spell. We found that smokey quartz adds a cloaking element when powered with Bloodroot. It creates a sort of veil that those with evil in their eyes cannot see through," he explained.

Fallon sagged her shoulders in relief. "Elma."

Arlo nodded. "We made the spell together, not long ago."

"Her weird Overseer powers must have known she would need it." Ronen laughed.

Ronen went to follow everyone down the hill, but felt a *whack* on his shin before he fell to the ground. He groaned, looking up at the boots that had tripped him. Fallon squatted down, her mean Viking face making its usual appearance.

"If you ever throw me off anything again, I'll make you dig your own grave before I put you in it."

He was still spitting the dirt from his mouth as she turned and trudged down the hill without another word. Frans and Jerrick followed, but Conall stayed to help him up.

The dark-haired man scanned him carefully. He was older than Jerrick, closer to Bhaltair's age. He might be handsome if he ever smiled. "I thought you two were supposed to be friends," he said.

"Well, you see," Ronen rubbed his sore chin. "I never really had friends. I thought the-Hulder-who-can-do-no-harm and Princess Uppercut were a good start. Sometimes I think I was wrong."

Conall didn't laugh. "You are the Nøkken from Athol?"

Here we go. "Yes. I'll give you a head start if you want to start running."

"I was never allowed to visit Athol Village because of you," he stated simply.

Ronen patted the strange man on the shoulder. "You're welcome."

Conall eyed him carefully. His tone was always so flat, Ronen didn't know if he was angry or sad or maybe even happy. "Why are you here?" he asked.

"Same as you," Ronen shrugged as they started down the hill. "Fritjof is wrong. He is lying to everyone about our history and about the gods. Fallon is royal, half-mortal or not," he said.

Conall's skin was so tan, so it took until just now for Ronen to notice the scars. Partially obscured by dark stubble, there were thick patches of scarred skin around his mouth. As if someone had tried to cut off his lips but gave up halfway through.

"Do you think it's real? The Godflame?" Conall asked, keeping his head low.

Ronen shook his head. "No. There was something wrong with that Sentinel, and I know you noticed it too. Whatever show Fritjof put on, I don't buy it."

"But what if it was real?"

"Doesn't matter. He could have the power of death itself for all I care. Because we are going to take back the castle and put Fallon on the throne where she belongs." Ronen assured him.

"You truly believe that?"

"I must. Because Fritjof was right about one thing." Ronen had never actually said these thoughts out loud. "We are going to war again. I don't know when, or with who, but I just have this unshakable feeling that if we lose … all of Lysserah will lose."

THIRTY-SEVEN

Fallon walked, and walked, refusing to turn around.

She could still feel their eyes on her. In fact, that's all she felt since the moment her power finally left the confinements of her skin: watched. Followed.

How did her mother run an entire kingdom? Fallon only had a small group of people relying on her, and she was ready to run back to Barwyn just to take a full breath again. The way they looked at her … the way they asked her questions as if she was supposed to have an answer … it made her queasy.

But Fallon chose this. She asked for this. In Barwyn, she was ready to do anything to take back her birthright. Crumbling now, right as she got her hands on just that, wasn't an option. She had to say *something* to them. She just didn't know how. What do you say to somebody who risked everything for you? Who chose faith, in her mother and her kingdom, over the fear of the unknown?

As she begrudgingly trotted down a large hill, she found herself leading everyone into a bowl of knolls. A large open field, flower patches, a herd of Hempia in the distance; the usual. Only when Fallon took a few more steps did she notice it.

A twinkling *whoosh* passed her ears, and a sudden stillness filled the air. Fallon cursed as she tripped over a chunk of stone the size of her fist. A few yards away she saw another, then a single white flower. More and more strange, out of place objects outlined the field.

Fallon smiled, whispering to herself, "A Faerie circle."

"Indeed," a familiar voice spoke.

Elma was still in her favorite green robes, dreaded hair in a high knot as she approached. "I was starting to worry," she rambled, checking all of them for any signs of harm. She grabbed Ronen forcefully by the face. "What took you so long?" She demanded.

Fallon laughed, and the tight ball in her chest loosened enough for her to take a full breath. "We brought some company," she explained, gesturing to the Light Court standing awkwardly behind them.

"Wilhelmina." Arlo bowed with a smile. He went around the circle introducing everyone. Little did they know, Elma had once been a vital member of the King's Court. When Asta died and Fritjof took over, he was quick to weed out the biggest threat.

Honeymaren bowed her shaved head, eyeing Elma curiously. "I have heard of the Overseer before. My daughter has a book about one, but his name was Ch ... Chross, Chrosos—"

"Chronos Dorian. He was the first Overseer in two-hundred years after the Elphynian War. Until him, it was believed that Ondorr swallowed the magic that protects the Temple of Wisdom. It got dangerously close, but the Temple still stands," she said proudly.

Arlo looked around, lanky arms tucked into his sides. "I am pleased to see the spell worked. So, what is this place?"

"Home," Fallon answered for her.

Once again, everyone turned toward Fallon. They were together, they were safe, there was no excuse anymore. Nowhere to run. Why was facing them so hard? Why did she not feel worthy of their trust?

Fallon cleared her stinging throat. "I know it's not much now, but we will make it a home. We will put up tents, huts, maybe even eventually cabins. It will be safe here. I will bring in more people strategically, starting with your families," she assured them.

Well, no one backed out so far. She might as well keep going. "I want to hear everything you have to say. If you don't agree with one of my decisions, say so. Because to tell you the truth, I—" she shook her head, fiddling with the arrow tip in her pocket. "I don't know how to be a princess, but I know how to survive. I know how to get back up after the whole world came down on top of you. Loss, tragedy, despair, pain, none of that is new to me. But *this*—being in a team, a family, this is new. So, I can teach you how to rise again, if you teach me how to be your leader. It will be long and hard, but … but we can go on that journey together if you'd like," she choked.

Everyone was quiet for a moment, long enough to make Fallon's palms sweat. *Please.* Please give her a chance. Fallon knew she could do it. She could muster herself up into some kind of leader for them. A queen.

Finally, Honeymaren placed a hand over her heart. "I think I speak for everyone when I say that you are off to a great start, young princess," she said.

Fallon beamed. Her heart was a bird that was finally released from its cage—free, light as air, and boundless. This was the first time she actually called Elphyne her home, and it felt more right than anything she had ever done. That iron throne would have left nothing but cold blisters on her skin.

Ronen opened his mouth to say something, but Conall gasped and shouted, "Valdyr!"

Her axe was in her hand before the word even left his mouth. Fallon whipped to where he was pointing, but then her arm dropped. She could only imagine what it looked like to the others when she and Ronen waved at the Valdyr with happy smiles on their faces.

Honeymaren shook her head in disbelief. "This kingdom just keeps surprising me. The General of the Valdyr, who has been loyal to Fritjof all these years, comes to our aid?"

"Loyal to the throne," Fallon corrected, "Not Fritjof."

But Bhaltair and Enok did not share her excitement. They wore grisly expressions as they approached. At least Enok had the decency to *act* happy to see them alive and well.

Fallon crossed her arms, knowing Bhaltair would appreciate a hug and a kiss on the cheek no more than she would. "How is the castle?"

"Absolute chaos?" Ronen guessed.

"Worse. Complete and total silence. No one has seen or heard from Fritjof since the meeting. He locked himself in his chambers and has not come out since," Bhaltair explained.

Ronen squinted his mismatched eyes. "Are you sure he's even in there? What if he got scared and ran away?" He asked.

"The smoke constantly pouring from under the door states otherwise."

Everyone murmured a curse or two. Right as they thought they got away unscathed, they were reminded that this was far from over. Relaxing was a luxury they could not afford. As soon as they made this Faerie circle livable, it was back to work.

Elowen held onto Enok's arm, gesturing to the group. "Everyone has had a long few days. So, can we focus on the positives right now?" she asked. It was the longest sentence Fallon has heard from her friend in days. Elowen was still rattled to the core by what happened at the castle.

The general nodded, releasing the tension in his shoulders. "You're right, my apologies." He turned to Ronen and Fallon. "Congratulations on being the most dumbfoundingly successful failures I've ever met. Your luck somehow always outweighs your irresponsibility in the end."

Ronen smiled from ear to ear. "Thank you!"

Bhaltair ignored him. "Explain to me how you managed to mess up such a perfectly laid out plan," he demanded.

Fallon obliged. But before she even got to the worst of it, Bhaltair's golden eyes widened. With no warning, he turned to Ronen and picked him up by the collar of his shirt.

"You controlled the river?" he demanded, shaking Ronen until his neck nearly snapped.

Ronen squeaked in surprise, "Yes, and it was probably the least controversial thing I've done this week. So why does it have your golden panties in a knot?" he tried to pry off Bhaltair's iron grip.

Enok kept signing the same word to Fallon, taking two fingers and individually tapping them on the same two fingers of his other hand. No one seemed to care about Ronen fighting for air.

"Drop him," Fallon warned quietly.

Bhaltair let go. "That river is fed by the waterfalls," he said slowly.

And the water pouring down the mountains was no ordinary water. "*Saltwater.*" Fallon laughed. She had been too busy before to even recognize the significance. She walked over and picked up where Bhaltair left off, shaking Ronen by the shoulders. "Ronen, you can control saltwater!"

Even Water Fae could not manipulate saltwater. Otherwise the Elphynian War would have gone quite differently.

Honeymaren placed her hands on her hips with a feline smile, "Surprises, surprises," she mumbled.

Only after every tent was pitched, a water source was established, and a fire was burning did Fallon let her guard down.

Elma only had six tents, so Fallon happily shared with Elowen while Jerrick volunteered to share with Frans. It wasn't much of a settlement yet, but it would do.

Ronen never stopped moving. He and Conall set up all the tents and went to find as much dry grass and twigs as possible. Which was difficult, given that there were no trees in the Knolls. Eventually, everyone found something to do. The hearth cave was a thirty-minute walk, so Honeymaren and Elowen went with Elma to get more food and supplies. Plus, after hearing about her powers, Elma was frantic to go to her endless library and find out more. This left Fallon alone in her tent with nothing but the storm of thoughts in her head and an ancient heartbeat in her chest.

She had her back against one of the posts, braiding a few strands of hair right by her ear. She was in a daze, watching the tent flap wave back and forth with the breeze. If she were mortal, she would have jumped as Bhaltair suddenly stepped into the tent. But she had scented him five seconds earlier.

Fallon closed her eyes. "The princess is taking a break," she muttered.

"Good," he said, sitting down in front of her, "Because it is Fallon I want to speak to." His chest and arm plates had been removed, showing more details of the beautifully designed green uniform underneath.

She peeked one eye open. "I already told Elma. I don't know where the power came from—"

"Where were you?" he asked calmly.

"What?"

"All these years, where were you? Where is Amory?"

Fallon sat forward, suddenly not interested in her braid. "It's a five day's walk from Halvar if you ignore the main roads. Why?"

Bhaltair rubbed his face, "Towards the end, your mother had many secrets. Even from me. The one that bothered me the most was how she survived it—the journey to see you," he said, staring at the grass between them.

Her heart turned into lead. "What do you mean?"

"The mortal sun is weak. It is enough to keep a Fae alive, but not enough to fuel our powers. We lose our gifts, our slow aging, and our healing. Then in your twelve hours of darkness, we gradually creep towards shade-poisoning. Even when the sun returns, it isn't enough to melt the shadows from us in time for the next nightfall. Three days was always our recommended limit in the mortal realm. A Fae *could not make it* to Amory," he explained.

Fallon just stared at him. "You're wrong. Elowen was there for years."

"Elowen's tree was being fed with our sunlight, their bond kept her alive. I thought Asta must have found a way for Fae to survive there, and that your mortal blood allowed you to tolerate the darkness. But I was wrong. After seeing what your powers did to everyone back there, I know now that it was *you*, Fallon. You saved your mother's life every single day in Amory," he explained.

Fallon's hands covered her mouth as a sob escaped her. Asta always held her close, always. They were never apart and even shared a bed at night. Flashes of memories so old they felt like dreams flooded her mind: Asta, pale as death, stumbling towards her bedside and taking Fallon into a tight embrace.

Fallon always thought her mother was just elated to see her. But her clammy skin ... her quivering hands reaching out for her the same way Elowen had that first day in Reinhart ...

"She knew," Fallon whispered. "She knew I was different. That's why she kept me so far away, where no one could ever find me—where my power could never develop." Not again. Not more truths she couldn't bear to hear.

A warm, steady hand rested on her shoulder. "We cannot make those assumptions. If even you did not know the nature of your powers until recently, how could she have known back then?" he asked.

The walls of the tent seemed to rise above her, spinning faster until she was trapped in a vortex of confusion and dead ends. "D-did you try to find me?" Her voice sounded so small, like the broken child still inside her crying out.

"I wanted to bring you home," he said quietly, unable to meet her eyes. "But after Asta died, I didn't even know where to start. As my responsibilities grew, I had less and less time to go searching." He wiped his hands down his face.

Fallon shook her head, letting out a breath through her nose. "You wouldn't have found me, Bhaltair. After Beowulf remarried, everyone forgot about me and my mother. No one could have directed you. Trust me, you had better odds finding that Shapeshifter than Barwyn's Bastard," she said solemnly.

She tried to not let herself dwell on the thoughts of what could have been. If Asta had not hidden her away, and Bhaltair had raised her as his own. How a body clear of scars would feel. How a peaceful night's sleep would be.

She tried for a smile. "I don't think you would have liked me much, anyways. I wasn't a very compliant child."

To her relief, he smiled back. "I hate to break it to you, but you're not a very compliant woman, either," he said.

A gentle breeze blew through the tent, and three Faeries followed. Elma and Elowen had returned, each carrying a full sack in their arms. Ronen, finally free of Conall, came and sat next to her. "Why do you seem so upset? We won," he said, tossing an apple into her lap.

"We won a battle, not the war." She took a large bite, still taken aback by how much better Elphynian food tasted. "I'll stop being upset when he's dead."

Elowen came to kneel by her, quickly undoing the sloppy braid Fallon had done and starting a new one. "You don't mean that."

Fallon just took another bite of her apple.

Bhaltair fetched a small crate for Elma to sit on. She was holding something tight to her side, but it was hidden within the waves of her robes. "It will take me time to find out more about this power, dear. Though I will say, the farther back in time I get, the closer I feel to the truth. Whatever this is, it is perhaps as old as the Firstborns themselves," she said, leaning forward. "May I see it?"

Even after all the questions Fallon had endured, no one asked her to do that yet. She didn't even know if she could. "I mean … I can try."

Feeling more than foolish, Fallon held up her hands. She could feel it just beneath her skin, like the current still moving under a frozen river. But it seemed rather content on staying there.

"Think about the last time you used it. How did you feel?" Elma asked gently.

Like four people weren't staring at me she wanted to say. Fallon thought about the Sentinel reaching for her friends, the look of hunger in its depthless eyes.

The air around them sizzled as a golden haze rose from her palms, swirling through her fingers and around her wrists. Its glow was dim, almost … lazy. As if it were none too pleased about being summoned during its nap.

"Remarkable," Elma breathed.

"So, you know what it is?" Fallon asked desperately. "It—I, healed my mother when she came to see me in Amory. Just as I healed everyone else's wounds and shade-poisoning. Whatever it is, it was enough to make my mother hide me away where no one would ever find me," she said.

The Overseer took a long, shaking breath. "Elin Alfrothul was the youngest Firstborn, given the Ash Throne as a gift from her parents. She was the first Winged Queen, leading a newborn kingdom and protecting them from Ondorr with the help of her four elder siblings."

Ronen whistled. "The Firstborns have names? I never knew that."

"Everyone has a name." Elowen chuckled.

"Indeed. And names have much, much power," Elma confirmed. "Elin passed on the throne to her children. But perhaps that was not the only thing she passed on," she said.

Bhaltair's eyes narrowed into thin slits. "You're speculating that this gift has gone unnoticed for thousands of years among the royal family?" he asked.

Elma closed her eyes. "Not unnoticed, son. Unneeded."

"I think everyone who died in the first Elphynian War would disagree with you," Ronen chimed in. Bhaltair growled.

Fallon scrunched her hands into fists, the light seeping back into her palms. "It was the call of her people that summoned the wings from a queen's back," she said quietly.

Elma pushed up her sleeves, revealing the old language engraved into her dark skin. She mumbled something, running her hands through the grass in front of her. "As I said before—the realm has been tilted into unbalance. I thought it was just the people's growing unhappiness, but that was dangerously naive of me," she continued to mumble to herself. What was causing this imbalance?

"Sunblood," Ronen blurted out. "When Fritjof saw her for the first time, he called Fallon a Sunblood."

Elma cocked her head to the side. "Did he? That is a very old term for royals. It was outdated even before my time. How strange indeed for Fritjof to even know it."

"Now it makes sense. The royals really are made of sunlight." Elowen smiled dreamily.

Everything had to be connected. The Sunbloods, Fritjof, her power, the upcoming war … it all came together somewhere. They were just missing too many pieces. What Fallon did know, though, was that they all seemed to lead back to one person.

"My mother." Fallon shook her head. "She was made of sunlight, and it wasn't good enough. Why would she let herself die when only she held the answer to every single question we have?" she raised her voice more than she should have.

Bhaltair hissed, "Watch your tongue."

"Why?" she snapped. "You have just as many secrets as she did. I need to know the truth—the *whole* truth, if I am to figure out how to save this realm," she demanded. She knew Bhaltair understood the real question she was asking.

For ten heartbeats, he said nothing. No one did. He must have seen her soul cracking in her eyes, because after a whole minute of silence, Bhaltair answered. "I had a meeting that day. It was to organize the yearly round of recruits into platoons for the upcoming training season. I was gone for no more than four hours when I returned to my rooms and knew something was wrong." For the first time, Fallon saw past the armor. For the first time, she saw her own anguish reflected back at her.

"I could smell her in the room. I followed it to my weapon cabinet, where I saw one of my swords was missing. If it were any other sword, I wouldn't have blinked an eye. I would have thought one of my men or Enok took it. But it was the sword her father used to knight me as her guard. I had never used it before, refusing to taint it with blood. So I got my Barguest and followed her scent. When I realized the direction we were going, I couldn't run fast enough. Even my Barguest could not keep up with me," he said.

The current under her skin ran still, and a cold chill rushed up her spine. "Ondorr," Ronen whispered for her. Fallon did not know if she was even capable of speaking. Her ears flexed, trying to hear Bhaltair's words before he even spoke them.

"She went alone. When she knew Enok and I could not follow. It was so unlike her, so random and zealous I thought she must have been forced against her will. I found the sword first; the tip was covered in black blood. Then," whatever words came next died in his throat. Fallon was surprised to see that it was Ronen who offered the general a comforting hand on the shoulder.

He took in a breath through his nose. "Then I found her. The veins in her hands were black, trailing up into her arms then down her front. The darkness had gone straight to her heart. I've never seen anything like it."

Fallon could not help but peer down at her own hands. She wanted to wash them in boiling water and scrub them until they bled. Why did Fallon get to summon the light and not Asta? It should have been her. She could have used it to save herself—

"Fallon?" Elowen pressed a small hand onto the top of her head, steadying her. Fallon did not realize she had been nearly hyperventilating. Her tongue was dry, sticking to her mouth as she tried to explain she was fine. But she wasn't. Not even close.

The only person who seemed more miserable than her was Bhaltair. "If Enok had not been right on my tail, I would have died there holding her. He pulled us both out, fighting off Sentinels while I did nothing." Shame and sorrow plagued his features.

Fallon had to step away from herself. She had to go back into that corner of her mind. Somewhere she had not been since childhood, where she'd endured hours of torment from Beowulf. It was quiet, it was warm, and it gave her enough room to think.

Pieces. More pieces of the puzzle.

Fallon went over every memory since she stepped foot in Elphyne. Every conversation. Tall grass, webbed hands, Shapeshifters, gold eyes, flying embers, wedding songs, peonies, saltwater, wisps, Sentinels—

Sentinels.

If someone was talking, she didn't hear it. Fallon stood up and grabbed *Himintelgya,* cracking her neck to either side. She stepped over Ronen, past Elma, and out of the tent.

Bhaltair rushed after her. "Where do you think you're going?" he demanded.

That voice that had never led her astray was warm and encouraging as it whispered in her ear, *connect the dots, north star.*

"On that day in the Sanctum, that Sentinel looked at me with eyes so full of abhorrence I could taste the malice in the air," she explained.

Everyone jogged to catch up to her. Ronen saw the way she was gripping her axe and wisely took a few steps back. "Fal, Sentinels don't even *have* eyes."

Fallon turned west, past the knolls and past the light of Lysserah.

"No, they don't."

YESTERDAY

August Alaric rested his face in his hands, trying to rub away the soot and ash burning in his eyes. Work was slow this morning, considering what happened last night.

Word traveled fast in Boudevijn, since all Orculli's voices were thunderous. The news came crashing through their mountain home like a flood: *The long-lost princess is here! She was in the castle!*

The giants seemed to have mixed emotions. Some of August's coworkers were afraid, some were suspicious, and some were downright angry. Not that any of them asked August how *he* felt about it, of course. No one ever cared what the only Fae in Boudevijn had to say. As far as any of them were concerned, allowing August to live was simply a business arrangement that worked in their favor.

August didn't know how he felt, or if he even believed the rumors. The queen died around the same time tragedy struck his own family, so he never really cared. With this new princess, maybe he could go back home. Maybe he could finally leave these damn mountains.

For now, though, he had to lie low. All these rumors resurfaced old tension between Orculli and Fae. Years of seclusion and borderline slavery left the three-legged giants bitter. When the reservoir ran dry five years ago, no Fae came to their aid. Since then, water was rationed out between homes and businesses. Yet the castle still demanded their supplies and merchandise.

August kept his head low and his emotions in check. The last thing he needed was another accident.

The bell of the clocktower rang, letting out four deafening *pangs*. Back to work. August grabbed his last bucket of water for the week and headed back to the forge. It was a dangerous place for a Fae: giants everywhere, hammers the size of his body flying around, and massive vats of molten metal. Unfortunately, August was the most dangerous thing in the room.

A room with no coal, no wood or steam.

The owner of the shop, Adelmar, knelt on three knees as August approached. "Adelmar is surprised you came," he said. August has lived here for ten years, and yet he was still not used to the Orculli's awful way of speaking in the third person.

He held up his shackled wrists. "I would happily parade around town in a dress and crown in honor of the long-lost princess if it meant a day off," he offered. Someone said she was young, perhaps she was around his age.

He laughed, scrunching his pig-like face. "Adelmar does not want to see that." He used a long key to take off the bar that kept August's hands from touching. As hard as it was to wipe his own ass, it was part of their agreement. It kept him alive.

"Suit yourselves," he mumbled, walking towards the first forge.

Easy now. August took deep breaths, trying to find that level ground within himself. He did this every day, and every day it was a fight. To own it. To not lose control.

All it took was one memory—one spark, and as soon as his palms touched, August's hands erupted into flames.

FOLLOW ON INSTAGRAM FOR UPDATES REGARDING **THE NAMELESS HEIR** AND ITS UPCOMING SEQUELS

@EMMAARCH.AUTHOR

ACKNOWLEDGEMENTS

This book has been a work in progress for over six years. It has seen me through the last two years of high school, the first four years of adulthood, and every tragically beautiful moment in between. I think every writer knows what I mean when I say publishing your book is like shouting into the void. The most important thing I've learned on this journey is that the real progress starts when you hear your own voice echo back. You need to be the biggest believer in your work. Cherish it. Champion it. If you do so, others will follow.

Which is why I would like to first and foremost thank you, the reader. These days there is so much fighting for our attention, yet you chose to give your time to my characters and their story. Thank you for walking that path of grief and forgiveness with Fallon. If you made it this far, I would like to officially welcome you into the Clan of Misfits. I claim you, too.

To my family, I thank you for your unwavering support. You have been my biggest advocates since the very first drafts of THE NAMELESS HEIR, offering constant reassurance and motivation. No one witnessed the lowest parts of my journey quite like my husband. He saw all the tears, temper tantrums, and bumps in the road. But he was also there to celebrate every small victory. Thanks to you, Carson, I understand the meaning of love and sacrifice. Thank you for your service to our country, and to our little family.

I would especially like to thank my followers on social media. Some of you have been around since my very first posts in June of 2023. After years in the query trenches, the welcoming embrace of the book community truly saved me. It was only because of your kindness that I decided to not only keep going, but to take matters into my own hands.

Printed in Great Britain
by Amazon